stitches in time

ALSO BY BARBARA MICHAELS

stitches in time

Barbara Michaels

HarperCollins*Publishers*

HarperCollins books may be purchased for educational, business, or sales promotional use. For information please write: Special Markets Department, HarperCollins Publishers, Inc., 10 East 53rd Street, New York, NY 10022.

FIRST EDITION

Designed by Caitlin Daniels

Library of Congress Cataloging-in-Publication Data

Michaels, Barbara, 1927–
    Stitches in time / by Barbara Michaels. — 1st ed.
      p.   cm.
    ISBN 0-06-017763-2
    I. Title.
    PS3563.E747S75   1995
    813'.54—dc20   95-4286

95 96 97 98 99 ❖/HC 10 9 8 7 6 5 4 3 2 1

For Benjamin James Brown Mertz
April 2, 1994
With love from Ammie

one

She cursed the needle, the cloth and the thread, fixing each stitch in place with a word of power. The murmured litany sounded so harmless, like a cat's purr or a low humming, but the other woman shivered and hunched her shoulders, like someone pelted by wind-driven sleet.

It had been a long time since she'd heard words like those, but she knew what they meant, and the hands that wielded her own needle felt stiff and clumsy. She had tried to remonstrate, to warn. Might as well talk to a stone, she thought, or one of the white marble statues the old man had put up all around the garden. Heathen images they were, statues of old gods and goddesses. Naked, too, some of them. It was against Scripture: You shall make unto yourself no heathen images. She'd read it herself in the Book, spelling out the words with slow, painful care. It was a prideful thing being able to read, and harder than anything she had ever undertaken, without help or encouragement, but she had wanted to read His words for herself. This was worse than heathen images, though. This was inviting the devil into your heart and feeding him on your hate. He was there in the room with them; she could feel him. Two women, sewing by the fire, and that Presence, not hot like the Bad Place was supposed to be, but icy-cold.

"You're stitching your soul into it." The words burst out of her. "There's *always a price to pay. You think it's her you'll hurt, but it'll come back on you."*

Like talking to a stone. The soft murmur continued unbroken. The needle gliding in and out reflected the firelight like a splinter of living flame.

"I can't stand it any longer."

Rachel had never heard her speak in that tone before: flat, dead, uninflected. Cheryl didn't believe in repressing her emotions. When she was angry she could swear like a marine sergeant, at the top of her lungs and at considerable length; when she laughed her whole body shook and dimples dented her rounded cheeks. Now she sounded like a tired old woman, forty years older than her real age—mid-thirties, Rachel assumed. The red-gold curls framed her gray face like an unsuitable wig.

Rachel glanced into the room they had just left—the hospital room where Cheryl's husband lay. He had roused long enough to acknowledge her presence and mutter a few words of reassurance, but now he was sleeping, stuffed full of painkillers.

"He's going to be fine. The doctor said he expects a full recovery."

"This time." Cheryl sagged, bracing herself against the wall. "He's been a cop for almost twenty years, sooner or later his luck was bound to run out. He could find another job, one that would pay better and wouldn't involve so much pressure. There was no need for him to answer this call. He wasn't even on duty, and it wasn't an emergency— a domestic argument, they happen all the time. But he won't quit and he won't stay safe. They've all got guns these days, and next time it may not be his leg. Next time . . . "

They were only acquaintances, not on hugging terms, but Rachel put an impulsive arm around the other woman. "Come on, Cheryl. I'll drive you home."

"Not yet. I told Kara I'd meet her here. Anyhow, I don't want the kids to see me like this." She straightened, took a deep breath, and produced a smile. "I'll wait in the cafeteria till Kara gets here and bum a ride home from her. Or walk—it's not far. You probably have things to do, you go on."

Rachel's eyes moved back to the open doorway. She couldn't see his face; it was hidden by the white mountain of sheets and cast. She didn't have to see it. Fifty years from now she would be able to close her eyes and remember how he had looked, gray-white skin drawn tight over the fine bones, dark eyes sunken and opaque. Drawn with shock and pain though it had been, his face was the kind that would stop any woman's breath, and the nurse's hands had lingered as she tucked the blankets around him.

"Lucky," the doctor had said. Lucky the guy who had been beating up on his wife had grabbed the .22 instead of the shotgun. A shotgun shell at close range would have shattered his kneecap as well as the bones of his thigh.

"Poor Rachel." Cheryl patted her shoulder—consoling her now. "This was a hell of a thing to dump on one of my best customers. I wouldn't blame you if you never came back."

It was stretching the truth to call Rachel a customer, much less one of the best. Most of the merchandise Cheryl sold was far beyond Rachel's means—antique linens and vintage clothing of such extraordinary quality that her customers came from all over the country. The shop occupied the lower floor of the rambling old house in which the Cardozas lived, in the small Virginia city of Leesburg. Though not far distant from Washington, it was hard to reach except by car. The drive was a long one even for Rachel, who lived on the Maryland side of the capital, but she made the trip frequently because for her the shop was as good as a museum—better, in some ways, because she was allowed to examine the objects closely, to linger and touch. Cheryl had spotted her immediately as a looker rather than a buyer, but she'd always treated Rachel with the same warmth she showed her regular customers, greeting her by name, answering her timid questions. Sometimes, when business was slow, she would close up for an hour and insist that Rachel join her in the family apartment for a sandwich or a cup of coffee. Rachel had found herself chatting as she seldom did to virtual strangers—about her boring job as a hostess in a local restaurant and her graduate work at the University of Maryland, and the difficulty of finding time to work on her doctoral dissertation. She had met Cheryl's pets and her three children. And her husband.

"I'm sorry you got stuck with this," Cheryl went on. "But I don't know what I'd have done if you hadn't been there when the call came Run the car into a tree, most likely."

Most likely she would have. The call, from the captain at the stat[·] had been cruelly vague—just that Tony had been shot while try[·]

break up a domestic argument. It wasn't until Cheryl reached the hospital that she learned the damage was "only" a shattered leg.

When they got out of the elevator Rachel saw a familiar face. Kara
was Cheryl's partner and sister-in-law, married to her brother Mark,
and Kara, standing at the admissions desk, was clearly upset. Rachel
could hear her clear across the lobby. "I am a member of the family,
dammit! I insist you tell me—"

Catching sight of them, she stopped shouting and ran to throw her
arms around Cheryl. They hugged each other and exchanged agitated
questions and responses, while Rachel stood awkwardly to one side.

She had always felt uncomfortable with Kara. She didn't know her
as well; Kara was the traveling partner, the Acquisitor, as Cheryl called
her—following up leads, attending sales and auctions, gathering the
merchandise Cheryl sold in the shop. It took a knowledgeable eye and
a great deal of expertise to spot potential prizes in a box-lot of crumpled linens or a pile of dirty old clothes. Kara had the expertise and the
connections. As the wife of a fourth-term congressman she knew
everyone in the political sphere; related by marriage to one of Washington's old families, she was accepted by people who wouldn't have
allowed a politician in their homes. She was all the things Rachel was
not—poised, sophisticated, mature—and she wore clothes as if they
had been designed specially for her.

She didn't look so sophisticated and soigné that day. Her suit jacket
was only half-buttoned and her makeup was smudged, especially
around the eyes, when she relaxed her grip on the other woman.

"Well, thank God it's no worse. Your message was so vague; I was
afraid . . . "

"Yeah," Cheryl said. "Me too."

"I'm sorry, honey, I didn't mean to sound critical. It must have been
horrible for you. That bastard Schroeder has the tact of an army mule."

"Did you call my only brother?"

Kara took a tissue from her purse and carefully blotted her eyes. "I
. . . age. Mark was in a meeting, as usual."

. . . back to normal, thinking about other people's needs
. . . better call again, tell him it's okay. He'll worry."

. . . close friends as well as related by marriage, but
. . . ugged. "There's plenty of time, the meeting will
. . . rnoon. What can I do for you? If you want to stay

here, I'll head back to the house, meet the school bus, tell the kids—"

"No. I have to tell them." Cheryl glanced at the clock. "We've got a couple of hours. What you can do for me is buy me a cup of coffee. And one for Rachel. She's been great. I don't know what I would have done without her."

Kara turned with a graceful gesture of apology and recognition. She did it well—she'd probably had lots of practice, pretending to remember her husband's constituents and aides—but Rachel could tell she didn't remember her. No reason why she should; Rachel had only met her three times, and on two of those occasions Kara had been busy with people who obviously were best customers—well-dressed professionals who didn't so much as blink at the high prices. After a quick, automatically appraising glance at Rachel's neat, nondesigner jeans and tailored shirt, she punched in the charm, smiling, extending her hand.

"You were there when Cheryl got the news? Thanks for coming to the rescue."

"She was wonderful," Cheryl said warmly. "I lost it, I was bawling and racing around trying to find my car keys and the phone so I could call you, and . . . It was a shock to her too, knowing Tony so well."

"I didn't realize that," Kara said.

Rachel poked a loosened strand of hair under the chiffon scarf that held it back from her face. She had been a fool to leave it hanging loose instead of braiding it as she usually did, but it was one of her few good features, thick and waving and walnut brown, and Tony worked odd hours, sometimes he was home during the day . . .

"He was very nice to me," she said primly, and forced herself to meet Kara's cool, knowing eyes.

"He is nice," Kara said. "No wonder you look so shaken. Let's get that coffee."

Rachel knew she should refuse. Cheryl didn't need her now. She could say she had to get back to work. Cheryl wouldn't remember what she had said earlier—that she had quit her job and had the whole day free. But she smiled and nodded and trailed along when they headed for the cafeteria.

After they settled down with coffee and sandwiches, and Kara had bullied Cheryl into eating something, Kara said briskly, "Do they have any idea how long it will be before he can go back to work?"

"I didn't ask," Cheryl admitted.

"Of course not. But even after he's released from the hospital he'll need therapy and attention and TLC. I'll arrange to take over at the shop."

"But you were going to Europe with Mark! You can't—"

"Certainly I can. A wife is just an ornamental encumbrance on trips like that. Mark would be the first to agree that your needs come first."

"Yeah, my needs," Cheryl said. "But not the shop. You know how he feels about it, Kara, he's been griping about—"

A glance from Kara stopped her. She looked embarrassed and then defiant. "Well, he has been, and I don't care who knows it. There's another possibility. We talked before about hiring someone part-time, and here's Rachel, she just quit her job so she could finish her dissertation, and her field is folklore—"

"Just a minute," Kara said gently. "Start again, from the beginning."

Cheryl hadn't forgotten a single detail. Rachel sat like a block of wood while she explained. "She's writing about women's work and traditions as a separate culture . . . Have I got it right, Rachel?" She stopped with a gurgle of self-deprecating laughter, and went on, "No, I can't explain things like that, but I understood it when you were telling me. Anyhow, she's concentrating on what they call the fabric arts— sewing and weaving, the patterns for quilts and embroidery and where they came from and the various techniques, and how they were passed on, and what they mean. She knows a lot about our kind of stuff—costume, too—and she's only got another year to finish, there's some kind of rule about how long you're allowed, and she's saved some money, but I'll bet she could use a little more, you always can."

She ran out of breath, and Rachel said it before Kara did. "You don't know me. You don't know my qualifications."

"I know more about you than I would about any other applicant. It wouldn't be hard work," Cheryl said earnestly. "There are long stretches when nobody's in the shop, you could work on your book—"

"ve the girl a break, Cheryl," Kara interrupted. "Don't rush her

on before she's had time to think it over. We can't pay

you might find your duties interfered with your

ry," Rachel said, trying to sound as cool and rea-

For a few weeks. You need somebody right away.

t, that would give you time to find someone else."

"It's very kind of you," Cheryl said earnestly.

It wasn't kind, and Rachel had a feeling Kara was well aware of that.

Cheryl had exaggerated when she praised Rachel's expertise. She was like that, giving people more than their due, seeing only the best in them. Rachel was glad she hadn't made any extravagant claims. The extent of her ignorance was embarrassingly evident to her once she got to work. She knew something about quilts and woven coverlets, since she had studied the patterns for her thesis, but her knowledge was purely academic. Her only knowledge of vintage clothing had come from her visits to the shop, and the other merchandise—antique jewelry, hats, fans, shawls—interested her not at all. Twinkling with gems faux and genuine, lavish with lace, feathered and embroidered and beflowered, the garments and accessories were too elaborate for her tastes and completely impractical. Imagine having to iron yards and yards of heavy cotton, eyelet-trimmed petticoats!

She did iron them, watched closely by Kara and perspiring with nervousness. She learned how to sew on buttons and repair hooks-and-eyes strained by customers who had underestimated their waist size. "If you don't replace a button immediately it may be lost," Kara had informed her. "And then we'd have to replace all of them." It was a sufficient threat; some of the Victorian and Edwardian blouses (Rachel learned to call them "waists") had long rows of buttons, all old and impossible to match.

In addition to demonstrating emergency cleaning techniques—"The sooner you get at a stain, the easier it is to remove"—Kara gave her a crash course in the history of costume. Luckily for Rachel the tags attached to each garment carried not only the price, but information about the date, the fabric and the approximate size. "Not that that deters chubbies from trying to squeeze themselves into a size three," Kara had commented wryly. "Try to talk them out of it if you can—tactfully. I usually point out that the armholes of the old garments are too tight for 'well-shaped modern females.' Women weren't supposed to have muscles in the bad old days."

Bias-cut, pongee, Lily Dache, Battenburg; celluloid versus torto shell, paste (paste?) versus rhinestone; at the end of a week Ra head rattled with information she knew she would never abso her wariness of Cheryl's partner had developed into heart

Kara was never flat-out rude . . . well, hardly ever; her comment on Rachel's first attempt at sewing on a button ("For God's sake, don't they teach kids anything useful these days?") was probably not meant to be taken personally. One day, watching Rachel rearrange the rack of lingerie a customer had left in disorder, Kara said suddenly, "You don't like these clothes, do you?"

Shaking out the twelve-inch flounce of a white petticoat, Rachel took her time about answering. "I admire the workmanship and the materials. But I'd never wear them. They aren't my style."

"Hmmm," said Kara. She didn't press the point.

Cheryl's standards were just as demanding, but her tutelage was a lot easier to take. She told funny stories about her own mistakes and interspersed instruction with compliments. "You sure are picking this up fast. Took me forever to learn all those designer names, and I still can't pronounce 'em right. Why do they all have to be French?"

Cheryl didn't have much time for Rachel, though. Not only did Tony require her attention, but ordinary domestic chores become more than doubly burdensome when the person who usually shares them is incapacitated. Cheryl seemed to spend half her time in the car, running errands, shopping, chauffeuring the children to various appointments. Occasionally she accepted Rachel's offer of help with gratitude so effusive it embarrassed Rachel, who was uncomfortably aware of her true motives. Any excuse to get away from the shop and Kara's bossiness!

By the time Tony came home from the hospital Cheryl was treating her like one of the family. It was impossible not to respond—rejecting Cheryl's overtures would have been like slapping a child—but Rachel almost preferred Kara's cool courtesy. She didn't want to hear Cheryl talk about her husband—about her fears for his safety, about his ~~ virtues and (few) failings. About how they had met, how she ~~ she could never care for another man as she had cared for ~~ she had been. Rachel listened with a sunny smile ~~ling darkly inside her. It wasn't fair. What had ~~ one but two such paragons? Her first mar- ~~ orce or desertion, but in her husband's pre-

Three children, all bright and healthy and ~~ouse filled with antiques, a loving brother and

fond friends. It was too good to be true, like a feature in some saccharine woman's magazine.

As "one of the family" she had come to know Cheryl's brother Mark, who was also Kara's husband, fairly well. Before he left for Europe he had helped Cheryl rearrange one of the downstairs rooms of the big, rambling house as a bedroom for Tony. The family living quarters were on the second floor, and Cheryl had decided—unilaterally—that the stairs would be too difficult for a man on crutches. She would, of course, sleep upstairs to be near the children. Once she had set her mind on something she was impossible to budge, so nobody argued with her, though Mark's raised eyebrows suggested he had some doubt of Tony's approval of the arrangement.

Rachel's initial wariness of Mark disappeared as she watched him carry furniture and wash windows, and listened to him exchange friendly insults with Alice, Cheryl's cleaning woman. All of them treated Alice like a friend instead of an employee, but Mark was obviously her favorite; he kept accusing her of being a feminist—a charge she vehemently denied—and she retaliated by repeating the current scandals about his fellow congressmen. There was always some scandal about some congressman, and Alice's expertise supported her claim that she read three newspapers a day.

Sometimes Rachel thought Mark was on better terms with Alice than with his own wife. There was something uneasy about that relationship, pleasant though it appeared on the surface. It couldn't be Kara's decision to stay in Washington instead of accompanying Mark to Europe; he had postponed his own departure for two days so he could be on hand to help bring Tony home from the hospital. They had been friends for years, even before Tony married Mark's sister, and their mutual affection was evident, though it took the typical masculine form of insults and rude jokes.

After Mark left, Tony had been visibly depressed. For a man who was accustomed to being active and in control, his enforced idleness was maddening, and with the best intentions in the world Cheryl kept saying and doing all the wrong things. Watching her, Rachel was torn between sympathy and exasperation. She understood, only too well, why Cheryl hovered over him, touching him and patting him; but couldn't Cheryl realize that he didn't want her to be bright and cheerful and uncomplaining all the time? He would have liked her to complain now and then, to prove she couldn't get on as well without him.

Tony had been home for about a week when Rachel found herself alone in the shop one gray December afternoon. It was the first time she had been on her own, and she was acutely conscious of Tony's presence, even though two closed doors and a short corridor separated them. Kara was out chasing down merchandise and Cheryl had taken young Jerry to the pediatrician—it was one of those ear infections that wouldn't go away—and there were no customers to occupy her attention. She was supposed to be reading one of her reference books but she hadn't turned a single page; she kept listening for sounds from the back room, and wondering what he was doing there all alone. Reading, sleeping, lying on his bed staring out the window in bored frustration? The view would be lovely in a few months, but the gray skies and withered grass of a December day would only depress a man who was already feeling low. Cheryl had put up a bird feeder outside the window. Rachel would never forget the look on Tony's face when his wife explained she was sure he'd enjoy watching the finches and the sparrows and the cute little tufted titmice.

It was no use trying to study, she couldn't concentrate. Perhaps there was something she ought to do in the shop. Brightly but softly lit, with pots of ferns and ivy hanging at the windows, it was a cheerful, summery room—a lot more cheerful than Tony's back bedroom. Once the double parlors of the house, it had been turned into a single large room by removing the French doors and replacing partition walls with square columns that provided additional display space. The graceful proportions and handsome old woodwork gave it a look of elegance that suited the merchandise on display—bright quilts, framed pieces of fragile old lace, designer gowns by great names like Worth and Vionnet. Rachel's gaze lingered on a garment that had struck her as epitomizing the frivolity and impracticality of vintage chic—a peignoir of fragile shell pink chiffon, its flowing sleeves and trailing skirts and low-cut neck trimmed with cascades of pink silk roses and green silk leaves. Why would a modern, sensible woman wear a thing like that? She certainly wouldn't; it was too frivolous and feminine, and far, far too expensive—another designer original, almost a century old. It was beautiful, though. The woman who had owned it must have worn it only a few times, on special occasions, for a special person, a husband or lover . . .

The footsteps on the porch outside were a welcome distraction from fantasies that had taken on an uncomfortable edge. Rachel swore under her breath. Those fantasies had gotten worse (or better?) since Tony came home. She'd have to do something about the situation–it wasn't fair to anyone, including herself.

Bracing herself to smile and look pleasant, she realized the footsteps had halted. Not retreated, just stopped, outside the door. There was a soft but solid thud, and then silence.

Rachel craned her neck, trying to get a glimpse of the person outside through one of the long glass panels flanking the door. The mailman, or UPS? If he had delivered something, he should have at least rung the bell. She was about to stand up when the door opened.

Not a customer, Rachel thought, unless the clientele was about to undergo a radical change. The usual male clients were either older men looking for a present for a wife or daughter, or younger men with sophisticated tastes in interior decoration. This man was in his late teens or early twenties, and if his clothes were any indication of his tastes, they weren't sophisticated. His sneakers had cost more than Rachel spent on clothes in a month, his jacket was covered with iridescent insignia, and his jeans were supported by a wide leather belt and gaudy brass buckle.

It wasn't his clothes that raised Rachel's hackles, it was the way his eyes shifted, searching the big room like a dog sniffing out a strange neighborhood. Not until he had looked the place over did he actually enter the room, giving the door a careless shove that slammed it into place. Then his eyes returned to Rachel.

One of Cheryl's first lessons had concerned potential buyers. "Just because a customer looks poor or ignorant doesn't mean she can't buy everything in the shop. Be polite. To everybody."

"Can I help you?" Rachel asked, politely.

"Depends on what you got in mind." Feet apart, thumbs hooked in his belt, he grinned insolently at her.

Oh, hell, Rachel thought. One of those. There was only one way to handle them—and for all she knew, he *could* buy everything in the shop. Holding her polite smile in place, she said, "Are you looking for something in particular?"

"Nah." He turned away, studying the garments on a rack nearby. When he began rummaging through them Rachel bit her lip to hold back a sharp protest. The clothes were vintage whites, Victorian and Edwardian undergarments and nightgowns. Their present snowy perfection was the result of hours of washing, bleaching, starching and ironing. She had ironed one of the petticoats herself, ruffle by ruffle by ruffle.

He wasn't looking at the clothes, he was yanking at the price tags. If he was a seller instead of a buyer, that would account for his behavior and his presence; sellers often checked the prices, especially people who were selling for the first time. They wanted to get an idea of how much they could ask. Most of them failed to take into account not only the difference between wholesale and retail, but the amount of work involved in restoring the garments. Cheryl had some funny stories about would-be sellers and their indignation when she tactfully declined to buy tattered family treasures for outrageous prices, but she had occasionally acquired good pieces from such sources. "Be polite to everybody."

Watching his dirty hands tugging at the fragile fabrics, Rachel was on the verge of breaking Cheryl's rule when he pulled one of the hangers off the rack. The sight of this particular garment had distracted him from his original purpose, whatever that may have been; it was a pair of lacy, ruffled underdrawers.

Like all the merchandise in the shop, they were in pristine condition and of rare quality—hand-stitched crepe de chine, the legs ending in deep frills of handmade lace and silk ribbons—but it was the label sewed inside the waistband that justified the high price. Lucile, whose real name was Lady Duff Gordon, had specialized in extravagant lingerie for wealthy aristocrats during the early 1900s. Following the fashion of the time, this pair of undies had separate legs, joined only at the waistband.

Turning, a broad grin on his face, the man inserted his hand into the front opening and wriggled his fingers.

Rachel felt a furious blush warm her face. She and Cheryl had laughed and exchanged mildly ribald comments over those open-legged panties, though the practicality of the arrangement in a period of long skirts and trailing petticoats could not be denied. It was not embarrassment but anger and shock that provoked her reaction. No doubt the man was just a stupid clod, like the characters who insist that the obscene remarks they yell at passing women aren't meant to sound threatening, but his fixed smile and intent unblinking stare underlined the crudeness of that gesture.

She couldn't do anything about the blush, but she managed to control her voice. "Please don't handle the merchandise. If it's torn or soiled you'll have to pay for repairs."

A sullen frown replaced the grin. "Aright, aright, you don't hafta be so snotty. I was just kidding around."

He slung the hanger into place and sauntered toward the back of the room, where rows of open shelves held folded quilts, coverlets and fabric. Rachel had spent hours folding the quilts just so. She clenched her hands. The hell with politeness, she thought. How could she get rid of him? Cheryl would be back soon . . .

She hadn't been frightened before. He was tall, a good foot taller than she, gawky and hollow-chested and pasty-faced—not a particularly formidable figure. But she was suddenly and unpleasantly conscious of the fact that the house was isolated, set back from the street in its own large lot, in a quiet residential district; and when she thought of Cheryl walking in the door with Jerry, five years old . . . Whatever this character had in mind, he wasn't likely to be deterred by another woman and a small child. Maybe he had a gun. Everybody had guns these days. He hadn't felt threatened, not by one undersized female, but if someone else came in . . .

He was standing with his back to her, examining one of the quilts Cheryl had hung on the wall—a spectacular Baltimore album quilt, each square showing a different pattern of flowers and birds—and Rachel was trying to nerve herself to speak, when the door into the hall opened.

Tony got out three words—"Excuse me, Rachel"—before the man spun around. At the sight of Tony his jaw dropped and his eyes bulged. With an inarticulate exclamation he bolted for the front door.

And Tony went after him.

It was pure unthinking reflex. When you're a cop, and people flee at the sight of you, you go after them. He moved too fast and too abruptly, and the hardwood floor had been polished to a slippery shine. One of the crutches skidded, and Tony fell with a crash.

Rachel ran to him and knelt down on the floor. He had landed on his right side, twisting as he fell in an instinctive attempt to spare his left leg and the cast that covered it from ankle to hip.

Gray-faced and sweating, Tony glared at her over his shoulder. "What the hell are you doing? Go after him. Stop him."

"How?" Rachel demanded.

A car door slammed and tires screeched. The roar of the engine faded fast; he must have been doing sixty. Tony's tight mouth relaxed. "Good question. I'm sorry, Rachel. Sorry I swore at you."

"That wasn't swearing." She laughed shakily. "Stay where you are. Don't move. I'll call the doctor—or the rescue squad—or—"

"No, it's okay. No damage done, except to my ego." He leaned back against the arm she had slipped under his shoulders. He was wearing a heavy sweatshirt—people feel the cold when they are lying still, bored and helpless—but even through the thick fabric she could feel the hard muscle and bone. He'd be forty next year—Cheryl had already started kidding him about it—but he was in better condition than most men half his age. The creep wouldn't have made it as far as the door if Tony had been able-bodied.

Rachel retrieved the crutches and, with their help, got him up and into a chair. "I still think I should call the doctor," she said anxiously. "Or do you want to go back to bed? Would you like some coffee or a glass of water?"

He smiled at her and her knees went weak. "I want you to sit down. That was an incredibly stupid performance. All I accomplished was to scare you half to death."

"You got rid of him." Rachel pulled up a chair and dropped into it. "I was getting worried. How did you know?"

"You had the intercom on."

She glanced at the desk. "I didn't know. Cheryl must have turned it on before she left. So you heard."

"The whole thing." His mouth twisted. "I was getting worried too. If it hadn't been for this damned leg I'd have been here sooner."

"Who was he?"

Tony shrugged. "Never saw him before."

"Then why did he run?"

Cautiously Tony shifted position. He didn't seem to be in pain; in fact, he looked more alert and cheerful than he had for some time. "The guilty flee where no man pursueth? I certainly couldn't pursue him. If he hadn't panicked, he'd have spotted the crutches and realized I was no threat to him."

"You might have been armed."

"Most people aren't. Unless they're cops. I think he recognized me."

"I think you're right," Rachel agreed. "Does that imply that he's from around here?"

Tony gave her an approving smile. "Smart girl. He wouldn't have reacted so dramatically if he hadn't encountered me before. I may even have arrested him. I can't remember every two-bit crook in the county."

"Well, thanks for rushing to the rescue. If you hadn't come when you did . . . " She stopped, realizing she was overdoing it and that he wasn't dumb enough to fall for the helpless female routine. He gave her a quizzical look.

"Yeah, I was a big help, wasn't I?" His brow wrinkled. "It's strange that he should come here. He couldn't know you'd be alone, and this isn't the sort of place a thief would hit, especially in daylight. I wonder . . . "

He broke off. "Don't tell Cheryl I fell," he said softly. "You know how she is."

His fingers closed over hers in a warm, warning grip. He had heard the car before she had. Speechless, Rachel swallowed and nodded, and Tony released her hand.

Cheryl was carrying a bag of groceries. Her face lit up when she saw Tony, and Jerry flung himself at his father, yelling, "The doctor stuck a needle in me and I didn't cry, and he said I couldn't have any candy 'cause it wasn't good for me, so can I have some?"

"Don't jump at your daddy like that," Cheryl exclaimed. "You'll hurt him."

Jerry, now on his father's knee, turned to stare at his mother. He had her stocky build and Tony's olive skin and black hair. His resemblance to his father had never been stronger than at that moment; both male faces bore identical scowls.

"It's all right," Tony said. "I think you deserve a reward, Jerry."

"He can have an apple," Cheryl said.

"I don't want a stinky apple, I want a choc'lit bar."

It turned into one of those idiotic, unproductive arguments bright children are so good at provoking, and which usually have undercurrents more complex than the immediate issue. Rachel took the groceries from Cheryl and escaped; when she came back, Jerry was eating cookies and looking maddeningly smug, and Cheryl was dragging a large black trash bag into the shop.

Rachel hurried to help her. The bag was heavy, the plastic strained by the weight of its contents. "What's this?" she asked.

"I was just about to ask you. Found it outside on the porch." She started to reach inside.

"Wait!" Rachel caught her arm.

Tony had stiffened. "Bring it over here. Please," he added.

Rachel knew what he was thinking. The unpleasant character who had left so hastily might have left an equally unpleasant souvenir—rotting trash laced with broken glass, for example. There was something wrong with that bag. She could feel it. The hairs on the back of her neck bristled.

Cheryl sat back on her heels. "What's the matter with you two? It's just old linens." Before Rachel could stop her, she pulled a crumpled bundle out of the bag.

"People bring things like this in all the time," she went on cheerfully. "Usually it's junk when it arrives in a trash bag, but you never know . . . Good gosh. Look at this."

The fabric she lifted between her hands was yellowed with age and badly wrinkled, but now Rachel saw the pattern Cheryl's better-educated eye had spotted. Delicate precise stitches shaped an elaborate tracery of intertwined scrolls.

"It's a quilt." Cheryl laid the fabric carefully out on the floor, smoothing the crumpled folds. "White work, trapunto, hand-stitched—though the stitching is so fine it looks machine-made. Look at the detail!"

The pattern covered the entire surface of the quilt, which was large enough for a double bed, in an intricate design of formalized flower and leaf shapes, scrolls and overlapping feathers. Certain elements had been raised by inserting cord or bits of cotton under the fabric of the top—the process called trapunto—so that it resembled low bas-relief. It was an astonishing piece of work and ordinarily Rachel would have been as rapt with admiration as Cheryl. But her irrational sense of something wrong had not diminished. If anything, it had grown stronger.

"Who brought this?" Cheryl demanded.

"Somebody you wouldn't want to meet," Tony said. His hands were clenched on the arms of the chair and Rachel sensed the frustration that filled him. If he had been able to move easily he'd have pushed his wife away and investigated the bag himself. "Hold it a minute, Cheryl," he continued. "It's probably all right. But Rachel just had a nasty encounter with the guy who left this—at least I assume it was he who left it—and I'd just as soon make sure there's nothing but old clothes inside."

He described the incident, making light of it and without mentioning his disastrous attempt at pursuit.

Cheryl jumped up, her eyes fixed on Jerry. "Oh, my God. A bomb?"

Tony laughed. "Nothing like that, honey. I was thinking more along the lines of something harmless but unpleasant, like the donor. I wonder . . . Is that old quilt worth money?"

"Once it's been cleaned, several thousand dollars."

"That much?"

"Maybe more." Torn between caution and fascination, Cheryl leaned closer to the quilt. "It's over a hundred years old and in excellent condition. The fabric is cotton and I don't see any bad stains. With careful cleaning it will be as good as new. Actually, I couldn't begin to put a price on it. We've only had one other of this type and it wasn't nearly as fine. Mid-nineteenth century at a guess."

"Hmmm." Tony stroked the piratical mustache framing his mouth.

"You think he stole it?" Rachel asked.

"The circumstances are suspicious, wouldn't you say? Trash bags have been a blessing to modern thieves. They're strong, you can cram a lot of stuff into them, and they are a lot less conspicuous than boxes or cartons. He had something on his shabby little conscience or he wouldn't have bolted when he recognized a cop. Let's see what else is in there. Carefully, babe; take hold of the bottom and spill it out."

Rachel's skin prickled as she watched Cheryl move slowly backward, tipping the contents of the bag out onto the floor. When it was empty she tossed it aside and straightened with a long breath of relief.

"No bomb. That was silly of me, wasn't it?"

"Not these days," Tony said. "You never know what people will think up next. So what have you got?"

There were two more bundles. At first glance they appeared to be the same white on white, but when Cheryl unfolded one of them a pattern of colored shapes was visible on the inner surface.

"Carolina Rose." Now relieved of her apprehension, Cheryl knelt to squint at the quilt. "At least I think that's what it is; I've never seen this particular variation. Patchwork, with some appliqué and the same exquisite quilting. Look at the way she uses color! Every flower is a different shade, but they blend perfectly."

Jerry came over to see what was going on and Rachel picked him up in time to keep him from walking across the quilt. He wriggled, trying to free himself.

"He's too heavy for you," Tony said. "Put him down before he kicks you—quite unintentionally. Jerry, how about another cookie?"

Cheryl was too preoccupied to comment on this flagrant violation of her rules. "Gosh, this is gorgeous. I'll bet it was made by the same woman. The pattern was popular during the mid-nineteenth century and the workmanship is almost as fine as the white quilt."

She went on crooning and commenting, but Rachel had stopped listening. There was one more bundle on the floor. The thief—the alleged thief—had crammed the quilts roughly into the bag. The third, on the bottom, had suffered most from careless handling and the weight of others on top of it. The fabric was filthy, covered with a peculiarly uniform grayish film. It didn't appear to be the normal yellowing of old linen, or ordinary dirt, and it certainly couldn't have been the original color of the cloth. No housewife would have chosen that nasty shade, even for backing.

Rachel spread it out on the floor and turned it over. Under the blurring gray film she saw colors and shapes—not the repetitive geometric shapes of patchwork, something quite different. Something wrong . . . She started violently when she heard Cheryl's voice.

"It's an album quilt, I guess. Each block has a different pattern—picture, rather, in appliqué. Is this a horse, with a rider and . . . a dog? It's so filthy I can't make out details. What a shame it's in such poor condition. Those stains probably won't come out."

Normally Rachel wouldn't have ventured to disagree. "They aren't stains. Look." Delicately, with one fingernail, she scraped at the gray film. It dissolved into a flaky powder. Bending closer, she blew gently at the spot. "I can get it clean, I'm sure I can. I'll try brushing it first, and then—"

"The hand vacuum." Cheryl peered at the area Rachel had cleaned. "Look at those minuscule stitches. I wonder how it got so dirty; the others aren't like that. I've never seen anything quite—"

She put out her hand, and then hesitated, her fingertip, like that of God in the Michelangelo painting, not quite touching the fabric. "I'll leave it to you, then."

"Thanks. I'll be careful, I promise. I know how to do it, you showed me."

"Just a minute," Tony said. He had one arm around Jerry, who was dribbling crumbs all over his lap. "Aren't you girls forgetting something? That may not be stolen property, but it certainly doesn't belong to you."

A dimple appeared at the corner of Cheryl's mouth. Rachel had seen this indentation before; it wasn't produced by laughter but by tightening lips. "Flotsam," she said. "Or is it jetsam?"

"Neither," said her husband. He was also familiar with that particular dimple.

"Oh, for God's sake, I was kidding," Cheryl snapped. "Although I'll bet there's some law that would support my argument. If unknown people dump things on other people's front porches—"

"We know who left it."

"No, we don't. That's just your guess."

"Not a guess. A reasonable hypothesis."

Rachel had never heard him raise his voice to anyone except his brother-in-law, in the course of one of their friendly arguments. But she knew the signs of rising temper—the way his eyebrows drew together, the soft, slightly rasping tone, the way his fingers tugged at the end of his mustache.

"Well, what am I supposed to do with the stuff?" Cheryl demanded. "I'm not running a free storage locker."

"Would you buy it?"

"If we could agree on a fair price. I've never cheated anybody in my life."

"I didn't mean—"

"I know." Cheryl moderated her voice. Jerry was looking uneasily from her to his father. She smiled at him. "Daddy and I are joking, Jerry."

Jerry went straight to the point. "Daddy will find the bad guy," he said confidently. "That's what Daddy does."

Tony's face relaxed. "Right, son. Daddy will find the bad guy and ask him very politely where he got the things."

"And then Mommy will buy them," Cheryl added. "Jerry, what a good idea. You are a very smart young man."

"Then can I have another cookie?"

Cheryl burst out laughing and hugged both of them.

Slowly and carefully, eyes averted, Rachel folded the quilt.

two

The black plastic bag Rachel was carrying when she left the shop that afternoon wasn't *the* trash bag. Tony had taken possession of that one after Rachel had folded the quilts neatly into a carton. From the careful way he handled it she assumed he meant to have it examined for fingerprints, though it didn't seem likely an identifiable print could have survived Cheryl's two-handed grip.

Rachel's bag held less intriguing items—a motley collection of linens from box-lots bought at auctions and yard sales that had failed to meet Cheryl's high standards. Kara had superb taste, but she was an auction freak and couldn't resist a bargain. Usually there would be one or two items in the collection that justified the price she had paid; she and Cheryl sold the rest to other dealers. Vintage fabrics, even fragments, were in demand by quilt makers, doll collectors and craftspeople.

Joe, the eldest of Cheryl's three children, arrived home from school in time to help Rachel carry the bag to her car. He wasn't Tony's son—Cheryl's first husband had died when Joe was four—but Tony treated him like his own, and Joe adored his stepfather, though of course he would never have been unmanly enough to say so. He was twelve, a skinny towhead with an enormous appetite and a serious view of the world. As he polished off two sandwiches and a glass of milk, he lectured Rachel and his mother about recycling and the wickedness of using plastic trash bags.

Cheryl had obviously heard it before. Her response was automatic. "I only use the biodegradable kind, honey, you know that. Rachel, don't bother dropping those scraps off tonight. Georgetown is so far out of your way, and it's later than I thought; the traffic will be terrible. Kara doesn't need the things right away."

"I don't mind."

"It will be dark by the time you get home." Cheryl persisted. "If you get home. Did you buy a new tire like I told you to? There wasn't a speck of tread on—"

"For gosh sakes, Mom!" Joe rolled his eyes. "She'll be even later if you don't shut . . . if you don't stop talking."

"Just promise you'll go straight home," Cheryl said anxiously. "Maybe you should spend the night. It looks like snow."

"Mo-om!"

"I'll take it to Kara tomorrow morning," Rachel said, seeing that Joe was about to violate the rules about being rude to his mother and/or using profanity in the presence of "ladies." Tony was strict about such things, and Joe tried to conform. He did pretty well; if Rachel hadn't happened to overhear him talking to a buddy on the telephone, she'd have feared he was being repressed.

"Drive carefully," Cheryl called after them.

"She always says that," Joe muttered. "Even to Dad. Like, he doesn't know how to drive?"

Rachel laughed and gave him a man-to-man slap on the back. "Thanks, Joe. Take care . . . I mean, so long."

It was later than Rachel had realized, and traffic was already heavy. Washington's rush hour starts at four p.m.; the suburban areas between Leesburg and the Capital Beltway had grown too fast for the roads that serviced them, and the Beltway itself was rapidly becoming notorious. Nervous drivers would go miles out of their way to avoid it, and there were legends about hapless tourists who had circled the city for days before they were able to exit. Traffic was no worse than usual that evening; it was about the same, bumper-to-bumper, and moving in fits and starts.

Rachel was used to it, but for some reason it got on her nerves that evening. She knew the reason, though. That incident had unnerved her, not only because encounters with slimy people are unpleasant, but because the scenario had all the elements of a banal romance novel: the leering villain, the wounded hero coming to the rescue.

The flare of brightening lights caught her eye, and she slammed on her brakes. An accident ahead? No; just the usual mess at the 270 interchange. Her neck muscles ached with tension. Spots of moisture appeared on the windshield. Great, she thought sourly. Washington drivers go completely to pieces when it rains. At least she wouldn't have to drive all the way through the city into Georgetown and all the way back to College Park. At that time of day it would have added an additional two hours to the trip. Cheryl was so considerate, always thinking of other people, offering help without having to be asked. Not that her mothering instincts couldn't drive a person crazy sometimes . . .

"Bitch," Rachel said, softly and savagely. She was referring to herself, not to Cheryl, and she sometimes wished she could cultivate the self-deception that allows many people to delude themselves about their real motives. No such comfort was available to her; she was clearly, painfully aware of how indefensible her feelings were. She couldn't conquer them, they were as basic and ungovernable as hunger, but at least she had had the decency to conceal them.

Cheryl didn't know—thank God she didn't know—why the idea of staying overnight was so distasteful. Rachel had spent the night a few times before Tony came home, babysitting (though that word was never used in Joe's hearing) so Cheryl could stay late at the hospital. She hadn't done it since, despite Cheryl's frequent offers. Imagining them together was bad enough without actually seeing it.

When had it happened? The time she had tripped over a teddy bear callously abandoned on the steps, and toppled into his arms? He had only held her for a moment before setting her on her feet and remarking, with a rueful grin, "If I've told Jerry once I've told him a hundred times not to leave his toys lying around. Lucky for Cheryl I arrived at the stragetic moment; you could have sued her for a hefty sum."

Or the time her car wouldn't start and he had insisted on driving her to the mall to buy a new battery after he had diagnosed the old one as beyond repair. He had helped her install it too. Cheryl must have told him she didn't have much money.

Or just the first time she had set eyes on him, arriving home in mid-morning after a long and obviously unpleasant night on the job. Despite the fatigue that lined his face, he was certainly the handsomest man she had ever seen—fifties' film-star handsome, the classic stereotype of the Latin lover of the old movies. But it hadn't been his looks, it had been his manner, the way he smiled at Cheryl, the tenderness with which he held his little boy . . .

And then there was Phil. Their relationship had gone sour so fast that its abrupt, ugly ending had left her groping for someone, something, to take . . . not Phil's place but the place she had hoped he would occupy. She had been trying to fill that place for several years, but in the other cases she had had sense enough to realize it wasn't going to work before she became intimately involved.

She had thought Phil would be different, but in the end it had been she who told him it was over. That was when things got ugly. His reaction had dealt the final blow to her infatuation. He wasn't hurt, he was furious—that she had dismissed him before he could walk out on her.

Tony was all the things she had wanted Phil to be, all the things she had deluded herself into believing that he was. Only one little problem there. Tony wasn't available.

When she got home the house was dark, not a light showing. She had shared the house with three other graduate students. Now that Phil had moved out there were only two, and both of them had gone home for the holidays. Rachel wasn't worried about being alone, but she could have kicked herself for failing to leave a few lights burning. It got dark so early these winter days and the house was on a side street, several blocks from the commercial strip of Route 1.

She opened the door and turned on the lights, including the one on the porch, and trudged wearily back to the car to get the bag of linens. This wasn't a particularly bad neighborhood, but no neighborhoods in and around big cities were free of crime and she didn't want to risk losing something that wasn't hers. The bag weighed a ton. Or maybe she was just tired.

Too tired, at any rate, to tackle the pile of reference books and notes on her desk. She hadn't made much progress on the dissertation these past weeks; she'd been too busy and too preoccupied to concentrate. Too tired to cook, too. Not that she needed to; Cheryl forced enough food on her during working hours to make a healthy dinner unnecessary. Nibbling on crackers and cheese, she decided to have a look at the discarded linens. That was research, of a sort.

There wasn't much of interest in the bag, though. The quilts were late in date, probably from the 1920s; Rachel had learned to recognize the cheap but cheerful cotton prints of that era. They would not rate as vintage classics even if they hadn't been torn and stained. She scraped at one spot with her fingernail. This time the only thing that flaked was the fabric itself; the disfiguring substance appeared to be rust, and it couldn't be removed without destroying the cloth. Perhaps one of the crafty types, as Kara called them, could recycle the unstained portions into a pillow or a stuffed toy.

Seeing the rich shine of black satin in the pile, she pulled it out. Her eye for vintage fabric had improved; this was heavy silk, the genuine article, not a modern synthetic, and it appeared to be a blouse—a waist, she corrected herself—with the leg-o'-mutton sleeves and high netted collar of the past century. When she held it up she understood why Cheryl had discarded it. The lace, fine as cobwebs, that cascaded down the front had turned brown and brittle and the underarm portions had rotted out—no way of repairing that damage, the armholes were usually too tight anyway—and all down the back . . . The stain appeared to be the same color as the black fabric, but it was stiff and hard. Higher up, just below the shoulder, gaped a gash that might have been made by a sharp knife.

Involuntarily Rachel dropped the waist, and then laughed at herself. The stain wasn't blood; the wearer must have leaned against a freshly painted wall or fence. There were other slits in the fabric, produced not by a knife but by the strong dyes used in that period. What had Kara called it? Shattering, that was the word.

There was something evocative and intriguing about old clothes, however; one couldn't help wondering about the women who had worn them. The black silk waist was of good quality; the owner must have been furious when she saw the stain. And what had distracted her, filled her thoughts to such an extent that she failed to notice the fresh paint? Black was for mourning. A grieving widow, an orphaned daughter?

She returned the scraps to the bag and dragged it into the corner out of her way. Television, even the multiple channels of cable, offered nothing that interested her, so she went to bed with one of her reference books.

"Denied outlets for their creative talents in literature and the fine arts, women poured their hidden frustration and suppressed need for expression into the spheres delegated to them by the dominant male society. Needlework has been, in most cultures, a traditional female occupation. Spinning and weaving, sewing and embroidery . . . "

Rachel tossed the book aside. Same old thing, she thought grumpily and unfairly. The thesis the author had expressed had become popular in recent years, especially among feminist scholars. What she hoped to prove was less obvious and more far-out: the theory that women had woven their own secret forms of magic into their creations—spells to guard against enemies, to attract and hold a lover, to protect the souls of the dead from demons. The magical use of weaving and spinning was well attested in ancient religions; in her introduction Rachel planned to discuss the well-known cases.

The Norns of Norse legend and the Moirai of the Greeks spun the threads of human lives. The Greek maiden Arachne had been turned into a spider for daring to challenge a goddess's skill in spinning—and in the magic that spinning wove? The Greek gods and goddesses were as spiteful and petty-minded as their human worshipers, but surely, Rachel argued, there had been more at stake in that contest than housewifely skill. The secret knowledge involved in such skills might have been passed down through the ages from mother to daughter, hidden from men because it was a source of power and therefore a threat to their domination. Even the patterns of quilting went back to ancient themes. Star and sun as symbols of light, flower and foliage representing the rebirth of spring life after the death of winter, the Drunkard's Path and similar patterns recalling the labyrinth, the maze in which an enemy could be trapped, unable to escape.

Like the Beltway, Rachel thought with a faint smile. Modern man is still trapped in a maze of roads that go nowhere.

There was no question about the fact that magic had been viewed by many cultures as a practical, pragmatic method of coping with the problems of life. In order to sprout and grow, crops had to be planted during the proper phase of the moon and with the proper spells; medicine would not be as effective without the incantations and prayers that accompanied it. In fact, there were few cultures, ancient and modern, that had not employed magic, and people who thought rational Western civilization had risen above such superstition were kidding themselves. It wasn't difficult to find examples of magical practices, but Rachel had not had much luck in identifying a secret, specific women's magic. That wasn't surprising. If the practices were secret, they wouldn't have been described to anthropologists, even female anthropologists, who would be viewed as foreigners, skeptics, outside the sisterhood of that particular culture.

She tossed the book aside and reached for another, on Ozark magic and superstition. Some of the superstitions connected with needlecraft were based on the principles of magic defined by the great nineteenth-century scholar Sir James Fraser. Knotting, braiding, and weaving were varieties of imitative magic; they could render a man impotent, or bind the affections of a faithless lover, or keep a woman writhing in the pangs of childbirth, unable to deliver. The magic of contagion or connection was based on the belief that an action performed on an object that had been in intimate contact with an individual, especially body parts like hair and fingernail clippings, would affect the individual himself. Never make a dress with a needle that has been used to sew a shroud; the contagion of death will affect the wearer of the dress.

Had Medea used such a needle when she embroidered the deadly garment she sent to the bride of her faithless lover? No; that was probably too farfetched. But Rachel felt sure Medea had steeped that garment in evil magic as well as in poison. Witch and sorceress they had called her, among other names—traitor, murderess, tiger. Well-merited names; her crimes had been unspeakable. And all for love . . . Rachel closed the book and turned out the light. So many spells, so many superstitions about love and marriage, winning a man and holding him. Women were fools. Including herself.

Her mind retraced the familiar labyrinth of indecision. She knew what she ought to do—give Cheryl her notice, find another job, or try to scrape along on her savings while she worked like mad on the dissertation.

If she stayed on she would give herself away sooner or later and that would settle the matter—in the most unpleasant, humiliating manner possible. There was no other possibility. Even if he . . .

It wasn't the first time she had allowed herself to entertain that fantasy—being alone with him, seeing his face change, his eyes soften, his hands reach out for her. Hearing him admit he had tried to fight his feelings but that they had proved too strong to resist . . . Rachel turned

over and buried her face in the pillow. She might be hopelessly infatu-
ated but she wasn't stupid or completely unprincipled. It would never
happen. He'd never leave his wife and children, not Tony, not even if
he fell in love with someone else. I wouldn't want him to, Rachel
thought. At least I hope I wouldn't. Oh, God, what am I going to do?

Eventually physical exhaustion overcame her and she fell into one of
those exasperating states of semiconsciousness, too tired to wake up
and too uptight to sleep soundly. If she had been deeply asleep she
might not have heard the faint creak of the opening door.

She was lying on her side facing the door, but she couldn't see anything, not even the light she had left burning in the hall. For several
seconds she heard nothing more, and she was trying to convince herself that the bulb had burned out and the sound had been the product
of dreaming when another sound put an end to those comfortable
assumptions. It was the sound of expelled breath.

Her heart was pounding so hard she felt sure the intruder could
hear it, and she almost regretted her refusal to buy a gun. Almost, but
not really. Phil had insisted on keeping his in the drawer of the bedside
table, and its proximity had always made her nervous. A loaded gun
was an invitation to accident or manslaughter, and an unloaded
weapon wasn't worth a damn. "What am I supposed to do, ask the
burglar to please wait till I find the bullets and put them in the gun?"
she had demanded of Phil. He had not thought it was funny.

The only potentially useful item in the drawer now was a flashlight.
Rachel's arms were under the bedclothes, and she knew she couldn't
extract them without making a noise. The flashlight was no good anyhow. He was already too close. Her eyes had adjusted and she could
see his outline, motionless in the open doorway. Ideas ran wildly
around in her head like a frantic animal trapped in a maze. How had
he gotten in? Silly question, there were no bars on the windows . . .
With a key? Phil still had one. There was no comfort in that thought;
he had been furious with her the day he left, mouthing curses and
threats. He'd been drunk, probably he hadn't meant it . . . She couldn't
think what to do, she couldn't move. Better lie still, pretend to be
asleep, let him find her purse, her few pieces of jewelry.

Coward.

The voice was as clear as if she had spoken aloud, but the words
leaped into her consciousness with the instantaneous speed of thought.

Hoping for a hero, are you? There are no heroes. Just you. Are you going to let him do whatever he wants—steal, rape you, hurt you? You can fight back.

The rustle of the sheets sounded as loud as an explosion to her, but the shapeless form didn't react. Perhaps he thought she was only turning over in her sleep. She knew the next sound would be louder. The drawer always stuck. She yanked it open, grabbed the flashlight, and switched it on. The beam struck him full in the face.

Rachel didn't get to Georgetown until almost ten a.m. She had hoped Kara would be gone by then and that she could leave the bag of linens with the maid. No such luck. Kara answered the door herself.

By her standards she was casually dressed, in loose slacks and an oversized shirt whose sleeves were rolled to the elbows. The shirt was Edwardian, a man's dress shirt with a starched pleated bib, and it looked sensational on her.

"Good God!" she exclaimed. "What happened to you?"

Involuntarily Rachel raised a hand to her face. "I ran into a door."

Kara grabbed the bag with one hand and Rachel with the other. "I had planned to offer you a cup of coffee, but I think an icebag or a slice of raw beefsteak—"

"I really can't stay. I'm late."

"Cheryl isn't expecting you till you get there." Moving with brisk efficiency she closed the door, divested Rachel of her wet coat, and draped it over a chair. "She called to tell me you were dropping off that parcel, but she didn't mention you'd had an accident. Come back to the kitchen and tell me about it."

There was no reason for reticence; Rachel had already reported the incident to the police, and she would have to tell Cheryl, if only to put her on her guard. But she resented Kara's authoritative manner, and she felt out of place in that house. It was as elegant as its mistress, one of the old Federal houses that gave the area its distinctive character, and as Rachel shuffled along the hall in Kara's wake she noticed details—a gracefully curved staircase, an antique Persian rug in the drawing room, floors polished to mirror smoothness except where her wet footprints marred them.

The kitchen wasn't as formal as the front part of the house; the warm red-brown tiles and the bright print of the curtains formed a cheerful contrast to the dead garden visible through the wide bay window. The table in the curve of the bay was set with woven mats, and at the moment its surface was comfortably cluttered with pottery mugs and dishes, a plate of doughnuts, magazines and papers. Rachel was starting to relax when she saw the woman who was sitting at the table, and felt herself freeze up again.

She was the daintiest of little ladies, exquisitely groomed and looking much younger than her probable age. The Chanel suit of soft blue matched her eyes and set off her porcelain skin and snowy hair; the outfit would have been more appropriate for a Junior League luncheon than a casual kitchen coffee klatch. When she saw Rachel she jumped up with a cry of sympathy.

"You poor girl! What happened?"

Rachel knew who she was even before Kara introduced them. Kara had often spoken of her Aunt Ruth, who had mothered her and encouraged her and helped her start her business. The house had once belonged to Ruth; she and her husband, a professor at a local university, now lived in the country.

She fussed over Rachel as Cheryl would have done, settling her in a chair, folding ice cubes in a towel and holding it against Rachel's bruised cheek. Kindness and sympathy had a demoralizing effect; Rachel felt tears come to her eyes.

She didn't want to show signs of weakness, so she fought back the tears and concentrated on producing a coherent story. Kara had obviously heard about the bag of quilts and the man who had left it; she nodded impatiently but didn't interrupt, since it was news to Ruth, who kept letting out little gasps of distress. Kara's interest revived when Rachel described what had happened the previous night.

"It was the same man?" she asked.

"Uh-huh."

"You were very brave," Ruth exclaimed. "I would have cowered under the covers and pretended I was asleep."

Kara's face softened. "No, you wouldn't. You'd have chased him, brandishing the flashlight."

"I hope I'd have had better sense," Ruth said indignantly. Then she gave Rachel an apologetic smile. "That wasn't meant as criticism. You didn't really chase him, did you?"

"I don't know what, if anything, I had in mind," Rachel admitted, with an answering smile. "It was sheer reflex—sheer terror, probably. You feel so helpless—you are helpless!—when you're lying down. I jumped up, yelling and waving the flashlight. He must have assumed I was asleep until the light hit him in the face, and it startled him so that he turned and ran. No, I wouldn't have chased him; I just wanted to slam the door and shove the furniture up against it. I miscalculated— ran smack into the edge of the door and almost knocked myself out. I managed to close and lock it, though."

"You called the police, of course." Kara reached for a doughnut and bit into it. Powdered sugar sifted down onto her chest.

"Of course."

"You told them the whole story?"

"Certainly."

"Don't be so defensive," Kara said mildly. "Have a doughnut."

She pushed the plate toward Rachel, who realized she was starved. No breakfast, only a few hours' sleep, and a headache the size of Mount Everest . . . She ate the doughnut, while Kara thought aloud.

"It's the bag he wants, obviously. He must have mistaken the one you took home for the one he abandoned. You didn't notice anyone following you?" She answered her own question before Rachel, her mouth full of doughnut, could do so. "No, why should you? Heavy traffic, dark, you were anxious to get home. You live alone?"

Rachel explained. Ruth said in a worried voice, "She can't go back there. Not until they catch the man."

"It might not be a good idea," Kara agreed. "Though if he was on your trail this morning he knows the bag isn't at your place now."

"Where is it?" Ruth asked.

Kara brushed at the sugar speckling her shirt front. "Here."

After a while she broke into Rachel's exclamations. "For God's sake stop apologizing. I know you had no intention of passing on the curse. And you stop fussing, Aunt Ruth. I don't think he'll be fool enough to try again; he's narrowly missed being caught twice already. If he does, I'd rather he came after me than after Rachel, or Cheryl and the kids."

"And Tony," Rachel said, without thinking.

"Right." Kara didn't look at her. "This house is as secure as bolts and bars and alarms can make it. And I've got Alexander."

"Oh, yes," Ruth said sarcastically. "How could I have forgotten about Alexander? With him on the premises you've nothing to worry about."

"Who's Alexander?" Rachel asked.

The other women turned to look at a basket on the far side of the room, close to the radiator. Rachel had taken the motionless, fuzzy mass in it for a pile of knitting—with a particularly ugly pattern. At the repetition of the name the bundle stirred and squirmed and a face appeared. It had to be a face—Rachel caught a glimpse of an eye before hair obscured it—but it didn't resemble the countenance of any creature, living or extinct, she had ever seen.

"Good Lord," she gasped. "What is it?"

The thing climbed slowly out of the basket and stood up. It resembled a small barrel or keg covered with orange and white and black and gray fur, except for its rump, which was obscenely bare. It inched forward, rolling from side to side; when it was a few feet away it stopped, tossed its head, and lunged.

Kara detached it from the leg of the table and lifted it onto her lap. "This is Alexander," she said. "Good dog, brave dog."

"Dog?" Rachel repeated in disbelief.

"He's old," Kara said defensively. "He can't see very well or move very fast, but he thinks he's defending me."

"Nonsense," Ruth said, eyeing Alexander askance. "He doesn't give a damn about you or anybody else. He just likes to bite things. He was aiming for your ankle, Rachel, but he can't see past the end of his nose and he's lost most of his teeth, so you weren't in any danger."

"He has so few pleasures," Kara murmured, cuddling the dog. It responded by clamping its jaws over her arm. "And he won't live much longer."

"He'll outlive the lot of us," Ruth said disgustedly. "He's too mean and ugly to die. Put him back in his basket, the sight of him spoils my appetite."

Kara did so without comment, although her compressed lips made it clear that pejorative comments about Alexander offended her. It wasn't unusual for a woman without children to lavish affection on a pet, but that anyone, much less fastidious Kara, could love a disaster like that dog, astonished Rachel.

Apparently unaware of the soggy spot on her sleeve, Kara said, "Where were we?" and went on without waiting for an answer. "Trying to figure out what the Alleged will do next. A futile exercise, really; he's obviously so much stupider than any of us that it would be impossible for us to predict his next move. Besides, we don't know whether he was following Rachel this morning. He may believe the bag of linens is still at her place."

"Which is precisely why I feel she shouldn't go back there," Ruth insisted.

"I agree."

"I don't," Rachel said. "There is absolutely no reason—"

Kara was on her feet, clearing the table. "You can't be certain it's the bag he's after. Maybe it's you."

"Don't frighten her," Ruth exclaimed.

"If I have to frighten her to convince her to act sensibly, I will," Kara said. "I can think of several theories that might explain this character's behavior, and all of them involve a potential threat to Rachel. I'm going to drive her back to her house so she can pack her things, and then I'll take her to Leesburg." Rachel started to protest. Again Kara cut her off. "Rachel, don't be stupid. You can stay here for a few days, if that's what you prefer. So long as you're not alone."

It wasn't the most gracious invitation Rachel had ever received. Though Kara's voice was neutral and her expression bland, Rachel felt sure the other woman knew her secret. Otherwise she wouldn't have suggested the alternative. Obviously it made better sense for Rachel to stay with the Cardozas, where there was ample room and she could be of help to Cheryl.

"She could come to us," Ruth said, innocently aware of undercurrents. "Pat and I rattle around in that big old house and it's not far from the shop."

That idea appealed even less than the prospect of moving in with Kara. Rachel could imagine what Ruth's house was like—a Virginia manor house, decorated with dainty chintzes and antique furniture. They probably had live-in servants. I'd be as out of place as Alexander the dog, Rachel thought; the only difference being that I know I'm a slob and Alexander doesn't know. Or care.

Before she could comment, Kara said impatiently, "We'll settle that later. Ruth, will you call Cheryl and explain the situation? Tell her we're on the way. Come on, Rachel, we've got a lot to do."

It was after noon by the time they left College Park. Arguing with Kara was a waste of breath; she had ignored or countered every protest

Rachel had made, helped her pack, hauled suitcases and boxes to the car. As they headed for the Beltway along the eccentric traffic of Route 1, Rachel tried one more time to talk Kara into taking her back to Georgetown and her car, but her heart wasn't in it. In the gray winter light the house had looked like a set for a horror movie, its paint peeling, its windows dark, the untrimmed shrubbery a wild tangle that provided concealment for an infinity of imaginary enemies. Rachel hadn't expected that the sight of her room would make her break into a cold sweat of remembered terror and morbid "what-ifs." What if he had had a gun? What if he had attacked instead of running away?

So when Kara told her not to be silly she settled back and relaxed. Kara was a good driver, and the car was warm and comfortable—quite a contrast to Rachel's drafty, springless wonder—and she had had only three hours' sleep. She dozed off and didn't wake up till they reached Leesburg.

Kara brushed her apologies aside. "I expect you were exhausted. I was watching; I'm almost certain no one was following us. Let's go in before Cheryl—. Too late, there she comes. Just look at her—no coat, no sweater, dashing out in the cold as if you were an abandoned baby. That woman needs to have her maternal instinct amputated."

Not until she had supplied them with hot coffee and hot soup, and Rachel had assured her no less than four times that she was fine, did Cheryl consent to sit down and stop talking. Tony hadn't spoken except to greet them; he was sitting in a rocking chair with one cushion behind his head and another one under his thigh. Several others had been inserted around him, more or less at random, and he looked horribly uncomfortable.

The room had been the kitchen of the house, and Cheryl had left the appliances in place when she turned it into a downstairs sitting or family room. The stove and refrigerator were butter-yellow; the rug was braided; the furniture was upholstered in a country print, with matching cottage curtains at the window; three cats and two dogs were curled up on the smaller rug next to the fireplace. It was cozy enough to turn a sensitive stomach, and the temperature of the room must have been close to eighty. Tony's face shone with perspiration.

He stopped Cheryl before she could add another log to the roaring fire. "Sit down, honey, and stop fussing. We have to talk."

"Right." Kara shed her jacket and rolled up her sleeves. "Kee-rist,

Cherry, it's a hundred degrees Fahrenheit in here already. I gather you talked to Aunt Ruth?"

"And the police," Cheryl said. "From D.C., I mean. They came out just before—"

"Let me tell it, okay?" Tony's voice was pleasant but tightly controlled.

"Okay," Cheryl said cheerfully. "Do you want another pillow behind—"

"No! I mean, no, thanks." He went on without drawing breath, addressing Rachel. "Ordinarily it might have taken them some time to follow up on your story, Rachel; they've got enough murders in D.C. to keep them busy, never mind a little attempted burglary. As it turns out, the cop you talked to last night remembered me, from the time when I worked for the department."

"I thought he gave me a funny look when I mentioned the shop."

"Yeah. I couldn't add much to what you had already told him. He agreed that the merchandise could be stolen property but he pointed out that the guy's subsequent behavior is a little whacko. Why would he take such risks to retrieve the stuff?"

"Because it's worth a lot of money," Cheryl said. "Ten, twenty, thirty thousand."

"That much?" Kara's eyes took on an acquisitive gleam.

"At least. And," Cheryl went on, "he might not think there was much risk involved. One woman, alone . . . After all, if criminals were sensible people they wouldn't be criminals."

Tony's frown turned to a smile. "You said it, babe."

"Makes sense to me," Kara agreed. "Your buddy doesn't buy that idea, Tony?"

Tony shrugged. "He's just a poor ignorant male like me. The idea of a bundle of old bedclothes being worth big bucks is hard to swallow."

"You ought to know better," Cheryl began.

"So what does he think?" Kara demanded.

Tony glanced at Rachel, and then looked away. One of the cats jumped onto her lap. It was a calico, named—by Megan, who was, after all, only four—Patches.

"You don't have to treat me like a child," she said, stroking the cat. "But that's stupid. Why would he go to all that trouble? There are plenty of women around and I'm not exactly Helen of Troy."

Tony's heavy black eyebrows drew together. "For God's sake, Rachel, don't make asinine jokes. This character got to you—don't deny it, I could hear it in your voice. Some people get a sexual kick out of evoking that reaction. If he thought—" He broke off. "Cheryl, will you stop making faces at me? I'm not trying to scare her, but I'm glad she's here, and I think she should stay here until they catch the guy."

"Suppose they don't?" Rachel demanded. "I can't stay here forever."

"The chances are pretty good that they will," Tony said. "I've asked the boys to check reports of break-ins and burglaries, not only here but in adjoining counties and the District. This one should be easy to spot; there can't be too many cases of stolen quilts. He may have a previous record, and if there's a mug shot on file I can probably pick him out. I got a good look at him."

"Anyhow, you're welcome to stay as long as you like," Cheryl declared. "That long drive is a killer, especially in bad weather, and we've got plenty of room. Oops—look at the time. I've got to go meet the school bus."

Kara rose to her feet. "I'd better get going too; we're supposed to attend a reception at the Japanese Embassy."

"You and Mark are coming for dinner tomorrow night, don't forget." Cheryl slipped into her coat.

"How could I forget the great annual tree-decorating ceremony? I don't know why you're bothering this year," Kara grumbled. "You won't even be here for Christmas. And you always work yourself into a frazzle and do too much."

"The kids enjoy it," Cheryl murmured. "See you tomorrow, then. I'll be right back, honey."

Rachel felt a sick mixture of relief and disappointment. She had heard Tony and Cheryl discussing their plans to spend the holidays with his mother in Ohio, but the fact had slipped her mind.

Despite her declared intention of leaving, Kara didn't seem to be in any hurry. As soon as Cheryl left the room she went to Tony, removed two of the most obtrusive pillows, and tossed them onto the couch. Neither of them commented, but the look they exchanged—not quite intimate, but a little warmer than friendly—made Rachel feel like an intruder.

"Do you really want to go to Ohio?" Kara asked.

"No way I can get out of it," Tony said. "The whole clan will be there this year, they planned it months ago. And Mama is dying to get her poor sick boy home."

"Poor sick boy," Kara murmured. She was smiling, making a joke of it, but her hand moved to his shoulder.

His eyes shifted, acknowledging—reminding her of—Rachel's presence. "What about you, Rachel? We're a bossy bunch, I never thought to ask about your plans. Are you going home for Christmas, or is someone coming to you?"

Kara turned. Her expression of polite inquiry didn't fool Rachel. Cheryl had taken her at face value, grateful for the help she needed so badly, but a sharp businesswoman like Kara would investigate anyone she hired to handle expensive objects. Kara undoubtedly knew all about her background. Not that there was anything shameful or embarrassing about it, but she was in no mood to explain to Kara, of all people, why she was alone during the holiday season.

"I have no plans," she said.

It sounded ruder and more abrupt than she had meant it to, and she realized, too late, that the brief speech might have been interpreted as a play for sympathy no plans, no friends, no family. Poor little me. She could have kicked herself when she saw Tony's expression—troubled, faintly guilty. He was blaming himself for insensitivity and lack of interest. Obviously it had never occurred to him to wonder about her personal life. Why should it?

Quickly Rachel went on, "I had talked with some of my friends about cooking dinner together—at my place—you know, one of us bringing the turkey and another making dessert, and . . . But we hadn't made definite plans. I'd be happy to stay here, if you need a housesitter."

"Even if you're staying here, which I think you should, you don't have to stick around twenty-four hours a day," Tony said pleasantly. "You could invite your friends to come here Christmas Day."

"Oh, no, I wouldn't do that." Kara's steady regard made her stumble into unnecessary explanations. "Not that they'd behave improperly, or anything. But this is your house, and you don't know them, so . . . I don't mind being alone."

"You won't be alone," Kara said.

"What?"

"I wouldn't have suggested you come here if I had thought you'd be alone. What would have been the point of that? Adam should be adequate protection."

She gave Tony another of those comradely grins, and his mustache twitched in responsive amusement. "I should think so."

"When is he coming?"

"His ETA is the twentieth, but that doesn't mean a thing with Adam; I've never known him to show up when he said he would. He always has the most fantastic stories to account for being late. Even more fantastic, they're usually true." Turning to Rachel, he added reassuringly, "I don't mean to imply he's unreliable. He'll certainly be here before we leave; he knows we're counting on him to look after the animals."

"Who is he?" Rachel asked.

"A former student of Pat's," Kara answered. Seeing Rachel's blank look, she explained. "Aunt Ruth's husband, Patrick MacDougal. He taught anthro at Johns Hopkins before he retired last year."

"I know who he is, of course," Rachel said. "I've read his books. The name didn't connect at first."

"Adam teaches too," Tony said. "In North Carolina. He's an orphan and a protégé of Pat's, so he often spends the holidays with them when he isn't out in the field. This year we conned him into pet-sitting for us. That suited him fine, because he's not . . . I mean, he prefers . . . Hmmm. I don't know exactly how to put this . . ."

"What Tony means is that he won't bother you," Kara said. "In any way."

Twenty-four hours later Rachel was still in the dark as to why the mysterious Adam wouldn't "bother" her. She had tried to find out, but the answers to her inquiries only confused her more. Her blunt question to Kara: "Is Adam gay?" got an equally blunt response. "I don't think so. Why do you ask? Are you homophobic?"

She tried Cheryl next. "He's not physically handicapped—I mean, 'challenged,' is he?"

Cheryl hooted with laughter. "Adam? Quite the contrary." She was about to elaborate when one of the cats let out a squawl of rage and she had to rush to rescue Jerry, who was trying, over the cat's emphatic protests, to tie a red bow and a bell around its neck.

The private kindergarten he and his four-year-old sister attended had closed for the holidays, but the public schools had not yet done so. Joe had left earlier, loudly berating the sadism of the board of education. Without him to ride herd on them, the younger children were racing around, yelling with excitement and getting in everybody's way. Alice, Cheryl's part-time housekeeper, had gone to Pennsylvania for a couple of weeks to spend the holidays with her daughter, and Cheryl was trying to do several things at once: bake cookies, set up the tree, prepare dinner for a dozen people, and deal with customers who had delayed their shopping till the last minute. The dogs wove in and out, hitting people with their tails and licking up the scraps of dough Cheryl dropped onto the floor; the cats all tried to get onto Tony's lap, since he was the only one sitting down. Abnormally sensitive to every expression that crossed his face, Rachel knew his enjoyment of the comfortable holiday bustle was marred by his inability to do anything except look on. Watching Cheryl wrestle with the tree, eight feet tall and too thick to fit into the stand, he appeared to be on the brink of apoplexy.

Kara arrived around noon, driving Rachel's car. She refused Cheryl's attempt to prepare lunch for her, saying she'd had a sandwich before she left, but accepted a chocolate chip cookie warm from the oven. "Anything new?" she asked.

Tony shook his head. His eyes, wide with alarm, were fixed on Cheryl, who was whacking at the trunk of the tree with a hatchet.

"Thomas is coming over this evening," he answered abstractedly. "He may have something . . . Honey, please don't wave that hatchet around. Leave it till Joe gets home, he'll do it."

The shop bell sounded. Kara reached for a towel and wiped her fingers. "I'll go."

"Take that plate of cookies," Cheryl said, her voice muffled by pine needles as she struggled with the recalcitrant tree. "You'd better check the punch, too, it's getting low."

"What plate of cookies?" Kara stopped, halfway to the door.

"Didn't I . . . Oh, darn, I forgot. Wait a minute." She tried to free herself from the affectionate grip of the tree.

"I'll do it," Rachel said quickly. Rolling her eyes, Kara hurried out, and Rachel got a plate from the shelf. It took some time to arrange the cookies to Cheryl's satisfaction—a paper doily underneath, sprigs of pine artistically arranged around the edges. She left Cheryl scolding one of the cats, a huge tabby with a perverse and perilous taste for chocolate, who had taken advantage of her distraction to steal a brownie.

Unruffled, her voice smooth as cream, Kara was entertaining a customer. Mrs. Baxter didn't buy for herself but she had a granddaughter on whom she doted and who was "into" vintage. She had been in twice before looking for a present for the girl, and she was still in the process of making up her mind. Accepting a cookie, she studied the garment Kara was holding.

"It's beautiful. But I don't know that green is her color. She's blonde, you know, with lovely blue eyes. Maybe the black would be better." She waved the cookie at the black dress, which had crystal and jet beads covering the bodice and hanging in festoons down the skirt. Kara moved discreetly back, avoiding the scattering of crumbs, and Mrs. Baxter went blithely on. "That twenties' style suits her, she has such a pretty slender figure. That one might be too big, though. She has such a slender—"

The door opened and a man entered. He was young, casually dressed in jeans and a down jacket, brown hair brushed back from a high forehead, horn-rimmed glasses riding low on his nose. Could this be the mysterious Adam, Rachel wondered? Apparently not. With a nod at Kara he sauntered toward the display case that contained jewelry.

Rachel hesitated, wondering whether she should withdraw or attend to the new customer. Mrs. Baxter obviously wasn't about to conclude her business in a hurry.

"I'll be with you in a minute, Mr. Dupuis," Kara said. "Mrs. Baxter, would you like Rachel to model the black dress? She's just Marian's size. What about another glass of punch?"

It was very smoothly done. By the time Rachel had changed, Mr. Dupuis had selected a garnet bracelet for his wife and Kara had boxed and wrapped it.

Mrs. Baxter loved the fashion show. Feeling like a fool, Rachel also modeled the green dress and the peignoir. After asking the price of the last, Mrs. Baxter decided on the black dress and Rachel was able to escape. Kara soon followed her into the kitchen.

"Sorry about that, Rachel," she said. "I didn't mean to put you on the spot, but I had to do something to force that woman to a decision. She'd sit all afternoon if I let her."

"What did she pick?" Cheryl asked. "Not the peignoir, I hope."

"No, the black flapper dress. We'd be a thousand bucks richer if she'd bought the peignoir."

"I don't care. I love that garment. It's Callot Soeurs—the only one we've ever had."

"If you like it so much why don't you keep it?" Tony asked.

Cheryl leaned over and gave him a quick kiss. "Too expensive. And too impractical. Besides, that pale pink is the wrong color for me."

"The wrong color for mousy Marian too," Kara said cattily. "With those washed-out blue eyes and wispy hair she'd be practically invisible. It looked fantastic on Rachel."

The compliment was too casual to be anything except genuine. The others studied Rachel with friendly interest and she felt herself blushing, not at Cheryl's additional compliments about her dark hair and eyes and "that pretty fresh complexion," or even at Tony's smiling agreement, but at the memory of how she had looked in the fabulous creation. She had had to take the pins and fasteners out of her hair so they wouldn't catch on the delicate fabric, and the image she had seen reflected in the long mirror was one she hardly recognized as herself. Like all inspired designers, the turn-of-the century sisters had created not just a dress but a mood, a fantasy. Loosened hair tumbling over her shoulders, cheeks pink and eyes wide, her reflection in the mirror had suggested the cover of a particularly sloppy regency romance.

"I'll take it," she said lightly, avoiding Tony's eyes. "On time, of course. Five bucks a week for the rest of my natural life."

By the time the guests began to arrive, things were more or less under control. The family room had been cleaned and swept, the animals banished to an upstairs room, and the buffet table covered with a lavish spread, turkey and ham and roast beef and all the accoutrements, salads and sauces and rolls. And cookies.

Cheryl hadn't forgotten a single cliché, not even the sprigs of mistletoe hung in strategic places. If any of the guests were inclined toward cynicism—and Rachel suspected at least one of them was—they kept their feelings to themselves. Everyone entered into the Dickensian spirit of the festivities, delivering and receiving brightly wrapped gifts, bellowing out carols, helping to decorate the tree, stuffing themselves with food, exchanging hugs and kisses and compliments.

While the others were gathered around the piano singing, Rachel retreated to a quiet corner to catch her breath. It had been a long time since she had been part of such a large, boisterous group and her brain was overflowing with names she would never remember—or have cause to remember. Only two of the people she had met had made a permanent impression: one was a stocky young man with steady brown eyes, whom Tony had introduced as one of his subordinates. "He'll keep an eye on you and the shop while I'm gone, Rachel."

Tom's expression indicated that the assignment was not unwelcome. "Sorry to say I've drawn a blank so far. But we'll track him down, don't worry. Call if anything at all happens."

The other man was sitting by himself on a sofa by the fire. If he was alone it was by choice; she had never seen anyone look so at ease, so comfortable with himself and his surroundings. He was a big man, heavily built and unbowed by age, though only a few streaks of the original carrot-red remained in his thick gray hair. Like most of the others he was casually dressed, in jeans and a wool shirt, and his face was as weathered as that of a farmer. The lines were deeply incised, and not all of them were lines of affability. He must scowl quite a lot, Rachel thought.

She had only exchanged a few words with him. Most of the time he had been the center of an animated group, whose conversation was dominated by his booming voice.

Catching her eye, he smiled, displaying a set of imposing teeth, and beckoned her to join him. "Not singing?" he asked.

"I can't," Rachel admitted.

"I can," said Patrick A. MacDougal, professor emeritus and former president of the American Anthropological Association. "But they won't let me. Spite and jealousy, that's the reason."

"You drown everybody else out, that's the reason," said his wife, leaving the group gathered around the piano. "And you sing flat."

"Spite and jealousy," MacDougal repeated. "So, Rachel, I understand you and I are in the same business."

"Hardly." Rachel let out a gasp of embarrassed laughter. "I've read your books, Dr. MacDougal—"

"Pat."

"Um . . . Thank you. They've been very helpful, especially the one on superstition, psychology, and folk medicine. But what I'm doing—hoping to do—is far less impressive."

"Tell me about it."

If she had met him in his professional capacity she might not have had the courage to talk at such length. His was one of the biggest names in the field, with a reputation that already equaled that of such icons as Malinowski and Fraser, and he was clearly not the kind of man who suffered fools gladly—or in any other way. He looked less formidable sprawled across the sofa with one long arm draped over the slim shoulders of his wife and a beer can in his other hand.

"Interesting idea," he said finally. "Female subcultures haven't received their proper attention—"

"That's because until a generation ago anthropologists were all men," Rachel said.

"Lay off me, kid," MacDougal said. "I'm already surrounded by hard-nosed feminists, including my own wife. Meade and Benedict, to name only two, were of your grandparents' generation, and there were others before them. Snubbed and ignored, most of them, but not by me."

"I'm sorry," Rachel began.

"Don't apologize," Ruth said. "He'll only despise you. He loves an argument. You're right, and he knows it."

MacDougal blandly ignored this put-down. "Interesting idea," he repeated. "I don't know that anyone's ever tackled it from quite that perspective. Sewing was employed in the most important and magical aspects of life—shrouds for the dead, clothing for newborn babies, wedding garments. What—" He broke off with a grunt as a small body toppled over the back of the couch and landed on his stomach. "God damn it!"

"Don't swear in front of the child," Ruth said, removing Jerry's left foot from her lap.

"Swear, hell, I'm going to give him a good hiding." Pat righted the child. "You ought to be in bed, you little monster."

Jerry grinned at the face that scowled hideously at him. "I'm not going to bed for a long time," he announced. "A long, long, long time."

By nine o'clock everyone had left except the family, and the younger children had been carried up to bed. Jerry went tucked under Pat's arm like a bundle of old clothes. He let out a few howls as a matter of principle, but he clearly enjoyed the process. Megan, looking like a Christmas fairy in a ruffled pinafore and a silver coronet, eluded capture for a full ten minutes before she was discovered in the coat closet sitting on a pile of boots and eating cookies. Once caught she went without protest, smiling angelically at the exasperated adults over her mother's shoulder.

His own friends having departed, Joe politely excused himself and went upstairs, though probably not to bed. Television was more interesting than adult conversation. The adults lounged in various stages of collapse. Rachel had started collecting glasses, plates, and crumpled napkins, but was driven back to her chair by a unanimous outcry.

"Don't do that or I'll feel as if I have to help," Ruth said. "And I don't feel like it."

"We'll all pitch in later," Mark added lazily. He had returned from Europe that evening and come straight to the house; now his suitcoat hung over the back of a chair and the head cat, a huge tabby named Figgin, was chewing on his discarded tie. "This is the best part, after everybody's gone home except us."

He smiled at his wife. Instead of responding, she said brusquely, "It was a great party, but I still think it was a stupid idea. Cheryl has that long drive ahead of her tomorrow, and I'll bet she hasn't finished packing yet."

"It's only a five—" An ear-splitting yawn interrupted Cheryl. "Hour drive. And I have too finished packing. Almost."

"And that's another thing," Kara said. "Where's that no-good friend of yours, Pat? If he doesn't show up, Rachel will be alone here."

The reminder was like a dash of cold water, spoiling the warm relaxed mood. The only calm face was that of Pat MacDougal. "He'll be here."

"If he isn't, Rachel can come to us," Mark said, frowning.

"And leave the animals alone?" Kara demanded.

"He'll be here, dammit!" Pat shouted. "But while we're on the subject, maybe one of you will explain to me precisely what has been going on. All I've heard so far is a lot of garbled gossip from various emotional females." He pointed a long finger, quelling the babble of indignant voices. "Tony."

Tony obliged, as methodically as if he were giving an official report. "So far nothing has turned up," he finished. "There have been the usual number of burglaries, but nobody's reported losing a bunch of old quilts."

"I can see," said Pat, "that it is high time someone of intelligence considered this business. Your Alleged must be a local boy—"

"Not necessarily," Tony began.

"Otherwise," Pat went on, raising his voice, "he wouldn't know about the shop. I assume you haven't had any parallel cases—burglars specializing in antique fabrics? I thought not. Nor, from your description of him, is he the sort of aesthete who would appreciate antiques of that esoteric variety. So the logical conclusion is that he knew in advance the stuff was worth stealing because he had a personal connection with the owner. Either he worked at a shop where such things are sold, or he swiped them from a friend or relative who had told him of their value."

"Even so," Tony argued, "the theft would have been reported."

"Not if the owner doesn't know the stuff is missing." Pat's teeth gleamed weirdly in the firelight. "Let's have a look at it."

He jumped briskly to his feet. The others stared at him with a conspicuous absence of enthusiasm.

"Not now," Mark said, with a groan. "Dammit, Pat, I want to sit and relax. Why'd you have to bring up the subject?"

"Pat's right," Tony said. "Much as I hate to inflate his ego by admitting it. Where'd you stow the loot, babe?"

"One of the cupboards in the shop." Cheryl rose stiffly. "I've been feeling bad about leaving Rachel here; if we can find out something that might help locate the man . . . "

The others followed her and she switched on the overhead lights before dragging the box out of the cupboard. Rachel helped her spread the contents over chairs and tables. Pat didn't even wait to see the collection before commenting, "As I thought. Five will get you ten that lot has been packed in a trunk or box for years. Smell the mothballs."

"Of course," Cheryl said.

"What do you mean, 'of course?'" Tony demanded. "You never bothered to mention—"

"A perfect example of the fact that men and women don't share the same cultural traditions," Pat said, grinning. "She didn't mention it because to her—and to you other ladies—the fact was self-evident."

"These things certainly didn't come from a commercial establishment," Kara agreed. "Nobody would put them out for sale in this condition." She leaned over to examine the white quilt more closely. "And I certainly wouldn't keep something as good as this in mothballs, I'd have it cleaned and on the shelf as soon as possible. Are the others as fine?"

"Even better. Show her the album quilt, Rachel."

Rachel realized that she was standing in front of the chair, blocking the view of the quilt—almost as if she were standing guard over it. Slowly she stepped back.

"Just look at the quilting," Cheryl urged. "And the designs. It's unique, I've never seen anything like it."

"I'll take your word for it." Kara studied the quilt from a safe distance, her nose crinkling. "It's filthy. Much dirtier than the others. And it stinks."

"Mothballs," Cheryl said.

"Mothballs and . . . something else."

"Rachel thinks she can clean it."

"Rather her than me," Kara said decisively. She moved away. "The white work is stunning. I'll bet we could get twelve thousand—"

"They're at it again," Tony shouted, his face reddening. "Look, girls, you don't own this stuff."

Mark burst out laughing. "Don't bother, buddy. This is another case of what Pat would call miscommunication between the sexes."

"But they're acting as if this was a fashion show! The condition of the merchandise is irrelevant and immaterial. What I want to know is where it came from."

"Somebody's attic," Cheryl said calmly. "Some little old lady, who has kept her family heirlooms all these years."

"That is an unsubstantiated theory," Tony insisted. "And you'd better hope it's false. We'll never catch this guy if—"

"Washing-up time," Mark said. "Come on, Tony. I'll clear, you stick the dishes in the dishwasher."

"Not the Haviland," Cheryl exclaimed. She followed them out of the room, expostulating.

"Leave them," Kara said, as Rachel started to fold the album quilt.

"They'll be all right here tonight, and they could certainly do with an airing." She went after the others.

Pat, who obviously had no intention of participating in menial chores, was slow to follow them. "Was I right or was I right?" he demanded of Rachel, the only audience left. "I'll bet granny doesn't even know she's been ripped off. We never discussed the most interesting aspect of this business. If the theft hasn't been reported, or even noticed, why is this guy so desperate to get the things back?"

three

The setting moon shone straight into her eyes, its light undimmed by leafless branches and thin lace curtains. For the tenth time Rachel shifted position. She couldn't sleep. Overfatigue, too much to eat and drink . . . and the question Pat MacDougal had tossed off so nonchalantly.

The question must have occurred to Tony. Asking questions like that was part of his job. He hadn't mentioned it to her because he hadn't wanted to worry her, for there was only one logical answer.

Why was the man so anxious to retrieve the quilts? Because they were evidence of a crime more serious than theft.

Her weary brain went over the same path it had traced a dozen times before. She and Tony could identify the Alleged, but they had not actually seen him with the trash bag in his hands, so evidence even of theft would be circumstantial. If he could retrieve it there would be no physical proof to connect him with a case of . . . aggravated assault? Rape?

The other crime, the one that carried the heaviest penalty, was one she shrank from naming even in thought.

So serious a case would surely have been reported. But Pat—damn him for having such a logical mind!—had accounted for that too. The theft of the quilts might not have been discovered. Even the owner might not realize something was missing from a seldom-visited storage area in an unused room. A police officer investigating another, more serious kind of crime wouldn't be likely to notice that a chest or box of linens was only half-filled. Especially a male police officer.

Rachel turned onto her back and glared at the ceiling. Such speculation was a waste of time and nervous energy. She had to get some sleep. It had been a tiring day, and tomorrow would be just as rushed; by now she was familiar enough with Cheryl's habits to anticipate the frantic scramble ahead, the last-minute packing, the forgotten tasks, the inevitable delays. Tony would be in a bad mood, fuming silently because he wasn't able to pitch in or help with the driving.

At first the voice was indistiguishable from the normal sounds of night, breathy as the movement of air in the branches, wordless as the wind. Then she heard, or thought she heard, words. Relaxing muscles tightened, propelling her out of bed. Without stopping to put on slippers or robe she headed for the stairs. Tony was down there, alone in his room, handicapped by the cast on his leg . . .

The night lights in the shop left the room in semidarkness. The garments hanging from hooks glimmered, ghost shapes in the shadows; the mannequins in their trailing skirts and big hats looked unnervingly lifelike. A lifted hand seemed to beckon, a parasol tilted at a coquettish angle hid sly, peering eyes. Rachel stopped in the doorway, every sense alert. Not a breath of air stirred. A good thing, too, she thought, trying to keep her composure. If a drapery had fluttered or a sleeve had moved, she would have dropped in her tracks.

She heard no sound, from within the house or outside it. She told herself she must have been dreaming. She was wide awake now, shivering in the night-cool air; but the sense of imminent intrusion, of something demanding entry, did not diminish. She pressed the switch and the track lights overhead shone out, lighting the room like a stage set.

She went from one window to another, shading her eyes, looking out, seeing only the normality of nighttime. But her skin was prickling and her mind denied the evidence of her eyes; she could feel it there, waiting, wanting—demanding—to come in.

The sound came, not from without, but from behind her. She

whirled around, lips parting in a cry she was too breathless with terror to utter.

"What's wrong?" His black hair was disheveled and his eyes were heavy with sleep, but he stood erect, steadying himself with the crutches instead of leaning on them. One hand rested on the pocket of his robe.

Rachel collapsed into the nearest chair. She was too short of breath to speak clearly; the words emerged in a whisper. "I'm sorry I woke you."

"I wasn't asleep." He swung himself toward her and stood by the chair looking down at her. "I'm the one who should apologize; I keep scaring you half to death, don't I? What are you doing down here?"

"I thought I heard something. A voice calling . . . I must have been dreaming."

Tilting her head back to meet his eyes, she was acutely aware of his nearness, and of the ragged condition of the old summer nightgown that left her arms and shoulders bare. She had a long-sleeved flannel nightshirt in one of her suitcases, but she had been too tired to look for it.

"You're shivering," Tony said. "It's freezing in here. Put this around you."

Balancing on one crutch he reached out for the nearest thing at hand and threw it clumsily over her shoulders.

Rachel rose to meet it, feeling the time-softened fabric settle around her like an embrace. The movement brought her so close to him that his face became a patchwork of isolated elements—the dark eyes, wide with surprise or some other, stronger emotion; a lock of black hair, lightly frosted with silver, curving over his temple; the thin, sensitive lips framed by his mustache. Her hand moved of its own volition, fingertips gliding lightly over the sharp outlines of cheekbone and temple till they reached his hair.

The crutch clattered to the floor as he pulled her roughly against him, pressing the folds of cloth tight across her back and hips. His mouth fumbled across her closed eyes and along her cheek before it found hers with a violence that would have snapped her head back if she had not met it with matching violence.

How long it went on she never knew—an immeasurable eternity, a few seconds of actual time. Then the entire length of his body stiffened, unyielding as stone, and he pushed her away, his hand hard against her breast. Disgust, contempt, and outrage transformed his face. His raised hand shook. For a moment she thought he was going to strike her.

Then she heard the knock at the door.

Without speaking or looking at her again, Tony retrieved the fallen crutch and started for the door. As Rachel fled she heard him say, in a voice whose gruffness might have been attributed to legitimate annoyance, "What's the idea of turning up this time of night, you inconsiderate son of a gun?"

"I wouldn't have knocked, but I saw the lights," a voice murmured apologetically.

The door she closed behind her cut off the rest of the conversation. Clutching the covering around her shivering body, she stumbled up the stairs. The old house was drafty; a finger of air from the window she had raised a healthy two inches curled around her face like an icy tentacle. She was about to drop the blanket—coverlet—whatever it was— that covered her shoulders to the floor when she identified it. The album quilt. Throwing it over a chair, she got into bed and curled herself into a tight knot under the blankets.

The late arrival must be the long-awaited Adam, living up to his reputation by turning up at a particularly inconvenient hour. What would he have done if he hadn't seen there were lights on in the house? Bunked down in the car? Gone to a motel?

It was possible that he had seen a lot more than the lights. Wouldn't a considerate visitor, turning up in the middle of the night, check to make sure someone was awake and receptive before he knocked? The glass panels on either side of the door would have given him a clear view of the interior of the room.

If he had seen them . . . Hot with shame and embarrassment, Rachel pushed the blankets back. He would certainly put the worst possible interpretation on that scene, and how could she blame him when she herself didn't understand why or how it had happened?

Sharing the same house with a man who had seen her for the first time in the arms of her friend's husband wouldn't be comfortable, but it was only a minor discomfort compared to the prospect of facing Tony the next day. The Cardozas were supposed to leave at noon. With luck she could avoid a direct confrontation for those few hours. Surely he would be as anxious to avoid it as she. Even if he didn't blame her for what had happened, the very sight of her would remind him of his moment of weakness. Another sort of man might shrug it off, but not Tony; his rigid conscience and old-fashioned values would give him hell.

A moment of weakness, nothing more. I am not going to blame myself, Rachel thought. It wasn't my fault, I didn't do it on purpose. It wasn't his fault either. It was no one's fault. It just happened. He hated himself for doing it, though. He looked as if he hated *me*. He pushed me away . . .

He pushed her away, so roughly she stumbled back and fell to the floor. Bruised and breathless she raised herself on her hands and looked up at him. He stood over her, his booted feet braced and his fists raised.

"God damn you! I warned you—"

"You wanted it too. You still want me. What's the harm in it? It's all I have, you can't take it away from me."

She raised herself to her knees, reaching out with both arms as if she would embrace his thighs. His breath caught harshly, but he moved back, beyond her grasp. "I can't risk it. Not any longer. It never was important—"

"Not to you?" Watching him, she said again, in a different voice. "No, not to you."

He hunched his shoulders uneasily, tried to avoid her eyes. "What did you expect? You're lucky to get off so easily. It could be worse, you know. It will be worse if you don't stop behaving this way."

Still on her knees she straightened her back and lifted her head. "Don't do this," she said, very softly. "I'm warning you."

"Are you threatening me?" His sullen, angry face relaxed into incredulous amusement. "Well. That settles it. I was willing to be accommodating if you behaved yourself, but that you should dare . . . You've only yourself to blame. I've done all I can."

Turning on his heel he strode out, slamming the door behind him. For several minutes she did not move. Then she rose slowly to her feet and went to the bureau. The objects on it were in wild disarray as they always were; mechanically she set them in order, bottles and jars and brushes. Before long she found what she wanted.

The clatter of childish footsteps and the babble of childish voices woke Rachel at dawn. Groggy from lack of sleep, at first she couldn't remember why she felt so terrible. A test for which she hadn't studied, gym class with that nasty Sue Collins making snotty remarks about her bra size . . . Maybe she could convince her mother she was sick . . .

When she got herself focused in time she felt even worse. There was no way of getting out of this one—no trusting parent to con, not even a hope of playing hooky. She heard Cheryl, trying vainly to hush the children—"You'll wake poor Rachel, let her sleep"—and let out a muffled groan.

They would have a nice day for the drive. The rays of the rising sun slipped into the room, strengthening the blues and greens of the braided rug, brightening the pattern of the quilt thrown over the chair. Averting her eyes from that reminder, Rachel headed for the bathroom.

The reflection of her drawn face and shadowed eyes made her turn from the mirror. How could anyone see that face and fail to suspect the truth? Only a few more hours, she reminded herself, and hid the dark circles with foundation, brightened the pale mouth with lipstick. Without makeup she looked so sickly Cheryl was bound to fuss over her. She couldn't stand sympathy from that source, not today.

Freezing her face into a smile, she went downstairs and was relieved to find only Cheryl, who was wiping the sink and looking infuriatingly relaxed. I'll go crazy if she dawdles like that all morning, Rachel thought. She had to force herself to speak casually.

"Don't bother with that, Cheryl, I'll finish cleaning up after you leave. You musn't be late getting off. What can I do to help?"

"My goodness, you're bright and cheerful this morning," Cheryl said with a laugh. "You must have had a good, sound night's sleep."

"Yes."

"I'm glad you weren't disturbed. That rotten Adam turned up at two a.m., can you imagine? He woke poor Tony, fumbling at the door. I guess I can't blame Adam; he had no way of knowing Tony would be on the alert for funny noises, but honestly!"

"So he's here," Rachel said.

"Yes, he's here. Tony made him sleep in the other twin bed in his room so he wouldn't disturb us tramping around upstairs." The coffee had finished dripping. Cheryl poured two cups and sat down at the table. "Relax while you can," she said cheerfully. "The thundering horde will be back soon. I sent them outside because they were making such a racket. They're excited about the trip, naturally; but I want to let Tony sleep as long as possible. He had such a disturbed night."

Some imp in the distant cupboards of Rachel's mind jeered, *She doesn't know the half of it.* Quickly, stupidly, she said, "He—they are still asleep then."

"I hope so. Adam was snoring like a buzzsaw when I looked in on Tony this morning. I just about jumped out of my sneakers when I heard him. Tony never snores, and of course I didn't know anyone else was there. Tony was awake, poor baby, but I think I persuaded him to go back to sleep."

If she doesn't stop calling him poor Tony, Rachel thought . . .

The children burst in, red-cheeked with cold and demanding hot cocoa. Joe followed them like a conscientious retriever. Giving his mother a critical look, he remarked with heavy sarcasm, "Hey, take it easy, Mom. Like, we don't have to get out of here till tonight. Dad really loves having you drive after dark."

"You're lucky he isn't here, young man," Cheryl said. "If you're in such a hurry, you'd better finish your own packing. Last time I saw your room you had junk all over the place. And don't try to sneak that football into your suitcase, I told you you can't take it."

"Aw, Mom—"

"Your cousins probably have a dozen footballs."

"But, like, this is a genuine NFL—"

"Stop saying 'like' every other word. And don't forget to make your bed."

"I can't. I have to watch the monsters. Or do you want 'em busting in on Dad?"

He made a grab for Jerry, who was edging toward the door. Jerry wriggled and yelled. "Daddy should wake up. We have to go see Grandma."

Cheryl collared her daughter, whose movements had been quieter but just as determined. Megan raised a cherubic face and crooned, "Daddy should wake up. We have to go see Grandma."

"She says everything I say," Jerry complained. "Make her shut up."

"Upstairs," Cheryl ordered. "All of you. And leave Daddy alone."

"How can I make my bed when—"

"Daddy should wake up. We have to go see Grandma."

"Shut up, shut up, shut up!"

"I'll go with them," Rachel offered. "Come on, guys, let's make sure you packed all Grandma's presents."

"Bless you," Cheryl said gratefully.

Rachel felt like the worst sort of hypocrite. It was impossible to hurry Cheryl; perhaps she would have better luck with the children.

She and the two younger children were in Jerry's room, trying—at least Rachel was trying—to reduce the chaos, when Cheryl came upstairs. "Good lord," she said, looking in.

"I'm sorry," Rachel said helplessly. "He keeps changing his mind about what clothes he wants to take."

"It's not your fault," Cheryl said. "Oh, Jerry, for goodness sake! You can't take these shorts. It's just as cold in Ohio as it is here. What did you do with the corduroys I packed?"

"I don't want the stinky old corduroys. I want my jeans." Jerry streaked for the door, yelling, "Daddy! Daddy, do I have to wear my stinky old corduroys?"

Megan had slipped out of the room. A soprano echo floated back through the open door. ". . . have to wear my stinky old . . . "

"It's all right," Cheryl said, as Rachel started to follow. "Tony's up and in the kitchen. He said to send the kids down if they were in the way. Why don't you join him, have another cup of coffee?"

"No, let me help you."

"I guess I could use some help at that, if I have to repack Megan's things too." Cheryl sighed. "Tony's in one of his moods this morning. Sometimes I wish he'd just yell and get it out in the open, instead of sitting there all tight-lipped and glowering. Poor guy— Excuse me?"

"I didn't say anything." Rachel busied herself replacing the collection of summer shorts and tees in the dresser drawer.

"Oh. I was going to say, it's hard on him having to watch me do all the work. I really would like to get off in good time, so he won't get more upset."

Megan had not substituted other clothes for the ones her mother had packed. The suitcase gaped empty; every doll and stuffed animal wore a pair of small panties or jeans, sometimes on its head, and Megan's best ruffled party dress had been wrapped around a large teddy bear and tied tightly in place with Christmas ribbons. For a moment Rachel thought Cheryl was going to burst into tears.

"I spent an hour ironing that dress," she whimpered, removing it from the teddy bear.

"I'm sure your mother-in-law has an iron," Rachel said. "And it would have been wrinkled anyway, packed in a suitcase."

They were still undressing the dolls when Joe yelled from his room. "Mom! Where's my Redskins Super Bowl shirt?"

"Honey, that shirt is five years old and in rags!" Cheryl yelled back.

"You didn't throw it away, did you?" His voice rose to a shriek.

Despite interruptions of a similar nature they managed to get the suitcases packed. Cheryl was in the bathroom the children shared, collecting toothbrushes and the bar of soap shaped like a cat, which was the only one Megan would use, when Rachel turned to see a shape looming in the doorway. She let out a squeak that brought Cheryl hurrying out of the bathroom.

"Oh," she said. "Hi, Adam. You haven't met Rachel, have you?"

He's HUGE, Rachel thought dazedly. He had to duck his head to enter the door. Some of his bulk might have been due to the fact that he was wearing at least three sweaters; she could see the edges of them at the neck and wrists. His head would have looked disproportionately small atop this structure if a springy mass of tight dark curls had not added an additional two inches of height and breadth, covering his forehead and ears and meeting the beard that hid the lower part of his face. The only features visible were a snub nose and a pair of half-closed eyes.

"Pleased to meet you," Rachel said insincerely.

He nodded in her general direction and looked out of the corner of his eye at Cheryl. "Ready?" he asked, nudging the suitcase with his foot. The foot was clad in a worn leather sandal and a bright orange sock with the toe out.

"Just let me put this in." Cheryl closed the suitcase. "Thanks, Adam, it's nice of you to help."

"More?" He tucked the suitcase under one arm.

"Yes, there are two in my room and one in Megan's; and you might see if you can persuade Joe to relinquish his."

The apparition turned and went out.

"So that's Adam." Rachel stared at the empty doorway. "Can't he talk?"

"Oh, sure. Once he gets started he never stops. But he's very shy. Tony says he isn't shy, he's just suspicious of people. Whatever it is, it will take him at least a week to talk to you in complete sentences."

"I'll try not to scare him," Rachel said drily. "I'm beginning to understand why you said he wouldn't bother me."

"He's got a girlfriend," Cheryl said. "Sort of."

"I suppose he's known her for twenty years?"

"Almost." Cheryl laughed. "And I'm not sure what the relationship is. Still developing, no doubt."

Footsteps clumped down the hall and Adam passed the door with a suitcase under each arm and one in each hand. He didn't look in.

Having seen her new housemate, Rachel's anxiety about his future behavior was somewhat lessened. He might turn into Mr. Hyde after the others had gone, but he didn't appear to be the type who meddled in other people's business. Quite the contrary. He hadn't looked directly at her or spoken more than a few words.

In his uncommunicative way he was more helpful than Rachel had expected; she heard him moving around downstairs, carrying things to the car, doing a number of the chores she had anticipated she would have to do, and allowing her to remain out of the way—Tony's way. Finally she knew she couldn't put it off any longer. The suitcases were packed and in the van; the only remaining job was to force the children to eat something before they hit the road. It would be a matter of force, unquestionably; she heard the raised voices as she approached the family room. Jerry was asking why they couldn't stop at a fast-food restaurant instead of eating stinky peanut butter sandwiches, and Megan was echoing him, although she never ate anything *but* peanut butter sandwiches.

A deep, unfamiliar male voice interrupted the argument. "You like worms, Jerry? That's what they make the hamburgers out of, ground-up worms."

Laughter, shrieks, and throw-up sounds followed this remark, which Rachel realized must have come from Adam. So he could talk in sentences when he chose—and he knew something about juvenile psychology.

Her face flushed with amusement, Cheryl turned from the counter when Rachel entered. "There you are. Would you rather have turkey or roast beef in your sandwich?"

"I'm not hungry. I'll have something later, after you go." Painfully conscious of Tony, enthroned at the head of the table—fingers tapping—she took the knife from Cheryl. "Shall I make some sandwiches for you to take with you?"

"That might be a good idea," Tony said. "At the rate we're going we'll still be in Pennsylvania at dinnertime. Cheryl, will you PLEASE sit down and eat something? It's eleven-thirty."

"Eat a worm sandwich," Jerry chanted. "Stinky worms, slimy worms, yucky worms—"

It was Adam who kept the situation from erupting. Unobtrusively and in virtual silence he somehow persuaded Cheryl to eat, and finished loading the van. It was only a few minutes past noon when Cheryl said in mild surprise, "I guess we're ready."

"Finally," Tony said. "Let's go, then."

He led the way, out of the family room and across the corridor. When they entered the shop Cheryl stopped.

"Darn, I forgot to put the quilts away. It will only take a minute—"

"I'll do it," Rachel said quickly.

Cheryl glanced at her husband. He didn't have to speak, his tight lips and lowering brows were as eloquent as a shout. "Thanks, Rachel. The acid-free tissue . . . But you know that. Adam, did you put the closed sign on the door? Make sure you lock it after we leave."

"Don't you want to keep the shop open until Christmas Eve?" Rachel asked. "Since I'll be here anyway—"

"Don't be a fool," Tony said roughly. "Keep this place locked and barred and don't let anybody in. Use the side door instead of this one. Is that clear?"

"Darling, you don't need to be so rude," Cheryl murmured. "It's nice of you to offer, Rachel, but we had already planned to close the shop over the holidays. Kara will cope with our regular customers. You don't have to do anything. Unless—"

"If we're ready," Tony said between his teeth.

"Okay. Here, darling, let me help you."

"I don't need you to help me. Get your coat."

Biting her lip, Cheryl went out. Rachel started to follow.

"Rachel," Tony said.

The sound of his voice pronouncing her name made her knees go weak. But Adam was within earshot, waiting at the door. Surely Tony wouldn't say anything in front of Adam. Unless they had already discussed it, unless Adam knew?

"Yes," she said, forcing herself to look directly at Tony.

"Excuse me for sounding peremptory just now," he said formally. "But you really have to be careful. I explained the situation to Adam, and Thomas will keep an eye on the place too. He'll let you know if they locate the guy. I've asked him to report progress to me as well."

"Thank you."

"Part of the job. Try not to worry," he added. "Something is bound to break sooner or later. Adam is taking my room, so he'll be downstairs."

He got slowly to his feet and reached for the crutches.

The worst was over, Rachel thought. A few more minutes and he'd be gone.

She should have known he wouldn't back away from it. It wasn't easy to find an opportunity for a private conversation, but he managed it, at the last minute, while Cheryl was trying to settle the children into the car and arbitrate the arguments as to where each would sit. They had been racing back and forth, up and down the steps, chasing one another, and since it was an unseasonably warm day their feet had left muddy smears on the stairs and the porch. Rachel was about to start down when the quiet voice pronouncing her name stopped her again. This time she couldn't bring herself to turn around. Face averted, she waited.

"I want you to know that I regret what happened last night. You may not believe me, but I've never—not since Cheryl and I—"

"I believe you. It's all right."

"No, it's not all right."

"I'll be gone when you get back," Rachel said. She hadn't meant to say it, but she knew the decision was inevitable and the words irretrievable.

He didn't respond immediately. Finally he said, "Perhaps that would be best. Surely by that time—"

Cheryl came trotting toward them and Tony started down the steps. If he was trying to prevent Cheryl from helping him the attempt backfired; moving clumsily and too quickly, he slipped on a patch of mud and might have fallen if she hadn't been there to steady him.

Rachel stood waving and smiling until the van turned the corner. It was a relief to let her face relax.

Adam wasn't the waving type. He had gone back into the house after hoisting Tony and the cast into the back seat of the van, and he was nowhere in sight when Rachel entered the shop. Methodically she locked and bolted the door and put up the chain. Then she went to her room.

The room was a mess. She hadn't made the bed or even finished unpacking. There hadn't been time. Vaguely she thought, I ought to have something to eat. I told Cheryl I'd clean up the kitchen. Did she put the butter away? The cats are probably licking it right now. The dogs are still outside, I ought to let them in, feed them.

The house was utterly silent. Apparently Adam intended to leave her strictly alone. That was fine with her. Maybe, after all, he hadn't seen anything. Guilty people become paranoid, she reminded herself.

"Perhaps that would be best." Well, what had she expected him to say? It could have been worse. He had waited for her to make the offer, he hadn't told her to get out. He wouldn't do that. He was fair and kind-hearted, not like . . .

Her thoughts dead-ended, as if they had run into a wall. For a terrifying second or two the room seemed to shiver, like an image embroidered on gauze shifted by a gust of wind. Rachel caught hold of a chair. No wonder she was giddy, not enough sleep, no lunch or breakfast.

The surface under her hand felt gritty, like fine sand. It wasn't wood she touched. The album quilt lay across the chair, where she had thrown it the night before.

She had forgotten about the quilt until that moment. Lucky for me Cheryl didn't see it, Rachel thought; she would have known I was downstairs last night and even she might wonder why neither Tony nor I mentioned that little detail.

The cats had licked the butter. The plate was clean and Figgin, the prize thief of the pride, was cleaning his whiskers. He looked hurt and indignant when Rachel scolded him.

She felt better after she had had a sandwich and a glass of milk. The dogs weren't supposed to be fed until later but they drove her crazy winding around her legs, so she filled their dishes and then went to work loading the dishwasher and tidying the room. She had already decided that this was where she would work—or try to work. The table in her room wasn't big enough to hold her laptop and the notes and reference books she would be using. And it was too close to the family apartment. She would give those rooms a good cleaning, but not now. Not yet.

The telephone rang and she picked it up. Cheryl had suggested that she screen calls, just in case—Cheryl's tactful euphemism for a threatening or obscene call—but at that moment Rachel would have considered an obscene phone call preferable to the painful treadmill of her own thoughts.

The caller was Ruth. After identifying herself she asked for Cheryl, and was pleased and surprised to find she was too late. "What on earth did you do to get them away so early?"

"They planned to leave around noon."

"Oh, yes, I know, but getting that bunch of rampant individualists organized isn't easy. Cheryl lets those kids get away with murder."

It wasn't meant as criticism, just as amused commentary, and its candor indicated that Ruth considered Rachel an adopted member of the family. Rachel didn't reply, and Ruth went on, "I wanted to talk to you anyhow. If your plans for Christmas Day aren't unalterable, Pat and I would like to have you join us. Adam is coming; you could ride with him."

Rachel knew what was behind the invitation—not a passionate desire for her company, but a way of making sure she was accompanied—guarded, to be blunt. She was about to make some excuse when she had second thoughts. She'd have to go somewhere, remaining alone in the house would prove she had lied about her plans, and why not take advantage of the opportunity to spend time with one of the foremost authorities in her field—pick his brain, get to know him?

"That's very kind of you. Are you sure Adam won't mind?"

"I never know what Adam minds," Ruth said calmly. "Pat claims he has some faint inkling of what goes on in that boy's head, but I certainly don't. Just don't talk to him. It would be a waste of time, all he does is grunt."

Ruth's kindness, and the prospect of having something to look forward to, raised Rachel's spirits a little. She was too restless to study, so she decided not to postpone the cleaning after all. Might as well get it over with. Then she could close the doors and not open them again, especially the door of the room Tony had shared with his wife, and would soon share again.

Anyhow, Joe's room probably needed immediate attention. Cheryl had retrieved two dirty glasses and a plate containing the remains of a petrified sandwich from under the bed, but there were probably other overlooked foodstuffs in various corners, breeding germs and green scum. Like many of his contemporaries, Joe considered the area under the bed appropriate storage space for everything from his gym socks to the bag of potato chips he intended to eat later.

As Rachel had hoped, cleaning Joe's room provided a useful distraction. Amusement and horror overcame other emotions as she made one appalling discovery after another. She had to lie flat on the floor and probe with a broom to reach the glass that had rolled into the farthest corner. It must have been there for days; a thick coating of dust had mixed with the film of—milk?—the identity of the original substance was no longer ascertainable—to produce an effect that turned even Rachel's unfastidious stomach. She dropped the glass into the wastebasket.

Said wastebasket was overflowing by the time she finished, and she had only tossed the objects that were rotting or in tatters. After carefully replacing the copy of *Hustler* that had slid from under the mattress, and finding the missing Redskins Super Bowl shirt wrapped around an oil-soaked bit of metal (its function eluded her, but it was obviously vital to Joe's very existence), she decided she had gone as far as she could without intruding on the boy's privacy. It had been a fascinating interlude, like studying the customs of an exotic, alien tribe. Obviously adolescent males had developed a culture of their own, only distantly related to the dominant culture of their society. The rites of passage, the initiation rituals, had an unnerving resemblance to those of so-called primitive societies. Driving too fast and competing to see who could drink the most beer in the shortest period of time weren't particularly sophisticated.

When she turned out the light preparatory to leaving the room she was surprised to see how dark it was—or rather, to realize how much time she had spent cleaning. The sun set early in winter, and this was the shortest day of the year—the Winter Solstice, when the earth was at its greatest distance from the sun. Or did it have something to do with the angle of declination? The scientific explanation had been irrelevant, unknown to ancient man, but the effect was clearly visible. Imperceptibly but steadily the hours of daylight had lessened; in all the northern mythologies and religions this was the dying time, when ice and cold and darkness threatened the world, and it would require prayer and ritual to start the sun back on its reviving journey.

Rachel carried the disgusting wastebasket downstairs and out onto the back porch. It was enclosed but unheated, and the cold made her catch her breath. The temperature must have dropped thirty degrees since noon. No sign of snow, though; the rim of the sun was visible through the naked tree limbs, a glaring crimson that spread its rays across the horizon like the sign of a great fire. Rachel sorted the contents of the wastebasket into the various bins demanded by Joe's recycling standards, replaced the top, and hurried back inside.

She made two more trips upstairs, carrying down her laptop and an armful of books, which she arranged on the table. There had been no sign of life from Adam, and as the cats began to make unsubtle suggestions about food she wondered what to do about her own dinner and Adam's. Surely he didn't expect her to cook for him? A recluse like Adam would probably prefer to gnaw a cold bone in private. He could forage for his own bones, if that was his preference. There were enough leftovers from the party to feed both of them for days.

After feeding the cats she turned on the TV and inspected the refrigerator. She was tired, and in no mood to work. Why not take the evening off, relax—maybe get a little drunk? She deserved it. There was half a bottle of white wine in the fridge. She took it out, filled a plate with hors d'oeuvres, and settled down on the lumpy old couch to watch the news.

She had to fight Figgin for the smoked oysters and Patches for the deviled eggs. After he had licked the empty plate thoroughly, Figgin settled down on her stomach and went to sleep. The other cats lined the top of the couch like a furry frieze, and the dogs settled down on the hearth rug. Snores and purrs and the weight of Figgin, warm as a hot-water bottle, had a soporific effect that was augmented by two glasses of wine. Sleep came over her so gently she wasn't aware of dropping off until she woke, stiff and disoriented, some hours later.

Rachel blinked sleepily at the clock over the sink. It couldn't be that late. Almost one a.m. Had she slept, solidly and without moving, for five hours?

She must have moved or shifted position at some point. And reached, half-conscious, for the afghan that had been folded across the arm of the couch. It was spread over her now. Yawning, she sat up and stretched, and then realized she was the focus of several pairs of staring eyes. Two of the cats still slept, curled in a huddle on the chair, but Figgin sat bolt upright on the arm of the couch, his glowing orange-yellow eyes fixed on her. The dogs were awake too, and they were also watching her. Worth, the black labrador, looked like a sleek statue of *The Noble Dog,* ears pricked and alert. The little mixed-breed, part hound and part spaniel, whom Cheryl had named Poiret after another famous designer, stared back at Rachel with big mournful eyes.

Their final visit to the comfort station in the back yard must be overdue. "Sorry, guys," she said, heading for the back door. There were a lot of doors in the house—too many doors, if one were inclined to be nervous about burglars. The family room had two, the "side door" the family normally used and another opening onto the porch and the fenced yard. The dogs were so anxious to get out they shoved past her when she opened the porch door.

It was bitter cold. She could hear twigs and branches cracking. The moon looked like a globe of solid ice, and under its cold rays the frozen grass was colorless as snow. By the time the dogs consented to come back in, Rachel's teeth were chattering furiously. After locking and bolting both doors and distributing the final treat of cat and dog crunchies, she turned out all except one of the lights, selected a book with which to read herself to sleep, and left the room.

The long nap had been a mistake. It hadn't refreshed her; every muscle ached with weariness, but mentally she was keyed-up and edgy. She might as well be alone in the big, sprawling house for all the aid and comfort she had received from Adam. A lot of help he was, squatting in his quarters like a Neanderthal in his cave. Was he going to behave like this for the rest of the week? Gentlemanly reticence was all very well, but he didn't have to treat her like a leper.

Filled with righteous indignation and increasing uneasiness, she made the rounds of the downstairs, checking the doors. Had she locked the door of the shop securely, put up the chain? She had better make certain. Feeling the brush of soft fur against her calf, she realized that Figgin had slithered out of the kitchen before she closed the door; he was always trying to sneak into the shop, which was out of bounds to the animals; there were too many temptations, hanging fabrics and drooping ruffles and feather trim. She pushed him gently away with her foot and slipped into the shop, closing the door behind her. Figgin let out an indignant yowl. It was echoed by a furious burst of barking from the family room.

"Shut up," Rachel hissed.

There was no comment from Figgin, but the barking continued, loud enough and continuous enough to cover lesser sounds. It was not until the front door started to open that Rachel realized the dogs weren't barking for the fun of it. They were sounding the alarm.

The light from the lamps at either end of the room left the doorway in shadow. She saw him as a dark bulk, menacing and motionless. Then he stepped forward and the light rippled along the blade of the long knife in his hand.

If she had been thinking sensibly she would have known a book, even a book two inches thick, was an ineffective weapon. Her action was completely instinctive; the book hurtled across the room, pages flapping, and hit him square in the chest. Recoiling in a movement as instinctive as hers, he slipped and fell over backward. The crash shook everything in the room and set the crystal dangles of the chandelier to chiming. Rachel pressed the light switch.

The fallen form looked like a bear wearing jeans. From the waist up it was a featureless expanse of furry brown.

"God damn it!" Rachel shouted. "What—what—" Fury and relief choked further comment.

A paw-like hand rose and waved feebly at her. He was wearing mittens—brown mittens. Pushing away the hair that had covered his eyes, he blinked at her and then looked at the book lying on the floor next to him.

"How appropriate. Pat has threatened me with this particular volume before, but this is the first time I've ever had the book thrown at me. Why couldn't you have been reading a paperback romance?"

four

Cheryl had been right about one thing. Once Adam got started talking he never stopped. As he hoisted himself to his feet and closed and locked the door, he delivered a lecture on her carelessness and folly. It was a very well-organized lecture.

"Obviously," he remarked, pushing the hair out of his eyes and tossing his brown, furry jacket over a chair, "you are under a certain amount of nervous strain. That's comprehensible, but if you didn't know it was me at the door your behavior was irresponsible. And if you knew it was me, as you ought to have done, you shouldn't have tried to brain me."

Rachel got her breath back. "How the hell was I supposed to know it was you? I didn't know you'd left the house. I thought you were in your room."

"Didn't you get my note?"

"What note?"

"I pinned it on your door."

"I've been in the family room all evening. Why in heaven's name couldn't you have told me you were going out? What's the idea of going out anyhow? Where have you been? Can't you talk?"

"I could if you'd shut up for a minute," Adam said coolly. "Your counterargument is irrelevant to my original premise. If you believed I was here your behavior becomes even less rational. Observing what you took to be an unauthorized intruder actually in the house, you should have retreated immediately and gone for help. Screaming might also have been a sensible action."

Even if she hadn't been angry, Rachel would have taken offense at that suggestion. "Oh, sure. That's what women are supposed to do, scream and run for help. Fat lot of help you'd have been, dead asleep and snoring; by the time you arrived, if you ever did, he would have caught up with me and . . . He had a knife! He—you—"

"Me," Adam said. "As it turned out. But your counterargument has some merit. I did have a knife. Found it on the porch. If I'd known you were in the shop I might have considered the effect, but since I didn't know . . . "

"You found it on the porch?"

"I'm not in the habit of carrying a carving knife around with me." Adam looked askance at the weapon, which lay on the floor where he had dropped it. He didn't pick it up. Instead he peeled off a cable-knit sweater, exposing the next layer—tan, with a Fairlane pattern—and threw it over a chair.

"Don't put your dirty clothes on that chair," Rachel said automatically.

Adam swept the sweater and the jacket onto the floor. When he spoke again he had abandoned his defensive tone. "Suppose we start all over, omitting the superfluous accusations and apologies? Would you care to join me in a cup of coffee, or any other beverage that suits your fancy? Or a belated supper? I'll cook."

"Supper? It's one a.m."

"I'm hungry," Adam said.

The dogs were delighted to see them and even happier to share the food. Adam didn't cook; as he sat gnawing on a turkey drumstick, his hair in his eyes, and a green sweater (the third layer down) covering his torso, he reminded Rachel irresistibly of the "cavemen" she had studied in grade school.

"Where were you?" she asked, watching in awe as he reduced the drumstick to bare bones and dug into a bowl of salad. She knew she had no right to ask, but Adam answered promptly, if indistinctly, "At an Esbat."

"At a what?"

"Esbat. It's one of the Great Festivals of Witchcraft. They occur on May Eve, Hallowe'en, February first, and August first, plus the winter and summer solstices. Today is December twenty-first . . ."

His voice trailed away and he sat quite still, the fork poised in his hand. A piece of lettuce fell with a plop, spraying his front with oil and vinegar.

"I know what an Esbat is," Rachel said, still dumbfounded.

"Oh, yeah." Adam peered at her through his hair. His eyes were bright and narrowed, like those of a furtive animal looking through a hedge. "You're supposed to be studying folklore. Why did you—"

"And I thought you were supposed to be a teacher. Why are you hobnobbing with witches? Have you joined a coven?"

"I was researching for Pat," Adam answered. "Modern witches are a harmless crowd, bless their innocent little hearts—it's all white magic, or so they claim. But they don't enjoy being laughed at any more than the rest of us, and Pat has made fun of them in print too often. They wouldn't have admitted him to the ceremony."

"I can see why you'd blend right in," Rachel admitted.

Frowning, Adam changed the subject. "Did you hear anybody out there tonight?"

"Just you."

"Somebody was there who wasn't me. What about the dogs?"

"That is odd," Rachel said. "They barked when you came. Not before."

"If you were asleep you might not have heard them."

"I was asleep part of the time but it was on the couch—" She indicated that article of furniture with a gesture—"and they were in the same room. I couldn't have missed hearing them."

"Interesting."

"Maybe he arrived just before you did, and you scared him off. Where was the knife?"

He hesitated briefly before he said, "On the top step. Standing upright. It had been driven into the wood."

Rachel understood why he had been reluctant to tell her. The simple description presented a picture ugly with overtones. "A threat?" she said.

"That's one possibility."

"What other possibility is there? If he had meant to break in he wouldn't have abandoned a weapon. You should have left it where it was. There might have been fingerprints. You probably wiped them off."

"You're right," Adam admitted. "I should have left it in situ. I'm not very experienced at this sort of thing."

"Well, the damage is done. I'll call the police—that friend of Tony's—in the morning. No sense doing it now."

Adam pitched the turkey bones into the trash can, to the visible chagrin of dogs and cats, and opened the refrigerator. "Want a piece of pie?"

"No, I'm going to bed."

"Sleep tight."

"How can I not, with you on guard?"

And, somewhat to her surprise, she did.

Next morning she called the number Tony had given her and asked for Thomas. A bored voice informed her he was out of the office. It volunteered nothing more, so Rachel left a message and tried to settle down to work. It was no betrayal of her feminist principles to admit she felt better knowing there was a man in the house—particularly a man the size of Adam. Peculiar was certainly a mild word for him, but now that he had been reminded so emphatically of the danger, he might be more reliable. He might even bring himself to inform her of his plans instead of sneaking around with little notes. Curt little notes, at that; the one stuck on her door had read, "Going out. Back later."

Out to a witches' sabbath. In retrospect it struck her as rather funny, and not as surprising as others might have found it. She knew a number of anthropologists; though some were as conventional as bankers, the percentage of eccentrics among them was rather high.

At nine-thirty Adam still hadn't made his appearance. It was a bleak, cold morning; after a few tentative sorties the animals decided they preferred the warmth of the house. Rachel began to regret she had decided to work in the family room; the dogs snored and twitched, the cats walked across her keyboard and wanted to sit on her lap, and she kept expecting a huge form to appear in the doorway, looking for breakfast and/or conversation.

After another unproductive half hour Rachel gave up trying to concentrate. Making sure the animals were confined in the family room, she went to the workroom. Located behind the shop, it was Cheryl's pride and joy, equipped with every item needed for the sometimes painstaking work of restoration old fabrics might need. In addition to sinks and drying racks, an ironing board and sewing machine, it contained cupboards for storage and supplies, two long worktables, and several comfortable chairs.

Under Cheryl's tutelage Rachel had begun to tackle some of the simpler cleaning and mending tasks. The techniques required considerable skill—accurate matching of colors and fabric, precise, almost invisible stitches, selection of the proper thread. The cobwebby silks and chiffons needed silk thread and a needle so fine it was maddeningly hard to thread. The silk knotted easily, and a false stitch was difficult to remove without leaving holes in the delicate fabric.

Sewing repairs were easier than cleaning, though. Treating the white cotton of Victorian petticoats and nightgowns was comparatively safe; they could be washed and even bleached. Even on these garments spots and stains presented a problem, however. Some obediently disappeared with careful bleaching; others disappeared but left a large, depressing hole. Rachel knew better than to tackle silks or rayons or wool, or even colored cloth. Some of the old dyes weren't fast, and would run if they got wet. Cheryl always tested them first with a damp cloth or Q-tip, but even she had made mistakes. One of them hung on the wall of the workroom as a reminder and a warning—a once-valuable sampler, dated 1793, whose blues and greens had run devastatingly and irreparably.

A pile of "whites" awaited Rachel's attentions—"only if you're in the mood, there's no hurry," Cheryl had told her. After rummaging through them, Rachel decided she wasn't in the mood. She tossed the whites back into their box. She had promised Cheryl she would put the quilts away; might as well get it done now.

Ripping off a long sheet from the heavy roll of acid-free tissue, she carried it into the shop and spread it across the floor. She paused for a moment to admire the white quilt before folding it in the paper; it was as beautiful as Cheryl had claimed, museum quality without a doubt.

After wrapping the patchwork quilt with equal care she carried both into the workroom. One more to go—the album quilt. It was still in her room. Rachel closed the workroom door and went along the corridor toward the stairs, her steps slow and reluctant. She didn't want to see the quilt, much less touch it, but she couldn't leave it where it was. Once it was put away, out of sight, it would no longer be a constant reminder of the incident that gnawed at her conscience like a worm in an apple.

Adam's room—Tony's former room—was on the same corridor, beyond the stairs. The door was closed.

She went on up the stairs, bundled the quilt into her arms, and carried it to the workshop. The paper in which it would be wrapped was ready, lying across one of the long worktables. She put the quilt down on top of the paper and spread it out.

Under the bright, shadowless fluorescents the pattern was clearer, though the strange gray film still dulled it. Her curiosity piqued, Rachel bent over the table, trying to make out details. Paired hearts, arrangements of flowers and leaves—other less conventional designs, oddly provocative. It couldn't do any harm to brush it, she thought, picking absently at the gray film with her fingernail. The stuff seems to come off easily enough.

Using the softest and finest brush she could find, she began on one corner, barely touching the fabric, alert for the slightest sign of damage. The gray didn't so much brush off as dissolve, leaving no residue on fabric or table. The underlying design took shape behind the slow sweep of the brush as if it were being freshly created instead of cleaned. The colors were soft, faded by time, but clear and pure.

Rachel finished one entire square before stepping back and examining the result.

This certainly was not a Baltimore album quilt. As was the case with all album quilts, each block had a different pattern, but the Baltimore quilt designs were distinctive and unmistakable—formal, complex flower and fruit arrangments, wreaths and birds so detailed that a single flower might utilize twenty or thirty separate pieces of fabric. The colors were strong and vivid, and sometimes ink shading was used to give a more naturalistic effect. After the blocks were sewed together an equally complex and bright colored border was added and the whole thing was covered with quilting.

The stiches on this one were as fine as any she had seen, but the appliquéd designs were nothing like the formal patterns of the Baltimore quilts. The block Rachel had cleaned—astonishingly, magically clean now, the creamy white background unsmirched—showed a flower arrangement, but the arranger had been Nature herself. Forget-me-nots, their petals shaped from pieces of fabric no larger than a baby's fingernail, and sprays of some pink flower she couldn't identify grew from a tuft of green grass. The flower petals had been appliquéd, the stems and grass embroidered. And half concealed by the grass . . . What was it? The shape was hard to make out, since it was of a shade only slightly darker than that of the grass. A sinuous curve of apple-green, twining around and through the perpendicular stalks in a pattern that pleased the eye even as it frustrated the viewer's attempt to trace its outline . . .

She was squinting at it, deep in concentration, when the ringing of the telephone made her start. At first she ignored the sound. Why didn't Adam answer the damned thing? It was probably for him, she wasn't expecting a call. Then she remembered that she was.

The voice was that of Thomas, or as he requested she call him, Tom. "Tony's the only one who uses my full name. It's his idea of a joke, has something to do with Doubting Thomas in the Bible, I guess."

The apostle in question had been the only one to demand proof of the identity of the resurrected Christ. An appropriate patron saint for a police officer, Rachel thought, but she hoped Tom wasn't too skeptical to believe her story. In the cold light of day it sounded like the sort of thing a nervous woman might have invented to get attention.

Tom listened without interrupting. The silence continued for several seconds after she finished. Then he said, "I intended to get in touch with you anyhow. Is it all right if I come by in, say, half an hour?"

"Has something happened?"

"I'll tell you about it when I get there." Before she could expostulate, he added, "I'll come to the side door. Don't open it until you're sure it's me."

He hung up. Rachel slammed the phone back into the cradle. Damn men anyhow, she thought unjustly. If he had deliberately set out to worry her, he couldn't have chosen a better way. A blunt statement, no matter how nasty, would have been easier to accept than vague hints and dire warnings.

Leaving the album quilt spread out on the table, she stormed out of the workroom and found herself nose to nose—or rather nose to sweater—with Adam.

"Oh, there you are," he said.

"Obviously." Rachel stepped back and rubbed her nose. The wool of the sweater was as stiff and harsh as burlap—the result of age and care-less laundering methods. "Were you looking for me?"

"I deduced that you were in the workroom since you weren't any-where else in the house and your coat is in the closet. So I came here and waited in the hall till you came out."

"Why didn't you . . . " Rachel stopped herself. It would have been a waste of time to ask why he hadn't knocked, or simply walked in. He never did the sensible thing. "What do you want?" she demanded.

"I want to talk to you. If the cops are coming, we should get our story straight before they arrive."

"What do you mean, straight? You tell your version, I tell mine. There's nothing to . . . " Then it hit her, and she began sputtering. "How did you know that was . . . Were you eavesdropping?"

"Sure." Adam looked mildly surprised. Then it seemed to dawn on him that she was upset about something. "I picked up the phone and you were talking to the cop and so I figured—"

"That you could just listen in on a private conversation?"

"But it wasn't a personal conversation. I mean, you and he aren't . . . Are you?"

"None of your business."

Adam considered this. "Ordinarily that response means 'yes.' In this case, however, I am inclined to take it literally. You certainly didn't say anything to him, or him to you, that would indicate you have a close, much less intimate, relationship."

"How would you know?" Rachel demanded.

Anger prompted this piece of rudeness and she regretted the words as soon as they had been spoken; but Adam's face gave no indication that she had offended him. In a slightly less aggressive tone she said, "In the future please don't pick up the phone after I've answered it. Or apologize and get off the line."

"I was going to, but he hung up before—"

"Would you mind getting out of my way?"

"What?"

"You are standing in the doorway," Rachel pointed out. "You fill the doorway. I can't get past you."

"Oh. Were you leaving the room?"

"No, I just opened the door because . . . " She took a deep breath. "Yes. I was leaving the room."

"Okay."

He followed her to the kitchen, so closely she could feel him, like a rock about to fall on her. She quickened her pace. Adam quickened his. "Have you had breakfast?" he asked.

"Hours ago." I will be damned, Rachel thought, if I offer to get his.

To judge by the evidence—crumbs on the table, an egg-stained plate in the sink—he had already prepared and eaten it. He had also made a fresh pot of coffee. Picking up a sponge, he swept the crumbs from the table onto the floor. "Want some coffee?"

Rachel was about to refuse when she realized she was being childish. With a muttered "Thanks," she helped herself and sat down at the table. Poiret was licking the floor. She nudged him with her foot. "Stop that."

"Don't discourage him," Adam said. "He's more effective than a mop or a vacuum cleaner. I don't understand why the human race is so reluctant to make use of a biodegradable, recyclable, natural resource like a dog. Think of all you'd save on—"

"What did you do with the knife?"

"It's in my room. I'll get it."

He put the dirty plate in the dishwasher, swabbed off the sink, and went out, leaving Rachel to deal with the cat that had jumped onto her lap and dipped its tail in her coffee.

What had he meant by that remark about getting their stories straight? She had nothing to conceal from the police; was he going to ask her to keep quiet about where he had been the night before? Maybe the meeting had been illegal. Maybe it hadn't been as harmless a gathering as he had claimed. From a former roommate, she had learned more than she wanted to know about "Wicca," as it was called; a religion, a spiritual path, a way of developing psychic and magical powers? Whatever, Rachel had thought, trying to think of a polite excuse to cut the lecture short. According to her enthusiastic friend, the religion of the "new witches" was not only harmless but positively high-minded, seeking the higher paths of understanding and self-development, looking to the good and abjuring evil. But there were other groups that weren't so well-intentioned, cults that sometimes made the news by sacrificing animals and desecrating churches, that might hold greater interest than a bunch of innocent white witches for a student of magic and religion like Pat MacDougal. If Adam had been playing nasty games with people like that . . .

She had no opportunity to demand further elucidation from Adam. Tom was early.

She didn't hear Adam coming, but he made it to the door first and moved her gently but firmly out of the way before he opened it. "Hello," he said amiably. "You must be the fuzz."

Tom stared at him, then at Rachel, then back, and up, at Adam, who hadn't stopped talking. "Interesting, the colloquialisms peple invent for the police. Do you know the derivation of fuzz? It comes from—"

"Perhaps you could tell me some other time," Tom said politely. "May I come in?"

Adam nodded approvingly. "Correct procedure. Yes, Officer, please come in. We were expecting you."

He stepped back. "Have a chair. How about a cup of coffee? Or tea, if you prefer. Nice to meet you."

"We haven't met," Tom pointed out. "You must be Dr. Nugent."

"That's right, though I only use the title when I'm forced to. Call me Adam. I'm a friend of—"

"Tony told me. Yes, thanks, I will have coffee." Tom settled into a chair and took a notebook from the breast pocket of his jacket. "Ms. Foley—"

"Milk, cream, sugar, sweetener?"

"Black, please. Now, Ms. Foley—"

"How about a muffin?"

"No, thank you," Tom said. "Rachel, tell me again what happened last night."

He took notes as she spoke, thanked her, and turned to Adam, who was twitching with repressed speech. "All right, Dr. Nugent."

If Adam had intended to lie about his noctural activities, he had changed his mind. He told all, ignoring—probably unaware of— Thomas's raised eyebrows.

"Wicca," he repeated, his voice carefully expressionless.

"You know about them?" Adam asked.

"Yes. They have to apply for permits to meet, like everyone else. Harmless bunch," he added with the air of a man who could have added other adjectives if he had been expressing a personal opinion rather than a professional judgment.

"Oh, sure," Adam agreed. "Some of them are very well informed, you know—not only about the history of the witchcraft cult, but about the various anthropological theories. Murray's work is generally discredited these days, of course."

"Of course," Tom murmured, making a note. "You saw no one near the house, Dr. Nugent?"

"Nope. I wasn't looking for anyone, though. The bushes by the front steps are evergreens, they're thick enough to—"

"Right. Where exactly did you find the knife?"

Adam looked uneasy and his answer was uncharacteristically brief. "Top step. Driven into the wood."

He had placed the knife on the table. It was an ordinary carving knife, the wooden haft polished and worn by use. Tom touched the blade with a careful finger. "Razor sharp."

"A good cook keeps his knives sharp," Adam said.

"I know. You handled it? How? Don't touch it, just show me."

Looking mortified, Adam demonstrated. "I didn't think—"

"No. It's unlikely there would have been usable prints, but of course we'll check. We'll need yours for comparison."

"I was wearing my mittens," Adam said.

"Mittens?" Tom's control slipped momentarily.

"I'm not used to this climate," Adam said. "The average temperature of Saudi Arabia—"

"He doesn't care about the climate of Saudi Arabia," Rachel said sharply. That would explain the sweaters, though . . . She went on, "You said you had planned to call me, Tom. What about?"

There was a cat on every lap by now; Tom, who seemed to be quite accustomed to this arrangement, carefully shifted his before leaning back in his chair. "We've identified the victim."

"Victim," Rachel repeated. She could have used one of Adam's sweaters; the temperature in the room seemed to have dropped a good ten degrees. "Of the burglary?"

Tom avoided her eyes. "I'm afraid it's not simple burglary any longer. She wasn't found till last night, but the coroner says she's been dead for almost a week."

"I don't want any brandy," Rachel said, pushing the glass away. "I don't need it."

"You're white as a sheet," Adam said.

"So are you." "Muddy brown" would have been more accurate; the climate of Saudi Arabia had produced a heavy tan.

"It was a shock." Adam drank the brandy. "Murder!"

"It wasn't premeditated, or violent," Tom said. "I'm sorry, Rachel, I shouldn't have broken it to you so abruptly."

"And I shouldn't have let it upset me. I didn't even know her. It's just that . . . Tell me."

"She was an old woman," Tom said. "Eighty-three. Lived alone, in a big old house a few miles south of here. It used to be in the country, but the town is spreading in that direction; there's a whole subdivision of new houses around hers. According to the neighbors she was active and independent despite her age, and her hearing was excellent. The thief may not have known that—or maybe he didn't care. We think she heard him rummaging around and came downstairs to confront him. She was in her nightgown and bathrobe. He tied her to a kitchen chair, gagged and blindfolded her, and then proceeded to take what he wanted. Except for tying her up he didn't molest her. The cause of death was a heart attack."

Adam's face faded from muddy brown to muddy gray. It was an ugly picture, as ugly in its way as brutal bloody assault. The thought of the old woman, blinded and mute and helpless, struggling to free herself, turned Rachel's stomach.

"How long," she began, and couldn't finish the sentence.

Tom wrenched the bottle of brandy away from Adam and splashed some into a glass. This time Rachel didn't refuse it.

"Not long," Tom said. "It may have been outrage rather than fear that brought on the attack. She had a reputation as a sour, unpleasant person. That's why she wasn't found for several days; the neighbors had given up trying to befriend her, they left her strictly alone, as she wanted."

"Nobody should die that way," Rachel whispered. "Nobody."

Tom patted her hand and then took his away, as if conscious of unprofessional behavior. But his voice was very gentle when he spoke. "Don't think of it as worse than it was, Rachel. The house was cold, she'd turned the thermostat down before she went to bed, so the body wasn't . . . And if she had been friendlier, more neighborly, someone would have found her sooner."

"Even so." Adam said no more, but Tom nodded.

"Even so, the charge will be murder, of one variety or another. Depends on the state's attorney, and on what we can wring out of him when we catch him."

"Did you find any fingerprints?" Adam asked.

"Too many. The place was filthy, every surface smeared with grease and dust. Most of the prints seem to be hers, but there were a few smudges that suggest he was wearing gloves. Every two-bit crook who watches television knows enough to wear gloves; you can buy 'em by the box in any drugstore. However," Tom added, "thanks to you and Tony, we know what he looks like."

"How do you know it's him?" Rachel asked. The question wasn't well phrased, but Tom knew what she meant.

"Took us a while to figure out what was missing from the house; that's why I didn't inform you earlier. She was no more friendly with her kin than with her neighbors, but we finally located a grand-niece who had visited her occasionally and was familiar with the inventory. The inventory," Tom added sardonically, "was the reason for the visits. She hoped to inherit a number of things, including the quilts. Her description of them was detailed."

"Will she inherit?" Adam asked.

"I don't know," Tom said. "I haven't seen the will yet. Her lawyer has been notified of her death, so the customary procedures are under way. I'll keep you informed, of course, but I thought you'd want to know about this right away."

"Does Tony know?" Rachel asked.

"Yes, I called him first thing this morning. He offered to come back—"

"No need for that," Adam said, squaring his shoulders. "I'm here."

"He seems to have great confidence in you." Tom's expression suggested he did not share Tony's opinion. "Anyhow, I convinced him we didn't need him, not at the moment. Rachel can identify the guy—"

"And he has identified her," Adam interrupted. "What are you doing about protection for her?"

"We feel sure Rachel is no longer in any danger," Tom said. "At least she won't be after the story hits the evening news broadcasts. She's not the only one who can identify him; Tony saw him too. It won't do him any good to retrieve the goods, half a dozen witnesses, including me, can testify to the fact that they ended up here. The news stories will emphasize the fact that they have been impounded by the police—"

"What?" Rachel's voice rose. "You're taking them?"

Tom looked at her in surprise. "They're stolen goods, Rachel. Evidence."

"You can't be absolutely certain yet. The—niece?—hasn't even seen them."

"Grand-niece. She's supposed to come in this afternoon to identify the objects." Tom hesitated. "If you're going to go by the book, I suppose I could bring her here."

"I'd prefer that. After all," Rachel said, "Cheryl left me in charge. I'm responsible, and I don't think I'm being unreasonable to insist that we follow the rules."

It sounded convincing, even to her.

Tom shrugged. "If that's how you want it . . . "

"What if this guy doesn't watch the news?" Adam asked. "Or draw the logical conclusions? Criminals are not, by definition, logical persons."

"Obviously you should continue taking sensible precautions. Don't go out alone. Keep the house locked and the dogs inside at night. Don't open the door to strangers—any strangers, he could be wearing a disguise. Call if you see anything out of line, and if I'm not there tell them to contact me immediately. Okay?"

Rachel wondered if he knew that the precise instructions and the gravity of his voice negated his earlier reassurance. "Okay," she said faintly.

"Don't worry, Rachel. This was a stupid, unnecessary crime but it means we'll be giving it top priority. We'll get him."

Adam had been eating doughnuts, assisted by the dogs. He offered the plate to Tom, who shook his head. "I have to get back. Come and show me exactly where you found this, Dr. Nugent." Wrapping a handkerchief around it, he dropped the knife into a plastic bag.

Uninvited, Rachel followed the men out onto the porch. I should sweep it, she thought, noting the smears of mud and dried grass. There was no danger of anyone slipping that morning; the cold snap had continued, and the ground looked hard as iron. She wrapped her arms around her shivering body.

"Go back in the house," Tom said, without looking directly at her. He had dropped to one knee and was staring at the top step.

Rachel ignored the suggestion—or was it an order?—and moved closer.

The place wasn't hard to find. A straight, inch-long slit broke the surface of the wood, which was dulled by a patch of dried mud. Flaking paint outlined the edges of the cut.

Tom took a thin steel probe from his pocket and inserted it delicately into the gash. When he withdrew it, his thumb marking the depth, he let out a whistle. "At least three inches. The blade went straight through."

"I had a hell of a time getting it out," Adam said.

The implications weren't lost on Rachel. "He must be stronger than he looks."

"Or very, very angry," said Adam.

Tom stood up. The look he gave Adam was decidedly unfriendly. "Is that the kind of theorizing anthropologists are taught?"

"Just a suggestion," Adam said meekly. "I was also going to mention—"

"Don't." Tom glanced at Rachel. "You'll catch cold. Go inside."

"Is that an order?"

"Just a suggestion." He smiled.

"Goodbye, then. And thank you."

"I'll let you know when to expect us. And don't worry."

After she had closed the door Rachel stood watching through the glass panel. The conversation didn't last long. Tom appeared to be asking questions and cutting off Adam's expansive answers in mid-sentence. Then Tom started down the steps, giving the slit in the wood a wide berth, and Adam came in.

"I'm chilled to the bone," he announced, with appropriate, exaggerated gestures. "Why anyone would choose to live in the so-called temperate zone—"

"What did he say?"

"Huh? Oh. Among other things, he wanted to know the address of the Esbat."

"So you need an alibi?"

Hugging himself and shivering, Adam watched her lock the door.

"Don't be dense. What kind of alibi would that be? Nothing happened until I got here."

"Then why—"

"It's obvious, isn't it? He thinks I may have been the one who drove that knife into the step. I'm big enough and strong enough," Adam said, without false modesty. "Unlike your burglar."

"But why—"

"If you'll stop interrupting, I'll tell you. It's rather shrewd of him, in fact; he's got more imagination than your average cop. That patch of mud on the step could have been—most probably was—a footprint. The use of footprints in sympathetic magic is well documented; like a man's shadow or his name, they are extensions of his soul, and any harm done to the extension can—with the proper spells and rituals—be duplicated on his body. Stab a footprint, and you stab the man himself. It's common practice in—" He broke off, seeing Rachel's expression. "I guess you know that. Well, there I was last night, fraternizing with a bunch of people who call themselves witches. Who's to know I'm not a believer, instead of the detached observer I claim to be? I'm not, as it happens, and the group doesn't practice or approve of Black Magic, but Tom isn't familiar with the Wicca creed or with my personal beliefs. He's right to check it out."

Rachel started to speak. Before she could get the first word out, Adam hurried on. "As for why I should do such an idiotic thing—that's what you were going to ask, wasn't it?—the police don't worry a lot about motive. They've seen too many people do too many bizarre things for inadequate or irrational reasons. Could be I resent your presence here, when I had expected to be alone—free to loot the place or throw wild parties or entertain the low-life of Leesburg. Could be I'm madly in love with Cheryl, and wildly jealous of Tony. Or vice versa."

"Could be you're crazy."

"That too. And don't forget the interesting fact that the dogs didn't bark till I showed up. I was here and so far there's no concrete evidence that anybody else was here. In short," Adam said, looking idiotically pleased, "I am a logical suspect."

"In short my foot," Rachel snapped. "Did Tom tell you all that?"

"Of course not. You don't tell suspects you suspect them."

"So he went off leaving me at the mercy of a demented witch?"

"Warlock," Adam said. "Although some nonsexist groups do use the word *witch* for male and female participants. He's just considering all the possibilities, as is his duty. He doesn't really believe it."

"Neither do I. And I don't believe the idea ever entered Tom's head! You're the one who has too much imagination. If you think you can scare me—"

"Scare you?" Adam's jaw dropped. "You're a sensible, adult female and a scholar; I assumed you'd see the flaws in that theory even if I hadn't pointed them out."

Rachel didn't know whether to be furious or flattered. He hadn't spared her tender female feelings, any more than he would have minced words with another man. How could she complain about that?

"Forget it," she said ungraciously. "Come out of the shop, I want to lock up. You don't see any of the cats, do you?"

"No." He followed her toward the rear door. "I suggest we keep it locked and use the side door from now on. Is there any reason why you have to go into the shop for the next few days?"

"I guess not. The things I should be working on are in the work-room."

"Which is where?"

"That door." Rachel pointed, adding, "The one Figgin is staring at. I swear, that damned animal has learned how to teleport himself. I thought I shut him in the kitchen."

"He materialized on my bed this morning." Adam picked up the cat, which had been sitting absolutely still except for its twitching tail, its eyes fixed unblinkingly on the workroom door. As soon as he lifted it, it began to kick and complain. Adam tightened his grip. "Cut it out, you monster. What does he want in there?"

"In," Rachel said. "Just *in*. It's forbidden territory, like the shop. The animals could damage the garments, and there are some dangerous substances in the workroom."

Adam opened the door of the family room and propelled a protesting Figgin through it. "Is the stolen merchandise in the workroom?"

"Yes."

"Can I have a look?"

"Why?"

"Why not?"

There was no reason why he shouldn't. Rachel shrugged, opened the door, and turned on the light.

Adam stood in the doorway, his eyes moving around the room. "Quite an elaborate arrangement."

"What did you expect?"

"A rocking chair and a sewing basket, I guess." Adam grinned. "What's all this stuff for? And where are those dangerous chemicals you mentioned?"

Enjoying the opportunity to monopolize the conversation for once, Rachel unlocked the cupboard above the stainless steel sinks and gave him a brief lecture. "Even common household cleaning materials can be dangerous when taken internally or combined with other substances, and some of them, like dry-cleaning solvents, are highly flammable. There have been cases of fanatical housecleaners being knocked out by breathing a mixture of ammonia and bleach. The fumes are deadly."

"You've got an outside vent and exhaust, I see."

"Cheryl believes in being extra careful. That's why she keeps this cupboard locked, so the kids and the pets can't get into it. The vent also helps control the humidity. Mold and mildew can ruin a garment."

"Very professional." Adam picked up a can of insect spray. "Fleas?"

"No, moths and silverfish. Everything that comes in, especially from Karen's auctions and flea markets, is inspected and, if necessary, treated, before it's brought into the shop. The darned insects spread like crazy. Cheryl usually puts suspect garments into an airtight container with the insecticide, and leaves it for a couple of weeks. Don't touch that," she added sharply, as Adam leaned over to inspect the quilt she had left spread across the table.

"Evidence?"

"It's one of the stolen pieces, yes. The others are here."

She displayed them. Adam gave them only a cursory glance before returning to the table and the album quilt.

"I don't understand what all the fuss is about. They're just scraps of cloth. And this one is dirty. Except for . . . You cleaned this part?"

"Just brushed it." She stood with hands tightly clasped, fighting the urge to pull him away.

"Just brushed it? I wish my laundry would respond so well to a simple brushing. Save me a bundle on laundromats and cleaning. It's kind of pretty, I guess—if you like pretty. But diamonds and rubies it ain't."

"It's quite valuable."

"I'll have to take your word for it. Well, how about lunch? I'll cook."

"I'm not hungry."

"Spaghetti? I make a mean marinara sauce."

She got him out of the room finally, and at once set to work. It was already after noon. She would have to hurry. Tom hadn't said when he expected to bring the murdered woman's niece to identify the quilts.

Later the phone rang. Rachel ignored it. A few minutes later Adam knocked at the door. "Cheryl wants to talk to you."

Rachel had locked the door. She went on working. "I'm in the middle of something, I can't stop now. Tell her I'll call back."

Adam went away. The phone rang again; with a murmured curse, Rachel unplugged it. She was working at top speed, with a recklessness Cheryl would have deplored, but without visible damage to the quilt. In her haste she didn't pause to examine the results of her labors, getting only hasty impressions of unusual and exquisite images—bluebirds nesting, a spray of roses, paired hearts pierced by an arrow feathered with stitches fine as hair . . .

Hair soft as yellow silk slipped through the bristles of the brush as it moved in rhythmic strokes. Her eyes were fixed on the mirror and on the other face it reflected.

"What else did you expect?" Her delicate, arched eyebrows rose in mocking inquiry. "Did you think I wouldn't put a stop to it?"

"A stop to . . . Then you knew."

"Of course I did." She sounded surprised, as if the answer should have been obvious. "I know everything that happens here. There was no reason for me to interfere then. After all, he wasn't the first, now was he?"

"You can't blame me for that! My Lord, I never wanted—"

"Blame?" Her laughter was light and indifferent. "Men have different needs. It was his right. But you wanted this, didn't you? You got what you wanted. Now I want it, and I don't share with anyone. Especially the likes of you."

Rachel hung the quilt over a drying rack and got out the camera—not the Polaroid Cheryl sometimes used, but the expensive thirty-five millimeter. After taking close-ups of each square in turn, she finished the roll with several overall views. She took the film out and put it in her pocket before replacing it with an unused roll.

The feeling of frantic haste, as if some enemy were in hot pursuit and closing in, began to diminish, and her taut muscles relaxed, leaving her weak-kneed and exhausted. A wave of dizziness swept over her and her vision blurred. Blinking, she focused on the clock. Almost three o'clock! Where had the time gone?

five

Adam was in the family room. "You look sort of green around the gills," he remarked tactlessly. "Have something to eat before Kara and the fuzz get here."

The words made no impression at first; she was too outraged at what she saw. Seated in front of her word processor, Adam was pounding energetically at the keyboard, using the clumsy-looking but effective four-fingered method of an amateur typist.

"What the hell do you think you're doing?" she demanded.

"Writing a letter. I have to get it off right away and I haven't unpacked my stuff yet. I didn't think you'd mind . . . " His voice trailed off into silence as it dawned on him that she did mind. In a misguided attempt to improve matters he added, "I didn't look at any of your personal files, just your thesis notes. I think you may be onto something."

"Do you?"

His smile faded. "What's the matter?"

"Does the word *private* mean anything to you?"

"Well, sure. I said, I didn't look at anything except your notes. Where'd you get that stuff about coded messages in quilts? I ran into a similar case in Guatemala."

"I thought you had been in . . . Never mind, I don't care where you've been." Rachel looked over his shoulder. Adam obligingly leaned back so she could see the screen. "My dear Rosamund," the letter began. "How are you? I am fine. The weather is cold. Snow is predicted for . . . "

"I haven't finished it," Adam explained.

"So I see." Yelling at him would have been as ineffectual as hitting a rock with a feather duster. Rosamund must be the girlfriend, question-mark, Cheryl had mentioned. If that was the sort of letter he wrote the love of his life, it was no wonder he wasn't concerned about privacy.

"Did you say Kara is coming? Why didn't you tell me?"

"I just did." Adam resumed typing.

"Before this. Why is she coming?"

"She wants to meet the grand-niece. Cheryl called her—Tom called her—everybody's been calling everybody," he added. "Including you. You told me you were busy, so I didn't interrupt you."

"Considerate of you."

"I made a pot of coffee."

"You didn't put the peanut butter away." It was on the counter, open, with a knife protruding from it.

"I thought you might prefer it to spaghetti," Adam said. "In view of the fact that there isn't time for a proper meal before our guests arrive."

Rachel wasn't in the mood for spaghetti or peanut butter, but she decided she had better eat something, so she spread some of the latter on a piece of bread, folded it over, and leaned against the counter while she ate. His tongue protruding with the effort of composition, Adam rattled off a few more sentences, let out a long "whew" and punched the print key.

"That's that. Maybe I should run to the store and get some cookies for our company."

"There's a bag of them in the cupboard."

"Not anymore. I ate 'em." He started to slip into his jacket.

"You said they'd be here any minute," Rachel pointed out. "Besides, this isn't a social occasion."

"Strictly speaking, that is correct, but even business meetings can be facilitated by a display of social—" The dogs began to bark and Adam said brightly, "Somebody's here."

The new arrival was Kara. Shedding her coat, she tossed it carelessly

over a chair and fixed Rachel with a cold stare. One of the cats headed
for the trailing folds of mink and was about to claw them into a comfortable nest when Rachel rescued the coat.

"I'll hang it up."

"It's not valuable," Kara said. "I picked it up at an auction. Don't try to
distract me, Rachel, I'm going to bawl you out. Why didn't you tell me?"

Rachel didn't ask what she meant. She had had time to reflect on her
mistake, and wonder why on earth she hadn't reported immediately to
Kara. As an employee, she had assumed a responsibility she had no
right to assume. As a guest—an unwanted guest at that—she had been
guilty of a breach of basic good manners. Since there was no reasonable excuse for her behavior, she remained silent.

"After all, I am one of the owners of this establishment," Kara went
on. "You ought to have contacted me and let me deal with the police.
Your involvement in this very unpleasant situation is a direct conse-
quence of your employment here, and although we may not be legally
responsible for your safety, it is a matter of concern to us."

She sounded more angry than concerned, and resentment replaced
Rachel's feeling of guilt. "I'm sorry," she said stiffly.

"She's been busy," Adam said. "Want a cup of coffee?"

Kara turned her inimical stare on him. The look and the tapping
foot would have cowed most people, but Adam, amiably unperturbed,
went on, "I was going to get cookies, but Rachel said there wasn't time.
How about cinnamon toast?"

Kara's lips relaxed into an unwilling smile. "For God's sake, Adam,
this isn't a tea party. I should be yelling at you, too. Why didn't you . . .
Oh, hell, what's the use? Put the damn coat down, Rachel, and relax.
How much time have we got before Tom arrives?"

"None," Adam said calmly as the dogs hurled themselves, howling,
at the side door. Opening the door to the porch, he urged them out.

"Let me do the talking," Kara said. Tucking a strand of hair back in
place, she sat down in the rocking chair, crossed her legs, smoothed
her skirt, and leaned back.

It was a calculated pose, designed to display not only cool self-pos-
session but her well-cut skirt and raw silk blouse and understated jewelry—gold chains and bracelet, no rings except the wide gold band on
her left hand. The contrast between her appearance and that of the

woman who entered couldn't have been more emphatic if Kara had planned it. Maybe she had, Rachel thought in reluctant admiration.

Mrs. Wilson, like all women, knew that fine feathers increase confidence. Unfortunately her taste didn't match her instincts. She was short, only an inch or two taller than five feet, but the word *petite* didn't describe any of her measurements except her height. She had made the common error of buying clothes that were a size too small; the tight skirt hugged her thighs and the extravagantly ruffled red blouse clashed with her orange hair. She was wearing too much jewelry—dangling earrings, a pearl choker, several gaudy rings.

Tom's face was particularly impassive. His dour expression brightened momentarily as he greeted Rachel but settled back into a frozen mask when he introduced Mrs. Wilson. It wasn't hard to deduce that she had been giving him a hard time.

Mrs. Wilson sat down, her skirt folding into horizontal pleats across her stomach, and looked at Kara. "You're the one who wants to buy—"

Smoothly Kara cut her off. "I'm so sorry about your aunt, Mrs. Wilson. Please accept my condolences."

Thus reminded of her bereavement, Mrs. Wilson took out a handkerchief and raised it cautiously to her eyes. "It was a terrible shock. Poor Auntie Ora. If she'd been in a nursing home like she should of been this wouldn't have happened. I told her over and over she should sell that big old house. My boy Rocky would of helped her get moved, though it would of been a terrible job getting rid of all that junk she'd collected over the years. We could have had a real nice auction." She glared at Tom. "Now he tells me we can't have her things back. That's not right. What kind of country is this when the police can take a person's property?"

"I've explained that, Mrs. Wilson," Tom said wearily. "You—if you are the heir—will get the quilts back as soon as possible. They are evidence."

"Yeah, and what about the TV and the other things? You never found those."

Kara had been listening with a faint smile. Now she said, "What else was taken?"

"Not much," Tom answered. "The television set was the only modern appliance. She didn't have a stereo or CD player, just a radio, and her jewelry was in a safe deposit box. A few pieces of furniture and bric-a-brac appear to be missing. We haven't located them yet, but we've put out a description."

"They was valuable antiques," Mrs. Wilson interrupted. "That old radio cabinet—"

"We're working on that, Mrs. Wilson." Tom looked at his watch. "I don't want to take up any more of your time or Mrs. Brinckley's. If you'll make a formal identification of the quilts I'll take them with me."

"Certainly." Kara responded as if the speech had been addressed to her. "They're in the workshop. This way."

She led the way to the door, her heels clicking decisively. The others trailed after her, including Adam, who brought up the rear. Rachel started to close the door and heard Kara say sharply, "Grab him, Adam, and put him back in the kitchen."

"Him" was Figgin, of course. Cursing and squirming, he was reimprisoned, and after making certain the kitchen door was shut tight, Rachel followed Adam to the workroom.

Tom had taken the carton from the cupboard. Rachel stared blankly at it. She couldn't remember folding and repacking the quilts after she had showed them to Adam. She must have done so; the table and racks were bare.

"Let me do that," she said, as Kara reached for the first neatly wrapped bundle. "You'll get dirty."

The tissue came away to display the Carolina Rose quilt. Rachel spread it out across the table and Mrs. Wilson pounced. "That's hers. That's Auntie's." Her long, scarlet nail picked at one of the patches. "It's tore. It was perfect before."

"Before what?" Kara inquired coldly. "I noticed that rent when I first examined the quilt. The fabric must have caught on something—a pin or a nail—during the robbery."

Mrs. Wilson gave her a shrewd glance and realized that the trick wasn't going to work. "I'm sure you took good care of it," she said in a syrupy voice.

Tom had taken out a list and a pencil. "Okay, that's one. Next, please."

Mrs. Wilson identified the white quilt as another of Auntie's treasures. The album quilt was the last. Rachel didn't stop to wonder why it was at the bottom of the box. She was anticipating a reprimand, or at least a question; if Mrs. Wilson didn't notice that the quilt had been cleaned, Kara certainly would. I'll say Cheryl told me to, Rachel thought. Cheryl had authorized it. Not in so many words, maybe, but . . .

Pencil poised, Tom said, "Well, Mrs. Wilson?"

The woman was slow to answer, and Rachel held her breath. Finally Mrs. Wilson muttered, "That has to be one of hers. It looks different. . . . "

"Yes or no?" Tom demanded.

"Yes." Mrs. Wilson smiled like a shark at Kara. "Beautiful, isn't it?"

Even Rachel recognized the gambit. Kara, who had been hardened by innumerable encounters with prospective sellers, braced herself for combat.

"Badly faded," she drawled. "A pity; it would be worth money if it were in good condition. She must have stored it in a hot attic or a damp basement. Look at the mold."

"That's not mold, just dust," Mrs. Wilson retorted.

Whatever it was, it was there—not as heavy as the film Rachel had removed only a few hours earlier, but the same dulling gray.

"You can wrap them up again," Tom said, tucking the list into his pocket. "Rachel?"

"What? Oh. Yes, of course." She waved aside Adam's offer of help and began folding the album quilt. How strange and how infuriating, the return of the dulling film. It must be seeping out to the surface from the filling, cotton batting permeated with decades of dust. Obviously more intensive cleaning than simple brushing would be required. The hand vacuum, or . . .

The mercantile duel between Kara and Mrs. Wilson was interrupted by Tom. "You ladies can make any arrangements you want, but you'll have to do it on your own time. I suggest you consult your lawyer, Mrs. Wilson; he can tell you how long it will be before you can dispose of your aunt's property."

"Quite right," Kara said.

"But you are interested?"

"I might be. At the proper time and under the proper conditions."

"I'll bet other people would be interested, too," Mrs. Wilson said. "Those quilts are famous. One of them was in a book. A lady came around to see them one time, and she put one of them in a book."

"Really." Kara's polite indifference parried that thrust. "It was nice meeting you, Mrs. Wilson. Let me know what you decide."

After Tom had removed Mrs. Wilson and the quilts, Kara dropped into the rocking chair and kicked off her shoes. "You did a nice job on the album quilt, Rachel."

"I just brushed it."

"So I assumed. You didn't get all the dirt out, but you were wise not to tackle anything more extensive. It will require careful handling. It is gorgeous, though."

"Are you going to buy it?" Rachel asked.

"I think so." Kara accepted a triangle of toast, thickly spread with melted butter and cinnamon sugar, from Adam. "She'll try to hold me up for an outlandish price, but I can deal with her. I know the type."

"She isn't a very nice woman," Rachel said.

"She's a greedy, crude, selfish woman," Kara corrected. "Who won't shed a tear over poor old Auntie. She's probably had her eye on those quilts ever since Miss Ora told her about the lady and the book and how valuable they were. I won't get any bargains." She dusted off her hands and reached for another piece of toast. "But we can make a reasonable profit on the deal, I think. That album quilt is really quite remarkable. I wish I'd had a chance to examine it more closely. Cheryl should have photographed it."

The roll of film in Rachel's pocket weighed like lead. She concentrated on eating cinnamon toast.

"I'll make some more toast," Adam said, pleased at how well his offering had been received.

"Not for me, I've got to be on my way." Kara slid her feet into her shoes. "That hit the spot, Adam; I can't remember when I last had cinnamon toast. Where'd you put my coat, Rachel?"

Rachel retrieved the coat and helped Kara into it. It was almost ankle-length and very full, with a deep shawl collar that could open up into a hood. "You got this at an auction?"

"Three hundred bucks," Kara said. "The lining was shot; I made a new one. And don't give me any grief about animal rights, I get enough of that from Joe." A fond, reminiscent smile transformed her face. "He's a slick debater, that kid. He's got me so brainwashed I'd never buy a new fur coat even if I wanted to spend the money. But these unfortunate minks passed on thirty years ago. I told Joe I was honoring their memory by wearing the coat."

"What did he say?" Rachel asked.

Kara laughed. "That my arguments were specious and my attitude hypocritical. In those precise words! I've been arguing with Little Joe—I used to call him that before he informed me he was too old for pet names—since he was four. I keep telling him vintage is very P.C. We're the ultimate recyclers. I haven't bought a new dress for ten years; everything I own is second-hand."

"Including that blouse?" Rachel asked. "It looks brand new."

"Estate sale," Kara said. "The woman was a compulsive clothes buyer; she had closets full of things she'd never worn. Want to make the rounds with me sometime? I can show you some of the tricks of the trade."

Rachel realized Kara was making an effort to be friendly, to compensate for her scolding. "Thanks. That would be fun."

"It's hard work. But the triumph of the occasional bargain makes it all worthwhile." She drew on her gloves. "Call Cheryl, will you please? You know what a worrier she is."

"I will."

"Good. Well, I'd better be going. We're having our usual Christmas Eve open house tomorrow night and I haven't even finished decorating the tree. If either of you is free, join the crowd. Six to whenever."

"We're busy," Adam said quickly.

"Never mind inventing appointments, I knew you wouldn't come. I don't blame you for refusing to mingle with a bunch of politicians. I'd get out of it myself if I could. Rachel . . . " Her face became serious. "You're more than welcome if you want to bring a guest. But don't come alone."

"I wouldn't want—"

"You know what I mean." Kara lingered at the door, smoothing her gloves. "Tom thinks the danger to you is over, but I'm not entirely convinced. This guy has done some peculiar things, even for a dim-witted criminal. Need I point out what they could imply?"

"No," Rachel said shortly.

"So be careful. Continue to take precautions. And Adam—"

"Fear not, kind lady, I will watch over all the helpless females that wander onto my turf. Wait till I get my coat and I'll walk you to your car."

"I was about to ask you to. I picked up your mail, Rachel; there are a couple of big boxes." She waved Rachel's thanks aside. "It was one of

Mark's aides who played mailman, actually, he lives in Hyattsville. I'll see you Christmas Day."

Adam went out with her. The early twilight had closed in, and their forms were hidden by darkness before they had gone ten feet. Rachel wondered how Kara liked being included in a list of helpless females. The words had been meant as a joke, but the offer had been genuine, and serious. Rachel had no objection to being protected, by anyone or anything—the more the merrier, in fact—but she could have wished her protector were someone other than Adam. He was big enough and willing enough, but he was so damned absentminded!

He hadn't even thought to turn on the outside lights. Typical of Adam, gallantly insisting on escorting a lady to her car and letting her stumble through the dark. Rachel pressed the switch and watched the lights spring up, illuminating bare branches and yellowed grass. They had been strategically placed to bathe the entire perimeter of the house in their glow—an effective deterrent to potential thieves. Rachel had asked why there was no security system, particularly for the shop, and Cheryl, laughing at her own inadequacies as she usually did, had admitted Tony made her shut it down after she had turned in three false alarms in a week. The lights and the dogs worked as well or better, he claimed, and he was certainly in a position to know.

Rachel waited to open the door for Adam, whose arms were loaded with two good-sized cartons and a shopping bag full of mail—mostly catalogues, Rachel observed. Stowing them in a corner, he murmured pathetically, "I was going to the grocery store, but I have to thaw out first."

"You were only out there for five minutes."

"That was four and a half minutes too long. Brrrr."

"There's no need for you to go to the store. The freezer is stuffed with leftovers from the party. Including cookies. Cheryl took most of the ones she made, but she left a few boxes for us."

"Why didn't you tell me that when I was trying to be hospitable?"

"Why should we waste Cheryl's cookies on people like Mrs. Wilson? We'll go shopping tomorrow," she added, remembering the roll of film. Even on Christmas Eve she could probably find a place that would develop it in an hour. "Sit down. I want to talk to you."

"What about?" Adam fumbled nervously with his beard.

"That damned beard, for one thing," Rachel said, to her surprise.

Adam's beard certainly hadn't been the most important thing on her mind.

"What's wrong with it?"

"You look like a Neanderthal."

"It keeps my face warm."

"You could at least trim it. Oh, hell, why am I talking about your beard? What plans have you made for tomorrow night?"

"I don't have any plans for tomorrow night. I just didn't want to go to that party." His eyes widened ingenuously. "Did you?"

"No. Though it might have occurred to you to ask me before you turned down the invitation. You said 'we,' and Kara assumed you were speaking for both of us."

"Where do you want to go?"

"I don't want to go anyplace! I just want to know what you're going to do."

"Whatever you're doing," Adam said simply.

"Oh."

"That's what Tony told me. Stick with her." Adam admitted, "I didn't take the situation seriously at first, and I had promised Pat I'd check out the Esbat, and I figured you'd be okay here for a few hours, with the dogs and the house locked up. I'm sorry about that. It won't happen again."

"What made you change your mind?"

"The knife. I don't like the way this guy is behaving. Kara thinks he's not after the quilts anymore, he's after you. I'm beginning to agree with her."

"Thanks for cheering me up."

"Would you rather we patted you on the head and told you not to worry? You can't even tell that comforting lie to a child these days, it's too dangerous to allow him to feel safe. God," Adam said, with sudden bitterness. "What a world it is."

"Yeah."

"So from now on you're stuck with me. Whither thou goest I will go. With strict observance of the proprieties, of course," he added. "I won't insist on sleeping with you."

"Oh," Rachel said blankly. "Thanks."

"You should thank me. I snore. Not all the time, just when I'm tired."

It was hard to tell what was going on under the beard; the vibrations could indicate a smile or a leer or a sneer. Rachel decided it was safe to laugh. "I meant, thanks for playing bodyguard. I'm not going to be heroic."

"Good. I respect courage and the principles of modern feminism, but this situation has nothing to do with either. If I were in your shoes I'd demand protection too. So let's consider our schedule and enjoy the festal season, undeterred by grinches of any variety. Christmas Day we're spending with Pat and Ruth. We better go shopping tomorrow, I haven't got anything for them yet."

"I haven't either," Rachel said guiltily. "I'm glad you reminded me."

"You've had other things on your mind."

"That's no excuse."

"Well, we'll do it tomorrow. Maybe you can give me some ideas. I never know what to get for women, they have such peculiar tastes."

Rachel laughed. "What did you—"

The telephone interrupted her and reminded her of a broken promise. As she might have known, the caller was Cheryl, spouting questions. When she could get a word in, she said, "I was about to call you. Kara just left, and Adam and I got to talking . . . Yes. Yes, he's here. Everything is fine. Mrs. Wilson identified the things and Tom—"

Cheryl knew what had happened; she had already had a long talk with Kara. Cheryl didn't scold her for failing to report, but Rachel would have preferred a lecture to the outpouring of warm sympathy and concern.

"Really," she said, as soon as she could get a word in, "there's nothing to worry about and absolutely no need for you to cut your holiday short. Adam is here and he's been . . . " She glanced at Adam, who was mouthing silent comments. "He's been . . . Do you want to talk to him?"

Adam handed her a bottle of wine and a corkscrew and took the phone. "We're about to get drunk," he announced. "So talk fast. She'll have the cork out in a second and if I let her get a few drinks ahead . . . What? No. Yes. I said so, didn't I? All right." He handed the phone back to Rachel and retrieved the bottle.

"What did you do to him?" Cheryl demanded.

"I don't understand."

"He's talking! And making insulting remarks. It usually takes him at least six months to get to that point with another man, much less a female. What did you do, put a spell on him?"

"I'll tell you about it some time," Rachel said.

She had to endure more friendly teasing from Cheryl, and an even more uncomfortable, if brief, discussion with Tony. It was only her guilty conscience, she told herself, that lent double meanings to some of his statements. He was glad she and Adam were getting on so well.

Rachel was on her second glass of wine and Adam was investigating the leftovers in the refrigerator when the telephone rang again. She recognized Tom's voice before he identified himself.

"Are you watching the news?" he asked.

The question jolted Rachel out of her mellow mood. "I forgot. Is it . . . Will there be something on about . . . "

The words and the tone of her voice alerted Adam; muttering under his breath, he went to the television set and switched it on.

"Channel four." Rachel repeated what Tom had said, and Adam settled down in front of the set to watch. The announcer was talking about a local resident whose neighbors had complained about his Christmas decorations. The ten thousand bulbs shining all night long kept them awake, and they were tired of listening to endless repetitions of "Have Yourself a Merry Little Christmas."

"They'll repeat the story at six," Tom said, when Rachel had reported this. "I—uh—I didn't get a chance to talk to you today. Alone, I mean."

"No," Rachel agreed. She was watching Adam, who appeared to be absorbed by the story about the Christmas decorations. She had no doubt as to whose side he was on.

"I thought maybe we could have a drink tomorrow night, or maybe an early dinner. I'm going to my sister's later, to help them put the toys together—you know, the ones that say, 'Some assembly required.' My brother-in-law is a good guy, but he doesn't know a screwdriver from a wrench. But I'm not supposed to show up till the kids are in bed, so I thought maybe . . . "

"I'd love to," Rachel said.

"Great. Suppose I pick you up at five."

Adam turned toward her and began waving his arms urgently.

"It's on," Rachel said. "I'll see you tomorrow."

The police officer who was being interviewed wasn't Tom; she realized she shouldn't have expected to see him, he was probably in the wrong department or not important enough to rate public exposure. The grizzled veteran who was probably a captain or deputy sheriff made the most of the pathos of the story and asked for the cooperation of the viewing audience. He didn't mention Rachel's name or the name of the shop, but he emphasized that "several" people had seen the presumed thief.

Adam switched off the set. "What is it you'd love to do?" he asked.

"None of your business."

"As your bodyguard, I am entitled to know your future plans," Adam said with great dignity. "When is he picking you up? Are you going shopping with me tomorrow?"

Adam insisted on shopping at the biggest and gaudiest mall in the area, which involved a twenty-mile drive that took twice as long as usual because too many other people had left their shopping until the day before Christmas. He also insisted on driving. They hadn't gone a block before Rachel realized she had made a serious error in letting him get behind the wheel. He handled the car as if it were a Jeep or Landrover, hitting bumps and potholes at full speed, and never yielding the right of way. She managed to talk him into removing his mittens so he could get a firm grip on the wheel, but her other remonstrations had little effect.

"Haven't driven in the States for a long time," Adam explained. "Takes a while to change old habits. Don't worry, I'm an excellent driver. Never had an accident."

That seemed improbable. Rachel closed her eyes and abandoned the subject. "How do you feel about malls?" she asked. "Most of the men I know avoid them like the plague."

"They're fascinating studies in sociological development." Adam fumbled in his pocket and withdrew a crumpled piece of paper. "I start screaming with claustrophobia after about an hour, though. Let's get organized. I made a list."

Rachel opened her eyes, but she got only a glimpse before he covered the paper with his hand. "You're not supposed to see what I'm getting for you," he explained indignantly.

"I didn't. Manure for Ruth?"

"She's a dedicated gardener," Adam explained.

"Yes, but . . . You aren't going to find manure or any other gardening things this time of year."

"Oh." Adam looked chagrined. "Any suggestions?"

"You're on your own, buster."

They had to circle the parking garage for twenty minutes before they found a space, and they wouldn't have gotten that one if Adam had not outbluffed two other drivers. One of them got out of his car, prepared to debate the case, but when Adam emerged and rose to his full height, his beard bristling, the combative gentleman beat a hasty retreat.

Otherwise Adam was the soul of courtesy, stopping to pick up a parcel a woman had dropped, holding the door for laden shoppers.

"I'll meet you here in an hour," he said. "Right inside the door."

"Make it an hour and a half."

The stores were crowded, the clerks harried, and the merchandise limited, but carols blared from the loudspeakers and people were in a holiday mood, good-natured and smiling. Even the cheap decorations, the swags of plastic holly and gold tinsel, had a tacky, insouciant charm. After Rachel had dropped off her film she squared her shoulders and plunged into the crowd. She knew it wouldn't be easy to find appropriate gifts; the others were well-to-do people with excellent taste.

Except Adam. She rather enjoyed selecting gifts for him—a new pair of mittens, a heavy cap with ear flaps, a bright tartan muffler and, the pièce de résistance, a pair of socks with a smirking blonde female on one and a grinning Santa on the other, with a concealed tape that played "I Saw Mommy Kissing Santa Claus." The presents she chose for the others were boring but safe—gloves, scarves, stationery.

When she returned to the photo shop the pictures weren't ready; she had to wait another fifteen minutes, and since she was already late she didn't examine them closely, only shuffled quickly through the pack to make sure they had come out. Hurrying to the door, she saw Adam waiting. His promptness surprised her a little; even more surprising was the fact that Adam the unsociable was deep in animated conversation with another man. Then the latter let out a booming laugh that rang out over the Christmas music, and she recognized Pat MacDougal.

"Look who I found," Adam said happily.

"Wrong. He didn't find me, I found him—wild-eyed and aimlessly wandering." He held out his hand. "Hello, Rachel. Somebody should have warned you not to go out in public with this—"

Rachel shifted her shopping bag to her left hand and offered her right. As he took it in his, he stopped speaking so suddenly that the last word ended in a gasp of expelled breath, and his grip tightened like a tourniquet. Rachel cried out.

He released her at once. "Sorry. Don't know my own strength." He was smiling, but he had stepped back, a quick, involuntary movement, and his narrowed eyes, intent on her face, were cold and unsmiling.

Adam stared at Pat. "What's the matter?"

"What's the matter with what? Take him home, Rachel, he's becoming incoherent. See you both tomorrow."

He moved quickly and rather clumsily, shouldering his way through the crowds of people, not looking back.

He knows. Watch out for him.

The words sounded so distinctly Rachel glanced over her shoulder to see who had spoken. No one was looking at her or talking to her. Except Adam, and he was saying something quite different in quite a different tone of voice.

"Quick, let's get out of here before she sees me."

"Who?" Rachel grabbed her shopping bag and let him tow her toward the exit.

"One of the Wiccas." He let out a breath of relief when they reached the parking garage unaccosted. "I was at that meeting under what you might call false pretenses, and I'd just as soon not—"

"You used a false name?"

She meant it as a joke until she saw his sheepish expression. "One of them might have known who I was. As I told Tom, they're a well-informed lot, they read the literature, and—well, uh . . . "

"What would they do, curse you?"

"They don't do curses," Adam said seriously. "They're very high-minded and pure. But it would have been embarrassing. It was kind of a low-down trick." He brightened. "She didn't notice me, though, so it's okay."

Rachel looked up at him. Big as a bear, covered with hair . . . "I don't see how she could have missed you."

She unlocked the car; he had two shopping bags in each hand and a large lumpy parcel—could it be manure?—under one arm. A roll of gaudy green and red wrapping protruded from one of the bags.

Adam ignored this rude remark. "We need to find a liquor store," he said cheerfully, tossing his purchases into the back seat. "I'm going to get Pat a bottle of whisky. Tonight we'll wrap presents and listen to carols and I'll make eggnog and chowder—"

"I'm going out."

"Oh, yeah, that's right." Adam started the wipers as snowflakes appeared on the windshield. "It's supposed to snow tonight. Maybe we'll have a blizzard and then you'll have to stay home."

Home. A strange word for him to use; the Leesburg house was home to neither of them.

Snow began to fall heavily during the afternoon, but the weather was not responsible for the alteration of her plans. Tom called shortly before five to say he had to work.

"On Christmas Eve?" Rachel exclaimed.

"A policeman's lot. And," Tom said, "the lot of a policeman's wife. Ask Cheryl. I'm sorry, Rachel."

"It's not your fault. I hope it's nothing serious?"

"All in a day's work," Tom said. There was a note in his voice that warned her not to pursue the subject. "Rain check?"

She reassured him, sympathized, and hung up to find Adam watching her.

"Well, you got your wish," she said shortly.

"I admit I was thinking negative thoughts, but I don't know enough magic to implement them. What happened?"

"It must have been something grisly, he wouldn't tell me."

She turned on the television. The story was the lead feature on the local news; murders always claim top spot. A liquor store hold-up gone awry, a semiautomatic rifle, a store full of holiday shoppers . . .

Adam reached the set in a single long stride and switched it off. "Not tonight," he said.

"My God." Rachel dropped into a chair and covered her face with her hands.

"I said, not tonight. You can't do the victims, or Tom, any good by agonizing over them. Come here." He lifted her, unresisting, out of the chair and led her to the door. The dogs took its opening as an invitation and rushed out; Adam drew her onto the porch and held her there, one arm around her. "Look."

Falling snow made a lacy curtain against the dark. The ground was already covered and every twig was outlined in white. The dogs ran in delighted circles, rolling and kicking the soft covering into drifts. Bright against the dark and the snow, the lighted trees along the street shone scarlet and green, blue and golden yellow. Barely audible, on the farthest boundary of hearing, came faint sounds that might have been bird song or the distant echo of music.

"It's so beautiful," Rachel murmured. "So peaceful. And less than five miles away—"

"Cut it out." His arm tightened, drawing her closer. It was a friendly, passionless embrace and she yielded to it, resting her head against his shoulder. "There's plenty of tragedy and sorrow out there. You've had your share and you'll have more, and so will I and a lot of other people. All the more reason to enjoy the good times."

"You're quite the philosopher, aren't you?"

"I have many talents," Adam said. "Want me to say some poetry?"

"'The Night Before Christmas'?"

Expecting a joke or a flippant response, she was surprised to hear something quite different.

"'Some say that ever 'gainst that season comes, Wherein our Saviour's birth is celebrated, This bird of dawning singeth all night long; And then, they say, no spirit dare stir abroad; The nights are wholesome; then no planets strike, No fairy takes, nor witch hath power to charm.'"

"That's lovely," Rachel said.

"It's an incantation. Against the powers of darkness. Not witches and fairies, dark thoughts and nasty people."

"Then . . . " Rachel had to stop and take a deep breath. "Then it's not working."

"Huh?"

He saw it, and let out a faint scream. Pale against the night, enveloped in white from its shoulders to its feet, it glided slowly toward the gate. Long silvery hair floated out around its head, which was crowned with a wreath of dark leaves.

Adam recovered his breath. "Shades of Charlie Dickens! It's the Spirit of Christmas Past!"

six

"I didn't mean to do that," Adam mumbled. "How did I do that? A harmless snatch of poetry! If Shakespeare's not safe, who is?"

"Stop babbling." She kicked him firmly but impersonally in the shin, as she would have kicked a malfunctioning machine.

Two other figures followed the first. They wore prosaic, practical coats, one of fuzzy faux fur, the other of padded blue down, over what appeared to be long robes. No spirits these, Rachel thought, ashamed of that moment of weakness. A magical moment though, in its way.

The dogs, belatedly aware of their responsibilities, rushed toward the fence, and the visitors stopped at a safe distance from the gate, huddling nervously together. The leader looked up. The light fell clearly and unflatteringly on features that were unquestionably female and on the red berries and dark green leaves on her head. Straightening the wreath, which had slipped over one eye, she raised her hand.

Rachel saw her lips move, but couldn't hear the words because of the racket the dogs were making. One of the acolytes jumped back as Worth reared up on his hind legs, front paws on the fence, massive head thrust forward.

Adam had recovered himself. "Dogs in!" he bellowed.

The dogs loved company. They were reluctant to leave their new-found friends, but eventually Adam persuaded them onto the porch and the little group bravely advanced.

"Come in and close the door," Rachel said out of the corner of her mouth.

"That would be rude."

"Rude, schmude. You know who they are, don't you?"

"Uh-huh. The least I can do is listen to what they have to say." He raised his voice. "Good evening, ladies and—uh."

The Spirit of Christmas Past cleared her throat and tried again. "May Her blessing be upon you," she intoned.

"Thank you," Adam said politely.

"We come in love," the woman went on.

An unconvincing murmur from the other two seconded the sentiment. Both had long dark hair and long white skirts, but Adam's uncertainty as to their gender was understandable. The leader had to be wearing several layers of woollies under her robe; she wasn't shivering, though her face was so red with cold that it rivaled the holly berries.

"May we enter this house?" She put her hand on the gate.

"No."

The word came promptly and forcibly, not from Adam but from Rachel.

Seeing him that afternoon with Pat, one of the "witches" must have realized their new recruit was a spy and an unbeliever. They had tracked him down—followed him, perhaps—and now they had come to tell him what they thought of him—in the kindest possible terms, of course. Adam was such a soft touch, he was already squirming and looking guilty. If she hadn't spoken up, Adam would have let them in, Rachel thought.

Once you invite them in they have power over you. They can't come in unless you let them.

Adam was poking her and murmuring under his breath. One of the acolytes had fixed her with a glare that didn't look very loving. "I'm sorry," Rachel said firmly. "But we're busy this evening. What do you want?"

She sensed that the leader was accustomed to such rebuffs. With a shrug, she launched into a speech. There were a number of references to the Goddess, to love, forgiveness, and the spirit of peace. The gist of it seemed to be that they had come to forgive Adam for the cruel trick he had played upon them, to return good for evil, and to assure him they would pray for him.

"That's nice," Rachel said. "Good night and happy . . . whatever it is you celebrate."

She shoved Adam back into the house and slammed the door.

"Did you have to be so rude?" he asked reproachfully.

"Yes. Have they gone?"

Adam peered out through the window. "They're holding hands and chanting. Or singing. It's freezing out there, shouldn't we at least offer them—"

"No! If they want to stand around and catch pneumonia that's their decision."

"They're going now," Adam said, relieved. "How about a hot buttered rum to start the festivities?"

He hadn't overlooked a single holiday cliché. Since he hadn't known she would be there, Rachel had to assume the schedule had been arranged for his solitary enjoyment, but he was delighted to have someone to share it with, and his enjoyment was contagious. Sipping their drinks and eating cookies, with Christmas music playing in the background, they wrapped their presents. Adam made her go into the hall while he wrapped hers. She was tempted to peek; after seeing what he had bought for the others, she was immensely curious.

"Why did you get Mark a sausage?" she demanded.

"It's not a sausage, it's some fancy kind of wurst." Adam swathed the fat foot-long cylinder in gold paper and tied a ribbon around its middle.

"You got one for Pat too?"

"I got one for everybody," Adam said. "I couldn't find any of the things on my list. Can you imagine a huge mall like that not having any manure or dried fish? I was lucky to find the wurst place."

He looked so pleased Rachel had to laugh, but she said firmly, "I don't like wurst."

"It's a good thing I didn't get you one, then."

After the presents had been wrapped Adam served his clam chowder, settled her in a chair in front of the television set, and put on a tape. *The Nutcracker.* Of course, Rachel thought; what else? Tschaikovsky was too saccharine for her tastes, and it had been years since she had seen the ballet; but that night the magic took hold, and the sheer beauty of the final pas de deux brought tears to her eyes. Even the sight of Adam solemnly sucking a candy cane didn't spoil her mood. He had turned the lights low and they sat in silence for a few moments after it ended.

"My mother took me to see it every year," Rachel said softly.

"Is she dead?" It was like Adam to avoid the cowardly euphemisms—deceased, gone, departed.

"Oh, no. Alive and flourishing." Her laugh struck a jarring note. "She lives in England with her second husband and their family."

"Oh. That's who the packages are from. I couldn't help noticing," he added hastily. "The stamps and the customs forms and—"

"Of course you couldn't help noticing. Don't be so defensive."

"Aren't you going to open them?"

"Now?"

"Well, you don't want to drag them all the way out to Ruth's and back again, do you? Come on, I want to see what's in them even if you don't."

"Why?"

"I love presents," Adam said happily. "Everybody's presents."

An anticipatory grin appeared in the middle of the beard. Rachel shrugged. "Oh, all right."

"Don't get up. I'll bring them."

He carried them to her, opened the outer boxes, and unloaded the contents, package by package. They had been beautifully wrapped, with bright bows and tags bearing affectionate messages. "To my dearest daughter with love from Mum"; "To Rachel from Alison, have a happy Christmas."

Adam had given up all pretense of respecting her privacy. There was a childish greediness in his interest. "Who's Alison?" he asked, watching Rachel unwrap a white jeweler's box.

"My half sister."

The box contained a bracelet of twisted gold mesh. Adam took it from her hand and fastened it on her wrist. "Looks good on you. She's got good taste."

"Mother picked it out. Alison is only three."

The gifts piled up—a cashmere sweater, a necklace to match the bracelet, a stuffed cat wearing a straw hat and an imbecilic expression, books, tins of tea and cookies and crackers from a famous London shop—and a bed of tissue from which Rachel drew a cloud of filmy pink chiffon.

Adam had been chuckling over the cat. He let out a low whistle. "Wow. That's the fanciest party dress I ever saw. Are you going to wear it tomorrow?"

"It's not a dress, you idiot. It's a robe." Pink chiffon—polyester, probably, not even her mother would be silly enough to send a garment that would have to be dry-cleaned every time it was worn—trimmed with satin rosebuds, it bore a striking and certainly coincidental resemblance to the Callot Soeurs peignoir.

Rachel bundled the full sleeves and flowing skirts back into the box. The yards of fabric were so fine they compressed into a small space. "I'll probably never wear it. What a waste of money."

"It's pretty," Adam said. One big finger stroked a satin rosebud.

"I never wear things like this. That's the last, isn't it?"

She tossed the box onto the floor and settled back.

"You want more?" He put the cat on a shelf near the TV, straightened its hat, and then began picking up the discarded wrappings. "'We'll miss you,'" he read aloud. "'Sorry you couldn't make it . . . ?'" The questioning note in his voice elicited a grudging response from Rachel.

"They sent me a plane ticket."

"And you didn't use it?"

"I couldn't spare the time." She met his mild, astonished gaze squarely, and he caught the message this time, closing his mouth on the words he had been about to say.

He had been more fascinated by the gifts than she—laughing over the cat, admiring the bracelet, skimming through the books. Smarting under his unspoken criticism, Rachel was tempted to retaliate by asking him about his family; but watching his absorbed face as he folded the bright wrapping paper and smoothed the ribbons, she couldn't commit that cruelty. It was odd, though, that he hadn't responded to her statements, grudging though they had been, with reminiscences about his parents. Had he cared so deeply for them that the loss was still unbearable? None of my business, she told herself.

When Rachel announced her intention of going to bed it was still early, but she had had as much seasonal jollity as she could stand, and Adam's suggestion that they watch *Miracle on Thirty-Fourth Street* was the last straw. He looked disappointed, but rallied bravely. "I'll read *A Christmas Carol* instead." Ignoring Rachel's nauseated expression, he went on, "Um—if it's all right with you I'm going to sleep upstairs from now on. Tony said it would be okay. In fact, he suggested it."

"I don't see the need for it, but it's all right with me. So long as you don't insist on reading aloud."

"You won't hear me, I'll be at the other end of the hall." He looked at the cats. "Any of you guys want to listen to *A Christmas Carol*?"

Figgin appeared receptive to the idea, or possibly to the glass of milk and plate of cookies Adam carried. Tail switching, he preceded them up the stairs.

"Which room are you using?" Rachel asked.

"The master bedroom, what else? Nothing but the best."

"I haven't cleaned it. Or changed the sheets, or—"

"Lady, you are speaking to a man who slept on the floor of a tent in the desert for three months. But if it will make you happier, I'll change the sheets. Where's the linen closet?"

"Oh, I'll do it," Rachel said irritably. "No, don't put that glass of milk on the floor, Figgin will knock it over. I'll get the door for you."

Both hands encumbered, Adam allowed her to open it and switch on the light. "Looks clean to me," he said.

In fact, the room was immaculate. The rug still showed the tracks of the vacuum cleaner, the surfaces of the furniture gleamed with polish. The bed had been made and not a wrinkle marred the smooth surfaces of the ruffled and embroidered pillows. Cheryl liked to use the lovely old linens, even if they did require hours of ironing. Rachel doubted that Tony, masculine to the core, appreciated the ruffles and lace and frilly bed curtains tied back by big bows, but his protests, if any, had been private and ineffectual.

Adam was less critical. "Wow! I never slept in a fancy antique bed like that. Is that what you call a canopy?"

"Half canopy." In Rachel's opinion the bed was a particularly ugly piece of furniture, dating from a period when the austere influence of Chippendale and Hepplewhite was being replaced by Victorian extravagance. The heavy posts and brackets that supported the half-tester were carved with vines and fat flowers. "The sheets certainly don't need changing. Cheryl must have done it before she left. Well . . . Good night. Try not to spill the milk or get crumbs all over that knit bedspread."

She left him admiring the bed with a grin of childish pleasure. All that innocent enjoyment had to be an act, she thought sourly. No grown man could be so ingenuous. *A Christmas Carol,* yet.

Her own bedtime reading was a heavy, folio-sized volume about quilts, which she had borrowed from Cheryl's collection. Earlier that afternoon she had retreated to her room and examined the snapshots of the album quilt, spreading them out across the table and arranging them in the original order. The photos had turned out quite well; most of the details were clean and clear.

It had to be a bride's quilt; the theme of love and/or marriage recurred in almost every block. Unlike patchwork quilts, in which the pieces of the pattern were seamed together, the designs had been appliquéd, sewn to the background of plain fabric. Embroidery added fine details. Traditionally the squares were made by different friends of the bride. Sewn together and enclosed in an appliquéd border, they formed the top of the quilt, which was composed of three layers: the upper surface, the inner padding, and the plain back. An overall pattern of fine stitches, the quilting, held the three layers together. The trick to good quilting was to keep the stitches even and close together. It wasn't so hard to accomplish this with a single layer of thin fabric, but when the needle had to penetrate three layers, one of them fairly thick, the technique took practice and a lot of skill.

This example had been beautifully quilted, but Rachel was more interested in the patterns of the blocks. Unlike the Baltimore album quilts with their complex formalized patterns, these designs were unique and more naturalistic. A pair of bluebirds had been rendered with such fidelity that the female's paler coloring was distinguished from the brighter blue of the male. The birds' eyes were French knots, the feathers delicately indicated by embroidery in a slightly darker blue. Cheryl had been correct; the quilt was a masterpiece, worth thousands of dollars to a serious collector. If they could just get rid of that strange, dulling gray film . . .

Rachel got into bed and began leafing through the book, looking for similar examples. So far she had found nothing to compare with the quilt, and she found nothing in this book either. Finally she put it aside and turned out the light.

She was still in the shadowy interface between waking and sleep when a reverberating crash brought her abruptly back to consciousness. Whether it was courage or the knowledge of Adam's nearness or some deeper instinct that moved her, she didn't know, but she reacted instantaneously, jumping out of bed and running to the door. Opening it, she encountered Figgin, whose headlong rush set her staggering as he bolted for the bed and went under it.

Another louder crash oriented her. It had come from the master bedroom.

The door was open and the room was dark until her hand found the light switch.

What she saw left her speechless, but there was no need to ask what had happened. It was only too evident.

The frame of the canopy lay on the floor beside the bed. The attached curtains had fallen with it; they were twisted around the wooden rectangle and around Adam, who had raised himself on one elbow. His eyes were hazel. She hadn't noticed their color before, but now his eyes were wide with surprise and shock.

Rachel found her voice. "Thank God it missed you."

"Actually, it didn't," Adam said. He sat up, slowly and carefully. Instead of pajamas he was wearing a heavy wool shirt over a pair of sweats. "I pushed it off onto the floor after it landed on top of me. Luckily I was lying on my face with a pillow over my head. I always sleep that way," he added defensively, mistaking her expression for one of criticism.

"Luckily." Rachel's voice shook. "How could it have happened? Did you lean against one of the posts, or jar it in some way?"

"I didn't do anything," Adam said plaintively. "Except roll over. Some of the screws must have worked loose. Is the cat all right? He was on the pillow next to me."

The concern in his voice touched her. "His reflexes must be better than yours. He was already at my door before you shoved the thing off you. Are you sure you're all right? Even with a pillow over it, your head took quite a blow."

"Not really. The framework is almost a foot deep and it only goes around three sides of the thing—the canopy. It was the lower edge of the frame that landed on my back."

"Let me see."

Meekly, trying not to wince, Adam stretched out across the bed.

"Why do you have to wear so many clothes?" she demanded, pushing the shirt and sweatshirt up.

"I'm cold-blooded. Ow," he added, his voice muffled by the comforter.

"Does this hurt?" She pressed down on a lower rib.

"Yes!"

The reddening mark ran in an uneven line from his left hip to his right side, midway between waist and armpit. The screws on one side of the canopy must have given way and pulled the others out when it collapsed. Instead of falling straight down it had struck on the diagonal; the lower part of the long bruise was more sharply defined.

Adam continued to complain as she pressed and poked, but the scream of pain she feared didn't materialize. His body was less heavily built than the multilayered garments had led her to expect. No wonder he felt the cold; there wasn't an ounce of fat over those bones and well-developed muscles. There were a number of scars, though.

"What have you been doing?" she asked, tracing a long white line with her forefinger.

Adam let out a muffled gurgle of laughter. "Don't do that, I'm very ticklish. What do you mean, what have I been doing?"

"All those scratches and scars."

"Nothing romantic or adventurous, I'm afraid. I fall over and into things a lot. Rocks, thorny bushes, goats—"

"Oh. Well, I don't think anything is broken, but I'm no doctor. Maybe you should get some X-rays."

"No, thanks. I'm damned if I'll spend Christmas Day sitting around some emergency room. That feels good," he added. "Don't stop. A little higher and to your right, please."

Rachel removed her hands from his shoulder blades. "You don't need a back rub, you need an ice pack. Reduce the swelling. I'll fix one for you."

Adam refused to examine the ruins of the canopy or even move to another room. "What for?" he asked reasonably. "There's nothing else to fall on me here and I wouldn't try to repair that thing even if it weren't two o'clock in the morning. It's a job for an expert. I'm pretty good at putting up tents, but—"

"Shut up and go to sleep," Rachel said, recognizing the start of another monologue.

It wasn't easy for her to follow her own advice. Even if he did have a cracked rib or three, Adam had been incredibly fortunate. The framework of the canopy was deep, but it was backed with solid pieces of wood. If it had fallen on a sleeper's upturned, unprotected face . . .

Cheryl's face. She slept upstairs to be near the children. Adam was heavier than Cheryl, and maybe he was a restless sleeper, but if the canopy was that unstable it would have fallen sooner or later. Probably sooner. It would be several weeks before the cast was removed and Tony joined his wife in the antique bed.

"You sure it's big enough? That's a right wide bed."

"It will be." The needle moved in and out, mechanical as a machine and almost as quickly. "When I put the border on."

The other woman picked up one of the four strips that would form the border. The appliqué was done: a pattern of vines and flowers, butterflies and bees and birds. "Never seen this kind of leaf before. Not around here."

"Maybe it's not from around here." She pulled the thread tight and knotted it, reached for another block.

"You got it from a book?"

She didn't answer right away. "From . . . someplace. I don't know where ideas come from."

"It's right pretty." The older woman watched the flashing needle. "Don't know how you're gonna get it done in time, though. I could help, if you want."

"I'll get it done," she said softly. "I don't need help. I have to do this all by myself."

Adam was already in the family room when Rachel came down the next morning. His movements were slow and cautious, but when Rachel asked how he felt he assured her he was suffering from nothing worse than aches and pains.

"What's that?" she asked as he bent carefully to open the oven door and remove a round baking pan.

"I thought I'd take Ruth a cake. For dessert." Adam studied the object doubtfully. A pale yellow mound, it had overflowed the pan, and to judge by the strong smell of burned batter that permeated the room, dripped down onto the bottom of the oven.

"The pan's too small."

"So it would appear. Oh, well, I'll just trim it, and the frosting will cover the rough spots." Adam picked up a knife and plunged it into the cake.

"What on earth are you doing?"

"Taking it out of the pan. It's run over the edges and I need to—"

"Don't do that!"

Adam stopped sawing and looked hopefully at her over his shoulder. Rachel's mouth twitched. "It has to cool before you take it out," she said. "I'll do it. What kind of frosting do you want?"

"White. The decorations will show up better on white. I found some cherries and sprinkles and stuff."

"Are you doing this deliberately?" Rachel asked.

"What?"

"Making a big show of your ineptness so I'll offer to take over a traditionally female job."

"Oh." Adam thought about it. "Like one of those coded messages women send when they burn the dinner or sew buttons on backward? Fascinating idea. I don't think I did it deliberately—"

"That's the whole point about coded messages, they are often unconscious. Protests."

"'All over America there is the smell of burning food.'"

Rachel stared at him in surprise. "You've read Adrienne Rich? She's a feminist."

"I read all sorts of things," Adam said equably. "In order to prove that I am consciously unencumbered by macho prejudices, I will make the frosting. Where's the powdered sugar?"

They managed to put the cake together. Since it was Christmas Day, Rachel refrained from pointing out that Ruth probably had already planned dessert, and that the end product of Adam's labors would not appeal to anyone over ten years old. He used all the cherries and all the sprinkles and finished it off with a scattering of silver dragées. Rachel grabbed the cake while he was considering the pros and cons of a handful of chocolate kisses, and put it in the refrigerator to harden the icing.

"What time are we supposed to be there?" she asked.

"Any time."

"I'll go and change, then."

"Why? You look fine."

"I can't wear jeans and a ratty old sweater to their house!"

"I always do." He studied his ensemble doubtfully. "You think I should—"

"No. I expect your back is pretty sore," she added charitably. "You could use that as an excuse if you feel the need for one."

"I hadn't planned to mention it."

"All right, if you'd rather not. Did you look at the canopy?"

"Uh-huh." His eyes were fixed on her face. There was the oddest look in them—questioning, even challenging, as if he were waiting for her to speak. When she didn't, he said, "The screws pulled out. It's getting late, we'd better hurry. I'll load the car while you change."

Snow had whitened the ground, and continued to fall gently as they drove. Gleefully and unnecessarily Adam pointed out that they were having a white Christmas. He started to sing. Holding the cake, whose icing was still in a tenuous condition, Rachel gamely joined in. She felt she owed him something for Adrienne Rich.

The MacDougal house was between Leesburg and Middleburg, in an area known to Washingtonians as "horse country," and when they passed between two stone gateposts onto a winding drive, Rachel braced herself for an uncomfortably elegant and expensive ambience. Since she was old enough to know that defiance of convention is sometimes not courageous but just plain rude, she was wearing pantyhose and a skirt and sweater. The sweater was the one her mother had sent. It was a little too small, but the soft golden brown set off her dark hair.

The house was less pretentious than she had expected, a simple two-story wooden structure with a screened porch on one side. The plantings were more indicative of the age of the place: high hedges of boxwood, and a tall oak that had taken at least a century to reach its present girth. Adam pulled up behind another car and stopped. "The others are already here."

"Who else is coming?" Rachel asked, with a prickle of stage fright.

"Just the Brinckleys."

"That's his car?" It was a Ford Taurus, several years old.

Easing himself out from behind the steering wheel, Adam grinned. "Unpretentious and American made. What else would you expect a smart politician to drive?"

It was a surprisingly cynical statement from that source, Rachel thought, and then realized she was guilty of superficial judgments. Adam might be sentimental but he wasn't stupid.

Pat had been watching for them. He had the door open before they reached it. "Late again," he said, reaching for the cake tin Rachel carried.

She held onto it. "I can manage, thanks. It needs to be kept level, the frosting isn't completely set. I'm sorry we're late."

"I wasn't blaming you." He was smiling, but his keen blue eyes fixed her with an intent stare.

"Aren't you going to let us in?" Adam demanded, clutching his armful of packages.

Pat stepped back. "Welcome," he said, waving them in with a formal, almost ritualistic gesture.

The room into which he led them had the graceful proportions and fine details of eighteenth-century manor house architecture, but the furniture was a comfortable blend of antique and modern. The overstuffed chairs and long sofa were covered with faded chintz and dog hairs. A fire burned bright under the carved mantel, and a golden retriever lay stretched on the hearth, its tail moving in rapturous circles as Kara, seated cross-legged on the floor next to it, stroked its head.

Following Pat's directions, Rachel carried the cake into the kitchen. Shirt sleeves rolled up, a ruffled apron tied around his waist, Mark was peeling potatoes while Ruth basted the turkey. She closed the oven door and turned, face becomingly flushed, to greet Rachel.

"How nice of you, dear," she said, taking the cake tin.

"The thanks are due to Adam. It was his idea."

"I could have deduced that." Mark laughed as Ruth removed the top to display Adam's decorating. "What, no chocolate kisses?"

"I stopped him in time," Rachel said. "What can I do to help?"

"Not a thing," Ruth said. "Everything is under control. You two join the others, I'll be with you in a minute."

Mark held the door for Rachel and they went through the butler's pantry, lined with cupboards filled with glass and china, into the hall. "Aren't you going to take off your apron?" she asked.

"I think it looks rather fetching, don't you?" He twirled in a pirouette, arms extended, and Rachel laughed, appreciating his effort to make her feel at ease.

"Unquestionably. Where are the servants?"

"At home with their families." He didn't add, "Of course," but his tone implied it.

They reached the living room in time to hear Kara say loudly, "I don't want to talk about witches. Not on Christmas Day."

"But they're good witches," Adam said. "They don't—"

Pat interrupted, waving his glass. "What'll you have, Rachel? Wine, beer, scotch—"

After he had served drinks all around and Ruth had joined them, he returned to the subject, addressing Rachel. "Adam says you had a visit from the good witches last night."

"Were they wearing pink tutus and waving wands?" Mark asked.

"It isn't funny," his wife said severely. "Those people are crazy, and now they know where Adam is living. How could you have been so careless, Adam?"

"If it's anyone's fault, it's mine," Pat said. "I shouldn't have greeted Adam so noisily in a public place. But you're making a big deal of nothing, Kara. There are some Satanic cultists who desecrate graves and sacrifice animals—psychopaths who get a sick pleasure out of defying law and convention—but in the eyes of its believers Wicca is a religion, the Old Religion, in fact. It worships pagan deities that pre-ceded Christianity by thousands of years. The Goddess in her three aspects of Maiden, Mother, and Crone, the Horned God who is both consort and son of the Goddess. You've read Margaret Murray?"

The question was directed at Rachel. Startled, she said, "Yes. But her books are discredited—"

"Questioned. And with reason. Like many scholars she became enamored of her own theories—which were not original with her—and carried them too far. But the identification of the God of the Witches with Cernunnos and other horned deities can't be wholly dis-missed."

"The Devil had horns too," Kara muttered.

"That's the point," Pat said. "Christianity, which was an exclusive religion, couldn't absorb the aggressively phallic horned god as it did the virgin mother goddess, so it turned him into a demon. To the early church fathers there were no shades of gray, only black and white, good and evil. The old pagan religions were more tolerant, and modern witches view the godhead as having many different aspects. It looks to the good and believes that every individual has psychic powers that can be used to influence events—"

"He does miss his captive audience of students, doesn't he?" Kara demanded of the room at large. "Enough with the lecturing, Pat. I don't care what these people believe or what they call it, they practice magic, and anybody who believes in magic is loony."

Pat's brows drew together, but before he could speak his wife said affectionately but firmly, "Kara, you ought to know better than to take that approach. Pat will argue on either side of an argument. Change the subject, darling."

"Huh," said Pat.

The silence was broken by Adam. "Can we open the presents now?"

They made him wait until after dinner. It was a gargantuan, unhealthy meal into which everyone, including Rachel, tucked with complete disregard for cholesterol and fat. Ruth had prepared both pumpkin and apple pie, but everyone gamely accepted a piece of Adam's cake instead. Adam was the only one who finished his.

"Don't you like it?" he asked anxiously.

"It's wonderful, dear," Ruth said warmly. "I'm too full to do it justice right now."

"So am I," Rachel said. "Everything was delicious. Especially your cranberry sauce, Ruth. That didn't come out of a can or jar, surely."

"No, I made it from scratch. It takes forever—you have to put the cooked berries through a sieve and then cook them again—but it's become a tradition. Tony is addicted to it. I'll send some home with you; it freezes quite well."

"Now can we open the presents?" Adam asked.

All of them except Adam and Mark, the designated drivers, had had quite a lot of wine; clearing the table was a joint project which inspired good-natured hilarity, most of it at the expense of the dog, who followed them back and forth to the kitchen in the hope that someone would drop a plate or leave the platter with the remains of the turkey unguarded for a few minutes. Pat did manage to drop a glass, which spattered into fragments on the brick floor. Cursing amiably, he swept up the pieces while Mark held the dog back. After the dishes had been stacked and the food put away, they retired to the living room and Pat opened another bottle of wine.

Adam didn't need alcohol to increase his good spirits; appointing himself Santa Claus, he trotted back and forth delivering presents and watching with breathless interest as they were unwrapped. The sausages, as Rachel insisted on calling them, aroused considerable laughter and a few anthropological jokes about phallus worship from Pat.

Rachel's gift from Adam was not sausage. After she had unwrapped it, she held it cradled in her hands, staring with admiration and surprise. It was a small statue, about six inches high, unglazed and painted in soft earth colors, depicting two women with their arms around one another. The embrace was gentle and loving; the two tiny faces smiled.

"It's beautiful," she said. "You didn't find this at the mall, surely."

"There's a potter in Ankara who makes them," Adam said. "I hadn't decided who I was going to give it to till I met you. The younger one looks a lot like you."

"Younger?" Rachel repeated. "They look about the same age to me."

"I thought they were mother and daughter," Adam said. "Women have babies at an early age down there."

"No, it's a depiction of friendship," Kara said. "Sisterhood."

Pat hooted, and Ruth said, smiling, "Whatever the intent, it's a lovely thing, Adam. Loving and lovely. And you're right, there is a resemblance to Rachel."

When the floor was littered with bright ribbon and paper Kara turned from the window. "It's starting to snow harder, Mark. We'd better head for home."

"You're worried about that disgusting old dog," Mark said lazily. "There's no hurry. We can't leave Ruth with that stack of dishes."

"Don't worry about that," Ruth said.

She wasn't the only one who had seen Kara's face darken and her lips draw tight over her teeth. "Let me do the dishes," Rachel said. "I didn't contribute anything to that wonderful meal; I'd like to help."

Visibly annoyed but trying to hide it, Mark got to his feet. "Thanks, Rachel. You can wear my apron."

After the Brinckleys had left, the others returned to the living room and Pat said briskly, "Now that we won't offend Kara's sensibilities, how about giving me a blow-by-blow of the proceedings the other night, Adam. Did you have to strip?"

Ruth let out a gasp of outraged laughter, and the visible portion of Adam's face turned red. "I wasn't initiated," he mumbled.

"Why not?"

"Oh, well, hell, Pat!"

"They wouldn't let you wear your mittens?" Rachel suggested. The wine was bubbling pleasantly in her veins and the picture of a naked Adam, covered with goosebumps and blue with cold, was irresistibly funny.

"This group allows people to attend as passive observers if they are willing to make a verbal commitment," Adam said. His voice was quite serious, though he was still blushing. "They want potential members to be absolutely certain before they go through the first, formal stage of initiation. I wouldn't have done it any other way; I mean, dammit, once you've taken the vows you're sworn to secrecy and I couldn't—I wouldn't—"

"Hell of an ethnologist you are," Pat said.

"I'm not an ethnologist. I'm a—"

"Sentimental idiot," Pat said. "Your scruples are unnecessary, you jackass; the process has been written up in a number of books. How does the ritual compare with the one described in *The Book of Shadows?*"

Ruth got up from her chair. "I don't think I want to hear about it."

"Neither do I," Rachel said.

Ordinarily she hated housework, but that evening the domestic ritual was soothing. Ruth had used her best crystal and china; the cutglass goblets and gold-trimmed dishes had to be washed and dried by hand. They hadn't finished when Pat appeared in the doorway.

"I don't want to be accused of copping out on the chores," he announced. "Want some help?"

"A token gesture," his wife jeered. "You know I won't let you touch these dishes. You're too clumsy."

"I picked up the trick from you feminists," Pat said. "Isn't that how you operate? Don't refuse outright, just do the job so badly that people won't ask you to do it again."

He grinned provocatively at Rachel.

"Feminists refuse outright," she said.

"I stand corrected." He moved to the sink and put his arm around Ruth's waist. She looked up at him with a smile that brought a sharp stab of pain to Rachel's insides.

"You look tired, honey," he said. "Go talk to Adam, I'll take over."

"I can finish," Rachel said. "Please, Ruth—both of you—let me do it. Unless you're afraid I'll pocket the silver."

She couldn't imagine why she had said that. It didn't sound like the joke she had intended, and the faces that turned to her were momentarily blank with surprise. It had the effect, however, of a request that could not in decency be denied.

"We always search our guests before they leave," Pat said. "Come on, you poor old lady, lean on me."

Meticulously and mechanically Rachel finished washing the plates and rinsed them in hot water. There were only the serving platters and bowls to be done; Ruth had already packed the leftover food in containers. Leaving the bowls to soak, Rachel began to wipe the glasses. They were beautiful fragile old goblets; a pity one had been broken. Ruth hadn't complained about it, she had just laughed and warned Pat to be careful not to cut himself when he swept up the pieces and put them in the trash.

They touched one another a lot. Sitting close, hands clasping, his arm around her . . .

"What in God's name are you doing?"

The words penetrated her consciousness like a shout and the hand that fell on her shoulder made her start convulsively. The container slipped from her hand and fell, spreading a pool of crimson across the floor.

The hand was Adam's, heavy and hard. She cried out in protest, tried to pull away. He transferred his grip to her arm, held her with her back against the counter.

She looked from his horrified face to the faces of the MacDougals, standing nearby, and saw the same expression of shock and disbelief. Ruth wasn't looking at her. She was looking at the puddle of cranberry sauce on the floor. Amid its crimson viscosity, sparks winked in the light.

"Glass," Adam said hoarsely. "She was putting it in the container. Stirring it."

"No," Rachel gasped. "No. I didn't. Pat must have missed some of the bits when he swept up the broken glass."

"I saw you," Adam said. "I stood watching you for several minutes."

Ruth came forward. "That's the container I filled for Cheryl and Tony."

"I thought so," Adam said. "She was responsible for the collapse of the canopy too. It wasn't an accident, the screws had been tampered with. Don't deny it, Rachel; no one else could have done it. You didn't know I'd be sleeping in that bed. You thought it would be . . . "

"Let her go." Pat spoke for the first time. "You're hurting her. She didn't intend to do any of those things, Adam. She probably doesn't even know she did them."

"I'd like to believe that," Adam said miserably. "But I saw them, the night I arrived. Her and Tony, in each other's arms."

"He pushed me away," Rachel whispered. The room was shivering, like a picture painted on gauze. Her voice sounded strange and distant.

"He heard me at the door," Adam said. "But before that he was holding her like . . . I can't handle this. What are we going to do? If she's sick—mentally ill—"

"She's not sick," Pat said quietly. "Or mentally ill. She's been overshadowed."

"What?" Adam's hand loosened its grip and then tightened again, less painfully, as Rachel swayed forward.

"I felt it yesterday," Pat said. "When we shook hands. Unmistakable, like an electric shock. I didn't feel it earlier, at the Christmas party." As if asking for support against the incredulity that fairly radiated from Adam, he held out his hand and Ruth took it in hers.

"He's right, Adam," she said quietly. "He told me when he came home. I can't feel it as strongly as he can because—"

"Because it takes one to know one," Pat said. "The same thing happened to me."

seven

"It happened almost twenty years ago," Pat said. "I had just met Ruth, through one of my students—Ruth's niece Sara, who is Kara's older sister. Sara was the first of us to feel the influence that haunted that old house in Georgetown. It was a classic case of possession; the girl who had come to a tragic end in the same house two centuries earlier occupied Sara's body and spoke through her. I happened to match the—well, call them the emotional patterns—of another individual who had been involved in the same tragedy. On at least three occasions he took over control of my mind and my actions. Sara's lover, who is now her husband, was also affected, though not to the same extent she and I were. We came horribly close to repeating the old pattern, with its grisly ending, before we found out what had happened and how to resolve it."

"You resolved it?" Adam repeated skeptically.

Pat nodded. "So successfully that the house, which was the focus of the influence, is harmless. It's the same one Kara and Mark own now. Ruth sold it to them after my mother died and we inherited this place."

"If I had heard a story like that from anybody but you . . . " For once

Adam's extensive vocabulary failed him. He flapped his hands help-lessly.

They had returned to the living room. Rachel sat on the couch, with a MacDougal on either side. It was their way of indicating support and sympathy, she supposed, but she felt hemmed in, and the afghan Ruth had tucked around her was tight as a cocoon or a baby's bunting. Bolt upright in his chair, Adam faced the three. His pose was confronta-tional, but his eyes were as miserable as those of a child who has just been told there is no Santa Claus.

"I can't say I blame you," Pat said calmly. "The first time I ran into a situation like this, I was the skeptic. It took personal experience to convince me. After I tried to rape Ruth and kill a man who was as close as a son to me, I became a convert."

He had chosen the words deliberately for their shock value. Adam's breath went out in a harsh gasp. "You'd never—"

"Not if I was in my right mind. I wasn't. Something else was. I call it overshadowing because that's what it felt like—the submergence of my own will, my very identity, by an alien personality. I think the same thing has happened to Rachel. I didn't sense anything wrong when I met her at the Christmas party, so it must have begun later that night—possibly when she and Tony enjoyed their first passionate embrace. It was the first time, wasn't it, Rachel?"

"Adam had no right to tell you about that," Rachel said furiously. "It wasn't . . . it wasn't the way he made it sound."

"Don't blame Adam. The incident obviously bothered him—he's eas-ily shocked, poor innocent kid—but he would never have mentioned it to me or anyone else if we hadn't caught you red-handed just now. Excuse the pun."

Adam's nose was crimson with embarrassment and fury. "God damn it, Pat, how can you joke about this? I wasn't shocked. Surprised, maybe—"

"So surprised that you still can't see the significance of that inci-dent." Pat leaned forward. "Tony's moral code is as tediously rigid as any Calvinist's. He wouldn't make love to another woman in his own house, with his wife sleeping only a few feet away. If you don't know him well enough to be sure of that, you'll have to take my word for it."

"There's always a first time," Adam said stubbornly. His eyes avoided Rachel's.

"Especially when the temptation is, as in this case, so uniquely irresistible." The amusement in Pat's voice made Adam go even redder. "What was that about a canopy being tampered with?"

Adam told him. "It was deliberate," he finished. "Had to be. And nobody else had the opportunity."

"Not necessarily true," Pat said calmly. "Oh, I agree Rachel is the most obvious suspect. But even if it was her hands that loosened the screws, her mind wasn't directing those hands. I can't prove my theory, Adam. The one incontrovertible piece of evidence is one you can't admit—my personal experience. You're like a man who has lost his hearing, watching an orchestra at a concert. I can tell you they're playing Beethoven but if you don't trust me—"

"I trust your integrity. I'm sure you believe what you're telling me."

"That's good enough to start with." He gave Ruth a companionable grin. "This is a tough one, isn't it? The first case was simple, by comparison. We stumbled, apparently by accident, into an unfinished, unresolved pattern. Three of the four of us who were involved happened to fit the personality types of three people who had lived in the house before. The pattern had to be worked out to its conclusion, the old tragedy resolved."

"It wasn't an accident," Ruth murmured. "It didn't just happen. It wasn't coincidence."

"Let's not start talking about the meaning of life," Pat said. Ruth smiled faintly; this was obviously an ongoing, and generally amiable, argument. "The best our limited senses can produce are analogies. I find it easier to think in terms of patterns. It's a concept with which Rachel should be familiar, since it fits her thesis topic—the Fates, spinning the web of a man's life. All lives are interwoven, and sometimes the immortal weavers get careless, so that the web is tangled or cut prematurely."

"Very poetic," Adam muttered.

"I said it was only an analogy. To continue in the same vein, our best hope of dealing with something like this is to trace the pattern and tie off the broken threads."

He looked at Adam, eyebrows raised in inquiry. The younger man raised *his* eyebrows. "Are you implying that this is the same sort of thing you ran into before? Even admitting your basic premise, which is insane, seems to me you're jumping to conclusions."

"Very good," Pat said approvingly. "I don't know whether this is the same sort of thing. I propose to find out. You do remember the rudiments of the scientific method, I hope? Form a hypothesis, run tests—"

"What kind of tests, for God's sake?"

Pat had his answer ready. "Rachel is our best source; she has to be aware, on some level, of what's happening. If she'll cooperate, answer questions—"

"Of course I'll cooperate." Rachel freed her arms from the folds of the afghan. "Don't you think I'd like to believe I didn't do those things deliberately? I'd give anything to find a scapegoat. Almost anything. I agree with Adam, what you've suggested is insane. I'm insane!"

Adam hadn't expected that response. He started to speak, but Pat beat him to it.

"Another skeptic? Good. If you were one of those suggestible sentimentalists who believes in reincarnation and angelic guides, we wouldn't have a prayer."

Coming from a man who had just asserted his belief in demonic possession, this statement struck Rachel as unduly critical. But when he turned to her she saw him brace himself, as if in anticipation of physical attack, before he held out his hands; and when she placed her hands in his, she felt him recoil before his fingers closed over hers. He drew a long breath. "Okay, kid, let's get at it. What happened that night?"

"Pat," Ruth said uneasily. "I don't think you should do this. You're pushing. It isn't going to be that easy."

"I'm not pushing," Pat insisted. "It's up to Rachel. Would you feel more comfortable talking about it if Adam left the room?"

"What would be the point of that?" Rachel said drearily. "He knows about it already, and I don't blame him for despising me. But I never intended . . . "

"Tell me."

"It was that same night, the night of the Christmas party. I thought . . . I thought I heard something. Outside. I couldn't sleep, I was nervous— we all were, about the burglar. So I went downstairs."

"You're a gutsy lady," Pat said. "Gutsy but stupid. You didn't wake the others?"

"I didn't want to scare Cheryl or the kids. And he—Tony—was downstairs alone, encumbered by that cast, possibly drugged; sometimes he took painkillers to help him sleep."

"But he wasn't asleep?"

He was leading her gently, like an attorney for the defense. "No," Rachel said. "He heard me in the shop. At least that's what he said. He didn't know who it was, he thought someone had broken in. He scared me half to death when he appeared. He apologized, told me to sit down . . ."

Her throat started to close up. She swallowed noisily, and Pat said, "You're doing fine, kid. If it's any consolation, I'm not enjoying this either. Up to that time had Tony ever made a pass at you—any kind of pass, verbal, physical, even a meaningful look?"

"No, never. And I never said or did anything to let him know . . ."

"That you were in love with him?"

"Stop it," Ruth ordered angrily. "You can't ask the girl to strip herself naked in front of us."

"It could be important," Pat said.

"It's not important," Rachel whispered. "But it's true. I didn't mean to. It just happened. He didn't know. Nobody knew except . . ."

"Who? Cheryl?"

"No! At least I hope she didn't. But I think Kara suspected."

"Interesting," Pat said thoughtfully.

"Get on with it," Ruth snapped. "If you're determined to do this."

Pat's fingers tightened. "Okay, Rachel. You're sitting in a chair, he's apologizing. Standing?"

"Yes."

"And then?"

Her throat felt constricted, as if she were coming down with a cold. It hurt to swallow. She had to force the words out. "He said, 'You're . . . '"

"Hang on, kid, we're almost there. 'You're . . . ' what?"

"'. . . shivering. It's freezing in here.' And then he reached for—"

No effort of will could shape the next word or pronounce it. She felt her lips stretch wide in a painful rictus, heard the rattling sound of air trying to pass the obstruction that blocked her throat, felt the muscles of limbs and body contract in a spasm that would have thrown her from the couch if Pat had not caught hold of her.

When her senses came back to her she was lying on the couch. Ruth was tucking the afghan around her and talking, in a soft, venomous monologue.

"Talk about rushing in where angels fear to tread! I told you it wasn't going to be that easy, but no, you knew better, you never listen."

"Now, honey." Rachel had never heard Pat MacDougal sound so meek. "I'm sorry. Is she all right?"

Rachel opened her eyes. They were all hovering, Ruth kneeling on the floor beside her, the two men bending over the couch.

"Of course she's not all right," Ruth snapped. "Leave her alone, you—you big bully! First you drive her into a convulsion, then you squeeze the breath out of her, and now you want her to relieve your guilty conscience by telling you no damage was done."

"I had to grab her, she would have hurt herself," Pat protested. "Rachel—"

"I'm fine." It was true. Except for slightly sore muscles, from Pat's bear hug, she felt quite normal. The painful constriction of her throat was gone. She sat up. "Really."

Not for the first time, Rachel wished Adam's face wasn't so veiled by hair. The only part of it she could see clearly was his nose, and noses are not particularly expressive features. His voice sounded peculiar, though "It looked like an epileptic seizure."

"It wasn't," Pat said. "I think I know what happened. Rachel, can you tell me—"

"Patrick MacDougal!" Ruth turned on her husband, her eyes blazing. "Not one more word, do you hear? I'm putting this child to bed, right this minute. Adam, you'd better spend the night too."

"The animals have to be fed and the dogs let out," Adam said. When Ruth would have objected he interrupted her, with uncharacteristic rudeness. "I don't want to leave the house empty, even for one night. You seem to have forgotten that there's a murderer wandering around loose."

"Oh, yeah." Pat scratched his chin. "I wonder how he fits into this. Okay, Adam, you go back to Leesburg. I'll bring Rachel—"

"No!" Rachel exclaimed. "Don't let him go."

"Do you think I can't handle your burglar?" Adam demanded. "I hope the little bastard does turn up."

"Oh, for God's sake, stop showing off!" Rachel shouted. They glared at one another. He was still leaning over the couch, so close she could see his dilated pupils and the circles of bright hazel around them. "I'm not worried about burglars. If I did that to the bed canopy—and I must have, no one else could have done it—what else may I have done? There could be booby traps in every room."

"I'll be careful," Adam said.

"Do." Pat's voice was dry. "I'd go with you, but I don't want to leave the girls alone."

"You've been a great help so far," Ruth said sarcastically. "And the epitome of tact. 'Girls!'"

"He is being tactful," Rachel said. "What he really means is he doesn't want to leave me alone with Ruth. He doesn't trust me, and he's absolutely right. I don't trust myself."

"No, I didn't mean that," Pat said. "It has no reason to harm Ruth. Or me."

The simple change of pronoun, from the personal to the impersonal, carried more conviction than anything he had said thus far. He believes it, Rachel thought. He's on my side. The only one who's completely, unequivocally on my side.

Whose side?

"Pat," his wife said warningly.

"Yeah, okay. You were right, you are always right. Put the kid to bed. Want me to carry you, Rachel?"

"I can walk."

Adam didn't offer. He stood motionless and silent as Rachel left the room, with Ruth's arm around her.

The guest room was simply, almost sparsely furnished. The walls were painted a soft shade of blue, the floor was bare except for a braided rug next to the bed. It looked quiet and peaceful, and suddenly Rachel was so tired she could hardly keep her eyes open. She accepted Ruth's offerings of nightgown and toothbrush but refused a sleeping pill, and then Ruth left her, saying only, "I'm right down the hall. Don't hesitate to wake me if you want anything."

The only thing she wanted was to be alone. The soft mattress and warm blankets welcomed her exhausted body, but her thoughts raced wildly, running from one dead end to another, unable to find relief or resolution. The evidence was incontrovertible, all the explanations equally frightening. One word blocked all efforts at reason. *It.* How could one small word be so terrifying? *It* was ambiguous, undefined; it could be anything. Shapeless, crouching, a small huddled shadow . . .

He's the one to watch out for now. He knows. Be careful, don't let him in.

She got out of bed. The sloping, uneven floorboards creaked underfoot. *Be careful, step softly. They mustn't hear.*

They were still in the living room. She heard voices but could not
make out what they were saying. She crept cautiously down the stairs
until the words became distinct, and leaned over the bannister, listening.

Adam hadn't left. The first complete sentence she heard came from
him.

"I don't know what they're calling it these days. Split personality?"

"The jargon changes from year to year." Pat's voice was rich with sarcasm. "Psychiatry is not an exact science, Adam, and in some ways it
hasn't advanced past the time when Mesmer and Freud were playing
around with hypnotic regression. With the right shrink and a lot of luck,
Rachel could develop eight or nine more personalities. At least you are
willing to admit that she is not consciously aware of what she has done?"

"I guess so. It's hard to believe she would deliberately try to harm
anyone."

"Then give me a chance to test my hypothesis before you condemn
the girl to a lifetime of expensive misery."

"How?" Adam demanded. "You can't set up scientific controls. You
can't apply logic to a situation like this one."

"Oh, yes, I can," Pat said.

Ruth said something, her soft voice indistinct. Pat interrupted. "I
said I was sorry. But that violent reaction was a clue in itself. Now
think. Remember her exact words. Tony said 'You're shivering, it's
freezing in here,' and then he reached for . . . What?"

The sound that came from Adam might have been a laugh. The listener on the stair flinched, and Pat said irritably, "We knew what the
end result was. Why should she balk at telling us what we already
knew? Something happened before they embraced, and that's what she
couldn't express. She was getting too close. *It* stopped her."

"You can't ask her," Ruth began.

"Good God, no. I don't have to. We can get at it another way. If you
thought someone was cold, shivering with cold, what would you do?
What did you do tonight after she passed out?"

"Put something around her," Ruth said slowly. "A blanket, an
afghan—"

"Something," Pat agreed. "A chivalrous gent might take off his coat.
But Tony was wearing a bathrobe, or so I assume, and even if he were

inclined to make a romantic gesture, he couldn't get out of the damned thing gracefully, not with those crutches."

"The haunted afghan," Adam muttered. "Pat, if you could hear yourself—"

"I can hear myself perfectly well. You're the one who won't listen. Honest to God, your generation is so incredibly arrogant! You've got all the answers, haven't you? What the hell gives you the right—" He broke off in mid-roar, and the listener deduced Ruth must have remonstrated, verbally or by gesture. He went on, in a lower but equally intense voice. "I'm not asking for your cooperation, Adam, I'm demanding it. You have no authority over Rachel."

"Neither do you."

"Damn straight. If she chooses to walk away, from the situation and from us, there is no way we can stop her. Or were you planning to swear out a warrant for assault?"

"For God's sake, Pat!"

"I take it that means you weren't. Down, boy, don't lose your temper. I was only attempting to demonstrate that there is no reasonable course of action other than the one I've proposed. Even if we were brutal enough to do so we couldn't take legal action; there's not enough evidence. We can't force her to seek medical attention. If we persuaded her to leave her job and move out of the house, she could still be a threat to Tony and Cheryl—and herself. The only hope is to find out what brought this on and put a stop to it. I believe it can be done. At any rate I intend to give it a damn good try, and the chances of success are much greater if you'll go along with me. We need you. Well?"

The silence stretched out for a long time. Finally Adam spoke in a voice so low the listener had to strain to hear it. "All right. I'll cooperate. What else can I say? You've got me over a barrel."

"Not me," Pat said smugly. "My inexorable, irrefutable logic."

"Inexorable bullshit. What do you want me to do?"

"Check that house from cellar to attic," Pat said promptly. "Make sure there aren't any other little surprises. Do it tonight."

"And then?"

"We'll discuss the next step tomorrow, when I drive Rachel home. You'll have enough to do tonight, searching the house," he added maliciously.

"I'd better go then."

The listener tensed, prepared to beat a hasty retreat, but Pat wasn't finished.

"Yes, you had better. Be thorough and be careful. Concentrate on the rooms Rachel doesn't ordinarily enter. *It* wouldn't set up a trap she might stumble into."

"I wish you'd stop saying *it,*" Adam protested.

"The feminine pronoun would be more accurate," Pat said. "But that would lead to confusion. You wouldn't know which of them I was referring to."

"Feminine," Adam repeated blankly.

"It's female. Or to be more accurate—it *was* female."

Rachel hadn't thought to bring sunglasses. She shielded her eyes against the dazzle of the white-blanketed fields. The snow was melting fast; the roads were already clear except for ridges of slush pushed to the shoulders by the plows. Pat had insisted on driving his pickup, despite Ruth's objections, and as they wended their way toward Leesburg she grumbled, "I told you the roads would be all right. We could have taken the car."

"What's wrong with this?" Pat demanded. "Plenty of room."

Ruth sighed. "It's a male fixation," she explained to Rachel. "Makes them feel macho, one of the good old boys."

Rachel smiled politely. They were being kind, trying to make her feel at ease. They must have sensed the nervous tension that filled her, increasing with every mile. How could she go back into that house, knowing what she now knew?

At least Adam was all right. He had called earlier to report that his search of the house had been without result. Rachel had come downstairs in time to hear Pat say, "Nothing? That's good. We'll see you in about an hour."

He hung up and waved Rachel to a chair at the breakfast table. "Did you sleep well?"

She sensed that the question was more than a meaningless courtesy, and answered promptly and truthfully. "Very well. I was dead to the world, as the saying goes."

Already seated, Ruth remarked, "That omelet is burning, Pat."

"Just nicely browned," was the complacent reply, accompanied by a sizzle and a spatter as he flipped the omelet.

After he had served it and filled the coffee cups he addressed Rachel. "We continued our conversation last night after you went to bed. Arrived at some interesting conclusions."

"Oh?" She waited for him to go on, but he appeared to expect a response from her. His steady, unblinking regard made her uncomfortable, though she could not have said why. Her eyes fell, and she muttered, "You don't have to tell me if you think I shouldn't know. I appreciate what you're trying to do."

"I don't want appreciation, I want your active, intelligent cooperation—insofar as you are able to give it. Feel free to make suggestions, disagree with me, argue—but only if you're comfortable doing so. Don't force it, as you did last night. I'm not going to question you. I'll try to get the information I need from other people."

"What other people?" Rachel demanded. "I guess I have no right to ask that you refrain from mentioning to Cheryl that I tried to brain her, but I couldn't face her if she knew . . . If she knew any of this. I'll leave town, move away, rather than do that."

"And spend the rest of your life wondering when it will happen again?"

Rachel abandoned any pretense of trying to eat. She pushed her plate away. "Last night you talked about broken, interrupted patterns. Suppose, for the sake of argument, that this is such a case, and that Tony and Cheryl are the other—well—the other strands in the web. If I stay away from them, never see either of them again . . . "

"It might work," Pat admitted. "And it might not. Do you want to take the risk? The situation is more complex than you realize. In my considered opinion there's a good chance we can resolve it if you'll cooperate."

"I'll cooperate. What else can I say? You've got me over a barrel."

The words sounded familiar, as if she had heard them spoken in that same order quite recently. Pat glanced sharply at her, but said only, "All right. Let's get going, then."

Traffic thickened as they approached the town. Most of it seemed to be headed for the shopping centers on Route 7, and Rachel had to interrupt Pat's diatribe on greed and meaningless consumerism in order to speak. There was one thing she hadn't said, one thing that had to be made clear.

"I will cooperate, Pat, as best I can. But I will leave the house or turn myself in to—to a psychiatric hospital, if anything else happens. I won't risk danger to another person."

"You mean to Tony or Cheryl."

"Any person," Rachel repeated. "You, Ruth, Adam . . . the children."

She was watching Ruth and she knew, by the latter's expression, that the possibility had already occurred to her.

Pat let out a surprising whoop of laughter. "You do have guts, don't you? And brains. The same thing had occurred to me, of course—another instance of great minds thinking alike. Don't worry about me and Ruth. We're forewarned and hence forearmed. So is Adam. He's a big boy, he can take care of himself."

"What about the others?"

Pat pulled into the driveway and brought the pickup to a stop. "They won't be back until the end of the week. Let's see what happens."

"Whatever happens, I'm moving out," Rachel declared. "Before they come back."

Pat got out and came around to her side. She opened her own door and jumped down, ignoring the hand he offered. With a smile and a shrug he reached up to help his wife descend from the high seat, giving her a hearty hug before he set her on her feet.

"We'll see," he said, and started up the walk.

"Dammit!" Rachel glared after him.

"He can be very exasperating at times," Ruth said apologetically. "But don't be misled by his manner. He's enjoying the intellectual challenge, but this isn't just a game to him, he is genuinely concerned. He has a high opinion of you. He told me so."

"He didn't say that."

Ruth smiled. "What he actually said was, 'If she'd been one of my students I could have made something of her.'"

Adam had let the dogs out. Their challenging barks and howls changed to equally vociferous barks and whines when they recognized the newcomers. Pat shook his fist at the Labrador, who responded by grinning idiotically and trying to climb the fence.

Adam opened the door. "Good morning," he said formally.

"So far," Pat said, giving him a sardonic look. "Look, Adam, I know you're uncomfortable but try to relax. If Rachel can adjust to this, you can."

"I'm trying." Adam tugged his beard. A shower of crumbs drifted down. "I made muffins," he explained, brushing ineffectually at the front of his sweater. "Want one? Or a cup of coffee?"

"Not that relaxed," Pat said in disgust. "Let's get at it. I want to reconstruct the crime."

"Which one?" Rachel asked, trying not to wince.

"The first one. The kiss, the clinch, the mad passionate embrace."

"For Pete's sake, Pat." It was Adam who protested; he carefully refrained from looking at Rachel. "Do you have to be so—"

"It's all right," Rachel said steadily. "I prefer honest tactlessness to useless sympathy."

Pat ignored the exchange. "Our terminus a quo is the Christmas party." He turned slowly, surveying the room. "We were sitting around in various stages of collapse after the other guests had left. Then I asked about your burglar."

"More honest tactlessness," Adam grunted. "It may have been that discussion that got Rachel so on edge she couldn't sleep."

"We'll get to that in due course," Pat said. "What happened next?"

Adam sighed. "I don't know. I wasn't here."

Ruth said, "You were your usual aggressive, dogmatic self, darling. You started an argument with Tony about the proper method of investigating the case, and then you insisted on viewing the evidence."

"It wasn't an argument, it was an amiable discussion. And I was right, too. So," Pat went on, before his wife could comment, "we went into the shop and the girls dragged the things out of the cupboard. Right?"

"Right," Ruth agreed. "What are you getting at?"

"Setting the stage," Pat said. "Let's go to the shop."

He led the way.

The shop had its own thermostat, which had been thriftily lowered; the temperature was fifteen degrees below that of the family room. Sunlight streaming through the high windows gave a false illusion of warmth.

"Is this the way it usually looks?" Pat asked.

It was the first time he had asked Rachel a direct question. She understood and appreciated his caution and she took her time about answering, half dreading a repetition of the vocal paralysis that had struck her the night before. But the words came easily, without restraint.

"Yes. Cheryl rearranges the furniture and displays from time to time, but it's been like this for several weeks."

"Except for the night of the Christmas party."

It wasn't a question. After a moment Ruth said, "What do you mean?"

"The doodads—quilts, whatever they were—were draped over various pieces of furniture. They were still there when we went back to the family room. Somebody—Kara, wasn't it?—said to leave them, they needed airing."

"That's right," Ruth said.

"It was late before we left," Pat went on. "Everybody was tired. I doubt Cheryl would have bothered putting them away that night."

Adam began, "Why don't you ask . . . " and then stopped with a gulp. "Oops."

"Oops is right," Pat said. "I'm walking a tightrope here, one I can't even see. Don't throw rotten eggs at the performer. You okay, kid?"

Rachel nodded dumbly. Pat was perspiring, despite the cool temperature, and Ruth's face was drawn and anxious. Their concern touched her, but it also puzzled her. What were they afraid of? *They aren't kin, they don't care about you, this is a game he's playing. Like that children's game, hot and cold. He's warm, getting warmer.*

"Rachel," Pat said.

"Yes?"

"I can do this without you. For a number of reasons I'd prefer that you were present, but if you start to feel uncomfortable let me know. I'll back off."

He's clever, oh, so clever. He's trying to make you think he cares. We can't stop him. But we don't have to help.

Rachel nodded.

"Okay," Pat said. "We can't set the scene, since the quilts are now in police custody. I can't even remember what the damned things looked like, much less where they were that night. Ruth?"

"There were three quilts," Ruth said. "But if you're asking for their exact location I can't say for sure."

"Try."

"Well . . . One of them, the white one, was on that table. I remember Cheryl moved the vase before she unfolded the quilt. The others were spread over the chairs—not those little straight chairs, the armchairs."

"This one?" Pat indicated the chair nearest the desk.

"I think so."

"Good." Pat rubbed his hands together like Sherlock Holmes. "Next witness. Adam, go out onto the porch."

"It's cold out there," Adam protested.

"You're wearing at least five sweaters," Pat said. "Move it."

Muttering, Adam shuffled toward the door, and Pat went on, "I'll be Tony, Ruth had better stand in for Rachel. Come here, honey. Leave the door open, Adam. Which window were you looking through?"

"The left one."

"Get into position then, don't stand there gaping like a fish. Can you see us?"

He put an arm around Ruth and led her behind the desk.

"No. Where are you?"

"How about now?"

He tried several different positions before he got the answer he wanted. "That's about right," Adam called. He came back to the doorway. "The field of vision is quite limited, in fact. The window is only a foot wide."

"That's what I thought," Pat said with visible satisfaction. "So they were standing here. In front of this chair. Describe what you saw."

"Damned if I will."

"This is no time for gentlemanly reticence. I want details. Where were Tony's crutches?"

"He was leaning on one of them. I don't know where the other . . . " Adam groaned. "Can I close the door? I'm frozen stiff."

"Yes, come in." He was still holding Ruth. She pulled away from him and went to Rachel.

"You don't have to listen to this. Let's go back to the family room."

"It's all right."

"You're sure?"

"Yes."

Pat went on with the interrogation. "He had one arm around her, right? Or both?"

"One."

"So he had dropped one crutch or laid it aside. What was he wearing?"

"A bathrobe, I guess. It was a dark color."

"Pajamas?"

Adam's nose turned pink. "Uh—I think so."

"What color?"

"How the hell should . . . Blue."

"What did Rachel have on?"

"Clothes!" Adam shouted.

"Bathrobe? Negligee?"

"I don't remember!"

"You mean you don't want to remember. Close your eyes. See it. See her. Where were her arms?"

"Around . . . " He swallowed. "Around his neck."

"Long sleeves? Short sleeves? No sleeves?"

Adam's nose, even his eyelids, were crimson. The words came out in a rush. "No sleeves. Bare arms. Slender, white . . . " His eyes popped open. "What am I saying? Did you hypnotize me? Damn you, Pat—"

"What—was—she—wearing?"

"Something. Don't hassle me, Pat, I can see it—visualize it—but I can't identify it. White or pale gray background, with some kind of colored print. It covered her from just below her shoulders clear down to the floor, even her feet."

"Could you see the pattern?"

"I was not in the mood to linger over artistic details," Adam said bitterly. "I jumped back from the window as soon as I realized what was going on. When I first looked in, I thought it was Cheryl he was holding, and then I saw the dark brown hair, streaming down her back, caught under his . . . Do you want me to go on? I can spare a few more layers of skin."

"That's enough," Pat said mildly. "That's what I expected. What you saw wrapped around her was one of the quilts. There's nothing else it could have been—no shawls, no afghans lying on the chair now. It was on the chair that night. He reached for it when he saw she was cold, and put it around her, and—"

"Stop," Ruth said firmly. "You've got what you wanted. Don't push it."

"All right. We'll adjourn. I could use a cup of coffee."

Adam hung back when they left the room. He avoided Rachel's eyes, and she realized she wasn't the only one whose privacy had been invaded. She shouldn't have been pleased about it, but she was.

"Adam, you're a terrible cook," Pat declared, studying with obvious disfavor the muffin from which he had taken a bite. "What's this supposed to be?"

"I didn't have any blueberries," Adam explained. "So I used cranberries."

"You're supposed to cook them before you add them to the mix," Rachel said.

"Oh."

"We'd better be getting home," Ruth said.

Pat stared at her in surprise. "What are you talking about? I've barely begun." He took a notebook and a pair of glasses from his pocket. Adjusting the latter on his nose, he opened the notebook and looked at Adam.

"You found nothing when you searched the house?"

"No."

"Where did you look?"

"Basement, upstairs bedrooms, and kitchen . . . "

When he finished the list Pat asked, "Not Rachel's room?"

"You said *it* wouldn't . . . " Adam caught himself. "You said not to bother with the places where she normally goes."

"So we've only got two confirmed attempts at—" Pat paused, and said delicately—"at causing harm. I'd like to have a look at that bed canopy."

Several of the cats accompanied them upstairs. The heavy canopy still lay on the floor beside the bed.

"I didn't realize it was so massive," Ruth murmured. Her voice was unsteady. "How could Cheryl stand to sleep under something so dangerous?"

"She must have had it repaired and braced quite recently," Adam said. "There are four separate sets of screws, each six inches long, plus a heavy bolt and nut on either end. There's no way screws and bolts could have worked loose."

Pat lowered himself to his hands and knees and squinted at the end of the canopy. "Some of the screws are still in place."

"She only had to loosen the screws on one end. When that end fell, the weight pulled the others away from the bed frame." He picked up an object from the table. "The nut had been removed. I found it under the bed. You can see the marks of the pliers."

The traces of tampering were obvious. The pliers had scored and brightened the metal. The head of the screw Adam offered next had the same sort of marks.

"It would take a great deal of strength to do that," Ruth protested. "Surely only a man—"

"With the proper tools, anyone could have done it," Adam said. "Tony's got long-handled pliers and an electric screwdriver in his workshop downstairs."

Pat got stiffly to his feet. "Damned arthritis . . . She didn't know you were going to sleep here?"

"It was a spur-of-the-moment decision."

"So cheer up. She isn't out to get you. So far."

"Your levity is disgusting," Adam snarled. "In front of Rachel—"

"I wasn't talking about Rachel," Pat said.

"Then who, or what, are you talking about? You're giving this—this thing—gender, and thus, by implication, identity. What are you basing that on?"

"Past experience," Pat said. "I don't buy the idea of an abstract demonic intelligence. There must be some spiritual connection between the invading entity and the host it occupies. In the earlier situation Sara was susceptible because she was the same age and sex as the girl who spoke through her. I'm assuming that the same thing applies to Rachel. I admit it's only a hypothesis so far, but several things support it. First, the sexual attraction that moved a puritanical man like Tony to violate his moral code."

"Oh, come on," Adam said angrily.

"I said it was only a hypothesis," Pat repeated. "The second point is stronger. The source of the contamination seems to be the quilt. Women make quilts."

"That's a sexist—" Ruth began.

"You know any men who make them?" Pat demanded.

"Not personally. But now that it's become an accepted art form—"

"It wasn't an art form when this quilt was made. Sewing was woman's work. Still is, on the whole."

They went on arguing, more for the fun of it than for any other reason; Pat's point was valid, and Ruth knew it.

Rachel didn't know whether to be relieved or sorry when Pat was finally persuaded to leave. It had been painful to see the evidence of her deadly intent, and to relive an experience from which memory shrank. His hand on her breast, hard, hurting, pushing her away . . .

Only you know about that. He doesn't know. And you won't tell him. Why should you? It only matters to you.

"What?" She started. Pat was speaking to her.

"I said, what's the name of that friend of Tony's at the station?"

"Tom Hardesty. Why?"

"I want to have a look at those quilts."

"Why?"

"Because," Pat said patiently, "there's got to be a connection. And before you start sneering at my deductive abilities, Adam, let me point out the underlying logic. The theft—which is now a case of theft and murder—has several peculiar aspects. Why haven't the police been able to find the thief? From the description of his appearance and behavior he would seem to be an ordinary stupid crook, without intelligence or subtlety. You've got two out-of-the-ordinary situations here—the theft, and the anomalies of Rachel's behavior, which began the night Tony wrapped her in the quilt. We are justified in assuming that the two are somehow connected."

"You always did reason like a Jesuit," Adam said rudely. "And you never listen to counterarguments. Play your little games. What do you want me to do?"

"You promised me a report on the Wiccas."

"Very funny," Adam said.

"I mean it. There's nothing else you can do at the moment."

"We really must get back, Pat," Ruth said. "I have things to do."

"What things? Oh, all right." He removed a cat from his lap, stood up, and put the cat on the seat he had vacated. The cat promptly jumped down.

"What about me?" Rachel asked.

"What about you? Follow your normal routine. Keep busy." He moved to the table that held Rachel's books and papers. "Work on your dissertation."

"Fat chance," Rachel said. "With Adam thumping around and cats sitting on the keyboard and my mental processes distracted by wondering what I'm going to do next."

Pat picked up one of the books. "Maybe I should read something about quilts. The subject has never had much attraction for me. Mind if I borrow this?"

"Take anything you like," Rachel said.

"Thanks." He put the book in his pocket. "All right, Ruth, we're off. Just one more stop."

"Pat!"

"It won't take long. I want to have a look at the front steps. We'll go outside and around."

Her lips a thin line, Ruth let him help her into her coat and preceded him out the door.

"You told him about the knife," Rachel said. Her voice was neutral, but Adam reacted as if the speech had been an accusation.

"I told him everything. Any objections?"

Without answering, Rachel followed the others.

Adam joined Pat, who was peering at the gash in the step with absorbed concentration. Ruth waited at the bottom of the steps, foot tapping and arms folded. The bright sunlight brought out lines in her forehead and cheeks Rachel hadn't noticed before.

"He's really into this, isn't he?" she said.

"Yes."

"You're both being very kind."

Ruth shook her head, frowning, and Rachel said hesitantly, "Are you angry about something? Have I done something?"

A flush of ugly color darkened the older woman's cheeks. She took Rachel's arm and led her away from the steps.

"It's not your fault. I'm a little worried, that's all."

"About me?"

"It happened to him once before." Ruth might have been talking to herself. "He's been exposed. Does that make him more susceptible? I couldn't go through that again. I couldn't stand it if he . . . " She looked at Rachel and said bluntly, "You're a nice girl, Rachel. I like you, and I'm very sorry for you, and I know you're not responsible for this. But I'd abandon you, this day, this moment, if I could persuade Pat to do the same. I'd hate myself for the rest of my life, but I'd do it."

eight

After the MacDougals left, Rachel settled herself in front of her word processor and tried to look as if she were working. She couldn't face Adam's clumsy attempts at casual chitchat, or his questions.

Ruth's blunt statement had left her speechless. She wouldn't have known what to say even if Ruth had given her a chance to respond, which she had not; collaring her husband, she had led him, protesting but unresisting, to the truck. It had been a fascinating demonstration of how that relationship worked. Ruth didn't assert herself often, but when she put her small foot down, Pat MacDougal obeyed.

What had struck Rachel dumb wasn't Ruth's candor, unexpected though it had been, but her realization that Ruth—intelligent, sophisticated, gentle Ruth—really *believed* Pat's hypothesis.

Pat claimed to believe it too, and Rachel didn't doubt his sincerity, but nothing he had said affected her as Ruth's blunt statement had done. In his own way Pat was enjoying the intellectual challenge; as he kept saying, he was testing a hypothesis. Ruth was not enjoying the situation. She was afraid—afraid because she believed. Believed wholeheartedly and without reservations, as some cultures believed in the efficacy of magic, as devoutly religious people believed in God and angels and the literal interpretation of Scripture. That intensity of belief was one of the strongest forces in the world, and one of the most dangerous. Old women had been burned alive because of it, heretics and sinners had been tortured to death when they refused to conform to a particular creed. Witches were fair game in almost all cultures; the most effective way of canceling evil spells that could cause illness, bad luck, accident, or death was to kill the witch.

She couldn't concentrate on her work when thoughts like those were squirming around in her head, and when Adam kept tiptoeing loudly past the door, pausing only long enough to look in before he went on.

The next time his shadow darkened the doorway Rachel called out to him.

"Pat told you to watch me, didn't he? So come in and sit down and watch."

"I thought you were working. I was trying not to bother you."

"Oh, stop being so damned tactful. How can I possibly get any work done? Admit it, he did order you to play watchdog."

"He didn't have to tell me." Adam came into the room, sat down on the edge of a chair, and stared fixedly at her. "I should think you'd find it reassuring to know I'm—uh—monitoring your activities. *It* won't try anything while I'm around."

At first she didn't believe her own ears. "*It?*" she repeated.

"Maybe we ought to give *it* a name," Adam mused. "Lilith? Medea? Susybelle?"

"Who was Susybelle?"

"Nobody. I just threw that innocuous name in to be fair. *It's* activities thus far have been reminiscent of some of the nastier ladies in literature and myth, but we shouldn't leap to conclusions without more evidence than—"

"I think you've lost your mind," Rachel said flatly. "Am I the only skeptic left?"

"My skepticism has been somewhat shaken. There are a couple of things that have led me to support Pat's lunatic hypothesis."

"Oh?"

"The first is the peculiar incident of the knife thrust into the step. It bothered me from the start, but I couldn't figure out why. It wasn't until last night, when I was going over things in my mind—and a damned uncomfortable process it was, I might add—that I realized the perpetrator probably wasn't your burglar. I think you did it. Now don't start yelling, let me explain. What would be the sense of a vague, melodramatic threat like that? If he were stalking you, he'd be more direct and more obtrusive. And there's the significant clue of the dogs that didn't bark."

Rachel had wondered about those points herself, but she was still on the defensive. "Why would I do such a thing?"

"Ah, that's the question, isn't it? Think. The incident happened on the night of the Winter Solstice. That's one of the great festivals of witchcraft—Esbats, as they are called. The smears of mud around the knife could have been a footprint. Hell's bells, woman, this is your field! Surely you've heard about sympathetic magic."

Rachel's strained temper gave way. "Dammit, Adam, don't patronize me! I get enough of that from Pat MacDougal, but at least he's a recognized authority. What you're talking about is the Law of Contagion or Connection. Objects that have been in contact with a person's body retain his identity, his soul, if you prefer, even after they are no longer in contact. Clothes, teeth, hair—"

"And the impressions of his body. I've read Fraser too," Adam said coolly. "He gives innumerable examples of the belief that you can harm a person by attacking his footprint."

"Laming him," Rachel said. She laughed harshly. "He already had one bad leg. Do you suppose I was trying for the other one?"

"Now you're the one who is fighting this," Adam said. "Try not to take it personally."

"Oh, sure. No problem."

"If Pat is correct, it's not you—it's something else trying to work through you. Stop wallowing in self-pity and use your intelligence and your training."

The criticism was like a slap in the face of a hysteric—painful but therapeutic. She tried to think, forced herself to sound calm and reasonable. "That doesn't make sense, even by Pat's theory. I—she—doesn't want to hurt Tony. Footprints are used in love spells too. Thrusting a needle into the footprint a man has left in your dooryard forces him to remain faithful. Ozark magic."

"Oh, yeah? I never heard that one."

"But I had. A knife is more—more emphatic than a needle, isn't it?"

"Mmm-hmmm." Adam pondered the idea. "I like it. It reinforces my theory. You didn't want to harm him, you wanted to—"

"You said there were a couple of things. What else?"

"The other isn't rational," Adam said. "I suspect that I am falling in love with you. It's only a hypothesis so far, but all the evidence seems to point that way."

Rachel's jaw dropped. Never in her wildest imaginings could she have anticipated such a declaration. "What—what evidence?"

"My emotional reactions are becoming abnormal," Adam said seriously. "When I saw you and Tony that night, I wasn't shocked, though I was surprised. He never struck me as the philandering type. However, that sort of thing happens all the time and it was none of my business. As time passed and I became better acquainted with you, I realized to my consternation that my attitude had drastically altered. I thought about that incident constantly, picturing you in his arms and feeling a variety of violently irrational emotions."

Rachel found it hard to imagine Adam experiencing violently irrational emotions. His cool, long-winded analysis was so typical and so inappropriate that she felt an equally inappropriate desire to laugh. "What kind of emotions?" she inquired.

"Rage, lust—"

"Lust?"

"Sexual desire."

"Oh, I see." A gurgle escaped her before she could stop it. What was wrong with her? This was no laughing matter. Adam was completely in earnest.

"It's not just sex, though," he said gloomily. "All the signs point to a classic case of old-fashioned romantic attachment. I've never felt anything quite like it, but I've read about it. I keep wanting to fight people on your behalf, rescue you from danger, stuff like that."

"You have a peculiar way of showing it. The things you said last night—"

"Oh, that was normal. I was fighting my irrational impulses. When you went into that spasm I wanted to kill Pat because he'd hurt you, and I wanted to smash his face in because it was he who was holding you, instead of me. Another overreaction, you see," he added. "That was when it dawned on me that I might be in love with you."

Rachel shook her head dazedly. "This is the craziest conversation."

"I'm glad we had it, though." Adam folded his arms, leaned back in his chair, and smiled amiably at her. "Cleared the air. I feel a lot better."

"I don't."

"You will, once the initial shock wears off. Like me, you are basically an honest, forthright person. There's nothing to worry about, you know; I mean, I'm not going to *do* anything unless you want me to. You'll have to make the first move."

"That's not likely," Rachel gasped.

"Would it help if I cut off my beard?"

After an hour spent staring blankly back at the blank screen of her computer, Rachel realized Adam was right. That extraordinary conversation had cleared the air, though not in the way he had meant. She couldn't take seriously his declaration of—what had he called it? Classic romantic attachment? What sort of background did the man come from, that he could make a remark like that with a straight face? It was certainly a contrast to the most recent declaration of "romantic attachment" she had received. Phil had initiated their affair with a statement consisting of five monosyllabic words. "Love" had not been one of them. Well, but she hadn't been in love with him either. Who was it who had said that these days love was one of the few four-letter words sophisticates were embarrassed to employ? Love wasn't relevant, love had nothing to do with a relationship like theirs.

It was over now, and maybe she had learned something from it. If Phil showed up again, she could and would deal with him.

The most important thing Adam had done was force her to recognize her refusal to confront her present problem head-on. If people like Patrick MacDougal and Ruth—and Adam—were willing to suspend rational disbelief, she was in no position to jeer at them. Especially when she knew . . .

Absently she stroked the cat that had settled on her lap. What did she know? Nothing that could be expressed in words. The impressions that had come to her weren't susceptible to definition; they were as difficult to describe as a half-remembered dream. Pat was right about one thing, though. *It* was female. She would never be able to tell him, not only because she couldn't explain that certainty, but because The Other wouldn't let . . . No. It wasn't a threat or prohibition that stopped her tongue, it was something else. Her mind fumbled with words. Reluctance, caution, distaste, fear . . . Fear. A wall, opaque and impenetrable, and behind it a huddled shape crouching, waiting.

The cat yowled and stuck its claws into her leg. "I'm sorry," Rachel muttered, relaxing her grip. The apology was not accepted; Patches jumped to the floor and began indignantly licking the place where Rachel's fingers had pressed.

No use trying to force that process; it made her feel disoriented and slightly sick. But perhaps there was another way, the one Adam had suggested. "It's your field," he had said offhandedly—and correctly. She was supposed to know about subjects like superstition and magic. At least, she thought cynically, going at it from that angle would give her new insights for her dissertation.

She turned to look at Adam, who had settled down in a chair some distance away. He was trying, unsuccessfully, to look smaller than he really was.

"I'm going out," she announced. "I suppose you want to go with me."

"Where are you going?"

"College Park. I haven't been back to the house for a week. I should collect my mail and check my answering machine. And I need some things. I packed in a hurry."

Adam closed the book he had been pretending to read and smiled at her. It was the first time she had spoken to him since she had rejected his offer to remove his beard, and his pleasure at her overture was obvious and a little pathetic. "I will come. If you don't mind?"

"I don't mind. But I'll drive."

Enveloped in layers of sweaters, Adam settled down in the passenger seat. He was wearing the mittens and muffler Rachel had given him, but not the Santa Claus socks; he had informed her he was going to save them for special occasions.

Traffic was lighter than usual and they made good time, but it was midafternoon before they reached College Park. The winter sun was low in the sky and the house was dark, shadowed by overgrown shrubbery. A light covering of snow still whitened the grass, but the feet of pedestrians had left only dirty slush on the sidewalk. When Rachel turned into the walk that led from the street to the front steps, Adam stopped her.

"Wait a minute."

"What's the problem?" Rachel demanded. "The burglar wouldn't hang around here; the house has been deserted for days."

"Somebody's been here, though."

He indicated the overlapping footprints.

"The mailman," Rachel said.

"Oh." Adam's face registered disappointment, but he rallied bravely. "Let me have a look at them before you go tramping over the evidence."

"For heaven's sake, Adam! Who do you think you are, Sherlock Holmes?"

"What's the harm in looking? It snowed again last night. That would have covered up any earlier footprints, so the ones we see had to have been made today. Right?"

"I suppose so."

"So, Watson, observe." He set her gently aside and paced slowly along the unmarked snow beside the walk, his head bent. "There are two different sets of prints—four in all, going and coming. I'll bet these are the mailman's. They look like old-style galoshes. Older man, is he? Heavy? His feet are almost as big as mine."

"The mailman is a mailwoman," Rachel said in a stifled voice.

Adam laughed. "So I guessed wrong. I'll bet Holmes occasionally did too, and Watson tactfully refrained from mentioning it. Yes, these appear to be a woman's prints. Narrower, smaller. I wonder whose the others are."

He carried on a casual, running commentary as he proceeded. "Dog crossing. Big dog. I'd take a wild stab at the breed, if it weren't for the fact that you are probably acquainted with the creature and would contradict me. Birds, cat . . . Yours is a busy neighborhood."

Rachel followed him. She didn't look at the male footprints. They could have been made by a delivery man or door-to-door salesman or a friend who had not heard that she and the others were away. But she knew someone who wore oversized, old-fashioned galoshes. Their housemates had often kidded him about them.

She unlocked the door, but when she would have opened it, Adam took her arm. "Let me go first."

Rachel didn't argue. Even a cheerful modern house has a depressing air about it when it has been unoccupied for some days, and this house was neither cheerful nor modern. The door opened halfway, into a space of dusky, stale-smelling silence, and then stuck.

Adam's eyes widened. "There's . . . something . . . behind the door," he breathed. Squaring his shoulders, he edged through the opening.

"Probably a body," Rachel said sarcastically.

There was a brief silence before Adam responded. "You sure get a lot of mail."

Rachel went in and switched on the overhead light. It didn't improve the general atmosphere, bringing into stark detail the stained, scuffed bare boards of the floor and the cobwebs hanging from the ceiling. Adam stood staring at the pile of envelopes and periodicals that had been pushed through the mail slot. A magazine had caught under the door, jamming it.

"One of my housemates is a catalogue freak," Rachel said. "Talk about junk mail! It's a wonder the world isn't buried under the stuff. I'll do that," she added, as Adam knelt and began sorting the accumulation into piles.

"I'll have a look around," Adam said, rising impressively to his feet. The small hallway looked even smaller with Adam and his sweaters occupying so much of the space. Small, shabby, and odorous; the ghosts of former meals and antique plumbing haunted the air. Wrinkling her nose, Rachel sat down on the floor. Tossing magazines and catalogues aside, she glanced through the envelopes. There was nothing for her except bills, a few belated Christmas cards . . . and a note, written on lined paper and folded twice.

She was still staring at it when Adam returned from his investigation of the kitchen and living room. "What's that?" he asked.

"Nothing important." Rachel stood up and shoved the paper into her jacket pocket. "A—a friend stopped by looking for me. That takes care of the mail. I'll see if there are any messages on the answering machine."

At least the note had prepared her. He had called five times, twice on Christmas Eve, three times on Christmas Day, leaving a number each time. The conciliatory tone of the first message turned to anger and accusation at the end. "I know you're there. Probably standing by the phone listening. Call me."

Hands in his pockets, shoulders hunched, Adam watched her curiously. "Same—friend?" he inquired.

"Yes."

"You didn't write down the number. Shall I play it back?"

"No." She jabbed at the rewind button, wiping out the messages. Except for Phil's tirades the only call had been a Christmas Day greeting from her family in England. Each of them had spoken a few words.

She let Adam precede her up the stairs. He moved lightly and quickly for a man of his size; when she reached the top of the stairs he had opened a door and was looking into the room.

"That's not my room," she said.

"I deduced that, from the intimate male garments lying on the unmade bed. Your housemates aren't very neat, are they?" Calmly, ignoring her protests, he looked into the other rooms. "How many people live here?"

"Four—I mean, three. They've all gone home for the holidays."

"I don't see any signs of unauthorized intrusion. This your room?"

"Yes."

All at once she was gripped by violent distaste—for her small, comfortless room, for the entire house. She wanted to get out of it as fast as possible and never come back. How could she have tolerated such a dirty, depressing place? Wherever she went after she left Tony . . . after she left Leesburg . . . it wouldn't be here.

Rapidly she emptied drawers and tossed clothing into the cartons she had stored in the closet. There weren't enough of them to hold all her possessions, she'd have to come back one more time. It didn't matter. What mattered was getting away, quickly.

"Can you carry this one?" she asked, indicating the box that held books and papers. "I'm afraid it's pretty heavy."

"No problem." Adam hoisted the box onto his shoulder.

Together they carried the cartons to the porch. Adam insisted on transporting them to the car and Rachel stood by the door, under the sheltering shadows of the porch, while he did so. When he came back for the last one she locked the door and followed slowly after him, scuffing her feet, blurring each footprint as she walked. *Maybe the snow will melt, but it's better to be safe than sorry.*

"What are you doing?" Adam asked.

Rachel looked up with a start. He was waiting by the car, frowning as he watched her.

Without answering she got in the car and started the engine. Adam climbed in beside her. He didn't speak until she had negotiated the stop-and-start traffic of Route 1 and turned onto the Beltway.

"Maybe you'd better tell me about this guy."

"There's nothing to tell. It's over."

"Doesn't sound as if he thinks so."

"Oh, he was just . . . in one of his moods. Probably bored and at loose ends. I haven't heard from him for weeks, and I don't expect I will again."

"You're afraid of him. Look at your hands." Rachel relaxed her white-knuckled grip on the wheel, and Adam went on gently but inexorably, "I'd just like to know how many threatening characters I have to watch out for. We're up to two now. Anybody else you'd care to mention?"

"I didn't mention Phil because my private affairs are none of your business," Rachel retorted hotly. "He is not a threat. He's a selfish, moody, irritating boor, but he's not dangerous. I am not afraid of him!"

"Then why were you scuffing out your footprints when you left? Watch out for that van," he added in the same mild voice. "He's about to move over into your lane."

Rachel slowed, leaving enough space for the impatient driver to cut in ahead of her. He hadn't bothered with turn signals, but if she hadn't been distracted she would have anticipated his intention too.

"You're right," she said, after a moment. "I wasn't aware of what I was doing. How ridiculous! All that talk about footprints and superstition must have been preying on my mind. Even if he came back and even if he knew I'd been there and even if he could identify footprints with the snow melting so fast, it wouldn't matter."

"Does he know where you work?"

"Let's drop the subject, all right?"

"Okay." Adam held out his hands. "Did I tell you how much I like my mittens? Great colors."

"It's not that I don't appreciate your concern," Rachel said awkwardly.

"It's purely selfish. I have these fantasies about rescuing you."

Rachel decided the only way she could deal with comments like that was to ignore them.

It was dark before they reached Leesburg. Christmas lights blazed out from houses along the way, and the shop windows of the business section had been strung with tinsel and ropes of evergreen, holly and poinsettias. The homeowners of Cornwall Street favored more subdued decorative effects; blue and crimson, gold and white, the bulbs of the trees inside the houses twinkled through the darkness. Thanks to Joe, whose tastes ran to quantity rather than quality, their own decorations were the most conspicuous on the quiet street; he had strung lights along the fence and around the blue spruce in the front yard, and only his mother's outraged protests had prevented him from climbing onto the roof to outline the entire house.

Either Adam had remembered to leave the lamps in the family room turned on or he had forgotten to turn them off; the house welcomed them with warmth and mellow light. The answering machine was blinking insistently, but Rachel was able to ignore it until after she had helped Adam carry in the cartons and return the rapturous greetings of the dogs. She wasn't afraid of Phil—that was ridiculous—but she shrank from talking, or rather arguing, with him, especially with Adam around, and she didn't underestimate his intelligence. If he wanted to track her down he could.

"I'll carry those boxes upstairs for you after dinner, okay?" Adam asked. "I'm starved. How about spaghetti?"

"Again?"

"I like spaghetti. You didn't have any last time."

He was smiling but his eyes shifted, avoiding hers, and then she understood. The sauce came from a can, the spaghetti from an unopened box. It wouldn't be easy to tamper with either.

"All right."

"Sit down and relax. Crazy Glue is waiting for a lap."

His attempt to suggest that this was just a nice normal domestic evening was a little ludicrous under the circumstances, but it proved to be effective. All the small details that added up to create atmosphere of comfort—warmth instead of chilly cold, light instead of shadows—a cat purring on her lap—Adam bustling back and forth from the sink to the stove to the fridge. The glass of wine he handed her was another nice touch, but when he sat down opposite her with a glass of his own she cried out.

"Adam! Don't!"

Adam jumped. "Geez, don't yell like that! Everything's under control; I have to wait for the water to boil before—"

"You poured the wine from a bottle that was already open," Rachel said urgently.

"Ah." Adam hesitated and at first she thought he was going to leave it at that. But he went on. "Is there something wrong with it?"

One part of her consciousness was aware of the apprehension with which he awaited the response a direct question might evoke. Another part probed inward, delicately as a fingertip, ready to pull back at the first sign of opposition. The wall was still there, and behind it only a waiting silence.

She hadn't realized she was holding her breath until it came out in a long, uneven sigh. "I don't know," she said. "I can't tell. But why take chances?"

Adam had been holding his breath too. "Are you all right?"

"Yes."

"I took quite a chance myself." His eyes were bright and speculative, and Rachel wondered if the business of the wine had been a test—and whether she had passed or failed. He might have been referring to the risk of questioning her, or the chance that she would not have stopped him from drinking wine she knew to be tainted.

Irrationally and unreasonably angry, she returned his stare. "Put some of it in a bottle. We'll have it analyzed."

"Forget it." But he tipped both glasses into the sink and opened another bottle. "I agree that we should be cautious, but I doubt there was anything wrong with it. Remember what Pat said—she wouldn't do anything that might injure you."

"Pat is awfully damned sure of himself. And his hypothesis is unproven. If I'm psychotic and guilty instead of innocent and haunted, I might arrange a little accident in order to clear myself of suspicion. I wouldn't worry about hurting someone else, either."

"What a clear, logical mind you have," Adam said approvingly.

A sarcastic retort was on the tip of Rachel's tongue when the telephone rang and Adam reached for it.

The voice was clearly audible, even from where she sat. "Didn't you get my messages? Why didn't you call me back? Where have you been?"

Adam started to explain. Pat cut him off. "All right, okay. Is Rachel there? Anything new?"

"Yes and no, in that order. How are you?" Adam grinned at Rachel and held the phone out so she could hear the reply. It continued, typically, as a monologue.

"Never mind the social amenities. I had a look at the stolen goods today." He chuckled fiendishly. "The cop at the desk didn't want to show me, but I bullied him into it. It helps to have connections. I think I've identified the one we're interested in. As soon as I touched the damned thing I could feel the difference. It was impossible to make out the pattern, the fabric was so filthy, but I spotted a couple of curious details. I thought you girls were going to clean it."

He stopped to take a breath. Adam said, "I'm not one of the girls. Do you want to talk to Rachel?"

He handed her the phone and sat down next to her. "Hold the earpiece out a couple of inches or you'll get your eardrum blasted," he advised.

Pat was talking again. "Well? Rachel, are you there? Why don't you answer the question?"

"What question?" Rachel demanded, following Adam's advice. "You don't have to yell, Pat, I can hear you quite well."

"I'm not yelling," Pat said indignantly. "Why didn't you clean the quilt?"

The answer came smoothly and promptly to her lips. It was the truth, if not the whole truth. "As Tony kept telling Cheryl, it doesn't belong to her. She had no right to clean it or do anything else to it."

"We've got to get possession of it, then, or at least get permission to examine it. Who is the legal owner?"

"The old lady's niece, I guess. But the police are holding it and the other things until—"

"Yes, that's what they told me. Officious bastards," Pat added unfairly.

Rachel waited for him to ask the next, obvious question. She couldn't volunteer the answer. It was as simple as that—she could not. But if he asked . . . Her stomach knotted in anticipation.

Adam wrenched the phone from her grip. "Pat? It's me again. Kara is the one you want to talk to. She discussed the possibility of buying the things from Mrs. Wilson, and I presume she's got the woman's phone number. Look, we're about to eat. I'll call back if anything interesting develops. Otherwise we'll talk to you tomorrow."

"You'll probably see me tomorrow."

"Thanks for the warning. Good night."

He hung up and headed for the stove, grumbling aloud. "If I hadn't shut him up the water would have boiled away. Play back the messages, why don't you, while I cook? If the phone rings, let it ring."

Even a message from Phil would be a relief, Rachel thought, punching the playback button. If Adam had not distracted him, Pat would have asked if she had had a close look at the quilt, and then she would have told him—tried to tell him—about the photographs she had taken, and then . . . Would she have been able to speak or would that awful, throttling grip have seized her by the throat? She was coward enough to be relieved that she had not been forced to find out.

There was no message from Phil. Pat had called twice, Kara had called to say she would be there the following morning, and Tom Hardesty had left a message asking her if she would have dinner with him the following night. He had left a number. "If I'm not there, just say yes or no."

Adam turned, a strand of spaghetti dangling from his mouth. "Another rival," he said, biting through the spaghetti and catching the ends as they fell. "Do you always have two or three guys following you around?"

"No."

Seeing that she was not amused, Adam changed the subject. "Almost ready. How about setting the table?"

As they ate he tried another approach. "Why don't you invite Tom to have dinner here tomorrow? Cops don't make a lot of money."

"You are so thoughtful," Rachel murmured. "Are you offering to cook?"

"You don't think I would be rude enough to horn in on a date, do you? I will remain tactfully in my room."

"You can remain tactfully anywhere you like. I am not going to invite him here. You surely aren't worried about Tom; a policeman is the safest escort I could have."

"I'm afraid he'll rescue you before I have a chance to," Adam said seriously. He wound the last strands of spaghetti around his fork and popped them neatly into his mouth. Rachel had to admit his technique was refined; not a drop of sauce dripped. Catching her eye, Adam swallowed and reached for a napkin.

"Did I dribble? I'll get rid of the beard if you find it unsanitary."

"I don't want to have anything to do with your beard," Rachel said. "I don't even want to discuss it. Do you want coffee? Sit still, I'll get it. And I'll do the dishes. That's only fair."

After she had cleared the table she called Tom. He wasn't there, so she left a message saying she would see him at seven the next evening. They watched television for a while, or pretended to watch; Rachel knew Adam was paying as little attention as she. He didn't even join in the canned laughter. Finally she removed one of the ubiquitous cats from her lap and began unpacking the carton of books.

"I said I'd carry them upstairs for you," Adam said.

"The books stay down here." She hesitated and then said, "If you want to work in this room, feel free. We could bring in another table."

"Maybe I will. If you don't mind?"

"Stop asking me what I want!" Rachel burst out. She pressed her hands to her head. "I'm sorry."

"That's okay. I understand."

"That's nice. I don't." She began sorting the books into piles. Adam watched her for a while and then said firmly, "I am going to bring my work into this room. First I will get another table."

Assisted by both dogs and by Figgin, he proceeded to do so. It didn't take long; he had no books, only a battered laptop and a few notebooks that also looked as if they had been through a war.

"What are you working on?" Rachel asked. Common courtesy was partially responsible for her question, but the sight of his materials roused her curiosity.

"First thing I have to do is type up these notes." Adam flipped open one of the notebooks, whose corners looked as if they had been chewed by a rat. The page was closely filled with neat, minuscule writing, quite unlike the block printing of the note he had once left for her. A handwriting expert would have described the writer as painfully repressed. As she looked closer she realized the apparent neatness was deceptive; only a few words were legible.

"Nobody can read my notes," Adam admitted. "I use a kind of personal shorthand, to save paper and time, but I've been told that my handwriting is indecipherable even when I spell the words out. The departmental secretary went on strike when I gave her my stuff, so I had to learn to type."

"If that's a hint, I can't read your writing either. It looks like cuneiform."

"Naomi—the secretary—said it was more like Pali. And that was not a hint. Are you going to work or do you want to watch some more television? There's a special on Unsolved Mysteries of History—Easter Island, Nostradamus, the Pyramids—"

"The only mystery about the pyramids is why a lot of gullible fools think there is a mystery, and Nostradamus was an ordinary charlatan with a great press agent."

"But that's why programs of that sort are so much fun," Adam said, with a grin. "They collect a few solemn idiots who rant on in pseudo-scholarly language about Martians and refugees from lost Atlantis and mystic prophecies. I love it."

"Enjoy yourself, then. I'm going to bed. Kara will be here at the crack of dawn, if I know her."

"First I'll tote these bales." Adam hoisted two of the cartons onto his shoulder.

He is strong, Rachel thought, as she followed him. Strong as an ox, wasn't that the cliché? And big as an ox, too. Into her mind, unsought and unexpected, came a sense of how it would feel to have Adam take her in his arms, hold her close. *Arms heavy with muscle bruising her ribs, bristling hair muffling her breath and lacerating her face . . .*

Adam lowered the boxes to the floor and straightened in time to see her expression.

"Something wrong?"

"No." But she backed away until her retreat was halted by the table and her outstretched hand knocked something off onto the floor. The contents of the envelope spilled and scattered.

Rachel dropped to her hands and knees and began gathering up the photographs. Kneeling in his turn, Adam helpfully retrieved several that had scattered in his direction. Then he looked at them.

He sat back on his heels and stared at Rachel. Down at her. Rachel straightened, sitting tall, but his head was still six inches higher than hers.

"This is it," he said, making it a statement. "You photographed it."

"Yes."

Adam didn't move or speak. He waited.

He knows what they are. He can take them if he wants. With one hand. His wrist is as big around as my arm, five of his fingers could hold all ten of mine.

Her hand moved of its own accord, offering him the photographs on her flattened palm. Adam's movements were slow and deliberate, as if he were approaching a wary animal. Delicately he took the photographs, without touching her hand.

"Can I—" He stopped himself. "I'm going to look at them," he said in a murmur that had almost no breath behind it. "Right here, right now. I'm going to sit in that chair over there."

He got slowly and carefully to his feet and, after hesitating perceptibly, offered her his hand. There were beads of sweat on his forehead and Rachel felt a distant stir of amusement. It was the first time she had seen cold-blooded Adam perspire. He must feel like a tightrope walker over a pool of piranhas. And she had hurt his feelings; he hadn't missed her look of distaste, or misunderstood the reason for her hasty retreat.

"Okay," she said, and took his hand.

His touch was tentative, the pressure of his fingers only firm enough to steady her as she rose. In silence she watched him shuffle through the stack of photographs. "It's all here," he muttered. "Separate squares, or whatever you call 'em, and the composite."

"That's right," Rachel said calmly.

"The details are surprisingly sharp. You did clean it."

Still no questions. She nodded. "Brushed it. I wouldn't have risked anything more drastic."

"But Pat said . . . Well, never mind. I don't think I want to take any more chances tonight. I'm going to give these to Pat."

"I can't stop you."

"No." He put the snapshots into the pocket of his shirt and walked wide around her on his way to the door.

"Adam."

"What?"

"I want you to lock me in."

He turned abruptly and she saw his face soften as he looked from her twisting hands to her tight mouth. "Honey, I can't do that. It's too dangerous. What if there were a fire? Besides, you don't have a private bath."

She smiled back at him. Her smile may have been no more convincing than his, but give us credit for trying, she thought. "Cheryl must have a chamber pot somewhere."

"No such undignified expedient will be necessary. Trust me."

Rachel was in bed, reading, when she heard the dogs. Adam must have let them out; they were in the backyard, which her window overlooked, and they were sounding the alarm, deep bass barks and agitated yips blending. As Adam had said, they barked at squirrels, moths, the moon, and occasionally just for the hell of it. But Rachel got out of bed and went to the window.

She couldn't see anything, not even the dogs, but she could hear them loud and clear. They weren't barking just for the hell of it. She opened her door and went to the window at the end of the hall, over the front door.

If the earlier visit of the witches had not prepared her for what she saw, she would have thought she was still asleep and dreaming. Pale draperies billowed and fluttered as their wearers moved in rapid patterns, crossing and recrossing one another's paths. Then Adam appeared from the side of the house, and Rachel realized that the intruders weren't dancing; they were running, in confusion and panic. Some of them reached the vehicles they had left parked farther down the street, and tumbled in. Doors slammed.

The beam of the flashlight Adam carried focused on one of the retreating forms—the largest and slowest of the lot. It skidded to a stop and turned, raising both hands like a fugitive responding to police orders. Thick glasses and a high bald forehead reflected the light; a neatly trimmed white beard and mustache framed a mouth gaping wide with alarm or shortness of breath. Probably both, Rachel thought; he was too old and fat to run so fast.

Adam advanced on his captive and they stood talking for a few minutes. Then Adam slapped him on the back—it was meant to be a friendly gesture, Rachel supposed, but the older man retreated in haste, glancing back at Adam over his shoulder every few steps. Adam stood looking after him.

Rachel wrestled with the window before she remembered it was painted shut and had not been opened in years. Damn the man! He wasn't even wearing a coat. The white witches might be harmless, but other people weren't, and he was standing there, practically inviting attack. She was about to bang on the glass when Adam turned and went back the way he had come. Rachel returned to bed.

Knowing he was safely indoors, she could see the humor of the encounter. Poor Adam, rushing out to defend her and finding nothing more formidable than a terrified little old man in a nightshirt. She was still giggling when she heard Adam come upstairs and pause briefly at her door before going on. He had taken off his shoes and was trying to tiptoe, but he made as much noise as a prowling bear.

After a while he came padding back and Rachel listened with interest to the soft sounds that followed. They made his actions as clear as sight would have done. The floorboards creaked as a heavy weight pressed them down; a soft, interested feline comment was followed by a loud "sssh!" and a louder squawk from the cat. Additional squeaks and hissing comments, animal and human, were succeeded, at last, by silence. He didn't snore.

When Rachel opened her door the next morning, Adam was gone, but she did not doubt he had spent the night outside her room, wrapped in a blanket or in some equally romantic and uncomfortable position. Knowing he was there had enabled her to sleep soundly, but she doubted he had. The cats would have been fascinated by this radical departure from human custom. If the hard floor had not kept Adam awake, their prowling must have.

He had fed the animals and let the dogs out. When Rachel entered the room, he was watching television, his eyes wide and staring. The face on the screen, in dreadful close-up, was that of a woman, her eyes wide and staring. ". . . there was this white light, and this voice, and it was, like, Welcome, and people were, like, singing."

The picture changed to show the audience—eyes wide and staring.

"You'll watch anything, won't you?" Rachel inquired.

"Talk shows are almost as good as pseudo-science. A lot of them are about pseudo-science. Like," he added with a grin, "these people all died and came back to life."

"Anything to get on TV, I suppose."

"They're dead—you should excuse the pun—serious." Adam sobered. "I shouldn't make fun of them."

"Especially in view of the fact that you—" The dogs began to bark. "Damn, is that Kara already?"

"Uh—I'm afraid it's Pat. He said he'd be here at nine."

She should have expected it, Rachel realized. He'd be on fire to see those snapshots. "Let him in," she said shortly. "And don't look so sheepish and apologetic!"

Pat didn't bother with polite greetings. "Where are they?" he demanded, tossing his coat onto the sofa.

Adam indicated the table. "Have you had breakfast?"

"Hours ago. I'll take some coffee, though." Pat seated himself and grabbed the pile of photographs. As he sorted through them he let out exclamations of pleasure. "Great. Oh, yes. Perfect. Nice and clear. Now where . . . Aha! Come here, you two. Have a look at this."

Adam took the photograph. "It's a guy on a horse. A hunter? There's a dog—"

Pat snatched it from him and passed it to Rachel. "It's not a guy, you ignoramus. Unless he's wearing very baggy pants. What do you say, Rachel?"

"I thought it was a man too," Rachel admitted. "I didn't examine the details closely. But I think you're right, Pat. That's a long skirt—a riding habit. The hat is a woman's too. They wore those jaunty top hats at one period. Yes, of course it's a woman. The sewer has even created the impression of a veil. What incredible workmanship! The thread is as fine as a single hair. The features are . . . "

Her voice caught. Pat said sharply, "What?"

"She's blind," Rachel whispered. "Look. Mouth, nose . . . and the crossed threads of the veil, with not even a French knot to indicate an eye."

Pat snatched the photo from her. "Damned if you aren't right."

Adam shifted protestingly. "I don't know anything about sewing, but it must be hard to show details as small as that. The whole face isn't as big as my fingernail."

"A valid point," Pat muttered, squinting closely at the tiny face. "But I don't believe it. What caught my eye was something else. Look at the dog—the shape and placement of its head. Either it's about to take a bite out of the horse's shank or your seamstress is less skilled than she has shown herself to be elsewhere."

"That's really far out," Adam exclaimed.

"I don't think so. It was just a hunch at first, but these photographs confirm it. There's something wrong in almost every scene." He selected another picture, slapped it down on the table, and jabbed at it with a peremptory finger. "That's a snake—a cute little green snake coiled around the stems of the flowers. And this. It's a charming depiction of a columned summer house or gazebo, surrounded by flowering shrubs—but what's this thing peering out between the leaves? It's got eyes. Red eyes."

"They're flowers." But Adam's voice lacked conviction.

They were not flowers. The difference in shading and shape was so subtle Rachel would not have seen it if Pat had not pointed it out.

"I'll be willing to bet there are more little surprises," Pat said. "We need enlargements. I'll have them made, Rachel, if you'll give me the negatives."

Rachel was staring in horrified disgust at the demonic red eyes. She heard the dogs bark, but didn't react until Adam said, "That must be Kara."

"Good," Pat said. "I want to talk to her."

Rachel jumped up. "You musn't tell her, Pat. Swear to me you won't tell her."

"About these?" He indicated the photographs. "Why should she object? It was a smart idea, to photograph the quilt. I don't understand how you got such clear shots, with that dirty gray film—"

"I cleaned it. It came right off, no problem. Pat—"

"It's come back then," Pat said thoughtfully. "Interesting. I wonder what—"

"Listen to me!" Frantic, expecting at any second to hear a knock at the door, she caught at his arm. "I don't care if she knows about the photographs, but you musn't tell her what I—what I tried to do, the canopy and the ground glass and . . . She'll never believe your hypothesis; she's the most rational, skeptical person I've ever met and she doesn't like me anyhow; she'll think I did it deliberately and—oh, God, there she is! Promise me, Pat."

"What makes you think she doesn't like you? Oh, all right, calm down. I promise. I'll concoct some story to explain why I'm interested in the origin of the quilt. Follow my lead and back me up. Okay,

Adam, let her in before she kicks the door down. Patience is not one of her virtues."

Kara didn't kick the door, but her knocking was loud and peremptory, and she wasted no time in telling them why she was so impatient.

"There are a couple of big cardboard boxes on the front porch," she announced. "Another sales pitch from your burglar?"

nine

Adam charged toward the door.

"Go through the shop," Kara ordered. "I have to open it anyway. Rachel, try to keep the damned cats from following us."

Rachel had almost forgotten about the Alleged; a possibly homicidal thief was small potatoes compared to her most recent difficulty. Corralling cats, she was slow to follow the others; she found them on the porch, standing in a wary circle around the cartons. Joe would have approved of the person who had left them, for they had obviously been reused several times. The sagging boxes would have given way at the seams if they had not been wound with rope.

"Get back," Adam ordered in a heroic baritone. Taking out a pocketknife, he edged cautiously up to the nearest box and started to cut the cord. Then he said in surprise, "There's a note. Addressed to you, Kara."

Kara accepted the folded sheet of lined paper. After reading the message she began to sputter. "Oh, for God's sake! I should have known. It's just Mrs. Grossmuller."

"Who?" Adam's face fell. Heroics were obviously not required.

In her worn jeans and sneakers, with a scarf covering her hair and laughter softening her face, Kara looked younger and less formidable. "She's a crazy old lady we met when we started the business. We bought a few things from her and now we can't get her off our backs; she considers herself one of our pickers, though we never made a formal arrangement with her. Cherry is terrified of her but I rather like the old lunatic. She did me a big favor once . . . And she does turn up good stuff upon occasion. When was she here?"

Adam shrugged. "We were away from the house yesterday afternoon. Didn't get back till after dark. I didn't look to see if there was anything on the porch. Sorry; I hope the merchandise hasn't been damaged by being out all night."

"It would take more than a night in the cold to damage Mrs. Grossmuller's contributions," Kara said. "But you should check for packages daily; the UPS and FedEx people won't deliver at the back because of the dogs. Well, let's take the boxes inside. What a nuisance! We're trying to get rid of things, not acquire more, and Mrs. Grossmuller's stuff always needs drastic cleaning. That reminds me, Rachel; I've notified some of our select customers that we're having a private clearance sale, just for them, on Thursday and Friday. I'll be here. In fact, I'll probably stay over Thursday night."

Hands in his pockets, Pat allowed Adam to carry the boxes into the shop. Kara began to unpack them, giving each item a quick, measuring glance before she tossed it aside. "Worse than usual," she muttered. "Well . . . This piece of lace isn't bad. Maybe I can recycle this petticoat. And this, and this . . . " When she finished there were two piles. "Rags and possibles," Kara said, nudging each heap with her foot. "Help me get the possibles into the workroom, Rachel; we'll put the whites to soak, see if the stains will come out. We may be able to get rid of some of these things during the sale."

Pat cleared his throat. "Can I say something?"

"What's stopping you?"

"Your formidable energy and flapping tongue. You can spare ten minutes. Sit down, I want to show you something."

He took the photographs from his pocket.

As he had predicted, Kara was approving instead of annoyed. "Good thinking, Rachel. I've been kicking myself for not suggesting that someone take photos. If I had realized what a fantastic piece of work it was,

I'd have kicked myself harder. I'm amazed at how well these came out. What did you do, vacuum it?"

"Brushed it."

"Oh, lovely," Kara murmured. "We've got to have it. Unfortunately that awful woman seems to know the quilts are worth money. She said one of them was in a book—"

"What?" The word came out of Pat like an explosion. He turned a formidable glare on Rachel, who cringed. "Why didn't you tell me?"

"I forgot," Rachel said feebly.

"What book?"

"I don't know."

"Stop picking on her, Pat," Kara ordered. "Since when have you become so passionate about quilts?"

Pat caught himself. "It was Rachel's idea," he said, so glibly that Rachel would have believed him if she hadn't known he was lying. "For her dissertation. She has a theory that friendship quilts, especially the ones made for brides, might have incorporated various good luck charms and motifs. This quilt has—she informs me—some unusual designs. So I suggested that she try to trace the original owner, learn something about her and her circle of friends, her life history . . . "

He ran out of breath and ideas at about the same time. Much of what he had said was nonsense, but Rachel was relieved to see that Kara didn't realize that. Her interest in the quilt was pragmatic; vague academic theories didn't concern her.

"Sounds interesting," Kara said politely. "I don't think you'll have much luck, but you could try."

"I—we—she thought she might interview Mrs. Wilson," Pat explained. "You have her address, don't you?"

"Not with me."

"But you can find it?"

"Yes, of course. The police have it too," she added. "Why don't you ask that nice friend of Tony's, Rachel?"

"I didn't think of that," Pat muttered.

Kara stacked the photos and put them in the desk drawer. "I'll look them over again later. Right now I have to get to work. Can you give me a hand, Rachel?"

It was courteous of her to ask, Rachel thought wryly. What else could she say but yes?

Kara threw the discards back into one of the cartons and scooped up an armful of clothes. Adam opened the door for her and followed her out. Rachel gathered the remaining linens and was about to go after them when Pat took her by the shoulders and lifted her till she was standing on tiptoe and his face, flushed with temper, was only inches from hers.

"Dammit, girl, has your brain shut down? Don't you realize how important that book could be? It might give us the name of the woman who made the quilt. You've got to find it."

"I'll try. Let go, you're hurting me."

"Don't talk so loud. Do you want Kara to hear?"

He was taller and heavier than she, stronger than she had realized, his hands as hard as those of a younger man. Violent, unreasoning panic swamped her and she twisted, trying to free herself. *"Don't hurt me. I'll do anything you want. Please . . . "*

Had she spoken the words aloud, or only heard them in her mind? When the room came back into focus Pat was several feet away, his face lined and pale.

"Holy Mother of God," he said softly. "Sorry, kid. I didn't expect that."

But Ruth did, Rachel thought. This is what she was afraid of.

"What are you guys doing?"

Adam was standing in the doorway. Rachel dropped to her knees and began picking up the clothes that had fallen from her grasp. Pat's control was better than hers; when he answered, his voice sounded normal.

"Plotting, what do you suppose? I'm going to the station and extract that woman's address from Tom. Rachel will look for the book Kara mentioned."

"Well, she'd better get herself into the workroom," Adam said. "Kara is making peremptory noises about wanting help."

Face averted, Rachel slipped past him.

"Put them on the table," Kara ordered. The armload she had brought was already soaking in the sink. One of the cupboard doors stood open and Kara was wrestling with a quart-sized plastic bottle. "The damned top is stuck," she said, grunting with effort. "How are you at . . . Never mind, I've got it."

Rachel didn't realize she had moved until she heard Kara cry out and saw her reel back against the sink. The bottle hit the floor and bounced.

Kara's scream brought both men to the door. "What happened?" Adam asked.

Kara rubbed her arm. Outrage and incredulity raised her voice a good half octave. "She hit me. Knocked the bottle out of my hand. I was going to bleach—"

"That's not bleach," Pat said.

Liquid continued to gurgle from the bottle, which had lost its cap as it fell. The liquid was certainly not bleach. Viscous, reddish brown, it had a sharp pungent odor quite unlike the unmistakable if equally pungent smell of bleach.

"Don't touch it," Pat ordered, as Adam reached for the bottle. "Not with your bare hands. Use this."

He snatched a cloth from the pile Rachel had dropped and gave it to Adam. It was one of the petticoats Kara had hoped to salvage, but Kara was too dumbfounded to object. After Adam had righted the bottle and screwed the cap on, he put it gingerly on the counter and studied the stained cloth.

"What is it?" Kara's voice was still soprano with disbelief.

Involuntarily, as one man, Pat and Adam turned to look at Rachel.

"I don't know!" She backed away, hands raised as if to fend off a physical attack. "I don't know what it is."

"But you knew there was something wrong with it." Kara would not accept that feeble denial, not when all the evidence, including Rachel's guilty expression, contradicted it. "You couldn't have smelled it or seen it, I hadn't even removed the cap. The label says it's bleach. How could you have known unless . . . " Her eyes moved from Rachel's face to Pat's. "What the hell is going on?"

"She didn't mean to," Adam said. He went to Rachel and stood beside her, solid as a rock, but he didn't touch her.

Kara transferred her accusing stare to him. "You're in on this too? You're all in on it. Okay, I give up. What's the joke? Was it supposed to turn my hands a bright indelible orange or make me break out in warts?"

"I think we'd better tell her, Rachel," Pat said. "I gave you my promise. Do I have your permission to break it?"

"I'll tell her," Rachel said. Confession, she had heard, was good for the soul. There must be some truth in that. The only emotion she felt was depression so vast it amounted to utter physical exhaustion. Unburdening herself would be a relief. "I'd rather she thought I was crazy than—than vicious and crazy. I honestly don't know what that vile stuff is, Kara, but it was I who put it in the bleach bottle, and it was intended to do harm—not to you, but to Cheryl. I didn't mean to do it. I didn't even know I had done it. I don't know what's wrong with me. I can't accept Pat's theory, though I wish to God I could. He thinks it's . . . " She couldn't bring herself to say the word—any of the specific, unbelievable words.

Pat, never one to mince words or avoid confrontation, said them. "Overshadowing. Mental invasion. Spiritual intrusion. Possession."

Kara's jaw dropped. "Oh, for God's sake. Not again!"

"I'm sorry," Rachel mumbled. "I hate swooning heroines! I don't know why I keep doing this."

She pushed the afghan away and sat up. Kara, seated in the rocking chair with a mug in her hand and a cat on her lap, said pleasantly, "In this case it was probably anticlimax. You had braced yourself for howls of disbelief and outrage."

"So Sara told you." Pat ran his hand through his hair, which stood out around his face like a rusty halo.

Kara nodded. "At one of those late-night bull sessions, when she was visiting me and Mark was out of town. Sara is my older sister, Rachel. She and her husband both had experiences like yours some years ago. She's the most normal, well-adjusted person I know. I couldn't doubt her, especially when Bruce confirmed the story."

"My testimony would not, of course, have impressed you," Pat said with heavy sarcasm.

"That was the same case you mentioned the other night?" Adam asked. He had caught Rachel when her knees buckled and carried her into the family room. His breathing was still uneven.

"Uh-huh. Such things don't happen as frequently as Kara's nonchalance might lead you to believe. I didn't feel I had the right to gossip about it to outsiders, even Sara's family, but I'll be damned if I can understand why Kara was so close-mouthed with me. I've been running all around Robin Hood's barn trying to be tactful and thoughtful and considerate."

He scowled horribly at Kara, who said, "You're just mad because you were hoping for a big loud argument, and I didn't give you the opportunity. I'll make it up to you by letting you tell me what has happened. Try not to be as long-winded as you usually are, please."

His summary was concise and well organized, and delivered with a panache that made Rachel realize what a superb lecturer he must have been. No wonder his courses had been so popular. Though none of what he said was new to her, she found it as fascinating as if she were hearing it for the first time. He omitted only one incident—that traumatic moment when she had fought to free herself from his hard, possessive grasp.

Kara was less impressed. "So," she said. "What are you going to do?"

"Do?" Pat repeated.

"Do. You've put together a plausible and entertaining story, but as you have often informed me, plausible isn't proven. If I understand you correctly, you think the woman who made that quilt was moved by malice against the woman who was to receive it—malice so intense that the emotion survived, undying, until it found a receptive vehicle."

Rachel's clasped hands tightened. "I didn't intend—"

"Never mind that now," Kara said. "We're discussing Pat's intriguing but unproven hypothesis. I see one serious objection to it right off the bat. The quilt is almost a hundred and fifty years old. What's it been doing all those years, lurking and biding its time, lying in wait for Rachel? Is there something about her that makes her uniquely receptive?"

Rachel started to protest, but Pat cut her off. "How the flaming hell should I know? Maybe it was packed away all those years, in harmless obscurity. Maybe it has to be in direct physical contact with a suitable individual. Or maybe . . . "

He broke off, frowning.

"What?" Adam asked.

"There could be another factor," Pat muttered. "Something unknown to us as yet. Oh, forget it. Speculation of that sort is a waste of time. For all we know there have been other vehicles over the years. We haven't investigated its history—"

"Precisely," Kara interrupted. "Seems to me your first move should be to find out who made the quilt, and what she was like."

"But the damned—excuse me—thing is over a hundred years old,"

Adam protested. "There won't be documentation; women's work wasn't considered important enough to merit written records."

Kara gave him a sardonic smile. "Records made by male historians, you mean? How true. But sometimes there are diaries, notes written by proud daughters and granddaughters, even annotated photographs in old albums. An expert might be able to determine the approximate date, possibly even the region of the country where it originated, from the type of fabric, the prints, the dyes. I'm surprised at you, Pat—and you too, Adam. You're supposed to be scholars; if you ran into a problem in a field with which you weren't familiar—paleobotany or medieval French art, for example—you'd consult an expert. Why didn't you ask Rachel? She could have told you all this."

"If you're accusing me of male chauvinism," Pat began furiously.

"They were afraid to ask me," Rachel said. "I have a habit of going into fits when people ask me direct questions. It's unnerving."

After a moment Kara said, "Yes, I see. Sorry, Pat."

"You have a point, though," Pat admitted. "I wasn't thinking of this as a legitimate research project. Old habits die hard. So you're willing to accept my hypothesis?"

Instead of answering, Kara went to the bookshelf. Selecting a book, she found the page she wanted and began to read aloud. "'My whole life is in that quilt. All my joys and all my sorrows are stitched into those little pieces. My hopes and fears, my loves and hates. I tremble sometimes when I remember what that quilt knows about me.'"

"What's that?" Pat made a grab for the book.

"It has nothing to do with your quilt," Kara said. "But it supports your theory, doesn't it? I remember hearing another woman talk about her embroidery. There was one piece I wanted to buy, but she wouldn't sell it. 'There's too much in that tablecloth,' she said. 'The times I sat by the baby's crib, loving him and thanking the Lord for him; the days I watched over my girls while they played, safe and happy; the nights I waited for my son to come home, not knowing where he was or what kind of trouble he could be in, and my hands shaking so bad I couldn't hardly hold the needle. See that part there, how uneven the stiches are? I should have pulled them out, but I won't. Because he did come home, and he's a grown-up man now, and a good man.' Then she laughed, a little sheepishly, and she said, 'I stitched my soul into that tablecloth, Miz Brinckley. What price could I put on that?'"

"Stitched her soul into it," Pat repeated. "Did she really believe her sewing brought a wayward youth safe home to mama? Hell's bells, superstition is my speciality. How could I have missed this sort of thing?"

"Because you're a man," Kara said tolerantly. "Women don't talk about 'this sort of thing' to supercilious male scholars. They're afraid they will be laughed at."

Her eyes met Rachel's in a long look of understanding and private amusement.

"They don't think of it as working magic," Rachel explained. "They don't really believe in it, but . . . 'It don't do no harm.' Isn't that what people say, when they toss a pinch of spilled salt over their shoulders or walk wide around a black cat? Modern superstitions are based on ancient religious and magical practices."

"Don't lecture me on my own field, young woman!" Pat shouted.

"Seems to me you're not the expert you thought you were," Kara said. "And that what you need right now is a little more action and a little less theorizing."

Pat began, "That book—"

"Yes, that book. If the author did her research, and if she was lucky, she was able to trace the ownership of the quilt back to its maker. But we can't waste time looking through books at random; there are dozens, possibly hundreds, of them. The quickest way to find it is to ask Mrs. Wilson. Shut up, Pat, I can't hear with you swearing."

She had picked up the telephone and dialed. After a brief conversation with someone—her secretary or housekeeper—she reached for a pen, wrote down a telephone number, and dialed again. The ensuing conversation was also brief. Kara slammed the phone back into the cradle.

"What a bitch. 'Ah'm afraid Ah'm too busy right now, but Ah might could spare you a few minutes later today, if it's all that important to you.'"

Her imitation of Mrs. Wilson trying to sound like a southern lady was cruelly accurate. She added sourly, "This is probably going to cost me money, Pat. I had to let her think I was after the quilts, and it's a mistake to sound too eager."

"Now just a cotton-pickin' minute," Pat exclaimed.

"Oooh, how cute." Kara grinned offensively.

"Don't fight," Adam pleaded.

"We're not fighting." Pat's grin was equally provocative. "Just trying to settle a little matter of the chain of command. I'm obviously the best person to talk to Mrs. Bitch. I can get more out of her than you can. I'll tell her I'm writing an article. I'm a historian—"

"No, you're not, you're just a bloody anthropologist. And a man. Two strikes against you." Kara glanced at Rachel and her smile faded. "Don't be misled, Rachel. We go on like this all the time. It doesn't mean we aren't taking the situation seriously."

"I know." Rachel glanced at Pat's apoplectic countenance and added wryly, "I suppose I'll get used to it."

Kara sat down on the arm of the sofa. "Seriously, Pat, I have an edge with Mrs. Wilson you lack. You can talk to her about research till you're blue in the face. She's not interested in history or genealogy, she's interested in money, and she's not the type to give anything, including information, away for free. My pitch will be that I need to know where the quilts originated in order to establish a fair price. They're worth more if they have a provenance—that's true, and she probably knows it. She'll be anxious to cooperate."

"Huh." She was right and he was too honest to deny it, but the grunt was as much of an admission as she was likely to get. "So what are Adam and I supposed to do, follow you around and take notes?"

"You can start by cleaning up that mess in the workroom."

"Who, me?"

"If you can con Adam into doing it, that's fine with me. For heaven's sake, Pat, stop grunting and rolling your eyes and playing ego games. There's too much at stake."

"Okay, okay. Suppose I take a sample and have that stuff analyzed."

"Good idea. Then you and Adam can search the house. Obviously he didn't do a thorough job the first time."

"Pat told me to concentrate on places where Rachel wasn't likely to go," Adam protested. "She works in that room—"

"You don't know where she's likely to go or what she is likely to do," Kara said. "That's the trouble with your procedure, Pat; instead of looking for evidence on which to base a theory, you act as if your tentative hypothesis were a fact. You had better start with the workroom. Rachel and I will help you."

The job took over an hour. They cleared every cupboard and emptied every drawer and opened every bottle and jar. Adam even checked the wiring. Finally Kara said, "I don't think we've missed anything. Have you guys got the hang of it now? Can we trust you to do as thorough a job elsewhere?"

Pat got stiffly to his feet. "Don't push me too far, Kara. I don't mind eating a little crow but you're rubbing it in. And don't tell me I'm mixing my metaphors."

"Would I do that?" Kara tucked a loosened lock of hair back under her scarf and glanced at her watch. "We've got just enough time to finish in here before we call on Mrs. Wilson. Take this cloth, Pat, and dust those shelves before you replace the materials. And stop glowering. I'm going to tell Cheryl we decided to give the place a good cleaning if she notices, as she surely will, that things have been disturbed."

"You think of everything, don't you?" Pat didn't stop glowering, but he took the dust cloth and there was grudging admiration in his voice.

By the time Kara was satisfied, the room had been restored to order, Mrs. Grossmuller's "whites" were soaking in a mixture of water and bleach, and the mysterious bottle had been sealed in a plastic bag. The only remaining evidence was a stain on the tiled floor. Adam had wiped up the puddle, but the stain had proved resistant to soap and water.

"It is indelible," Kara murmured. "I wonder if bleach—"

"Leave it for now," Pat said. "Once we find out what it is, we can figure out what cleaning agent will be most effective."

"Very good." Kara gave him an approving smile. "Old dogs can be taught new tricks, I see."

"Oh, I'm loving every moment of this. Next you can teach me how to knit."

Kara allowed herself only ten minutes for lunch. "I have to change clothes," she explained. "Looking rich is part of the technique of intimidating a seller."

"I thought the idea was to look poor," Adam said interestedly.

"That may work in the bazaars of the Near East and in flea markets, but it's not effective with people like Mrs. Wilson. You have to intimidate them or they will try to intimidate you. You needn't bother changing, Rachel," she added. "I can intimidate enough for both of us."

Rachel hadn't realized she was expected to go along. The idea wasn't especially appealing, but she didn't argue. Might as well argue with a tornado. She was still dazed by Kara's calm acceptance of the incredible and by her energetic response.

When Kara came back she looked like Cinderella after the fairy godmother's visit. Rachel recognized the dress; it was a thirties silk print from the shop. Kara's hair was pinned up with a pair of faux tortoiseshell barrettes from the same source, and her makeup was impeccable.

"Lucky Cheryl and I wear the same size shoes," she said, seeing Rachel stare at the smart pumps. "Well—almost the same size. These pinch like hell but I can stand it for a couple of hours. Ready, Rachel? While we're gone, you guys can investigate the upstairs kitchen. Toss anything that looks suspicious."

Pat tugged at his forelock. "Yes, ma'am."

Kara seemed preoccupied, frowning as she drove. When they halted at the stoplight in the middle of town she reached into her purse and handed Rachel a small bottle.

"You don't remember this, I suppose."

According to the label the bottle contained foundation, a popular, moderately expensive brand. "It's not mine," Rachel said. She had a premonition of what Kara was going to say.

"No, it's Cheryl's." The light changed. A horn behind them blared and Kara rolled down the window and made a rude hand gesture before transferring her foot from the brake to the gas. "While I was up there I thought I might as well look through the medicine chest in her—their—bathroom."

"What—what's wrong with it?"

"Something gritty has been added." Kara rolled up the window. "Can't be ground glass, it doesn't sparkle. Can't be sand, it's too sharp."

"So if she put it on her face . . . "

"It wouldn't have done her complexion any good." Kara's voice was quite calm. "Ever seen her put on makeup? Hard and fast, the way she does everything. She probably wouldn't have noticed anything was wrong until after she slapped the first lot on."

Rachel eyed the little bottle as if it had been a snake coiled to strike. "I can't stand this," she muttered. "I've got to leave that house. Now, today."

"Copping out? No. You're not going anyplace until we've settled this business—one way or the other."

"Why are you doing this?" Rachel whispered.

Kara's eyes remained fixed on the road. "I'll let you know when I've figured it out myself. There's a notebook in my purse. Get it, and a pen if you don't have one with you. Do you take shorthand? No? Well, do the best you can. Write everything down. That's part of the intimidation process," she added with a tight smile.

Mrs. Wilson lived in one of the subdivisions that had grown up around the old town. The curving streets had names like Azalea Drive and Dogwood Lane and the houses sprawled pretentiously over a quarter-acre of land. After a wrong turn—"The damned woman doesn't know right from left," Kara grunted—they found Daffodil Court. Kara had a final word of instruction. "Let me do the talking."

If she hadn't been so distracted Rachel would have been amused at the unarmed combat between Kara and Mrs. Wilson. The latter was also familiar with the basic tactics; she just didn't employ them as skillfully as her opponent. Her dress was too fussy and too formal, glittering with sequins and beads, and she wore too much jewelry—all of it fake, except for her engagement and wedding rings. The living room was painfully neat, every cushion "plumped," every wooden surface slick with polish. The mantel over the fireplace (gas) held a row of family photographs. The "entertainment center" covered an entire wall, the single bookcase contained a few bestsellers and *Readers' Digest* condensed books plus a collection of collectors' plates featuring scenes from *Gone With the Wind*, and a two-foot-tall Scarlett O'Hara doll wearing the famous "barbecue" dress.

Rachel told herself not to be a snob.

Kara didn't bother concealing her feelings. The curl of her lip relaxed only once, when she admired a massive silver candelabrum.

"It was Auntie's," Mrs. Wilson said, eyes alert. "Been in the family for a hundred years. You and your partner interested in old silver?"

Kara parried with a denial that left open the possibility of a deal if the price was right. The duel went on while Mrs. Wilson poured tea and offered a plate of cookies. She gave Rachel a sharp look when the latter took out her notebook, but made no comment. The courtesies having been satisfied by the serving of tea, she got down to business.

"Auntie had a lot of nice things, but I just don't have the room for them. I spent a lot of time and money getting my place like I want it and her old things don't fit my day-cor. Besides, I've got a boy going off to college, and you know how much that costs these days."

Kara shifted position, grimacing slightly. The shoes must be pinching. "Yes, it's frightful, isn't it? I'd be happy to look over your aunt's furniture and other things, but my partner and I are primarily interested in fabrics. Vintage clothing—it has to be at least fifty years old and in excellent condition—"

"I don't think she had anything like that, but I can look. If the damned cops ever finish," she added spitefully. "How about jewelry?"

"If it's old and genuine. We don't buy costume jewelry."

"Oh. But you want the quilts?"

"Were the stolen quilts the only ones she had?"

"I guess so. They was the ones she made all the fuss about. They're worth quite a bit. One of them was in a book."

She couldn't remember what book it was. Yes, Auntie had a copy of it, but it was still back at the house, and there was no use asking the damned cops to let her have it; they said nothing could be taken away till they got through investigating.

Kara cut short a diatribe on the damned cops. She was beginning to lose patience and Mrs. Wilson, more sensitive to nuances than one might have supposed, took offense at her blunt questions. Her answers became brusque and even less informative. She didn't have the faintest notion who had made the quilts. They had come down from mother to daughter over many generations; Auntie was the last of the direct line. No, she didn't have any family albums. Maybe Auntie had some but there was no use asking the damned cops . . .

Rachel got up and went to the fireplace. "What a handsome little boy," she said, indicating one of the photos on the mantel. "Is this your son, Mrs. Wilson?"

The question distracted Mrs. Wilson from the iniquities of the cops. A smile of maternal pride spread over her face. "Yes, that's my Rocky. Six years old he was when that was made. That one at the end is the latest, he's seventeen now."

Several of the others showed the same face, at various ages. The features were clean-cut and not unattractive, though "handsome" had been a deliberate exaggeration on Rachel's part. The thing that struck her most forcefully was the self-satisfied expression. Not surprising, perhaps, in an only son who was obviously the apple of mummy's eye.

"He looks like you," Rachel lied. "And this gentleman—is he your father?"

Mrs. Wilson beamed. They examined the photographs one by one and Mrs. Wilson told her all about the subjects. Rachel saw that Kara had retrieved the abandoned notebook and was scribbling busily.

Mrs. Wilson was rambling happily on about her granddaddy (he had been mayor of a town Rachel had never heard of) when the front door opened and slammed, and a man appeared in the doorway. Rachel knew that face well by now, though its expression was more surprised than smug.

"Why, darlin', I didn't expect you back so soon," Mrs. Wilson exclaimed. "Didn't you have practice today? He's the star of the basketball team," she added, face aglow.

He was tall enough, at any rate—six five or six. Thick brown hair was brushed back from his face. He was wearing an expensive leather jacket and the regulation overpriced sneakers.

"I didn't feel like it," Rocky said. "Excuse me, Mam. I didn't know you had company."

"Come in and be introduced, honey. You don't know these ladies. This is Miz Brinckley—her husband is the congressman, and she's gonna buy those old quilts of Auntie's. And this . . . "

She had obviously forgotten not only her manners but Rachel's name. Rachel supplied it. Rocky murmured something but did not look directly at her. The photographs had done him an injustice, Rachel thought; he appeared to be rather shy.

Rocky declined an invitation to join them, shuffled his feet, directed a muttered, "Nice to meet you," at the air between Rachel and Kara, and withdrew. His mother sighed.

"He's such a good boy. A mother couldn't ask for a better son."

"He has nice manners," Kara said, trying to reestablish friendly relations.

She failed. "That's because he comes from a God-fearing nuc-lear family, with a daddy that works day and night to support his family and a mama that stays home like a woman should."

It was the first time Mrs. Wilson had referred to her husband. There was no photograph of him on the mantel. Looking from the spotless, sterile room to Mrs. Wilson's face, Rachel understood why Daddy put in a lot of overtime. If that was what he was doing.

Kara didn't respond to the veiled insult but she had had enough.

Rising with scarcely a wince, she said, "You probably have things to do, Mrs. Wilson. I didn't intend to keep you so long."

They parted with expressions of goodwill that were insincere on all sides, and Mrs. Wilson promised to let them know when the quilts would be available. "I'll see if I can dig up those old albums of Auntie's, too. You say the quilts are worth more if you can put a name to 'em?"

As soon as they were in the car Kara kicked off her shoes. "God, what a relief. Pride goeth before a blister on the toe. It was wasted effort, too. I pissed the old girl off. She wouldn't have given us any information if you hadn't buttered her up."

"It was a case of good cop, bad cop."

Kara shook her head. "No, I let my dislike get the better of me and I didn't bother hiding it. Overcompensation, I suppose. I used to be so meek and mealy-mouthed and wimpy—"

"You?" Rachel braced herself as Kara cut in ahead of another car.

Kara grinned. "Hard to believe, isn't it? I'll show you a picture sometime. I look the same in all of the ones from that time in my life— slumped and sloppy, with an expression like that of a worried hound. I threw most of them away, especially the ones of me and my ex—I was always behind him, sort of huddled, if you know what I mean—but I kept one to remind me of what I was, and hope never to be again. Maybe I've gone too far in the opposite direction. I didn't have to be so overbearing with Pat."

"I don't think he minded." Rachel studied the elegant figure beside her unbelievingly. "Sloppy?"

"Fat and sloppy. I'm still overweight," Kara added cheerfully. "The difference is I don't give a damn."

"You don't look overweight."

"That's because I don't give a damn. Wearing the right clothes helps. I had to learn how to do that too. It's not just vanity; knowing you look good makes you more confident. And being confident makes you look good. Sorry. I didn't mean to lecture."

She didn't speak again except to mutter curses at the other drivers who got in her way. The early winter dusk had fallen and traffic was thickening. When they reached the house they found only Adam.

"Pat had to go," he explained. "Any luck?"

"Some. Rachel will tell you, I have to leave too." She had obviously worked out her plans as she drove; her sentences were quick and decided, offering no opening for discussion. "I'll be back in the morning, and I'll plan to stay for a few days. You can spend the evening looking through Cheryl's quilt books, Rachel."

"She's got a date," Adam said.

"Oh, lord," Rachel exclaimed. "I'd forgotten about him."

"Who's him?" Kara asked.

"Tom. Tony's friend. It's not really a date, he's just being conscientious. I could call him and cancel."

"No, don't do that. It's always useful to have a cop for a friend." Kara studied her thoughtfully. "I don't know whether Cheryl mentioned it, Rachel, but you're welcome to borrow clothes from stock. So long as it's not one of the designer models."

Rachel felt herself stiffen. "That's very kind, but I'd rather not. I do have a few decent outfits, believe it or not."

"Then put one of them on." Kara's smile softened the blunt words. "I don't think Tom's motives are purely professional. Work your wiles and see what you can get out of him. They must have some ideas about the murder and theft, they just aren't talking to civilians."

"I could look at the books," Adam offered.

"You don't know what you're looking for. Come on, Rachel, I'll go up with you. If I walk one more step in these shoes I'll be crippled for life."

Rachel half expected Kara to stay and inspect her ensemble, like a critical big sister, but Kara put her head in the door only long enough to say good night before her sneakered feet proceeded on down the stairs. It had taken her only a few minutes to change. Rachel was still looking through her scanty wardrobe trying to decide what to wear.

There wasn't as much choice as she had claimed. In fact, the only thing she owned that would have met Kara's standards was the cashmere sweater her mother had sent for Christmas. It ought to be cleaned before being worn again, and the skirt that went with it had unpleasantly suggestive stains at the hem. The cranberry sauce had splashed.

Irritably Rachel tossed both garments onto a chair and pulled out a Viyella plaid shirt—another of her mother's contributions. Tom would have to put up with pants, she didn't have another decent skirt.

There was just time to shower and change before Tom arrived, if she hurried. It was too late to cancel now. She wished she had remembered the appointment earlier, in time to back out. She was so tired she could hardly move, so tired the very idea of bright conversation, much less womanly wiles, brought a groan to her lips. It had been quite a day. Just being around Kara was enough to wear a person out. All that energy—and the astonishing, unexpected, wholehearted acceptance. Kara might not like her, but for reasons Rachel could not fathom Kara was backing her one hundred percent.

The long mirror in the bathroom reflected a depressing image. It looked just the way she felt—slumped, sloppy, and morose. Maybe that was why Kara was taking her part—pity, laced with contempt, for a woman as wimpish and helpless as she had once been.

It was not a pleasant thought. But Kara had tried to be nice. In her way . . .

Tom had already arrived when Rachel came downstairs. Seated in the rocking chair with a cat on his lap, he was trying to fend off Adam's enthusiastic hospitality. "Coffee? Wine? How about a drink? Bourbon, scotch, vodka, cola, mineral water—"

"No, thanks." Tom got to his feet, one hand supporting the cat, which had attached itself, purring hysterically, to his shoulder. "Hi, Rachel. Do we take the cat with us? It seems to be stuck; I don't know how to get it off."

"That's why we call her Crazy Glue," Adam explained. "She's very affectionate."

Rachel detached the cat, claw by claw, and, with malicious intent, handed her to Adam. The fickle animal transferred the claws to Adam's sweater and purred even louder.

As the evening progressed, it dawned on Rachel that Tom wasn't just being conscientious, and that so far as he was concerned, this was a date. He didn't mention the case, and he kept apologizing for the restaurant. "It's not very fancy, but the food is good. I come here a lot and they know me, and . . . Is this table all right? That one over there might be better."

She suspected he had picked the restaurant because he was well known there. The hostess greeted him by name and the proprietor took their order himself. Men enjoy things like that, she thought, smothering a smile, and then realized she was being sexist. She was enjoying herself too, and for the same reasons—personal attention, a little flattery.

The conversation ranged from personal confidences to personal tastes and interests—the subjects people talk about when they want to know one another better. Tom's face lit up when she said she liked jazz and poetry, and fell when she admitted she considered baseball the most boring sport ever invented. "If you knew more about it you wouldn't feel that way. Tell you what; come with me to watch the Orioles play sometime, and I'll explain it to you."

"I thought baseball season didn't start till spring."

"That's not so far away. 'If winter comes, can spring be far behind?'"

He looked so childishly pleased with himself at having found an appropriate quotation that Rachel laughed, and then apologized.

"That's okay." His hand closed over hers. "I'd make a fool of myself any day to see you look like that."

Rachel's eyes fell, and he released her hand. "I know there's something bothering you, something that's made you wary and defensive. If you ever want to tell me—if I can do anything . . . "

Help me exorcise my ghost.

Rachel bit her lip. She could imagine how sensible, practical Tom would react to that statement. She didn't doubt he meant the offer though. It was the second such offer she had received in the past two days. Was it pure coincidence that she had met two men who talked like heroes of old-fashioned romances, or was there something about her?

"What did that guy do to you?"

Rachel stared at him. He looked down at his plate. "Damn. I didn't mean to say that. I didn't intend to talk about the case. I wanted to forget about it—let you forget about it for a while. But maybe . . . Is that what's bothering you?"

"Partly." She remembered what Kara had said. It was better than the truth, anyhow. "I don't mind talking about it, Tom. It doesn't bother me as much as you think, honestly, but I'd certainly be relieved to know you had located him."

"We will. We're following several promising leads." He hesitated, torn between professional discretion and personal feelings. "Rachel,

I'm ninety percent certain he's out of the picture. Out of state, out of your life. On the run."

"You've identified him?"

"Well . . . Not absolutely. But we've got a suspect who fits the criteria and there's an APB out on him. Some cop somewhere will pick him up sooner or later, and then we can get a positive ID. Tony agrees with me—"

"You've talked with Tony about this?"

"Sure. He calls at least once a day. So you can stop worrying. The guy is miles away by this time." .

"That's good news."

"Keep it confidential, will you?"

"Of course," Rachel said.

Tom beckoned the hovering waiter. "How about dessert? They make a great tiramisù."

He was determined, so she accepted. The tiramisù was excellent; Tom was glad to finish hers. They were drinking coffee when the waiter sidled up to the table and informed Tom he was wanted on the phone.

"I thought you were off duty," Rachel said, drawing the obvious and inevitable conclusion, not only from the interruption but from the change in his expression.

"Back in a minute."

He was, looking even grimmer. "So much for my brilliant deductions. Rachel, I hate to do this, but you'll have to come with me."

"To the station?"

"To the shop. Your friend Adam just called the station. He caught someone trying to break in."

ten

Warned by the dogs, Adam had the door open when they arrived. "It's okay," he said, when Tom would have held Rachel back. His tone was mildly indignant. "I told you I had the situation under control."

"You sure have." Tom studied the figure that lay on the floor. Overlapping coils of clothesline were wrapped around it, and a long woolen scarf—one of Adam's, to judge by its frizzled appearance—covered the lower part of its face. At the sight of Rachel it began to thrash around, dislodging Patches, who had been trying to curl up on its stomach.

"Did you have to use quite so much rope?" Tom inquired.

"I didn't want to hurt him."

"Considerate of you."

"He was fighting dirty and I was getting mad," Adam explained. "Then he started using vulgar language—"

"I see. Well, get that gag off so Rachel can have a look at him."

"I know who he is," Rachel said.

Adam yanked off the scarf, none too gently.

No man looks at his best in such a position, but if his face hadn't been so distorted by fury it would not have been unattractive. By conventional standards his features were better shaped than the comical conglomeration that occupied Adam's face. Funny, Rachel thought, with critical detachment, I used to think he was good-looking. It wasn't the bones and muscle and shape, it was the expression. Even when he smiled his eyes had been angry.

At the moment he was—with cause, she had to admit—extremely angry. Spitting out a mouthful of fuzz, he began to speak. After a while Tom said, "That's enough."

"Enough, hell! I haven't even started—"

Tom didn't raise his voice. "I'm a police officer. If you have a complaint it will be heard at the proper time. Rachel, is this guy who he says he is?"

Rachel's face felt as if it were on fire. Choked with rage and wool threads though they had been, the adjectives directed at her had been only too intelligible.

"His name is Philip Marshall. He's a former—friend of mine."

"Some friend," said Adam. "Sneaking around the house, peering in the windows—"

"That will do," Tom said wearily. "Untie him, Adam, and keep quiet. Mr. Marshall, let's hear your version of what happened."

Rachel could see that Phil had been drinking, but he was sober enough to realize that further outbursts would damage his position. He claimed he had come to the door like any normal caller, asking for her, and that Adam had first insulted and then attacked him. Unfortunately his attempt at dignified self-control was slightly marred by Adam, who had refused to cut the ropes—"Why ruin a perfectly good piece of clothesline?"—and was circling him like a dancer around a maypole, coiling the clothesline as he unwound it. Two of the cats followed him, pouncing on the dangling end. By the time he finished freeing his prisoner, Rachel's anger and embarrassment had been replaced by a wild desire to laugh, and Tom was having trouble controlling his mouth.

"Thank you, Mr. Marshall," he said, looking up from his notebook. "What do you have to say, Dr. Nugent?"

"It's a big fat lie from start to finish," Adam said. "I heard the dogs and went out to see what was going on. Caught this guy on the front porch trying to see in the window."

Rachel didn't doubt his version was the truth and Tom obviously shared her opinion, but after an exchange of denials and contradictions, he said wearily, "All right, enough. I can't hold him on anything,

Adam, it's your word against his. Mr. Marshall, do you want to prefer charges?"

"I just want to get away from this hairy Neanderthal," Phil growled. "Your tastes have certainly deteriorated, Rachel, but you've made your bed and if you choose to share it with—"

Adam took a step toward him and he scuttled out the door.

Adam closed it. "Well," he said. "Uh. Did you have a nice time? What about a cup of coffee?"

Tom closed his notebook and stood up. "Thanks, but I'd better be going. Good night, Rachel."

"Thank you for a lovely evening." They shook hands while Adam beamed paternally.

After Tom had left, Adam became very busy, letting the dogs out, wiping the sink, sweeping the floor. Absently stroking the omnipresent Crazy Glue, Rachel watched him in silence. Eventually Adam ran out of chores. He replaced the broom and turned to face Rachel.

"Did you have—"

"Yes."

"Look, I'm sorry about—"

"That's all right."

"Are you mad?"

"No," Rachel said. Getting mad at him was a waste of time. In some ways he was as naive as a child, in others as devious as an atheistic shaman. Even raging paranoia couldn't believe Adam had conjured up a presumed burglar as an excuse for getting her home early, but she was convinced he had known from the start who Phil was. It hadn't been necessary to call the police, or ask for Tom.

"I guess he won't be back," Adam said.

"I hope not. This situation is complicated enough without him."

"Yeah. Did you get any information out of Tom?"

"No."

She had promised not to repeat Tom's reassurance, and although she wasn't "mad" at Adam, she was annoyed. Her annoyance increased when Adam said shrewdly, "There's been no sign of the Alleged for days. He's probably skipped town."

"I hope so."

"Which leaves us with only one remaining difficulty."

"Is that what you call it?"

Adam ignored this. "And now we've got Kara on our side. She's an amazing woman, you know that? The way she put Pat in his place . . . You sure you don't want coffee or something? It's still early."

"It certainly is." How would the evening have ended, she wondered, if Phil hadn't turned up to disrupt it? Tom probably wouldn't have suggested they go to his place, not at this stage in a relationship which was in part professional, but he might not have considered a few friendly gestures unprofessional. She pictured them sitting in his car outside the house, with Tom's arm around her and his mouth searching for hers—and a large shadowy shape hovering in the doorway. Or would Adam have trotted out to the car with cheerful greetings and hospitable offerings of food and drink?

She laughed involuntarily. "Oh, all right. Coffee."

Adam's worried frown smoothed out. She watched him fill a cup and add a little milk—he already knew how she took her coffee, he didn't have to ask—acknowledging if only to herself that the comic relief Adam supplied had helped to maintain her mental balance. Who was it who said that sardonic laughter was a homeopathic protection against total disintegration? Or, to put it less pedantically, sometimes you have to laugh to keep from falling apart. Had Adam developed his lunatic habits as a means of protecting himself from emotional pressure, or was it the result of natural joie de vivre?

"You were looking at the quilt books," she said, glancing at the stack on the table. "I don't suppose you found anything."

"No. It was a waste of time, I guess. The only one I might recognize was the—what do you call it?"

"Album quilt," Rachel said, resisting the temptation to suggest a more theatrical name. She began leafing through one of the books. "I'm not sure I would spot the others either. Especially the white on white; I've forgotten the details of the quilting."

"You could ask Tom to check the old lady's bookshelf."

"I didn't think of that." Rachel thought about it. "Yes, why not? He wouldn't be breaking any rules by telling me the names of the quilt books she owned. I'll call him tomorrow."

"Why not now?" He added blandly, "It's still early."

Rachel was prepared to offer Tom a long complicated explanation for her interest in the books, but it wasn't necessary; he apparently saw nothing unreasonable about the question. "Sure, I'll see if I can get around to it tomorrow. I'm glad you called, Rachel, I wanted to apologize—"

"There's no need for you to apologize," Rachel murmured. "I'm sorry the evening ended as it did. I was having a lovely time."

She looked at Adam, who gave her a broad, unrepentant grin.

"Me too," Tom said. "Are you willing to give it another try?"

"Anytime."

"Great. I'll call you tomorrow, then."

"I'll look forward to it."

"That was disgusting," Adam said, as she returned the phone to its cradle. "You were purring like one of the cats."

This time his light tone struck a false note. The repetition of the word *tomorrow* had made Rachel realize how little time they had. Another comment of Adam's came back to her with an urgency that might or might not have been coincidental.

"There's something I want to do before I go to bed," she said. "I want you to help me. Watch me."

"What?"

"Search the children's rooms."

"I already did. While you were gone." He gave her a reassuring nod. "Nothing."

"I want to do it again. Now."

Joe's room looked as she had left it and she was glad she had gotten rid of the encrusted glasses and scraps of food. They had had a particularly evil look. Adam's vigorous probing under the bed with a broom dislodged an overlooked soft drink can, but nothing suspicious turned up, in the drawers or the closet or under the furniture. At Rachel's insistence they stripped the bed and turned the mattress (she knew by Adam's guilty look he hadn't thought of that). The copy of *Hustler* brought a smile to his face, but he replaced it without comment.

Megan's room took even longer. She had enough stuffed animals to equip a toy store, and Rachel made Adam squeeze each one of them from its furry head to its fuzzy legs. While he watched, she emptied the bureau drawers and inspected each miniature garment before replacing it. She probed the tiny shoes with her fingers, and checked the wooden toys for splinters and protruding nails. Megan's canopied bed looked like a wedding cake; smothered by ruffles, Rachel examined the legs and the supports of the box springs, shaking and tugging at them. She made Adam climb on a chair to inspect the frilly canopy and its frame.

"That wouldn't hurt her seriously even if it did fall down. It's too lightweight." But he did as she asked.

"Now the closet."

There were things at the back of Megan's closet that should not have been there. Rachel wondered whether Joe was still looking for his fielder's mitt; it was now serving as a mattress for plastic figures of six of the Seven Dwarfs. A pair of glittery evening pumps must be Cheryl's, and other souvenirs testified to Megan's affection for the remaining members of her family.

By the time they finished it was two a.m. and Rachel was shaking with fatigue and nerves. "No more tonight," Adam said firmly. "We'll do Jerry's room tomorrow."

"All right." But she stood still in the middle of the room and closed her eyes, reaching in toward the dark, closed-off place in her mind with a mental probe as emphatic as the physical probes she had employed earlier. There was nothing, not even a psychic wall—only emptiness and withdrawal and the faintest, vaguest impression of . . .

"Rachel." Adam's voice, low and urgent, pulled her back to reality before she could identify what she had felt. "Was there a particular reason why you wanted to do this tonight?"

"I . . . " Rachel rubbed her aching forehead. "I remembered what you said. About Medea."

"Son of a bitch." The words exploded out of him. "Me, I mean. I should learn to keep my big mouth shut."

"I would have thought of it sooner or later. I was going to mention her in my dissertation. The gown she sent her successful rival was embroidered as well as poisoned—poisoned by magic, by the curses she wove and sewed into it. But the revenge she took on her faithless husband was worse. Destroying his children—her children—"

"Stop it, Rachel. There's no parallel between the two cases. None at all. It isn't Tony you—she—"

"Whoever," Rachel said wearily. "I don't want to hurt any of them. But if I did want to inflict pain on a woman I hated, what more effective revenge could there be than striking at her children? If I were that demented, I wouldn't care who else was hurt."

•   •   •

When Rachel opened her door the next morning, Adam was still asleep. She would have tripped over him if she had not expected he would be there.

He was sleeping so soundly that he had not heard her alarm. She had set it because she didn't want Kara to find her still in bed, and she feared she might oversleep. It had taken her some time to fall asleep; lying open-eyed in the dark she had mentally searched the rooms again and again, wondering what she might have overlooked. How could she possibly allow the children to occupy those rooms again, if there was the slightest chance of danger?

Adam must have lain awake too. He had been even more disturbed than she by what she had said, and he was too intelligent and too honest to deny the possibility that she had been right. His breathing was deep and even, but he looked uncomfortable, probably because there was a cat on either side of him and a third on his chest. The effect of this, in the shadowy light of early morning, was to make it appear that his beard had grown a foot longer overnight. Rachel had developed a violent antagonism toward that beard; it was almost impossible to know what Adam was thinking when every feature except his nose was covered with hair. That was probably why he had grown the damned thing, so he could hide behind it.

She stepped over him and headed for the bathroom, followed by the cats. They were vocally annoyed when she refused to be herded toward the stairs. Their complaints woke Adam; when she came out of the bathroom he and the sleeping bag were gone.

But when she stopped on her way downstairs to try the door of Megan's room, she heard his door open.

"You locked it," she said.

"I thought you wanted me to."

"I did. Thanks."

Sunshine warmed the family room, brightening the cheerful yellow print of the curtains and setting the copper bottoms of the saucepans ablaze with reflected light. When Adam came back from letting the dogs out, he said, "It's going to be a nice day. Freezing cold but bright and sunny."

"I'm delighted to hear it." Hands braced on the counter, Rachel stared at the coffeemaker, willing it to drip faster.

"I wouldn't be surprised if—"

"Adam, will you please shut up?"

Rachel managed to get one cup of coffee before Kara arrived, which was just as well; the other woman's bright-eyed, firm-lipped efficiency was hard to take even with the artificial assistance of caffeine. Not that she didn't appreciate the support. But Kara's interest was impersonal and detached. She doesn't care about me, Rachel thought; in the last extremity, if there is no other way, she'll rid herself, and the ones she really cares about, of me. As she should.

After she had deposited an armload of books and papers on the table and removed her coat, Kara studied them critically. "You both look like hell," she remarked. "What did you do last night, if it's any of my business?"

Rachel let Adam tell her about Phil. He made a long dramatic story of it, but Kara's only reaction was amusement. "That's the trouble with life. It's so untidy. The characters in novels hardly ever seem to worry about eating and sleeping and earning a living—much less putting the investigation on hold while they wait for the plumber to come and unstop the toilet, or cope with rejected lovers."

"He has a gun," Rachel said. She was on her second cup of coffee, but it hadn't made her any less resentful of Kara's attitude.

Her announcement had the desired effect. The sober faces of her companions made her regret her childish attempt to shock them.

"At least he used to own one," she amended. "When we were— when he was living at the house in College Park."

"He wasn't carrying it on him," Adam said. "Why didn't you tell me?"

His voice was mild, but Rachel flinched, as if he had shouted at her. "I didn't think he'd come here. It never occurred to me that you might . . . It was only for self-defense, in case someone broke into the house. He wouldn't . . . I'm sorry, Adam. I never thought—"

"I wasn't criticizing you, I was just asking," Adam said cheerfully.

"You should have told him." Kara's tone was decidedly critical. "Is this character likely to come gunning for you, Rachel? We don't need this! How unstable is he? What did you do to him?"

"I didn't do anything to him. Unless you consider telling him I never wanted to see him again legitimate grounds for assault. Some judges and juries still do."

Kara's face froze and a wave of color rose from the open collar of her shirt to the roots of her hair. After a moment she let out her breath. "If you want to kick me, I'll bend over. Blame the victim, right? And from me of all people . . . I didn't mean it that way. What I meant—"

"I overreacted," Rachel admitted. "But I get so tired of hearing people say 'She asked for it.' I know what you meant, and the answer is no, I don't think he'll be back. Not after the way Adam humiliated him. An anonymous phone call or two, maybe."

"If he tries that, sic Tom onto him," Kara advised. "Okay, I'll take your word for it. Get your coat, Rachel. We're supposed to meet Mrs. Wilson in half an hour."

The abrupt change of subject left Rachel staring. "Where? What happened?"

"She called me last night." Kara's smile would have made Mrs. Wilson extremely uneasy. "I thought she would. We're meeting at Auntie's house. The police have finished there and told her she's free to enter. She's going to look for the quilt book and search for photos and family records. And try to sell me Auntie's old furniture, worn-out clothes, and tacky costume jewelry. I just hope to hell I can get out of this without buying any."

"Can I come?" Adam asked.

"No reason why not, I guess. If you hurry."

Rachel had never formed a clear mental image of the house, but the reality was quite different from anything she might have imagined, and when she saw it she understood why it might have taken even friendly neighbors several days to realize that something had happened to the occupant. As anomalous on that street of modest, modern split-levels as a peacock in a flock of geese, it was a well-proportioned brick house surrounded by trees and shrubbery of impressive age and proportions. The peacock was molting, however. The lawn had been abandoned to weeds, the porch steps sagged, only a few flaking sections of paint remained on the shutters and trim, and several windows had been boarded up. Overgrown untrimmed lilac bushes and evergreens hid the house from its neighbor on the south side; the lot on the north side was presumably empty, since it was surrounded by a rough wooden fence bearing the sign of a local construction company. The rooms inside must always be dark, even on a sunny day. Rachel's skin felt as if it were tightening over her bones, and she wished she hadn't eaten a hearty breakfast.

No such morbid thoughts troubled Kara. Eyes narrowed speculatively, she murmured, "It's an old house—late nineteenth century, probably. If some of the contents are as old . . . "

A car pulled up behind them and Mrs. Wilson got out. She was all smiles, and although she obviously hadn't expected Adam, she greeted him affably. Probably thinks Kara brought him along to haul away the furniture, Rachel thought cynically.

Adam was even more affable. "Wonderful old house," he said, with more enthusiasm than accuracy. "I suppose the land on which the subdivision was built was part of the original property."

"Yes." Mrs. Wilson was brusque. "Auntie sold it off bit by bit over the years. That lot next door was the last. I told her and told her she ought to hang onto it, property values was going up and up. And what did she need the money for?"

The reminder of lost profit had annoyed her. She stamped off toward the house without waiting for an answer.

If the house in College Park had smelled musty and disused, this was ten times worse. Some of it, Rachel knew, was the product of her unbridled imagination, but not all. It was not surprising. An old woman couldn't keep up with the necessary cleaning and obviously none of her kin had bothered to help her. Mrs. Wilson, who had expected to inherit, could have brought her vacuum cleaner over once a month.

"Sorry I can't offer you tea or coffee," Mrs. Wilson said, switching on lights. "The kitchen's in a terrible state and I haven't had a chance to clean."

"That's quite all right," Kara said. "We haven't much time and I expect you are busy too."

"Yeah. Meeting my lawyer at the police station at one. You sure the cops'll give me those quilts back?"

"If your lawyer is any good they will. I told you what to say: they haven't the proper facilities for safeguarding items of that sort and if the quilts are damaged while they are in police custody they will be responsible. So long as you promise to produce them if they are needed in court there shouldn't be any problem." Kara sounded impatient. She must have explained all that before, and her quick comprehensive survey of the contents of the hall and parlor had obviously disappointed her. The furniture was Depression era—solid, well-built pieces, but not of the caliber she and Cheryl would choose.

"I sure hope you're right," Mrs. Wilson said. "Lord knows how long all this legal business is going to take, and if—when—Rocky gets accepted at the university, he'll need a new car and lots of other things besides tuition. Soon as the will's cleared I'll put this house on the market. Now where was it she kept them books?"

The answer should have been obvious. Like any miserly old woman with a (legitimate) fear of burglars, the old lady had kept all her treasures close at hand. Her bedroom resembled a storeroom, with piled-up boxes, cartons, and trunks filling all the space except for narrow paths from the door to the bed and the bed to the closet. Rachel wondered how much of the mess had been endemic and how much had been created by the thieves and/or the police. The cartons piled haphazardly on the bed certainly hadn't been placed there by the old lady. Fighting the malaise that had seized her at the first sight of the house, Rachel reminded herself that the old lady hadn't died in this room. But the bed hadn't been made or stripped; under the cartons she could see crumpled sheets and a pillow flattened and hollowed by the pressure of the head that had rested on it. Catching Adam's eye, she saw that his face mirrored her discomfort.

Mrs. Wilson did not share it. "Damn cops. You'd think they could at least pick up after themselves."

"They asked you to check to see if anything else was missing?" Kara's voice was cool and businesslike.

"Yeah. But how the hell could anybody tell? She did keep her jewelry and legal papers in a safe deposit," Mrs. Wilson admitted grudgingly. "The rest of this is junk. I mean—"

She looked hopefully at Kara, who said briskly, "Well, let's have a look."

She kept up a running commentary as she investigated the closet and the boxes containing linens. "No use to us, I'm afraid. She must have thrown out or worn out any clothing she wore before she was married. Nothing here earlier than the sixties, and it's in poor condition. Damask tablecloths . . . mass produced, nobody uses them anymore. Crocheted doilies . . . someone might give you a few bucks for them, but it won't be me, they're a glut on the market. Is that where she had the quilts?"

Mrs. Wilson had lifted the lid of a brassbound trunk. A strong smell of mothballs filled the room. "Uh-huh. There was only the three. You sure there's nothing else you want?"

"I'm sure. In fact . . . " Kara hesitated, weighing her words. "I don't mean to sound disparaging, Mrs. Wilson, but I don't understand the discrepancy between those quilts and the quality of her other things. The quilts are quite unusual. This stuff . . . isn't."

Typically, Mrs. Wilson reacted as if Kara had questioned her or her aunt's honesty. "They was hers, if that's what you mean."

"I didn't—"

"Come down to her from her great-granny. They were gentry, the Janneys; had lots of fine things. That was before the Wo-ah." Indignation deepened Mrs. Wilson's voice and thickened her accent. She hurried on, ignoring Kara's apologetic murmurs. "The damyankees burned the house and stole everything they could lay their thieving hands on. The silver and some other things was hid but they was divided among the children and grandchildren. Auntie only had that silver candlestick thing I showed you. And the quilts."

"And the house?" Adam asked.

"The plantation house was burned down, like I said. This one wasn't built till later." Mrs. Wilson had lost interest. She glanced at her watch. "So all you want is the quilts?"

"Yes." The flat-out admission cost Kara quite a struggle. She added, "Of course the price will depend on the documentation you can supply."

They found the quilt book without difficulty—the old lady's library was no more extensive than her grand-niece's—and Mrs. Wilson located a carton filled with scrapbooks, photos, and clippings, for which Kara gave her a written receipt. She made one last attempt to interest Kara in the parlor furnishings, including a framed wreath made of human hair. Kara declined this last with a visible shudder.

Adam had preceded them with the box of photographs. When they came out of the house they saw him standing on tiptoe, looking over the construction fence next door. Kara had to call him twice before he joined them.

"What's the hurry?" he asked, folding himself into the back seat.

Kara barely waited until he had closed the door before slamming the car into gear and pulling away from the curb. "Rachel," she said. "She's so pale she's turning green. The place really got to you, didn't it?"

"It was horrible," Rachel muttered. "Living like that . . . Dying like that . . . "

Adam put a steadying hand on her shoulder. "Don't think about it. Was that what bothered you, or was there . . . something else?"

"I don't know. I felt sick as soon as I set eyes on the place and it got steadily worse." She moved slightly, dislodging his hand. "I'm all right now."

"We got what we wanted, anyhow," Kara said. "Have a look at the quilt book, Rachel. I can't wait till we get back, I'm dying of curiosity."

With Adam breathing heavily onto the back of her neck, Rachel reached for the book. She didn't have to look through it; several sheets of folded paper marked the desired page.

"It's not the album quilt," she said. "It's the other. The white one."

Kara didn't take her eyes off the road. "Read the description. Read it aloud."

Rachel had to clear her throat before she complied. The answer they had sought and scarcely hoped to find was there. It seemed too easy.

"'Exquisite quilting and a remarkable sense of design characterize this white work quilt. The trapunto was inserted between the threads of the backing, so that the material was uncut. It was made by Mary Elizabeth Janney of Virginia in 1859 and is still in the possession of a descendant. The quality of the workmanship is typical of quilts made by antebellum planatation mistresses.' That's all. But this isn't the one—"

"The others must have been made by the same woman," Kara said. "They all date from approximately the same period and the author of the book is wrong about the quality of the workmanship; it isn't typical, it's extraordinary."

"You're right." Adam had taken the folded papers and was reading them. "It's all here, in the old lady's own hand. Mary Elizabeth Janney was her great-grandmother. She left the quilts to her daughter, who left them to her daughter, who was Miss Ora's mother."

"Mary Elizabeth," Rachel repeated. She was conscious of an odd feeling of anticlimax. The name should have struck a chord, shouldn't it? Recognition, empathy, acknowledgment? "Does Miss Ora say anything about her?"

"Quite a bit."

"Well?"

"Well. Um. It would make a good opening paragraph for a sentimental Southern novel. Want to hear it?"

"Of couse," Kara said impatiently.

"'She was exquisitely beautiful, with silver-gilt hair and eyes as blue as the Virginia heavens, and as talented as she was lovely. Her mother having died when she was twelve years of age, she assumed the manifold duties of a plantation mistress, supervising the food, clothing, and medical needs of family and servants. Yet she found the time to become a skilled performer on harp and piano and a fine needlewoman—'"

"All the womanly arts," said Kara. "I wonder if she ever read a book?"

"She probably didn't have time," Adam said fairly. "'Unfortunately the only examples of her skill that have come down to me are the three quilts. Her other descendants did not appreciate them as I do.' Shall I go on? There's a pretty description of Mary Elizabeth sitting and sewing with her maids—a polite euphemism for the female slaves, I assume."

"Spare me." Kara's foot was heavy on the gas.

When they reached the house there was another vehicle parked in front. "Pat's truck," Adam said unnecessarily.

They found Pat comfortably ensconced in the family room, studying the quilt photographs, which he had laid out on the coffee table like a pack of cards. Two cats, unable to find room on his lap, crouched at his feet waiting for him to lean back.

"Where've you been?" he demanded. "You could at least leave a note."

"You could at least tell someone you're coming," Kara retorted. "Have you found anything interesting?"

"Oh, definitely." Pat leaned back. "Somebody really had it in for the recipient of this quilt. Take a look."

"With luck we'll have the quilt itself tonight or tomorrow." Kara slung her jacket onto a chair.

"What?"

"You heard me."

"What have you been up to? And what's that?" He indicated the carton Adam was carrying.

Kara gave him a concise summary of their recent activities while Adam investigated the refrigerator. "Turkey sandwiches?" he offered.

"Ham, cheese, bologna, anything but turkey." Pat grimaced. "I've eaten turkey for two days and Ruth is making soup out of the bones at this very moment. So you found the book, did you? If you're waiting for compliments, Kara, you won't get them. I prefer to sulk."

"You and Adam can sulk together—and investigate the contents of that carton." Kara whipped out her notebook. "You've got a date and a name now; concentrate on that, but don't overlook any possible reference—"

"Don't tell me how to do research." Pat bared his teeth and then bit into the sandwich Adam offered him. "What esoteric bit of evidence are you going to pursue while we're slogging?"

"I'm going to be working in the shop. Dammit, I'm already a day behind," she added defensively. "Life goes on. If Rachel can give me a hand . . . "

She didn't finish the sentence. Rachel said quietly, "Yes, of course. I'd forgotten about the inventory."

"It's not the inventory," Kara admitted. "Cheryl's got everything on the computer; she's good at that sort of thing, all I have to do is bring it up to date. The problem is the sale tomorrow. Had I but known I wouldn't have scheduled it, but it's too late to cancel now."

"Of course," Rachel repeated. "Shall we start right away?"

"Not until you've had something to eat," Kara said "You still look a little peaked."

Pat's eyes narrowed. "What happened?"

"Nothing of concern to you," Kara answered. "It was a depressing, neglected house and any sensitive person would have felt uncomfortable at the scene of the poor old woman's death."

"If it was her house—Mary Elizabeth's," Pat began.

"It's not that old," Kara said. "Honestly, Pat, your imagination is getting out of hand. Are you finished, Rachel? I don't want to hurry you—"

Rachel rose obediently. She wasn't hungry anyway.

Kara *was* in a hurry. She went through the racks and drawers at top speed, removing objects and handing them to Rachel. Her memory was remarkable; with only a few exceptions, for which she had to refer to the inventory, she knew when every article had been purchased and how long it had been in stock.

"That should do it," she said at last. "We'll make that the sale rack; get the other items off it and into the nonsale section. And clear another table. This luncheon cloth can go, it's been here for over six months. And the basket of fake flowers and feathers, and these gloves, and this . . . "

Rachel had already had occasion to admire Cheryl's methodical arrangement of the records. Everything was cross-referenced, by date, type, and number; all she had to do was find the number Kara read off and enter the new price, which Kara was writing on the tag attached to the garment or piece of linen.

She had just begun this process when the door opened and Pat put his head in. "Adam wants to know," he began.

"Close that door!" Kara swooped down on Figgin, who was heading for a silk nightgown draped over a chair, along with other items intended for the sale rack. His abstracted expression was meant to suggest he was just out for a stroll with no ulterior purpose in mind.

"If you want coffee," Pat went on imperturbably. "How much longer are you going to be at this?"

"At least another hour." Kara thrust the cat at him. "No coffee. Go away."

"Actually, we're going out," Pat said. "And don't ask me where."

"I don't care where. How long will you be gone?"

"Couple of hours." He took a firmer grip on Figgin and backed away. "Shall we meet for tea at four?"

"All right," Kara said ungraciously. "Where were we, Rachel?"

Pat slammed the door.

It was almost four before Kara was satisfied. The last item she added to the rack of sale items was a christening dress trimmed with eyelet embroidery and finished with a lace frill around the high neck. "Mark it down to ninety bucks," she said. "We sell a lot of these. Though why anybody would cram a poor inoffensive baby into a tight, scratchy, tickly thing like this I can't imagine."

Her hands lingered on the little dress, however, straightening the long skirt and smoothing the neck frill.

The men hadn't returned. Rachel put the kettle on and Kara headed for the answering machine. The telephone had rung several times, but she had refused to interrupt her work to answer it. Most of the messages were from customers inquiring about the sale; Kara jotted down the numbers, muttering disagreeably. "All the information was on the notice I sent. Can't they read?"

Her face brightened when she heard Mrs. Wilson's voice, oily with triumph. "I got 'em. My lawyer says there won't be any trouble about selling 'em to you, seeing as how your brother-in-law is a cop and all. So as soon as we can agree on a price . . . Are you there? I guess not. Well, you better call me back. There are a couple other people interested."

Kara switched off the machine. "That's a lie. She must really be hard up for cash. Her son probably wants a new pair of sneakers or a Jag . . . Oh, thanks." She took the cup Rachel offered her and sat back with a sigh. "I wonder what Pat and Adam are doing. I'm just as glad they aren't back, though; I could do with a breather, and I expect you could too. You're a hard worker. I appreciate your help."

Rachel seated herself on the couch. The photographs lay on the table, but they had been disarranged, probably by one of the cats. Slowly she began putting them back in order. "Why are you doing this?" she asked, too tired to be less than direct. "You could just fire me. I would, if I were in your shoes. Is it because I remind you of yourself as you used to be?"

A few sips of tea had restored Kara to her usual energy. She leaned forward, her eyes bright with amusement. "My dear girl, at your worst you weren't as frumpy and grumpy and unattractive as I was. And you've changed. You're more . . . Oh, hell, I don't know what it is, but I'm not the only one who's noticed it. Adam, Tom . . . " She hesitated only briefly before adding, "And Tony. Don't shy away, Rachel, we need to talk about it and I'm not anxious to let my hair down in front of Pat and Adam. I don't think even Pat realizes how extraordinary Tony's behavior that night was. He can't help being gorgeous and kind and lovable, but he goes out of his way to avoid problems because he's only too well aware of the effect he has on women. You aren't the first, not by a damn sight. I was half in love with him once myself."

"Was he in love with you?"

"He thought he was." Kara kicked off her shoes and curled up in the big chair. "Or to be more accurate, he tried to believe he was. It was Cherry he wanted all along, but he thought he couldn't have her. So . . . Luckily we both had sense enough to know it wouldn't work, but there's still a touch of the old feeling; there always will be. Tony's biggest problem is that he's the kind of guy a woman turns to when another relationship goes sour."

"I hadn't thought of that," Rachel said slowly. "But I think you're right. I had just broken up with Phil."

"The point is that since he was married Tony has never made a pass at another woman—including me. And there have been times when . . . "

"When you wanted him to?"

"I'd put it a little more strongly than that."

"You mean——"

"I mean I made a pass at *him*." Kara laughed shortly. "Nice, huh? My best friend's husband. I'd like to think I took the chance because I knew he wouldn't respond, and because all I really wanted was affection and understanding."

"And to get back at—" Rachel stopped with a gulp. Not since her undergraduate days had she had a conversation like this, with friends who weren't afraid to talk freely about their feelings and experiences. She had done it too—then. "I'm sorry!"

"There you go, apologizing again. I brought the subject up. And you're absolutely right. It's terrifying how closely love and anger can be interwoven. I do love Mark, but I get so furious with him sometimes. You can probably guess what the bone of contention is. You saw me pawing that baby dress."

"He doesn't want children?"

"He says he does. But somehow the time is never convenient, and my good old biological clock is running down, and he's never home, and his solution to that little difficulty is for me to give up the business. If I were a lawyer or a professor he probably wouldn't expect me to abandon my career, but a shop full of old clothes and castoffs . . . Mark can't understand why I won't give it up. You understand, though, don't you? It's a symbol of independence and achievement, a concrete demonstration of how far I've come from that crawling, spineless thing I once was. Something I did myself—oh, not without help, I couldn't have succeeded without Cherry, and Ruth's encouragement, and Pat's financial help, and the enthusiastic cooperation of Pat's mother, God rest her soul. Alexander belonged to her. I have several reasons for cherishing that disgusting old dog, but the chief reason is that he reminds me of Mrs. Mac." Kara laughed shakily. "Even his looks; she was one of the homeliest women I've ever seen. I miss her even more than Pat does, I think."

"I wish I'd known her."

"You'd have adored her. Or been terrified of her. Or both, as I was. I still have some of the designer clothes she gave me to start the business. I'll never sell them."

Kara reached for a tissue and blew her nose loudly. "Sorry," she muttered.

"Stop apologizing," Rachel said firmly.

They exchanged smiles. "I got off the subject, didn't I?" Kara said. "God, that felt good! I haven't unburdened myself for a long time. I can't let it all hang out with Cherry, Tony isn't too crazy about the business either, and she's so goofy about him she gets redfaced and defensive if I criticize him."

"She's worried about him," Rachel said. "About his job."

"I worry about that too. But she's going about it the wrong way. You don't get a man like Tony to do what you want by nagging him and fussing over him. Anyhow, that's a decision he has to make for himself. She knew what he did for a living before she married him, knew how much it meant to him. She has no right to demand that he give it up, any more than Mark has the right to expect me to give up the shop." Kara looked faintly surprised. "Funny, I never thought of it that way before. Well, enough of this. If you ever feel like dumping on me, remember I owe you."

"No, I still owe you. You don't have to do this." Rachel gestured at the photographs of the quilt. "I should get the hell out of here, leave all of you in peace."

"You're doing it again," Kara said in exasperation. "I just wanted you to know that you're not the only sucker in town, and that taking the blame for everything that happens to you is stupid."

Rachel began, "Responsibility—"

"That's different. Responsibility implies action. If you don't like your life it's up to you to change it. You may not be able to change some things, but sitting in a helpless huddle feeling guilty won't change anything." Kara laughed self-consciously. "I even changed my first name. Every time someone called me Karen, I heard my ex-husband saying it, in that critical, contemptuous voice of his. It was a small change, and I suppose rather silly, but—"

"No, not silly. Every little bit helps, right?"

One of the dogs jumped up, and Kara started. "Damn that animal!

The guys must be back. Let me conclude my lecture. You are not to blame for this situation. You *are* responsible for trying to get yourself out of it."

The dogs hurled themselves at the door. Kara had to yell to be heard over the barking. "There will be a quiz on Friday."

Adam came in. "You look cozy," he said approvingly. "Can a mere male join the circle?"

"Where's Pat?" Kara asked.

"Gone home. Ruth threatened him with violence if he didn't get there in time for dinner. He'll be back later, though." He shivered and rubbed his mittened hands together. "It's bitter cold tonight."

"I suppose you're starved," Rachel said, starting to rise.

"I'm always starved. Don't get up, dinner is already under way. A nice filling stew. I started it earlier; all I have to do is add the vegetables."

"You'll make some woman a great wife," Kara said. "Where did you learn to cook?"

It was a casual, friendly question, but Adam's face closed up and he didn't answer directly. "I've always known how to cook. Do you like turnips in your stew?"

"No, but I won't be eating it." Kara reached for the phone. "I need to make a few calls, then I'll be on my way. Chop as quietly as possible, please."

She dealt with the customers, most of whom seemed to be in search of conversation rather than information, with her usual efficiency, and then dialed Mrs. Wilson. Adam had not known she had called; when he heard what Kara was saying he let out an exclamation and turned. Blood spurted from his thumb.

Rachel dived at him with a handful of paper towels. "You're dripping on the potatoes!"

"I cut myself," Adam explained unnecessarily. "Has she got the quilt? Why didn't you tell me? Is Kara going to—"

"Ssssh. She's trying."

Kara's first tentative offer must have been rejected, with indignation. She listened for some time, rolling her eyes and tapping her foot, and then cut into the tirade. "I'll have to have another look before I can make a definite offer, Mrs. Wilson. Shall we say the end of the week— or next week? Oh. I don't think so, I have a lot to do tomorrow . . . Very well, then, as a favor to you. If you can make it early. Nine o'clock?"

"You're a smooth operator, I must say," Adam remarked admiringly.

"I'm going to lose money on this," Kara muttered.

"Whatever it takes," Adam said quietly.

Kara gave him a long, measuring look. "That's what I meant, Sir Galahad. We'll have it tomorrow. Whatever it takes. Where's that carton of Miss Ora's stuff?"

Adam blinked. "Pat's got it."

"I should have known. What's he up to? What did you do this afternoon?"

"Pat made me promise not to tell."

"What is this, a game?"

"He had a few more things to work out and he—uh—he wanted to explain it himself. He'll be here later."

"I can't wait for him, I've got too much to do." Kara's lips compressed. "He's just trying to get back at me."

"He wouldn't do that," Adam said earnestly.

"Yes, he would." Kara stood up. "If I'm going to stay here for a few days I have to get things organized at home. I'll be here early—probably around seven. Leave the door unbolted so I can get in if you aren't awake." Her tone strongly suggested that they had damned well better be awake. She went on, clipping the words off like staples. "Mrs. Wilson will be here at nine. I'll have the bloody woman out of here and the quilts in my hands by ten o'clock or know the reason why. The sale starts at eleven. If Patrick A. MacDougal cares to let me in on what he's doing, he can come at ten. On the dot. Got that?"

Adam snapped to attention. "Yes, ma'am."

"Good." She shrugged into her coat. "No, don't walk me to the car. I don't need protection. If anybody gets in my way, he'll be the one who needs protection."

The glass in the door rattled when she slammed it.

"I wouldn't want to be in Pat's shoes tomorrow," Adam murmured.

"Maybe she'll have cooled off by then."

"I'd have told her if she'd asked."

"I thought you promised Pat you wouldn't."

"Oh, yeah, but I can never hold out against women who try to worm secrets out of me."

"How's your thumb?"

"Agonizing." Adam groaned. "You're on the right track. A little more sympathy and I'll spill my guts."

While she applied sympathy and antiseptic, he spilled them. "The stuff in the carton wasn't much help. You know the sort of thing people accumulate over a lifetime—clippings, snapshots, letters—they always mean to put them in albums, but they never get around to it. So Pat got the idea of going to the county courthouse to look for deeds and birth and death certificates. He thinks he can work out a rough genealogy."

"What good will that do?" Rachel wound a Band-Aid around the afflicted member and went to the stove to stir the stew. The aroma, redolent of herbs and red wine, roused the appetite that had been dormant all day.

"You never know," Adam said. Rachel looked at him suspiciously. He shifted his weight, avoiding her eyes. "He's got a couple of ideas. He'll explain them later."

However, Pat called as they were sitting down to dinner, to explain that he couldn't make it. Ruth wasn't feeling well. No, nothing serious, but he didn't want to leave her alone. He'd see them in the morning. Seven a.m., and don't argue with me, you young whippersnapper, if Kara is going to be there at seven, I'll be there at seven.

"I hope Ruth is all right," Adam said, returning to the table.

Rachel felt no concern. She thought she knew why Ruth had managed to keep Pat at home that evening.

When she suggested they finish checking the children's rooms Adam refused with unexpected firmness. "I didn't try to stop you last night because you were upset, but it was a waste of time. Do you think Kara would overlook such an elementary precaution, or take the slightest chance of harm coming to the people she loves? They won't be back till Monday or Tuesday, and if I know Kara, she'll wait till the last minute before she strips those rooms down to the bare walls and floor. Whatever else happens."

He meant to reassure her. What he had said made perfect sense, but it made Rachel realize how little time they had, and how futile their activities had been. None of the things they had discovered brought them any closer to a solution. What was the point of pursuing meaningless research like Pat's stupid genealogy? What was the point of anything?

You can't always change things, but sitting in a helpless huddle won't change anything.

The words hadn't come from the recesses of her own mind. They were Kara's. Rachel took one of the books from her table and started to read.

Abnormally sensitive to her moods, Adam took this one for annoyance with him. He didn't venture to address her again, or even to turn on the television. The book he selected didn't seem to interest him very much.

Anticipating the predawn arrival of two very angry people, Rachel went upstairs early, with only a brief "good night." She wasn't annoyed with Adam, but she did wish he would stop being so apologetic. She kept feeling she ought to pat him on the head.

It must have been some sound that woke her a few hours later, but it was thirst that prevented her from dropping off again. The room was like an oven. She had neglected to open the window, and Adam must not have turned down the thermostat before going to bed. Cursing the climate of Saudi Arabia, she got out of bed and stumbled toward the door.

The light in the hall dazzled her eyes after the darkness of her bedroom, and her temporarily impaired vision gave her a blurred, misleading impression of the figure that stood looking out the front window. At first she assumed it was Adam; it was certainly large enough. Then she saw it was bare to the waist, its only covering a pair of light, loose pants. She had never known Adam to venture forth without at least three sweaters, and there was a distinct draft blowing along the hall.

"Adam?" she said uncertainly.

The figure turned. The face was one she had never seen before.

eleven

"This makes twice," Adam said indistinctly. "Do you think the third time will be the—"

"Put your head back."

"It's almost stopped." He pushed away the towel she held pressed against his face and raised a hand gingerly to his nose.

Rachel located an unstained section of the towel and wiped a trickle of blood from his upper lip. "Why the hell didn't you tell me you were going to shave off your beard? Strolling around half-naked in the middle of the night—how was I suppposed to recognize you? Why didn't you speak up, instead of coming at me that way? If I'd had a gun I probably would have shot you!"

They were in her room where she had led him, dripping blood from his nose and clutching at the drawstring of his pajama pants.

Adam glanced down, decided the pajamas were safely anchored, and leaned back in the chair. "It was a sudden impulse—the beard, I mean. I saw no reason why I should discuss it with you, particularly in view of the fact that you had indicated total disinterest in the subject. It is customary to remove one's upper garments when performing such an operation; the hair gets under them and itches. It is customary to remove all one's clothing when taking a shower. Except in the female religious communities of the Middle Ages, where, I have been told—"

"Do you have to lecture about everything?"

His nose had bled copiously all down his front. Rachel started to wipe the stains off his chest. The broad bands of muscle stretched and tensed as he drew in his breath. She scrambled to her feet and backed away, flushing. "I'll get a clean towel."

"What did you hit me with?" Adam asked curiously when she came back from the bathroom.

Rachel handed him the damp washcloth. "A glass. I hope it didn't break, it was an old one. Pressed glass."

She expected a sarcastic reply—he would have been justified in making one—but he only nodded and went on scrubbing at his chest. The basic structure wasn't as impressive as all those layers of sweaters might have led one to expect, but it was worth looking at—deeply tanned, laced with fading scratches like his back and, somewhat to her surprise, devoid of hair. Unless he'd shaved it too?

"I'm sorry," she said.

Adam looked up. The lower part of his face, white as that of a Southern belle, looked strange between his tanned forehead and throat. His features were refined to the point of delicacy—a narrow pointed chin, hollow cheeks, and a thin, flexible mouth. So much for stereotypes, Rachel thought, watching the last-named organ curve in a way that made her retreat another step or two.

Adam saw the movement. His lips tightened, but when he spoke his voice was determinedly casual. "It was my fault. Next time I'll announce my identity loud and clear. You don't need a gun, you have a good throwing arm for a . . . Oops. I'd better clear out before I get myself deeper in trouble."

He went out, taking the bloody towels with him, and leaving Rachel with her mouth open. She knew why he had retreated so precipitately and she knew the answer to the question he had not answered. She couldn't blame him for an involuntary movement; there was nothing wrong with his male hormones, and her sudden appearance, hair unbound and shoulders bare, had caught him off guard. He would have stopped, though, even if she hadn't pitched the glass at him. She felt certain of that. When he had told her she would have to make the first move he had meant it—and the move would have to be intentional and unmistakable.

Rachel got into bed and turned out the light. I'll have to watch it, she told herself. That wasn't fair.

Anything is fair where they're concerned. When are they ever fair?

He's been rather sweet.

They talk sweet to get what they want. They all want the same thing.

By the time Rachel came downstairs the next morning, the rest of the committee had arrived. She could hear Pat's roar through the closed door. She assumed he was arguing with Kara, probably trying to denigrate her activities in favor of his own; but when she entered the room she realized the debate was about something quite different.

Swathed in mink, her cheeks crimson and her mouth so compressed her lips were almost invisible, Kara held in her arms a bundle of pale pink knitted fabric. Neither she nor Pat so much as glanced at Rachel.

"I had to bring him!" Her voice wasn't as loud as Pat's, but it was shrill enough to override his. "Mark is out of town—as usual—and I don't trust the maid to look after him."

The back door opened, admitting Adam, whose arms were filled with miscellaneous objects, including a wicker basket. Rachel had already identified the misshaped object protruding from the bundle of pink fabric. Presumably it was Alexander's head, since it was covered with hair, which his hindquarters were not. The sound issuing from him was probably a growl. It sounded like chalk scraping across a blackboard.

"I hate that goddamn animal," Pat snarled. "I always did hate him."

"He doesn't like you either," Kara said. "It's none of your business, Pat. I'll keep him in my room."

"He won't be any trouble," Adam added. Juggling Alexander's luggage, he freed one hand and patted the shaggy mop of orange and black hair. "Poor old guy . . . Hey!"

Nearsighted people have excellent close-range vision. The same must have been true of dogs; Alexander struck hard and fast at Adam's hand, gumming it furiously.

"He hasn't got any teeth," Kara said, as Adam wiped his wet fingers on his sweater. "Bring his things, Adam."

They went out together. "Morning, Rachel," Pat said.

"Good morning."

He didn't rise or offer his hand. Rachel moved away from him, toward the counter and the coffeemaker. "How is Ruth?" she asked, reaching for a cup.

"Fine."

"Did you tell her?" She turned to face him, leaning against the counter.

Craggy was a trite adjective, but it was an accurate description of Pat's face. Some of the angles smoothed out when she spoke; he seemed to be relieved that she had introduced the subject. "About what happened yesterday? No, I didn't. I couldn't think of any objective way of describing it without recalling a memory that still haunts her. Small wonder. If someone hadn't interrupted us, I would have . . . " He took a long breath. "It haunts me too. I can never completely forgive myself, even though I know I wasn't responsible. Feeling the way I did about her, I should have been able to fight it off, control it somehow . . . Well, never mind that. You've got to believe me, Rachel—what happened yesterday was completely different. Grabbing you was stupid and rude, but all I meant to do was give you a friendly little shake. When you reacted so violently I dropped you like a hot potato and backed off. You scared the bejesus out of me. I'd rather you didn't mention it to Ruth, but if you—"

He broke off as the door opened and Kara came in, followed by Adam. She had taken off her coat—Rachel wouldn't have been surprised to learn that Alexander was now sleeping in a nest of mink—and looked every inch the upper-crust businesswoman, in a navy tweed suit and soft white blouse. Settling herself at the table, she opened her briefcase and took out a notebook.

"I've been trying to arrive at a price for those quilts," she explained, handing the notebook to Rachel. "These are records of prices we have paid for comparable items, plus notes of auction prices over the past few years."

"Never mind that," Pat said. "We'll pay whatever is necessary. I'll buy the damned things myself."

"Then I'd have to cut you in on the profit," Kara said. Her smile was affectionate. "Leave it to me, Pat. I'll get them. What did you find out about Mary Elizabeth?"

"I thought you'd never ask." Pat pulled a sheaf of crumpled papers from the pocket of his jacket.

Kara gave the papers a quick glance and tossed them aside. "This is all fairly recent material. Nothing earlier than 1890."

"That's as far back as the memorabilia in the carton went. There was one of those fancy plush albums with photographs of—"

"No one we'd be interested in," Kara said with a sniff.

"Miss Ora's grandparents," Pat continued doggedly. "Granddad did build the house. His name was Gerhardt. One photograph showed him in front of—"

"Who cares about Miss Ora's grandfather?"

"Will you quit interrupting me? This sort of thing takes time, dammit, and you have to start with known facts and work your way back. I only had a few—"

"Work your way back, hell. You had Mary Elizabeth's name. Why didn't you—"

"Because the older records aren't there!" The glass in the door vibrated, and the dogs rushed at him, barking. Pat lowered his voice slightly. "Not at the courthouse. There are other sources, which I fully intend to consult, but I just started this yesterday afternoon."

Kara handed the paper to Rachel. "I see what you mean. Sorry, Pat, I shouldn't have criticized."

"Feel her forehead," Pat said. "She must be sick. You, apologizing?"

"I'll un-apologize if you don't cut it out."

Pat's grin faded. "This isn't going to be easy, you know. Many records are missing—destroyed during the Wo-ah, as Mrs. Wilson calls it, or in the normal course of time. Counties have been divided and renamed—Loudon County used to be part of Fairfax. One thing we have going for us is that Mary Elizabeth was the common ancestress of several branches of the family. Her descendants could be scattered from New England to California."

"That's good?" Kara abandoned her attempt to be conciliatory. "Heavens, Pat, it could take years to track them down."

"But some of them—one of them—might be more interested in family history than Mrs. Wilson. The quilts survived; other portable property may have been inherited by other branches of the family. I'm going to Charlottesville this afternoon. The library at the university has—used to have, anyhow—a sizable collection of materials on Virginia genealogy, including microfilm copies of some county records. If I don't find what I want there, I may get a clue as to where to look next."

"Lots of luck," Kara said politely. It was clear that she had no great hopes of success from this approach. The dogs heralded a new arrival, and she went on, "That must be Mrs. Wilson. I might have known she'd be early."

Mrs. Wilson had not come alone. Rocky carried the carton containing the quilts, but he was probably there to lend moral support as well. He eyed the other men warily, responding to Adam's friendly greeting with a shy nod.

"We'll take them into the shop," Kara said, as Figgin headed purposefully for the carton Rocky had placed on the floor. "This way."

It took even longer than usual to keep the cats from following; Figgin struggled furiously when Rachel picked him up, and she had to shut him in the pantry before they could leave the room. "I don't know why you put up with those animals," Mrs. Wilson grumbled. "Dirty things, shedding all over."

She was in a bad temper, even for her. The reason for her ill humor became apparent after Kara had taken two of the quilts out of the box. The album quilt was on the bottom. At least . . . It had to be the album quilt, but the crumpled, wadded object bore little resemblance to the one Rachel had seen.

"My God!" Kara sounded as if she had been stabbed to the heart. "What . . . You didn't . . . You washed it?"

"It was filthy." Mrs. Wilson's face had turned bright red.

"It's ruined." Kara collapsed into the nearest chair.

Adam was bending over the quilt, trying to smooth out the wrinkles with his hands. Washing had not removed the gray film, it had set into a solid coating, like dried mud or thin plaster. The stitches had puckered and drawn so that the once-smooth surface was a mass of lumps.

Like any teenager embarrassed by the behavior of a parent, Rocky turned his back and pretended to examine the quilts hanging on the back wall. Rachel couldn't blame him; Mrs. Wilson continued to protest and complain and excuse herself. "You could of warned me," she shouted at Kara, who responded with a silent snarl.

"Maybe you can fix it," Adam said.

"It's beyond repair," Kara said flatly. "I wouldn't give you ten bucks for it."

From a commercial point of view the destruction of the album quilt served Kara well. A subdued Mrs. Wilson sold her the others without haggling, and accepted the ten dollars Kara had offered for the album quilt. As soon as the front door closed, they heard her voice raised in pained protestation. "How was I supposed to know? I'm so mad I could spit. It wasn't my fault!"

Rocky's reply was only audible as a soothing murmur.

"Is it as bad as you implied, or were you just trying to save a buck?" Pat inquired.

"It's that bad." Kara bundled the other quilts neatly but unceremoniously into the carton and turned to examine the album quilt. Her face was screwed up like that of a squeamish maiden lady forcing herself to deal with a dead and mangled mouse. Rachel realized her distress had nothing to do with the loss of potential profit.

After a closer look Kara groaned. "I'd like to kill her. If she'd deliberately set out to wreck it she couldn't have done a better job. I'll bet she used hot water and ordinary detergent—in the washing machine!—and then heaved it into the dryer." Delicately she scraped at the stained surface and curiosity overcame her wrath. "What is this? Looks like dried mud. But washing would have removed that."

"It kept coming back," Rachel said.

The others turned to stare at her. "I had it clean," Rachel went on. "The dust, or whatever it was, brushed right off. You saw the photographs. When you saw it a few days later, Pat, you said it was dirty again. Could the dirt be inside, permeating the wadding?"

"That's an idea." A section flaked off under Kara's nail. "But why weren't the other quilts affected?" She gathered the crumpled mass into her arms. "I'm going to try something. It can't do any harm, the damage has already been done. Come on, Rachel, we've got about twenty minutes before the thundering hordes descend."

It took almost that long to set up the arrangement she had in mind. Cheryl used fiberglass screening framed in wood to support delicate articles while they dried; the weight of the wet fabric could strain old threads. None of these were large enough or sturdy enough to suit Kara. "The fabric isn't a modern synthetic," she explained. "It's cotton, heavy as lead when it's wet. We'll try brushing and vacuuming first, before we wash it. In cold water! Put it on that long table, Adam. Don't try to pull it straight, you'll break the threads."

The soft brush Rachel had used earlier had no effect at all this time. Kara reached for another, stiffer-bristled brush, and attacked the fabric ruthlessly. Gray dust rose in a fine cloud, and she let out a murmur of satisfaction.

"You'll get your suit dirty," Rachel said. "Let me do that."

"It'll have to wait till later. Hear the dogs? One of the customers must be here. Mrs. Ferncliffe, I'll bet. She's always early, damn her eyes."

"Want me to give it a try?" Adam asked.

"No, keep your hands off it." Kara bent over and blew gently at the loosened dirt. "It's left a stain," she announced dispiritedly.

"We've got the photographs," Pat reminded her. "Come on, Adam, leave women's work to women. They won't thank you for . . . Kara? What's the matter?"

Raising her hands to her face, Kara bent over in a paroxysm of coughing. Rachel put an arm around her heaving shoulders.

"Slap her on the back," Pat suggested.

Kara straightened, lowering her hands. Her face was red and her eyes streamed with tears. "Something . . . caught in my throat," she gasped. "It's all right."

The shop bell was ringing, in long peremptory peals. "I'll get it," Rachel said. "Sit down and catch your breath."

"Wait." Kara's breath was still uneven. Instead of wiping away the tears that had overflowed her eyes, she went to the sink and washed her hands, scrubbing them like a surgeon preparing for an operation, before blotting her face with a paper towel.

"Okay," she said, drawing a deep breath. "Everybody out."

"Go ahead, I'll lock up," Adam offered.

"I said, everybody out. Don't touch that quilt. Don't even go near it."

Pat's heavy brows drew together. "What happened?"

"I don't know. I can't talk about it now, Pat. Louisa is going to break that door down if I don't answer it."

She herded them out. After she had locked the door she put the key in her pocket.

Mrs. Ferncliffe was not pleased to have been kept waiting and she kept up a grumbled monologue of complaint as she rummaged through the racks looking for bargains. She bought a number of items, however, including some that had not been on sale. Half a dozen other sale-wise customers arrived during the first hour; they knew the early birds got the choicest items. It was well after two o'clock before the last of them left.

Stacking the sales slips, Kara looked pleased. "We've done better than I expected. There will be a lull now, then another rush during the last hour, when people hope for further markdowns."

"Why don't you go and get something to eat?" Rachel suggested. "I can keep an eye on things here."

"All right. I guess I should take Alexander out. Straighten up the sales tables, will you please? What slobs people are! I'll bring you a sandwich, or maybe I can talk Adam into playing chef."

They had been too busy all morning to talk privately, but the task of refolding and rearranging the scattered linens wasn't demanding enough to keep Rachel's thoughts from returning to Kara's odd behavior. Inhaling some of that gritty dust might induce a coughing fit, but Kara's reaction had been more than a simple physical reflex. She didn't seem to be eager to discuss it.

The sound of footsteps on the porch made Rachel's heart jump, and she scolded herself silently as the door opened to admit a pair of giggling female teenagers. Would she ever stop starting at the sound of feet on that porch? The girls were "just looking," and they were still at it when Kara came back. She put the tray she carried on the desk and advanced, smiling fixedly, on one of the young women, who was reaching for the Callot Soeurs peignoir, ignoring the discreet sign that read, "Please ask for assistance."

"It is lovely, isn't it? There are a few like it in museums, but this is the only one of that quality we've ever had. Let me hold it for you."

Her tone, even more than the words themselves, got the point across. The girls left, without buying anything, and Rachel began, "I'm sorry. I thought they might be regulars, and Cheryl said—"

"Stop apologizing for everything." Kara took a bite of her sandwich. "You'll learn. Our regulars know better than to grab at expensive items, and girls that age aren't likely to buy designer originals. I don't mind them looking, but some kids treat the merchandise the same way they do the ready-mades in department stores—and the clerks will tell you how much damage they can do. Cheryl should have put the peignoir in a display case, like our other treasures."

There were three such garments on display, in shallow cases like oversized shadow boxes. The glass had been treated in order to cut out damaging sunlight. Rachel took a sandwich from the plate Kara offered and studied one of the gowns, a glittering shape of silver tissue. The paste gems studding the wide hip sash sparkled in the light—emerald and ruby, topaz and jet.

"Is that one of Mrs. Mac's?" she asked.

"Right. An Egyptian model of Poiret's. It's not for sale."

"I doubt if I could afford it anyhow."

"Do I detect a slight note of regret in your voice? I thought you didn't like vintage clothes."

"Seeing and handling them has changed my viewpoint," Rachel admitted. "They are so beautiful. Impractical, though, for a person like me."

"Not all of them." Kara hesitated and then said, "Would you be offended if I picked out a few for you? Just to try on, not to buy— unless you wanted to. You're entitled to a hefty discount."

A few weeks earlier the suggestion would have struck Rachel as both patronizing and insulting. Now she understood what had prompted it, and responded readily, "That's kind of you. Someday, maybe. After . . . "

"Okay." A shadow fell across Kara's face. She selected another sandwich, crustless, daintily frilled with lettuce.

"Adam didn't make these," Rachel said.

"He wasn't there. Neither was Pat."

"Pat said he was going to Charlottesville. Didn't Adam leave a note?"

"Uh-huh. 'Gone out. Back later.'"

"Sounds like Adam. What happened this morning, Kara?"

Kara took her time about answering, chewing methodically and swallowing before she spoke. "I breathed in some of the dust, as you probably surmised. Dumb of me, I wasn't thinking. The coughing was an involuntary reflex, but . . . It's hard to describe. Every time my breath went out, I felt something like . . . like cold, dank air touching my face."

"God bless you," Rachel murmured.

"What?"

"That's what people say when someone sneezes. When the breath goes out, the soul goes with it. You call down a blessing to keep the soul from getting lost and something . . . different . . . from going in."

"God." Kara stared at her. "What a horrible thought."

"That's the origin of the superstition. I know something about superstitions," Rachel said wryly. "They have an underlying logic—of sorts."

"Was it like that for you?"

The question came so naturally Rachel answered without thinking. "I did breathe in some of the dust. I must have, I was bending over the quilt and brushing it, just as you were. I didn't notice anything at the time, though. It wasn't until that night, when he put the quilt around my shoulders, that . . . " Rachel looked down at her clasped hands. "I made the first move. Not Tony. He barely touched me, it was only a kind gesture. I stood up. The quilt seemed to wrap itself around me, I don't even remember taking hold of it."

"Are you all right?" Kara asked apprehensively. "I shouldn't have asked. I forgot—"

"I wasn't expecting it the first time. *We* weren't expecting it. Anyway, he knows now—Pat—everybody knows, don't they? I can't talk to him the way I can to you," she added querulously. "He doesn't understand. You understand."

"Understand what?"

"How it is to love someone that way. When you've got no right, when it's wrong. When he hurts you and you want to hurt him back."

"Rachel? Rachel, can you hear me?"

The voice was barely audible, as distant as a whisper from another room. "He's so tall," Rachel said dreamily. "He had to lift me up, I was standing on tiptoe—I remember—I knew—how soft his hair felt, would feel, between my fingers, the curve of his head under my hands, the shape of his mouth and the way it fit, would fit, against mine, it hurt, but I didn't care, and his arm—his arms—held me so hard *I couldn't breathe, and I tried to get away and I couldn't, and then he—he . . .* "

Kara's palm struck her cheek with enough force to drive the remaining air from her straining lungs. Reflexively she sucked in her breath.

"God bless you!" Kara sounded the words like a shout.

"Thanks." Rachel rubbed her cheek. "What happened? What did I say?"

The skin framing Kara's mouth had gone white. "You weren't talking about Tony. Not after a while. The one sort of . . . flowed into the other. At the end your face was so distorted I wouldn't have recognized it if I hadn't seen it change. Did he strike you?"

"He pushed me away."

"I see." Kara's eyes were fixed on the hand Rachel had raised to her breast. "Okay. Enough already."

She went to the door, opened it, and turned the sign over.

"You're closing?" Rachel asked. "I thought you said—"

"The hell with the sale and the customers. I should have called it off. I didn't realize . . . " She was still pale and her voice was unsteady. "I never saw anything like that before. Sara told me and Pat told me, but it's impossible to understand unless you actually . . . Let's get at that quilt. I'd do it myself, but to tell the truth I'm terrified of being in there alone."

She wasn't joking. The precautions she took would not have been inappropriate for dealing with hazardous waste. They both wore rubber gloves and masks—Cheryl had a supply of the throwaway variety—and Kara used the vacuum cleaner instead of a brush, moving it hard and quickly across the fabric. When she had covered the entire surface she put the vacuum aside. Now restored to her normal self, she said sardonically, "God knows what I'm going to do with the bag. Bury it?"

"The quilt is still stained. The photographs are clearer than the original."

"We'll try one more trick." Kara gathered up the quilt, tossed it into the sink, and turned on the cold water. "It can't make it any worse."

When the fabric was thoroughly saturated she let the water out and lifted the soggy, dripping bundle onto the mesh frame. Between them they smoothed it out as best they could.

"It's a little better, but not much," Kara said. "Well, we've done all we can. Let's get out of here."

Someone, presumably a belated customer, was pounding on the front door, but Kara didn't even glance in that direction. "I'm going to shower and change. I'll bring Alexander downstairs with me, if that's all right with you. He gets lonely. And he hardly ever bites people more than once."

When she returned carrying the woolly bundle, Rachel was feeding the dogs. Alexander looked even nastier than usual; one eye was visible, set in a glare as cold and malevolent as that of a crocodile, and when he saw the dogs he started squirming and wheezing.

"I'll take him out," Kara said. "Then when I bring him in, you let the dogs out."

"They wouldn't attack him, would they?" Rachel held the door for her.

"No. He attacks them."

"But he hasn't got any teeth!"

"It's moral intimidation," Kara explained, rather proudly. "They cower and whine and try to climb in people's laps."

Rachel was inclined to sympathize with the dogs. Probably they didn't know what to make of Alexander; he didn't look or behave like any creature they had ever beheld.

The canine exchange was made without difficulty, and after the dogs had had their run Rachel shut them in the pantry. The cats had sensibly retreated to the tops of various articles of furniture, leaving Alexander in sole possession. Staggering purposefully around the room, he completed the survey of his temporary domain before collapsing onto the rug at Kara's feet.

She had the photographs spread out on the coffee table and was arranging them in order. "Would you like a cup of tea or coffee?" Rachel asked.

"No, I'd like a drink. But I'll have coffee. Did you look at these?"

"Not closely."

"There's a magnifying glass in the drawer. Get it."

Neither of them spoke for a long time. Finally Kara leaned back. "Well?"

"It's worse than I thought." Rachel put down the magnifying glass and replaced the photo she had been examining—a charming pink Cupid with feathery wings and a head of curls that almost hid the pointed horns. "There's something wrong with every one of them, isn't there?"

"Uh-huh. Maybe it's just as well Mrs. Wilson wrecked the quilt. I couldn't sell it in good conscience. Not to a bride, certainly."

"It is a bride's quilt, isn't it?"

"Has to be. Which raises an interesting question. Who was the bride?"

"I thought of that too." Rachel saw Kara stiffen, and smiled reassuringly. "No, I'm not getting psychic flashes. It's just common sense and familiarity with the field. According to Miss Ora, all three quilts were made by her ancestress. But brides didn't make these quilts for themselves. They were joint projects; each square was made by a different friend or relative. But in this case the blocks all appear to be the work of a single person. Mary Elizabeth was a remarkably gifted seamstress, so she might have made an entire quilt for a close friend, but if so, why didn't she give it to her?"

Kara nodded. "Professor Patrick A. MacDougal never thought of that, I'll bet. Of course," she added fairly, "it's not his field."

The smiles they exchanged had a new warmth and intimacy. "But you'll rub it in, won't you?" Rachel asked.

"Of course."

"It is odd," Rachel said thoughtfully. "Could someone else have made it for Mary Elizabeth?"

"Miss Ora said Mary Elizabeth made all three quilts. She was reporting a family tradition, which doesn't count for much; but the similarities are unmistakable—not just technique and design capability, but the repetition of certain unusual quilting patterns on all three." Her face sobered. "Whoever made them really hated the woman who was to receive the bride's quilt. I've never seen such concentrated, deliberate malice worked into a piece of sewing."

"Suppose Mary Elizabeth made it for someone who . . . " Rachel stopped. The idea was so melodramatic she shrank from expressing it, but Kara knew what she had been about to say. They were thinking the same language.

"Who died—as a result of the curse?" Kara laughed shortly. "Her descendants neglected to mention that Mary Elizabeth included black magic among her other talents. I guess I will have a drink. This is crazy."

"No crazier than the other things we've been thinking," Rachel pointed out. "Curses can kill, you know, if the intended victim believes in them."

Kara stepped carefully over the snoring bundle at her feet. Selecting a bottle from the shelf, she splashed liquid into a glass and turned to look at Rachel with new respect. "By George, you're right. I've heard of cases like that. Want some?" She held up her glass.

"No, thanks." Rachel was intent on her theory. "The literature of folklore is full of such cases; there was one in the United States less than fifty years ago, and I'll bet it still happens in some areas and subcultures, even in so-called civilized countries. People just don't talk about it or report it, for fear of being jeered at.

"We have to start with the assumption that Mary Elizabeth was the maker of the quilt. She sure as hell didn't make it for herself, it was designed to cause harm. If the recipient realized what it meant—if Mary Elizabeth told her—if she believed—"

"And Mary Elizabeth took the quilt back, or was given it back by the grieving family, after the girl died?"

"The girl may not have lived long enough to receive it. Knowledge of Mary Elizabeth's intent could be enough. *If* she believed."

Kara came back to her chair. "I can't think offhand of any other explanation that fits the facts," she admitted. "But if it's true, we're in deep trouble. It's going to be difficult enough learning more about Mary Elizabeth. Locating an unknown, hypothetical friend—"

"But that's not the point," Rachel said eagerly. "Don't you see—"

The incarcerated dogs interrupted her, hurling themselves against the closed door and howling in a dismally muffled fashion that sounded like wolves on the tundras. Alexander got up and creaked toward the door. Rachel couldn't decide whether the sound came from his joints or his mouth.

Adam came in, accompanied by a blast of icy air. "Close the door," Kara ordered.

Adam glanced down at the unseemly object wrapped around his right ankle. "You'll have to call off your dog first. He's slobbering all over my sock and I can't move without stepping on him."

Kara detached Alexander and put him down on the floor. His carnivorous instincts satisfied, he wandered off, grumbling happily to himself and running into pieces of furniture. Adam kicked the door shut and deposited two brown paper bags on the table. "I got Chinese. Figured you'd be too busy to cook."

"It was a kindly thought," Kara said. "Have I mentioned you look much better without the beard?"

"I thought you hadn't noticed," Adam said shyly. "Thank you. I appreciate the comment all the more because nobody else has bothered to compliment me on my good looks or acknowledged my noble sacrifice. I could have used some protection tonight. My face is a solid block of ice."

It looked like a solid block of cherry ice cream. Only prolonged exposure to the cold could have produced such a shade. "Where have you been?" Rachel asked curiously.

Adam shed a couple of sweaters and began unloading white cartons. "Around and about, hither and yon, to and fro, up and down the town."

"Are we going to tell him?" Kara asked.

"If he's going to be mysterious, I don't see why we should confide in him."

Adam added plates and silverware to the accumulation on the table and gestured hospitably. "Pull up your chairs, ladies. Dinner is served. I'm not being mysterious, only modest. I'm sure your accomplishments far exceed mine and that you will be kind enough to share them with me."

"We may as well," Rachel said. "Unlikely though it seems, he may have something to contribute."

Adam gave her an amiable grin and helped himself to chow mein.

He was sufficiently intrigued by their theory to stop eating for a full thirty seconds. "That's very ingenious. I don't know why I didn't think of it. Well, yes, I do know why I didn't think of it. Maybe Pat can dig up some more information in Charlottesville. He said he'd probably have to stay overnight, that he'd call tonight if—"

"He's wasting his time," Rachel said flatly. "That's what I was about to say to Kara just before you got here, Adam. This genealogical and historical research is all very well, but it takes forever and there's no guarantee that it will turn up anything useful, especially when there's so little to go on. We have to try another method."

In his haste to reply, Adam stopped chewing and swallowed too abruptly. His face turned purple. "No! Dammit, Rachel, if you're considering hypnosis—"

"Why not?" Kara asked. "It worked before. Sara told me—"

"It's too dangerous!" Adam got his breath under control. "Shut up, both of you, and listen to me. The popular belief that people can't lie under hypnosis is wrong. They lie all the time. Have you ever heard of a process called confabulation?"

"Yes," said Rachel.

"Oh." Momentarily deflated, Adam rallied. "I'm not talking about the conventional meaning of the word—a cozy, informal chat. Like this one," he added sarcastically.

"My goodness but you're in a fierce mood," Kara remarked. "You sound like Pat. If that's not what it means, then I don't know what you're talking about. Show off to me."

"It's what happens when an imaginative, cooperative subject is ques-tioned, under hypnosis or not. He invents answers—not consciously, he really believes what he's saying, but the answers are tailored to fit his preconceptions or the expectations of the questioner, as he con-ceives them to be. We're all biased, we'd feed her cues without mean-ing to, and we couldn't trust any information we might get from her."

"That's right," Rachel said quietly. "I have certain preconceptions of my own. They would undoubtedly color my responses to questions."

"Not to mention the fact that she tends to go into fits whenever—" Adam broke off. "What preconceptions?"

"I don't want to talk about them. They would prejudice you, and right now I don't know whether my impressions are genuine or—or self-confabulation." She planted both elbows on the table and leaned forward, intent on convincing them. "There's another way of going at this, the same method Kara and I were using this evening. We don't need to know names and dates. We know that the person for whom the quilt was made was a woman—a bride. We know the person who made it—another woman, obviously—wanted to hurt the first woman, who was almost certainly a close friend, or she wouldn't have rated such an extravagant gift. Why did Woman A hate Woman B?"

Kara shrugged. "Jealousy, of course. A was in love with B's fiancé. She wanted him, and she had lost him."

"Oh, come on," Adam exclaimed. "That's the wildest leap of logic I have ever heard, and demeaning besides. I thought you two considered yourself feminists."

"There weren't many feminists in the middle of the nineteenth cen-tury," Rachel said dryly. "What else would two women of that period compete for, except a man and everything that went with him—love, security, marriage? You're overlooking the most important confirmatory evidence, Adam. For the past week I've tried not once but several times to harm Cheryl. Lusting after her husband was my own fault . . . " She caught Kara's watchful eye and smiled faintly. "My own idea. It wasn't very nice but it was understandable; I didn't need any encouragement from the World Beyond to develop a normal if rather silly crush. But to believe I could 'get' Tony by destroying his wife—a woman who's been kind to me, whom I admire and respect—I'd have to be totally insane! Or . . . "

"Overshadowed." Adam's voice was carefully neutral.

"Influenced," Rachel corrected. "The term *overshadowed*, and Pat's theory, are based on his own preconceptions. Didn't that woman Kara mentioned say she had sewed her soul into her quilt? Some psychics believe strong emotions survive the person who felt them, that they can permeate the very fabric of a house. Why not the fabric of a dress or a quilt? It might not have affected me if I hadn't been in a similar if less violent emotional state."

"Huh." Adam pushed his plate away and pondered for a moment. Then he said in an aggrieved voice, "Women don't think the way men do."

"Don't be a sore loser," Kara said. "You know she's right."

"Another example of female logic," Adam mumbled. "I wasn't criticizing," he added quickly. "I was just wishing there wasn't this communication gap between the sexes. You two assumed from the first that sexual jealousy was the motive behind the creation of the quilt? Why didn't you say so?"

Rachel shrugged. "It was so obvious. There was no reason to spell it out, it should have been equally obvious to you."

"Huh. Well, you may be right at that. In fact, you have opened up a new and fascinating avenue of speculative thought. Why should Western rationalism be the best method of approaching a problem? We need fresh insights, different approaches, from women and other minority—"

He flinched back as a heavy object landed on the table, spilling cartons right and left and spraying him with soy sauce. "So I apologize. You didn't have to throw the cat at me."

Figgin had leaped from the top of the refrigerator, cannily avoiding Alexander, who was still looking for something to bite. One foot planted in a bowl of rice, he began gobbling sweet and sour pork, including the peppers.

"Oh, for God's sake," Kara said. "It's impossible to carry on a sane conversation in this house! Get him off the table, Adam."

The removal was not accomplished without more spillage and considerable complaint from Figgin. Mumbling angrily, he retreated to the refrigerator and began licking his paws while Adam dealt with the mess on the table.

"We were through eating anyway," he said. "Not that I have anything against your dog, Kara, but maybe you ought to put him to bed. I can't think with cats flying around the room and dogs having hysterics in the pantry."

Kara graciously admitted that the suggestion had some merit. She carried Alexander off. After order had been restored and the dogs released from the pantry, Adam said, "I see where you guys are heading, and I think you may be on the right track."

"You still don't get it," Rachel informed him. "There is no right track. That's the trouble with Western rational thought—which was, let me point out, defined by men. You assume there's only one way of proceeding and that all other ways are wrong. And you call yourself an anthropologist! Other cultures do things differently, and who are you to say they are mistaken?"

Adam grinned at her. "You ought to write a book. Or possibly a dissertation. Let's get down to specifics. You've found a motive and an explanation for the phenomenon, or at least a working hypothesis that makes as much sense as Pat's. So what do you propose to do about it?"

Kara's lips parted. Before she could speak, Rachel said, "He's catching on. That's the point, Adam. We may never know the name or the life story of the woman who began this this disaster. We may not need that information. There are other, more direct ways of counteracting the effect. And I'm not talking about hypnosis."

"No," Adam said, no longer amused. "You're talking about black magic."

twelve

Adam was trying hard, but old ingrained habits weren't easy to over-come. He continued to argue, with himself as much as with Rachel, as they wended their way to the workroom.

"Witchcraft. The Old Religion. Curses and spells and . . . All right, okay, I don't know as much about the subject as you and Pat do, but . . . What's that?"

"A mask," Kara said. "Put it on. And these gloves."

"And," Rachel added, "don't bother pointing out that she is using modern rational methods of dealing with an irrational theory. The con-tamination may be purely mental—psychic, rather—but there could be a physical source. I think there is. That's why I want to have a closer look at the quilt—not the patterns but the actual physical fabric of it."

The fabric had stopped dripping, but it was still waterlogged and heavy. Rachel bent over to examine one of the corner squares. Then she took a firm grip on the edges and looked at Kara.

"I'm going to tear it," she said. "I'll pay you back."

"Ten bucks?" Kara smiled wryly. "Do what you have to do."

Rachel gave the fabric a sharp yank. Transferring her grip to other parts of the cloth, she pulled and tugged and pressed until the corner section was almost as flat as it had been before Mrs. Wilson's disastrous attempt at cleaning. Heat had shrunk not the fabric but the threads that held it together. Already weakened, they snapped instead of stretching, leaving gaps in the even lines of quilting and freeing the shaped pieces of the appliquéd picture from the backing. An involuntary groan came from Kara.

"I'm sorry," Rachel murmured.

"It was ruined anyway. What are you looking for?" Kara asked, watching Rachel insert a finger under a loosened piece of fabric.

"Confirming a hypothesis." Before Kara could protest, Rachel stripped off the rubber glove. "Don't worry, I've already caught it— whatever it is—and I need bare hands for this. If what I expect to find is here, it is very small."

Turning to Adam, who was watching in open-mouthed fascination, she explained, "See the way the front columns of the little temple are raised, so that they look three dimensional, closer to the viewer than the columns in back? That's what they call trapunto—inserting cord or cotton under the fabric. Like this." Ruthlessly she ripped out the remaining threads and extracted the stuffing material. It retained its columnar shape, approximately two inches long and half an inch wide, until Rachel pulled it apart.

"Cotton," Kara said. "Raw cotton, straight from the fields. Typical of southern quilts of that period. Stained, like the quilt. What are you looking for?"

"I'm beginning to get an idea," Adam said in a stifled voice. "You won't find it in an architectural element, Rachel. Try this."

His gloved finger jabbed at the figure of the veiled rider.

Rachel turned to look at him. He had combed his hair back from his forehead, and his eyes, wide-set under curving dark brows, looked larger, the pupils bright greenish-brown against the clear white around them. His nose was wrinkled, as if he had smelled something unpleasant.

"You're right," she said. Picking up a pair of sharp scissors, she clipped the threads that held the rider's bodice to the cloth.

The three-dimensional effect was modest and subtle; only a small amount of stuffing had been used. It was not cotton. With a cry Rachel dropped the bundle of crushed threads.

"Hair!"

"Human hair," Adam corrected. Gloved fingers clumsy, he plucked at the intertwined mass until he separated a single strand. "It's too fine to be horsehair. And it is—was—blonde."

White-faced, Rachel wiped her fingers on her shirt. She had expected something of the sort, but had not anticipated it would take this precise form. Hair as brittle and dead as the bones of the woman from whose head it had come, hair that had once been sleek and shining, springing back under the strokes of the brush, clinging to the fingers . . .

She'd brush and play with it, curling the ends around her fingers, drawing it over her shoulders and then throwing it back, turning in front of the mirror so she could see it hanging down her back, clear to the waist. Fine hairs caught in the brush like a golden net, a net to bind her soul . . .

". . . Classic sympathetic magic," Adam said. "Hair and other body parts retain the identity, the soul imprint, of the person to whom they belonged. Strange, isn't it, that modern science has arrived at a similar conclusion? DNA—those tiny scraps of genetic material, unique to each individual, complete in each strand of hair and drop of blood . . . "

"Don't get philosophical on me," Kara said sharply. "Do you mean this was her hair—the woman for whom the quilt was made?"

"I'd bet money on it," Adam said. "And I'm not a betting man. You've heard about the dolls made by magicians for the purpose of injuring the person they represented? They would put hair, fingernail clippings, any body parts they could get, into the doll in order to make the connection stronger. Stick a pin in the doll and the person feels pain in the corresponding area of his body. Burn or bury or destroy the doll . . . Well, you get the idea. She didn't make a doll. She made this."

"The woman on the horse represents the recipient?"

"In the magical sense, the pictured rider *was* the woman. Blinded and under attack." Adam's eyes shone. He had forgotten his disgust in fascination. "I've read about it, but this is the first time I've seen an actual example. Can I borrow the scissors?"

He took them from Rachel's unresisting hand. "What do you think? The bleeding hearts? Symbolic, but then the whole thing is a matter of symbols."

"They aren't raised," Rachel murmured. "Try the bluebirds' wings."

Each wing contained, amid the cotton, a tiny scrap of translucent hornlike substance. "There are your fingernail clippings," Adam breathed. "Let's see what else we've got."

Some of the raised sections held nothing, at least nothing they could identify. The cord under a depiction of a golden ring—the break in its surface so small it could only be seen with a magnifying glass—proved to be a fine strand of braided hair. The shaped trunk of a stately oak tree, around which a rose twined coyly, yielded a tiny scrap of cloth bearing a dark stain, and the dried, flaking body of some sort of insect.

"Pricked herself with a needle, maybe?" Adam inquired, putting the scrap carefully into an envelope Kara had provided. "Can't identify the bug; I guess it was supposed to multiply and chew out the innards of the tree."

"That's enough," Kara said. She looked sick.

"Enough," Adam agreed, adding the other specimens to the collection in the envelope. "Rachel's proved her point."

"Not quite." Rachel hadn't spoken for so long her voice sounded strange to her. "One thing more. Help me turn it over."

The remains of what had been a unique piece of art flopped limply as they turned it, helpless and dead as a once-living body. The rips and stains were like wounds, and even though she knew it had to be done, even though the quilt was already beyond repair, Rachel had to force herself to insert the sharp tip of the tool into the homespun weave of the backing. The tool was one Cheryl used for ripping out stitches; it slid through the fabric with a faint tearing sound. Rachel cut another slit at right angles to the first and folded the fabric back.

"That's not the back of the front," Kara said with a puzzled frown. "I mean, it's not—"

"I know what you mean," Rachel said.

"I don't," Adam said.

"There are usually three layers in a quilt," Rachel explained. "The front, with its appliquéd or pieced pattern, the filling or batting, and the backing. In quilts like these, where the aim was beauty instead of utility, they sometimes omitted the filler. An additional layer would have made the fabric too thick for the tiny, even stitches that were demanded. But this quilt seems to have a layer of filler. What we're looking at is the back of that inner layer."

With even greater care she cut a section out of the inner layer. Underneath was what appeared to be a fourth layer of cloth—coarse, brownish-black instead of white.

"That's where the gray dust came from," Rachel said. "There are two inner layers, not one, with this between them. She sprinkled it on the fabric before she quilted the pieces together—wet it and let it dry, perhaps, so it would harden. They used a horizontal frame for the actual quilting, so the—the stuff stayed in place."

"What is it?" Kara asked.

A moonless night as the teaching said, only starlight to guide her through the maze of tree trunks, through the gate, into the enclosure dark with shadows and something worse. Stumbling over fallen stones, crouching to tear away the matted grass and weeds, the gritty soil settling deep under her nails . . .

Rachel swallowed. "Graveyard dirt."

Adam had made coffee, but he was the only one drinking it. Rachel had refused and Kara had gone straight to the liquor cabinet.

"I know I drink too much," she muttered. "It's an occupational hazard in Washington. But tonight I deserve it."

"How do you know?" Adam looked at Rachel.

Darkness, faint sounds in the night that might have been the wind or a muffled voice from deep underground . . .

The image came and went in a measureless interval of time, so quickly that not even Rachel was conscious of delay before she answered.

"It fits the pattern. Fingernail clippings and hair from the intended victim, dirt from a grave to cast a death spell. Magic is a pseudo-science; it has its own distorted logic, its rules and methodology. Pat wasn't the first scholar to point that out, but he discussed it at length in his last book."

"And in his notorious lectures on magic, science, and religion," Adam said. "It used to be one of the most popular courses on campus. He did demonstrations. In costume."

Diverted, Rachel demanded further details. "Surely he didn't mash toads or drain the blood of a white cockerel?"

"Good heavens, Rachel!" Kara exclaimed.

"Those are popular ingredients," Rachel said. "I haven't mentioned the most disgusting."

"He used a rubber chicken," Adam said reminiscently. "And tomato juice. He chanted, too. Some of the parents complained to the dean."

"I should think so," Kara murmured. "I hate to think what he'll do when he finds out about this. I suppose if there are standard formulae for cursing there are also formulae for removing a curse? I can't believe I'm saying this," she added morosely.

"That's right," Adam said eagerly. "Rachel is absolutely right. I've been reading up on it—"

"So why don't you let her talk?" Kara inquired. "You said she's the expert."

"Oh. Sorry."

"There are . . . ways," Rachel said slowly. "Different ways. Magic isn't a science, of course. There aren't any scientific formulae."

"What ways?" Adam demanded.

"Well . . . prayer."

"Prayer," Adam repeated. Rachel had never seen that look on his face, or heard such bitter cynicism in his voice.

"Counterspells, if you prefer. Appeals to the powers of light for protection."

"I do prefer," Adam said shortly. "But not by much. The quilt and the garbage we found in it are physical objects. There must be a physical response. What would happen if we destroyed the damned thing? Buried it, burned it—"

"I don't know!" Rachel shouted.

The others stared at her in surprise. She knew, or thought she knew, why Adam's suggestion had induced such a violent reaction, but she couldn't tell them. Not yet.

Moderating her voice, she explained, "We can't risk doing anything until we're sure. Destroying it might have precisely the wrong effect."

"Okay, okay," Adam said quickly. "You're right again. Our relationship may founder on that shoal, you know. It's very annoying to live with someone who is always right."

His attempt to lighten the atmosphere didn't succeed. Kara, nursing her drink, scowled at him, and Rachel snapped, "I'm just trying to be logical. Rushing into action could be a fatal mistake. We've got several more days, there's no sense in taking chances. Pat may come up with something useful."

"I thought you said he was wasting his time."

"I didn't say that, I said it wasn't the only way of going at this. There are . . ."

Her voice faded, and Adam watching her with concern, finished, "Other ways. Yeah, right. Speaking of Pat, did anyone check the answering machine? He said he'd call tonight."

Pat hadn't called, but there were several other messages, one of which almost succeeded in taking Rachel's mind off her more imminent problem. Phil was at his most pompous and precise. "I hope you've come to your senses and are ready to apologize for that outrageous business the other night. I've moved back into the house in College Park; the others are still away, and I saw no sense in paying good money for a motel. You can call me here. If you choose not to, you'll have to live with your decision. I won't call you again."

It wasn't the final message, but Adam pressed the stop switch and looked relieved. "That's good news. We've heard the last of him."

"Maybe not," Kara said slowly. "I don't like the sound of that. It could be an implicit threat."

"No, just one of Phil's famous ultimata." Rachel shook her head. "Dammit, now I can't go back there without risking another unpleasant encounter. I was going to move out anyhow, but some of my things are still there."

"Don't risk it." Kara hesitated, but only for a moment. "I know what I'm talking about, Rachel. I was married to a guy like that once. Same kind of voice—arrogant, cocksure, subtly threatening. We'll send someone to pack and pick up your things. Not you, Adam, you'd lose your temper and end up in jail."

"I probably would." He added awkwardly, "I never knew that, Kara. I'm sorry. Lucky you found somebody like Mark, you deserve the best."

Kara's face was unreadable. "Play on," she ordered, gesturing at the answering machine.

The final message infuriated Adam and roused the mirth of the two women. It was from someone calling herself Starflower or Stargazer—she mumbled—and informing Adam that she had forgiven him for what he had done and for what he might do. She was praying for him.

"One of the Wiccas?" Kara inquired, trying to control her voice. "What are you so mad about, Adam? It's a kindly thought."

"Wicca is the name of the—the thing, the religion, whatever," Adam muttered. "She's the high priestess. Dammit, she's got no business praying at me!"

"Better than the alternative. Maybe we ought to consult them. A little white magic could be just what we need."

"Ha ha," Adam said.

"You're losing your sense of humor, Adam." Kara sighed. "Mine is fading too. I think I'll hit the sack. I'd better call Cherry first, though, she expects to hear from me."

"I wondered why she hadn't called lately," Rachel said. "What did you tell her?"

"To leave you alone because you were busy."

"You were right about that. Tell her everything is . . . Can you bring yourself to say fine?"

"I can bring myself to say almost anything if it will have the desired effect." She picked up the phone.

The conversation took some time. Cheryl wanted to know how the sale had gone, what they had sold, who had bought what, how the dogs were doing, how the cats were doing, what they were eating, what the weather was like. Rachel was able to deduce the questions from Kara's answers. Kara's contributions were brief and conventional: how is everybody, are you having a good time, love to Tony and the kids. Then, at Cheryl's request, she handed the phone to Rachel.

"I won't talk long, I know you're busy," Cheryl said. "Kara says you've been working night and day on your thesis."

"Uh—"

"Don't work too hard." Cheryl's rich, friendly chuckle echoed along the line. "From what I hear, you have something nice to distract you. I'm real happy about it, Rachel. He's a sweet guy. Tony says I shouldn't worry about the burglar because he's probably split, but I would worry if I didn't know Adam was . . . Well, I promised I wouldn't say anything but I just had to tell you how happy I am about it. Gotta run, it's past Jerry's bedtime and he's driving his grandma crazy asking questions."

Hanging up the phone, Rachel turned an accusing eye on Kara.

"What did you tell her about me and Adam?"

"I had to think of something to keep her from bugging you," Kara said calmly. "Cheryl is a saint, but she wouldn't consider a little old doctoral dissertation sufficient reason for noninterference. A hot romance, on the other hand . . . "

"It's not very hot," Adam said in an aggrieved voice. "In fact, it's not a romance. Despite my best efforts."

"Really?" Kara was surprised and amused. "I must say you've been very discreet. I haven't noticed any efforts at all. I invented that to distract Cheryl."

"He's not serious," Rachel said.

"Oh, yes, I am. I'm just too much of a little gent to force unwelcome attentions on a lady." His voice was light but the level hazel eyes held no amusement. "Especially when she's being hassled by two other guys."

They dropped the subject by mutual if unspoken consent. Kara finished her drink and took Alexander out for his final run, or stagger, around the yard. Adam nobly offered to take the dog, but Alexander made it clear he did not approve of that arrangement. When Kara came back she was shivering, despite the folds of mink that swathed her and the dog.

"Cold?" Adam asked.

"Definitely a three dog night. If Pat calls, tell him . . . Tell him whatever you like. See you in the morning."

She and Alexander were sleeping in the room Tony had occupied. Rachel followed her; she didn't want to be alone with Adam just now, he'd be full of questions she didn't know how to answer, and there was something she wanted to discuss with Kara.

Opening the bedroom door and turning on the light for Kara, whose arms were full of dog, she said, "Did you search this room?"

"Should I?" Kara put the dog on the bed and took off her coat.

Rachel didn't answer.

"I had a quick look around," Kara said. "Changed the sheets, made sure there was nothing Alexander could knock over. Is there something you want to tell me?"

"Not about that. I wanted . . . But you're tired."

"Not that tired. Sit down." She began to undress, moving quickly because the room was cold but undeterred by Rachel's presence. Stripped, she was heavier than Rachel had realized, with a perceptible layer of fat under her firm skin. Like a Greek Venus, Rachel thought, a sturdy healthy Venus like the one from Milo. Standards of beauty differed from age to age and culture to culture, and, as Kara would probably put it, standards were a lot of b.s. anyhow.

"What do you want to talk about?" Kara asked, pulling a thick flannel nightgown over her head.

"Adam."

"He hasn't bothered you, has he?"

"Not in the way you mean. It's just that I know so little about him. And I think I should know—not out of idle curiosity, but so I can avoid saying or doing the wrong thing. Why did he get so uptight when we talked about praying?"

Kara climbed into bed and propped herself up with a couple of pillows. There was an odd expression on her face. "He didn't tell you about himself?"

"No." She had never given him the chance—indicated interest, asked a friendly question. Uncomfortably Rachel added, "Somebody, I forget who, mentioned that he's an orphan."

"Since his father died, two years ago. Adam hadn't seen him since he was seventeen. He didn't even go to the funeral." Kara hesitated for a moment and then shrugged. "I got this from Pat, Adam has never discussed it with me. But you're right, you should know, if only to avoid hurting him inadvertently. The old man was one of those self-appointed ministers of the Lord—no congregation, no formal affiliation, he just wandered around fulminating at anybody who'd sit still long enough to listen to him. Funny, isn't it, how some people who interpret the Bible literally concentrate on the Old Testament instead of the teachings of Christ? 'An eye for an eye and a tooth for a tooth,' not 'Love thy neighbor as thyself.' 'If thy right hand offend thee, cut it off,' not 'Let him who is without sin among you cast the first stone.' It's no wonder Adam hates prayer. He grew up connecting it with a belt across his backside."

"His father beat him?"

"Him and his mother. Didn't you know that's one way to cast out demons? Maybe we ought to try it on the quilt." Kara's smile was sardonic and short-lived. "When Adam was big enough to fight back the old bully stopped abusing him physically. He took it out on Adam's mother. She had two miscarriages as a result of those beatings. When Adam tried to interfere *she* told him to butt out."

"My God."

"Yes, indeed. I find that hard to believe too, in spite of the evidence—that women collaborate in their own abuse. It's understandable; if you've been taught to believe you're garbage you don't expect decent treatment. I know a little about that."

"But you broke away. You escaped."

"With a lot of help from a lot of people. And I never had it that bad. Jack never laid a hand on me; his abuse was verbal and emotional. I can't condemn women like Adam's mother, I don't know whether I'd have acted any differently in her place. She was too terrorized and too dependent to escape.

"Anyhow—Adam stuck around, doing what little he could to protect her, with no thanks or cooperation from her. I can't imagine what those years were like for him; it must have been hell on earth. After she died he left, straight from the cemetery, with all his wordly goods in a brown paper bag. The story of how he fought for the education he wanted is a saga in itself. Eventually he met Pat. That was the turning point; Pat recognized his quality and practically adopted him. Adam wasn't the first or the last stray Pat has picked up but he's the most successful. It's no wonder he idolizes Pat. He's not the only one. I think rather highly of the guy myself."

"So you criticize him and yell at him."

"Sure. He prefers it that way. Sentimentality makes him nervous."

Rachel was silent. She was remembering Adam's pleasure in the gifts her family had sent, the gentleness of his big hand smoothing the satin roses. There had been nothing for him, not even a memory of love.

"Don't say anything to Adam," Kara said.

"Of course not." Rachel got to her feet. "Thanks for telling me."

She waited until after she had left the room before she wiped her eyes, though she suspected Kara had spotted the tears. Kara had probably shed a tear or two herself when she first heard Adam's story; she wasn't as hard as she pretended, and anyone would be moved to pity by hearing of pain no child should ever have to endure. How could he have come out of that tormented childhood so untainted? Not unscathed—there must be scars, deep and still painful—but so gentle, so capable of laughter? There was no hate in him. Rachel squirmed internally. For years she had been sulking over a fancied injury that couldn't be mentioned in the same breath with what Adam had endured. How he would despise her if he knew how selfish, how petty-minded and self-pitying she had been.

"Looks like snow," Adam announced.

"I don't know why you sound so pleased," Kara grumbled. They were finishing a hasty breakfast in the warm light of electricity. The dark skies supported Adam's weather prediction, and a keen wind had ruffled the animals' fur when they ventured out. Alexander had looked particularly disgusting with his hair wildly awry and his hairless rump even more visible.

He had been returned to his basket in the bedroom and the other animals had taken their proper places, sprawled across the rug and the furniture. Adam was rinsing the dishes. Rachel watched him. Kara had already been in the family room when she got there, so she had not had to make conversation.

He looked perfectly at home as he went about his domestic chores, big hands slow and careful with the glasses he was putting into the dishwasher. "I like snow," he said over his shoulder. "Snow is nice. The more snow the better."

"We may not have so many customers if the weather is bad," Kara said, brightening. "I hope Pat doesn't get caught in a blizzard, though."

"He said he expected to be back by noon." Adam closed the dishwasher.

"That means two or three p.m. Pat always underestimates how long a job will take." Kara rose. "I'd better open up. Are you really going to see that woman, Adam?"

"Uh-huh," Adam said. The impromptu haircut he had perpetrated on himself badly needed professional repair; pushing the ragged locks out of his eyes, he went on, "Want to come, Rachel?"

It was the first time he had addressed her that morning. Meeting his gaze she found it as candid and direct as ever, and reminded herself she wasn't supposed to know . . . what she knew.

"Where are you going?" she asked.

"He made an appointment with Ms. Starwalker." Kara let out a gurgle of laughter. "If anybody had called me at eight a.m., I'd have blown him up, but she seems anxious to talk with him. You'd better go along, Rachel, to referee."

"You don't need me in the shop?"

"No. Take my car, that heap of yours is about to fall apart."

"In that case, I will go," Rachel said. "And drive."

"That's what I had in mind," Kara said. "Pat warned me about Adam's driving."

•　　•　　•

Sans robe, mistletoe, and other accoutrements, Stargazer turned out to be a middle-sized, middle-aged woman with mild dark eyes and a lined face. The name that appeared on her mailbox in the apartment house lobby, possibly because the U.S. Postal Service was confused enough without having to deliver letters to someone named Stargazer, was Hassenfuss. She worked out of her apartment; through an open door Rachel saw a room filled with computer paraphernalia and deduced that Ms. Hassenfuss operated some sort of desktop publishing company.

Except for the multilayered clutter of beads and chains around her neck, her attire was unremarkable—a long homespun skirt and a peasant blouse. Rachel realized that the jewelry was not meant solely for adornment; she identified an ankh sign, a Star of David, a cross, and beads of semiprecious stones such as lapis lazuli and turquoise, which probably had psychic import. Hanging from a silver chain was a tiny bag of blue flannel.

Apparently Adam had already made the necessary apologies, for they were welcomed and offered chairs and herbal tea. Rachel would have refused the latter if Adam hadn't accepted before she could do so. Serves him right, she thought, watching with amusement as he took the first sip.

"Delicious," he said, in a voice that would only have deceived a woman as innocent as his hostess.

"Steeped leaves of the holy lotus. It brings love, peace, and understanding." Stargazer leaned forward and looked earnestly at Adam. "I am so glad, Adam—I may call you that, I hope, it is a name full of spiritual meaning—I am so glad our prayers had their effect in softening your ill will."

"I wasn't hostile," Adam protested. "Just—uh—ignorant."

"And you have come to learn, to be informed. How wonderful! Deeper understanding can only lead to love and sympathy." She shook a playful finger at Adam. "But my psychic talents tell me more than you would disclose, Adam. You have another reason for coming here. You are in need of help. Confess! I will not think less of you, this world is given to us for our enjoyment, and the body is as important as the soul."

Adam started so that the cup wobbled in his hand, and Rachel was momentarily impressed. She reminded herself that it was the same method fortune-tellers and professional psychics employ—clever guesses, based on human psychology. Most people act out of self-interest, and in this case at least Adam was no exception.

Stargazer went wildly off the track with her next guess, though. "Something has disturbed the even course of your love. Do you doubt your young lady's fidelity? Does she question yours? Or is the trouble impotence?"

Rachel was afraid to look at Adam. He made a series of choking sounds before he was able to articulate clearly. "Uh—no. At least . . . No!"

Rachel decided to throw him to the wolves. He would probably prefer her suggestion to some of the alternatives. "I don't doubt him," she murmured. "Not really. I just want to make sure . . . There are spells to bind souls together, aren't there?"

There were indeed. Lots of spells. Their hostess, happy to have a receptive audience, might have rambled on indefinitely if the ringing of the doorbell had not reminded her of a previous engagement. She urged them to come back any time and, at Adam's request, supplied him with a reading list. She even pressed a few of her own precious books on them.

"I hoped you're satisfied," Rachel said, as they returned to the car.

"She's a nice lady," Adam said simply. "She was trying to help us."

"You're hopeless." But Rachel's voice was gentle. "It was a waste of time."

"I'm not so sure. Turn right at the corner."

"It's the wrong way."

"I want to stop by that store she mentioned."

"The one that sells herbs and amulets? You aren't serious."

"Weren't you the one who was talking about multiple approaches? It can't do any harm to try." Adam had opened one of the books. "I did some reading last night after you guys went to bed. I didn't know—or if I did, I'd forgotten—how widespread some of these ideas are. (Left here, and then left again onto King Street.) The same elements recur over and over, from cultures widely separated in time and place—mojo bags, like the one she was wearing—Native Americans called them medicine bundles, Europeans charm bags or witches' sachets, people of African ancestry gris-gris or hands."

"I told you, magic has its own internal, consistent rules. The logic is based on false premises—"

"Oh, yeah?"

Rachel said no more.

Leesburg had a thriving tourist trade; the magic shop, as Rachel insisted on calling it, was in an area well-supplied with restaurants, boutiques, and specialty shops. The Eye of Horus appeared more prosperous than some of its neighbors, perhaps because it was the only one of its kind. The craft shops all seemed to be selling the same pottery and misshapen stuffed animals.

"Got any money?" Adam inquired. "I forgot my wallet."

"Five or ten bucks."

Adam stopped to look in the shop window. The theme that month appeared to be based on Tolkien and/or the northern mythology that had inspired his work. Mistletoe and holly, statues of wizards with long beards and longer staffs, a tree stump on which perched elves and fairies of various varieties and materials, plus the usual beads, crystals, candles, and bundles of herbs.

"I have a feeling that won't be enough," Adam said.

Rachel sighed. "I just paid my credit card bill."

"Great. I'll pay you back."

He paused to inspect the notices and advertisements pinned to the door. "Somebody is giving a workshop on Sacred Drum Making."

"I don't think Kara would stand for sacred drums," Rachel said.

"Alexander wouldn't like 'em either," Adam admitted. "How about an Intuitive Channeling Class given by an Ascended Master?"

"If you insist on doing this, let's get it over with."

Once inside Rachel left him to his own devices while she wandered around. Native American must be hot in the magic business this year; silver and turquoise jewelry filled several showcases, and artistically arranged displays of tomahawks and arrows adorned the wall. She was tempted to get Adam a tomahawk trimmed with bits of fur, or a t-shirt featuring a naked goddess.

When he requested her assistance in paying for his purchases, she saw they filled several large bags. Observing the total on the slip she signed, she said out of the corner of her mouth, "You'd better be good for this. What in heaven's name did you buy?"

"I'll show you later." Adam picked up the bags, smiled broadly at the clerk, who smiled broadly back at him, and led the way out.

"It's getting darker," Rachel said, as they walked toward the parking gargage. "I hope Pat is back."

"He'll be all right." As soon as he got in the car Adam began digging around in one of the bags. He waited until she had stopped for a traffic light before looping something around her neck.

"What's that for?" Rachel looked cross-eyed at her chest. The beads were white and translucent and oddly shaped.

"Warding off evil," Adam said seriously. "They're pearls—baroque pearls, the lady said, that's why they're those funny shapes."

"Adam—"

"Well, it can't hurt, can it? Anyhow, I thought they were pretty. They look nice on you."

After a moment Rachel said, "Thank you. They are pretty."

Adam fished in the bag again. "I got lots of stuff," he said happily. "Including a few more books. This one looked interesting. She describes how to rob a graveyard."

"You're joking."

"No, no. And it's very practical, down-to-earth—excuse me—advice. You find an abandoned cemetery, like the old private cemeteries near eighteenth-century houses—plenty of them around here—and take a few friends with you to help with the digging. She recommends at least four flashlights, and pliers, and ropes to slip under the coffin once it's exposed."

"That's sick," Rachel said in disgust. "How old is that book?"

"Published in 1970."

"That's even sicker."

"She needed coffin nails for a spell. That's another of the recurring ingredients in hex magic." He turned a page. "Brandy."

"What?"

"Take along a flask of brandy. Yes, I suppose an occasional nip might be cheering under those circumstances . . . Wear jeans and a sweat-band . . . She's right, digging is hard work. But you don't have to pull the coffin clear out, just raise it enough to get at the nails. That's where the pliers come in."

Rachel glanced at him in alarm. "Adam, you aren't seriously consid-ering—"

"Well, no. We don't want to cast a death spell, we want to take one off." He skimmed the remaining pages. "She doesn't say anything about removing curses. This wasn't one of the books Stargazer recommended. I can see why. Her crowd doesn't approve of black magic."

"Neither do I."

"It's dangerous," Adam said. He sounded perfectly serious. "If you don't know what you're doing, or if your intended victim is properly protected, the curse can rebound onto you."

"Put that awful book away."

"There's Pat's truck," Adam said. "I can hardly wait to hear what he has to say about this."

thirteen

Pat had plenty to say, most of it profane, but the majority of his curses were directed at himself.

"I'm getting senile. Outthought by a chit of a girl, and in my own field! I don't know why the idea didn't occur to me. Yes, I do. I committed the same sin for which I have blasted innumerable quailing colleagues—forming a hypothesis without adequate evidence and then getting so stuck on my own theory I couldn't see anything else." He groaned dramatically, "'I am old, I am old; I shall wear the bottoms of my trousers rolled . . .'"

"Now that you've got that out of your system maybe we can proceed," Adam said unsympathetically. "Have you seen the quilt?"

Pat shook his head. He had been making himself a sandwich when they arrived; cartons, jars, bottles, and baggies littered the counter. "Don't put the pickles away," he ordered as Adam started to clear away the mess. "Hand 'em over. Thanks. No, I haven't. Kara had just finished telling me about your discoveries when a couple of customers arrived and she wouldn't give me the key to the workroom. As if I didn't have sense enough to be left in there alone!"

He bit savagely into his sandwich. Pickles crunched like dried bones.

"I'm with Kara," Adam said. "The damned thing is dangerous, Pat, and you do tend to rush in where angels fear to tread." Cheeks bulging, Pat glared at him, but he went on imperturbably. "We need to give this careful thought before we proceed. You want a sandwich, Rachel?"

"Yes. No. I don't care."

"I need something to take the taste of lotus leaves out of my mouth," Adam said. "Let's eat, and discuss the situation, and then we'll have show and tell."

Pat swallowed. "Might I inquire why you have been breakfasting on lotus leaves?"

Adam's account of how they had spent the morning produced another string of curses, directed this time at Adam. "You wasted your time, boy. And your money. What's all this junk?"

He reached for one of the bags. His face reddening, Adam snatched the bag away from him. "Never mind. Look, Pat, we're in no position to throw stones at anybody or discard any possible approach. Stop yelling and make like the expert you claim to be."

"Touché," Pat said mildly. He dusted the crumbs off his fingers. "If you guys are right, this case is not a parallel to the one in which I was involved some years ago. Mind you, I'm not saying you *are* right, but I am willing to admit that your hypothesis is worthy of consideration."

"I figured your humility and open-mindedness were only tempo-rary," Adam jeered. "Rachel has a stronger case than you. The evidence supports her theory."

Pat leaned back in his chair and fixed his eyes on Rachel. She knew what he was trying to do—stare her down, get her to start talking, defend her theory. She also knew what he was thinking. She hadn't proved her case. Not all the evidence supported it.

She pressed her lips firmly together and stared silently back at Pat.

Tacitly acknowledging defeat, Pat transferred his hard stare to Adam. "I said it was worth considering. What we would have, then, is a clas-sic example of ill-wishing, employing the standard ingredients of black magic. Theoretically the curse can be broken by employing the con-ventional counterspells."

"That's what I thought," Adam said, with a betraying glance at the bags of magical apparatus. "Such as?"

Pat's lecturer's pose wilted. "That's the trouble," he said querulously. "There are a lot of possibilities, some of them mutually contradictory."

"I might have known you'd start waffling as soon as we got down to practical advice." Adam's normally even temper appeared to be cracking. "What about burning the damned thing? Wouldn't that cancel the spell?"

"It might." Pat glanced at Rachel. He hadn't missed her involuntary movement of protest. "Or it might be the worst thing we could do. Burning one of the poppets—the magical dolls—killed the person it represented."

"This person is already dead," Adam said sourly.

"So, one may reasonably assume, is the individual who made the quilt."

"What does that have to do with it?" Adam demanded.

"Well." Pat shrugged. "In some cases the destruction of the ensorceled object—witches' ladder, hex bag, whatever—turns the curse back on the perpetrator."

"That would be fine with me," Adam said. "But what you seem to be saying, if I understand that welter of contradictions, is that burning the ensorceled object (what a pompous phrase!) could have one effect or its exact opposite—and you don't know which."

"Magic is not an exact science," Pat said, visibly amused.

"How about burying it?" Adam persisted.

"You're being too simplistic. The physical actions are only one part of a magical performance. The spoken spell, the words, are equally important. The third element is perhaps the most vital—the powerful emotion felt by the magician—passion and desire in the case of love magic, bitter hatred in cursing. The emotion must be intense, focused— hurled, like a spear, at the intended victim. According to some theories, this last is not only necessary but sufficient; the other elements, words and actions, only assist in concentrating the magician's mental powers." He was silent for a moment and then he said soberly, "Mind over matter. There's some truth in that; we are just beginning to learn how much. If a man can wish himself to death, or control certain functions of his body by positive thinking, what else may he be able to do?"

"I don't give a damn about empty theorizing," Adam said. His face was flushed. "I can project hate, all that's necessary. Tell me what else to do."

"Who, me?" Pat's open amusement made Adam flush more deeply. "You are uptight about this, aren't you? I wonder why. Now, Adam, you were the one who said we ought to go slow. At least we should ask Rachel what she thinks."

"You don't destroy hate with more hate," Rachel said, and felt her own cheeks burn. "Good lord, I'm talking like Stargazer."

"You've got a point, though," Pat said, watching her. "Not that I want to sound like a dog in the manger, Rachel, but you might have mentioned your brilliant deductions to me before I wasted a whole day tracking down useless information in a town with too many good restaurants. I still have heartburn."

"You didn't ask me," Rachel snapped.

Pat grinned at her.

"Did you have any luck?" Adam asked.

"Some. I found Mary Elizabeth's obituary."

"That's not useless," Rachel exclaimed. "Didn't you locate anything else?"

"Typical," Pat growled. "A compliment and a criticism, almost in the same breath. No, dear, I didn't locate anything else. I told you, the records are incomplete and they are scattered all over hell and gone. The obit is interesting, though. Janney was her maiden name. Her husband was a Charles King, who came from North Carolina. He was listed as missing, presumed dead, after Bull Run—or Manassas, as they call it south of the Mason-Dixon line."

There was something in his voice that kept the others silent for a few moments. Then Adam said tentatively, "Eighteen sixty-one. He was a Confederate?"

"Yep."

"So she died later."

"Uh-huh."

"Oh, for God's sake, Pat, stop being theatrical," Rachel burst out. "What is it?"

"Weeell," Pat drawled. "It is rather suggestive. She survived him—if he was dead—by only a few months. They were married in 1860. She died a year later. In childbirth."

Involuntarily Adam glanced at Rachel. Neither spoke.

"Screws up your theory, doesn't it?" Pat inquired politely. "If you believe in curses, Mary Elizabeth must have been the recipient of the quilt instead of its maker. It killed her young husband and then her. She was twenty-one."

"Did the child survive?" Rachel asked.

"Yes. A girl. That may have been part of the curse," Pat added maliciously. "Sons were the preferred variety."

"Then Miss Ora lied, or was mistaken, about who made the quilts," Adam began.

"Not necessarily," Rachel said. "One of the perils of black magic is that a curse can bounce back and affect the person who sent it. If she made the quilt for someone else, and it was returned to her . . . "

"That's all we need, an unknown second party. The chance of locating her, if she existed at all, are slim to zero." Pat tossed his notebook aside. "This is beginning to look less and less relevant. Dammit, what's keeping Kara? I want to have a look at that quilt. Go get the key from her, Adam, tell her Rachel will make sure I don't misbehave."

As soon as Adam had left the room Pat reached for Adam's bags of magical paraphernalia and began unloading the contents. "The lad does have an inquiring mind, doesn't he?" he said, grinning wolfishly. "Black candles, little packets of mystic herbs, staurolite yeah, right, that's supposed to protect the wearer against black magic . . . Aha. What have we here?"

"You shouldn't do that," Rachel exclaimed. "Adam won't like it."

"He certainly wouldn't like my finding this." Pat sat the fat pink candle down in the center of the table with a decisive plonk. "If I remember the procedure correctly, he'll scratch your name on the wax, maybe wrap a strand of your hair around it, and burn it as he chants something maudlin like, 'Aphrodite, goddess of love, consume this maiden's heart with love of me as this candle is consumed . . . ' "

His voice rose to a saccharine falsetto. "Stop it," Rachel gasped. "That is so cruel!"

"I'm not the one who is cruel. What have you done to the kid?"

"What do you mean, what have I done?" Rachel grabbed the pink candle and put it back in the sack, piling the other objects in helter-skelter. Among them was a packet of dried rose petals. It didn't require much imagination to understand their purpose, if not their precise function, in the ritual.

"I guess you aren't obliged to fall for him just because he's gone goofy over you," Pat conceded with magnificent tolerance. "But I've never seen him like this. He's been hiding behind that beard for years. Did you complain about it scratching you?"

"You're disgusting. I didn't complain about . . . "

She *had* expressed disapproval of the beard, though. Pat's complacent smile infuriated her and made her feel obscurely guilty. "I didn't lead him on or encourage him, and he isn't goofy over me. He's a little goofy, period. According to Cheryl and Kara—"

"Women," Pat said in disgust. "What do they know about him?"

"More than you suppose."

"Ah. Who told you, Kara?"

"Yes. I can understand why he's afraid of taking chances, he's been hurt too often—"

Pat brought his fist down on the table. "Women! You've got it bassackwards, girl. He's afraid of hurting other people. That's why he keeps himself under such tight control. He almost killed his father one time, after the old swine had taken a broom handle to Adam's mother. She expressed her appreciation by beating on him with her fists and telling him it was all his fault that the old man was violent."

Rachel's eyes fell. "I knew about that. But not about . . . "

"So now you do. Don't look so stricken. And for God's sake don't offer to go to bed with him out of pity."

The comment had the effect he intended. The color rushed back into Rachel's face. "Damn you!"

"Under the present circumstances," said Pat, "it might be better if you refrained from suggestions like that. Paste a smile on, kid, here they come. This is just between us."

Kara had put up the "Closed" sign in order to grab a quick lunch, as she explained, but it was obviously Alexander's needs that concerned her most. She was carrying him when she came in. He and Pat bared their teeth—or in Alexander's case, his gums—at one another.

"I'm sorry we were so long," Rachel said. "I'll walk Alexander or take over in the shop, whatever you want."

"It's been busy," Kara admitted. She looked tired, her eyes shadowed and her mouth drooping. "I'd appreciate your help in the shop, but first you'd better show Pat the evidence. He won't leave until after he's examined it."

"Sit down." Adam took Alexander from her with such an air of authority that Kara obeyed and even Alexander realized protest would be futile. They weren't gone long. When they returned Adam's hair stood up in wild disarray and Alexander looked like a dirty mop.

"It's blowing a gale," Adam announced, putting the dog down. "Maybe you had better get on home, Pat."

"Not till I've seen the quilt." Pat's lips set stubbornly.

Kara looked at Alexander, who was tottering around looking for something to terrorize. The dogs had retreated into a corner and the cats had dematerialized. With a sigh she took the key from her pocket and handed it to Rachel. "I'll be along in a minute. Don't let him—"

"Take your time," Rachel said. "I can handle him."

"Ha," said Pat.

However, he accepted without argument the plastic gloves Rachel insisted he wear. You've come a long way, baby, she thought; who would have believed a few weeks ago you'd be ordering the great Patrick MacDougal around and swearing at him?

The quilt was dry now. After Rachel had shown Pat the dark inner layer, he asked her to turn it over. When she saw the appliquéd surface Rachel felt less guilty about finishing the destruction of the quilt. The stains were set and permanent, not dust but a deeper darkness, ingrained into the fabric. The gentle cleaning methods she had used would be ineffective now. Was there some mineral in the earth, iron or copper or lead, that had reacted with hot water to produce an indelible stain? Ordinary garden soil should simply wash out.

But this wasn't ordinary garden soil.

Delicately, almost shrinkingly, Pat ran his fingers over the fabric. "Nasty," he muttered. "Very nasty. The gloves help, though. Don't know why they should, but they do . . . Is this where you found the hair?"

Adam got out his specimens and indicated their original location. His disgust overcome by growing interest, Pat nodded. "She didn't miss much, did she? Let's get the rest of them out."

"You think there are more?" Adam asked.

"Sure to be. The lady knew her stuff. Scissors." He held out his hand, palm up, like a surgeon.

"This works better." Rachel gave him the ripping tool. "Do you want me to do it?"

Pat glanced at her from under furrowed brows. "I think not. Show me how this gizmo works."

Kara didn't join them. Vaguely Rachel was aware of the constant ringing of the shop bell. She felt she ought to join her beleaguered employer, but she couldn't bring herself to leave. Pat's big, clumsy-looking hands moved with a surgeon's skill and he found things the others might have missed. One was a fragment of rotting silk that had been used, instead of the usual cotton, to stuff the petal of a rose. The greenish-black worm coiled in the heart of the flower had not been visible until Pat removed the overlapping petals.

"She didn't miss a trick," he said again, and there was something close to admiration coloring his voice. "I'd guess the silk came from some intimate garment, a nightgown or underwear. Worn next to the skin, it absorbed the owner's perspiration and personality."

"That's unusual," Rachel said. "I think Cheryl told me respectable women didn't wear silk underclothes at that period."

"Is that right?" Pat looked up. "Maybe she wasn't a respectable woman. Maybe she was—"

"Get on with it," Adam said shortly.

The deadly collection mounted up—bits of linen cloth that might have been clipped from handkerchiefs dampened with tears or sweat, more fingernail clippings and hair, and a length of knotted string that brought a crow of recognition from Pat.

"The witches' ladder. Oh, very nice. One, two, three . . . Seven knots. The number varies, but seven has magical properties."

"A curse with each knot, I suppose." Adam eyed the harmless-looking object askance.

"Or a prayer. To whatever gods or demons the witch worshiped." Pat squinted nearsightedly at the string. "One method of removing the curse is to untie the knots, but these are so tight and the string is so rotted I doubt it could be done. I think that's everything, but we'd have to remove every piece of—what do you call it? Appliqué?—to be certain."

"What would be the point?" Rachel demanded. Watching, she had felt as if she were witnessing the deliberate mutilation of a living thing. Evil, no doubt, but so beautiful . . . And oddly pathetic, in its ruined state.

"No point," Pat agreed. He weighed the envelope with its bizarre contents in his hand. It was very light. "The fabric is permeated; whatever we do has to be done to the entire quilt, not just the bits and pieces. Oh, hell. It's getting late, I'd better head for home before Ruth comes gunning for me. Have you got any inert plastic?"

"Why, yes," Rachel said. "Cheryl uses it for old textiles; regular plastic contains chemicals that may react with the cloth. What—"

"Do I have in mind? Very little," Pat said wryly. "But it can't do any harm. Wrap it and seal it tight. We'll start working on it tomorrow. Talk to Rachel," he added, anticipating Adam's question. "She knows as much about it as I do, and she has a pretty good collection of books on magic and superstition. Check the indexes under 'curses, how to cancel them.'"

"What if there isn't—" Adam began.

"I was joking! Use your imagination and your common sense." Pat looked thoughtful. "I wonder where I can lay my hands on some holy water. Me, that hasn't been to mass in fifty years."

After the quilt had been sealed in plastic and the workroom locked, Rachel went to the shop, where she found Kara trying to cope with a pair of her regulars, middle-aged women who had nothing else to do that afternoon and had settled down for a comfortable chat.

"Sorry to interrupt," Rachel said, "but there's a phone call for you, Kara. On the other line." ·

Kara was quick to pick up the cue. "It must be Aunt Ruth. Oh, dear, I hope she's not worse. Excuse me."

She went no farther than the hall, where she lurked until the customers, foiled of their prey, had departed. Returning, she dropped limply into a chair.

"It's been like that all day. No, don't apologize, that's taboo, remember? Where are Pat and Adam?"

"Pat's gone home." Rachel's lips twisted. "He found more—more things in the quilt. It's a total wreck."

"It already was. Did he have any sensible suggestions?"

"Most people wouldn't call them sensible. The standard procedures involve fighting black magic with white, countering curses with prayer and religious symbols."

"Crosses, holy water, exorcism?"

"Among others. Adam brought home two bags of magical doodads. He's probably planning his experiments right now."

"You don't think those methods will be effective?"

Rachel shrugged. "I don't see how we can tell whether they are effective or not. It would be handy if squirting the quilt with holy water produced a cloud of evil-smelling black smoke or a demonic voice screaming 'Okay, okay, I give up,' but I doubt anything that dramatic will occur."

"It certainly hasn't produced any impressive special effects so far," Kara agreed. "The only manifestations have been . . . "

The advent of another customer stopped her, but she looked as if she had already regretted what she had started to say. The only manifestations had been in Rachel's behavior. Rachel wondered whether the obvious corollary had occurred to Kara, as it had to her. How would she be affected by the countermeasures Pat proposed to use? And how would the others be affected—the disembodied minds, the wandering spirits, of the intended victims and the sorceress?

I don't care, Rachel thought. I should care, but I don't. I'm too tired. *It's been so long. I want to rest, I want it so bad, but I can't rest till I finish what I set out to do.*

"Thank God that's over," Kara said, locking the front door. "Don't bother straightening up, Rachel, we'll do it later."

"I'll just finish this first. They certainly left things in a mess." Rachel continued to fold lengths of lace and ribbon.

"Our customers aren't as bad as some. And they took a lot of things off our hands." With weary satisfaction Kara studied the depleted sale racks. "I'm supposed to be good at spotting salable merchandise, but every now and then I goof. Every buyer does, I suppose. I thought this dress was charming, but even on sale nobody wanted it. Too demure, do you think?"

She held up a navy blue and white calico print with a long skirt gathered tight to a fitted bodice. To its only trim, a collar and cuffs of Irish crochet, she had added a narrow navy ribbon belt.

"Too costumey," Rachel said ungrammatically. "It looks like *Little Women.*"

"It's not that old. Women wore clothes like these clear up to the turn of the century and beyond; Paris and New York fashions never made it into the hinterlands, the farms, the small towns. Do you want to try it on?"

"What?" Rachel stared at her.

"This is one of those dresses that looks like nothing on a hanger, but on the right person it would be smashing. Trust me, I have an instinct for these things. Give you a good price."

"Are you serious?"

"I am, as a matter of fact. I love picking out clothes for people. But I don't suppose you're in the mood right now." She returned the hanger to the rack. "Some other time. Come on, I want a cup of tea."

They found Adam busily making notes. A pile of books at his elbow bristled with markers, and the surface of the table was littered with a weird miscellany—piles of silver coins, a few cloves of garlic, white candles, packets of dried herbs, a handful of nails, a hammer, and two cats nosing curiously at the herbs.

"Are you planning to eat supper standing up?" Kara demanded.

"Is it that late?" Without interrupting his writing Adam pushed Figgin away from the packet he was sniffing.

"Not really. I was trying to make a little joke."

Adam put the pen down and looked up. Brow furrowed, he said curtly, "Mark called. Wanted to know when you were coming home."

"Oh, hell. I didn't expect him back till tomorrow."

"Are you going home tonight?" Rachel asked. Her voice was carefully neutral, but she awaited Kara's answer with an anxiety she would not have felt a few days ago. She had come to depend on the other woman's help, and on something else. Friendship, perhaps?

"What do you take me for?" Kara demanded. She sounded angry. "I'm not leaving until this business is settled."

"Thanks." Rachel didn't trust herself to say more. She turned away and busied herself with the tea kettle.

"What is this stuff?" Kara asked. "It's driving Figgin crazy."

"Get it away from him." Adam made a dive for the cat. Packet in mouth, Figgin eluded him, but was captured by Kara. "It's vervain, otherwise known as Witchwort. I need it."

"I always suspected this animal was in league with the Devil," Kara muttered. "Give it back, Figgin. Ouch." She handed the packet, more or less intact, to Adam. "Put it in the cupboard. I presume this junk has some bearing on your research, but do you have to clutter the table with it?"

"I guess not." Adam tossed the packages into a drawer. "According to the books, all these herbs are used in unhexing, or uncrossing, as it is sometimes called. Vervain, St. John's wort, frankincense and myrrh, belladonna, foxglove—"

"Those aren't herbs, they're poisons," Kara exclaimed.

"I'm not going to leave them lying around."

Which was precisely what he had done; but after glancing at his dour face Kara decided not to press the point. She accepted the cup of tea Rachel handed her with a nod of thanks and then asked, "What are these other things?"

"Are you going to call Mark?"

"Soon. I'm asking for enlightenment, Adam. With all due humility and respect."

After a moment his forehead smoothed out and he smiled faintly. "Sorry. I'm getting frustrated; the information is so vague. All these objects are used in protective spells. Silver is supposed to be deadly to supernatural forces—you've heard about werewolves and silver bullets? Same for garlic. The white candles occur in one of the Wicca books, but you need a lucky rabbit's foot for that particular spell, and I don't have one."

"The nails are Ozark magic, aren't they?" Rachel asked.

"Also West African and old English," Adam said. "Iron is anathema to supernatural beings, and horseshoes keep witches away. One source suggested driving three nails—three is a potent magical number, it represents the Trinity—in a triangle over each door." A sweep of his arm cleared the table, pushing candles, nails, and the other objects into a shopping bag. Rachel realized the abrupt movement was another demonstration of his frustration.

"I'm not questioning your methods," Kara said. "But—correct me if I'm wrong—none of this deals directly with the source of the contamination. You can't shoot the quilt with a silver bullet, or drive nails into it."

Words and tone had been conciliatory, but Adam glared wildly at her. "Don't bet on it, lady. Some of the ideas I've considered are even loonier than those. Ah, hell. You're right, of course. I found a number of unhexing spells, but they all depend on something we don't have and can't get."

Opening one of the books, he read aloud. "'Take a piece of blood-root and throw it on the doorstep of the person who hexed you.' Or this one: 'Get a photograph or draw a picture of the witch who has put the curse on you, fasten it to a tree, and drive a nail into it.' Another possibility is to make a doll, incorporating some part of the witch's body, give it the name of the witch, and stick pins into it."

He tossed the book aside with a grunt of disgust. Rachel picked it up and began reading as the others continued to talk.

"I see what you mean," Kara said. "We don't know what she looked like, or even her name."

Rachel read, "Press the hair, the fingernail parings, or whatever other body part can be obtained, into a small ball of beeswax. Bore a hole in an oak tree, insert the beeswax, and drive a wooden peg into the hole . . . "

They didn't know what she looked like, or even her name. But they had something even more effective. Pat hadn't observed it, Adam hadn't noticed it.

Rachel closed the book. "I'll set the table," she said.

Kara went to her room to make the call to Mark. When she came back, flushed and tight-lipped, she was carrying Alexander.

"He smells worse than usual," said Adam, hurrying to the door.

"He had a little accident," Kara said coldly. "It was my fault. I should have taken him out earlier."

Alexander didn't appear to be overcome by remorse. He started squirming, and both dogs hastily retreated into the pantry.

Adam opened the door and then stood staring open-mouthed into the darkness—a wet, warm, windy darkness. "It's raining!"

"Oh, hell," Kara said. "Hand me that umbrella."

"It's raining," Adam repeated stupidly.

"So give me the umbrella."

She went out. Adam remained by the open door, muttering. "It's warm. When did it get warm? God damn it, I thought it was going to snow."

"The newspaper said something about a warm front," Rachel said. "What are you raving about? I thought you hated cold weather."

Kara came back, drenched, smeared with mud and, for once, a trifle out of temper with Alexander. "He didn't want to do anything except roll in the mud and get it all over me. Excuse us. One of us will return shortly."

When she returned she was wearing jeans and a t-shirt urging prospective voters to send Brinckley back to Congress. Adam had wandered out, leaving Rachel to dish up the meal he had prepared earlier. Glancing at the shirt, Rachel asked, "Was Mark upset because you weren't coming home tonight?"

"Not really. Well, yes, he was, but considering the weather and the fact that I didn't know he was going to be there he refrained from saying so. He didn't blow up till I mentioned I wasn't coming home tomorrow either."

She bit into a carrot stick and chewed fiercely.

Rachel said, "Hadn't you better tell him the truth? If you're holding back on my account, you needn't."

"You wouldn't mind?"

"I'd mind. But I like him, he's always been nice to me. And I don't want to cause trouble for you."

"In this case, the truth would cause even more trouble," Kara said wryly. "Mark is rigidly rational—difficult as that is to believe about a member of Congress. He'd think I was making up excuses—and pretty feeble excuses at that."

Adam's reappearance ended the discussion and they sat down to eat. The main dish was stewed chicken and noodles, into which Adam had dumped a package of frozen peas; hardly gourmet fare, but it had been easy to prepare and it was undeniably filling. Knowing what she now knew, Rachel realized that he had probably learned to cook out of sheer necessity. Neither of his parents had been nurturing types.

They were interrupted once by a call from Pat. After a brief conversation, Adam reported, "He'll be here tomorrow morning—holy water in hand, to quote him."

"That too?" Kara shook her head. "Why not a formal exorcism, bell, book, and candle?"

"Pat's against that," Adam said. "I gather he tried it once and it backfired rather badly."

"That's right, Sara mentioned it." Kara frowned. "But the cases aren't the same. You're trying everything else, why not that?"

"Churches are as bureaucratic as other large organizations. It would take too long."

Two days. The words, unspoken but understood by all of them, seemed to hang in the empty air. That's all the time we've got. Two more days.

After dinner Adam retired to his room, ostensibly to continue his reading, and after watching Kara roam restlessly around the room for a while, Rachel suggested they finish cleaning up the shop.

"We may as well," Kara said with a sigh. "It seems absurd to waste time on something so trivial, but I guess there's nothing else we can do. Nothing I can do, I should say. I feel as if I ought to be reading those books of yours, looking for practical advice, but if you and Adam and Pat haven't found anything, an ignoramus like me certainly wouldn't."

"That's not necessarily true," Rachel said. "Amateurs have been known to spot things the so-called experts have overlooked, if only because they are so obvious. But we may as well get at the other job. It will have to be done sooner or later."

Before Cheryl comes home. She didn't have to say it, they were both thinking the same thing. Two more days . . .

The job took longer than Rachel had expected. By the time they had restored order, replaced the tags on the garments and the garments on the racks, and entered the day's transactions in the inventory, she was exhausted. Leaving Kara mumbling and cursing at the computer, she went to the window.

It was still raining, steadily and quietly. The street was a stretch of glistening black and the puddles on the lawn and sidewalk reflected the outdoor lights, shivering into fragments of shot gold as the rain-drops struck them.

"Did you turn on the outside lights?" she asked.

"No. Damn this thing! Don't tell me computers don't have minds of their own; this one behaves like a little lamb for Cherry, but it knows I haven't the faintest idea what I'm . . . Ah, that's got it." She punched keys with savage satisfaction and then rose, stretching. "I'll leave the rest to Cherry. She always enjoys discovering my mistakes."

She joined Rachel at the window. "Still raining. Perfect weather for melancholia. Let's have something alcoholic or fattening or both."

The hallway behind the shop was dark except for the light at the top of the stairs. They both heard the sound; it was only that of a board creaking under the pressure of someone's foot, but both of them were ready to start at shadows. Kara called out.

"Adam?"

Her voice sounded oddly muted, as if the hall was filled with some substance heavier than air—or as if she had been afraid to speak loudly. The only response was the sound of a door closing.

"I wish he wouldn't creep around like that," Kara said unfairly. "What's he doing up there?"

Remembering Adam's pathetic collection of charms, Rachel realized how far he had come—descended, as he might have said—from his comforting rationalism. Her own voice was sharp. "He's got a lot on his mind. Leave him alone."

"Okay, okay."

The exaggerated coziness of the family room, unsophisticated and unsubtle as Cheryl herself, had never looked more appealing, but it didn't improve Kara's mood. She threw the dresses she was carrying over a chair and stared at the dogs. Both were on their feet, staring hopefully at her.

"So what do you want?" she demanded.

Worth's tail moved in a tentative wag. "They probably want to go out," Rachel said.

"Rather them than me." Kara went to the porch and opened the door. When Poiret, who had belatedly realized it was wet out there, lingered on the threshold, she gave him a shove and returned to the family room.

"How about Alexander?" Rachel asked.

"He'll have to wait. I'm not in the mood. Let's have a party. Why don't you slip into something more comfortable?"

One of the dresses she had brought from the shop was the navy and white calico. "You're determined to get me into that, aren't you?" Rachel said, amused.

"Please." Kara ran her fingers through her hair. "I'm so uptight I feel stretched. Do something to entertain me."

"Oh, all right."

Rachel retired modestly behind the sofa. Stripping off her shirt and pants she slipped the dress over her head. It was surprisingly comfortable, the soft old fabric gentle on her skin, the fit easy around arms and bust.

"Need some help?" Kara turned, a bottle of wine in her hand.

"No. It buttons up the front. Does that mean she didn't have a maid?"

"That's not a society lady's dress," Kara said. "Sweet and simple small-town stuff. You're right, though; the type of fastening was one indication of social class. Those ball gowns with two dozen tiny buttons down the back required a maid. Aha! I was right again. Look at yourself."

Rachel turned to the mirror over the mantel. She had braided her hair that morning; the thick, shining rope hung down over her shoulder, emphasizing the curve of the fabric across her breasts and ribs. The tightly gathered skirt belled out becomingly as she pivoted.

"Sweet and simple," she repeated. "I don't know that this is the look I'm after, Kara. It is well cut, though."

"You look adorable." Kara's grin indicated that she knew Rachel wouldn't appreciate the compliment. "Fits like a glove, too. Yes, she was an excellent seamstress. There are no darts in that bodice, she used six separate pieces of—oh, damn!"

A soprano howl from Poiret made her start and spill the wine she was pouring. The other dog added his deeper tones. Kara cursed them both. Rachel was about to point out that they probably wanted in out of the rain when something happened to prove her wrong. The door to the hall opened.

She hadn't heard footsteps. He had taken care that neither of them would hear him.

His hand still on the knob, ready to retreat, he looked quickly and apprehensively around the room, though he must have known from the barking that the dogs were outside. He must have waited till they were outside. He had been drinking, not enough to blur his speech or make his steps unsteady, just enough to give him false courage. Rachel knew the signs. Shocked into paralyzed silence, she watched his hunched shoulders relax, saw a smile replace his worried frown when he saw they were alone.

"Hello, ladies. Yes, thanks, I will join you in a glass of wine."

"How did you get in?" Rachel gasped.

"Bedroom window." Phil gestured. "Nice place you have here, Mrs. Brinckley. Now why don't you go sit over there in the corner while Rachel and I have a little chat? I'd suggest you leave the room, but I don't trust you not to telephone the police. That would be foolish. We don't want them."

"Get out," Kara said.

"How rude." The wrinkles framing his mouth deepened. "Don't be afraid, Mrs. Brinckley, I'm not going to hurt you. Or Rachel. I just want to talk to her. She's behaved rather badly, but I'm willing to give her another chance. That dress suits you, Rachel; you look demure and feminine and sweetly simple-minded, the way a woman is supposed to look."

"It was you upstairs," Rachel said. She was still afraid, but not for herself.

"I've been all over the house," Phil said complacently. "Found your room, Rachel; it's a nice room, much more comfortable than your old one. You landed on your feet with this move, didn't you? Nice room, nice rich influential friends—"

"What have you done to Adam?"

"Nothing. Oh, I came prepared to deal with him—he owes me satisfaction, don't you think?—but your hero isn't here. How do you suppose I got in that window? I saw him leave the house before I tried it."

Rachel noted the blatant contradictions, the macho bragging and the cautious cowardice, but she was too stunned to comment on them. "Adam isn't here?"

Kara's eyes narrowed. "We don't need Adam," she said. Rachel looked at her. Kara's eyes met hers, and then rolled sideways. A slight jerk of the head accompanied the eye movement.

"Right," Rachel said. She wasn't sure what Kara intended to do, but the meaning of the gesture had been clear: move toward him, distract him, get him to turn.

At least I'm dressed for it, Rachel thought, with a coolness she would marvel at later. Sweet and demure and—what was the word Kara had used? Adorable. Nonthreatening. Her skirts swayed as she walked slowly into the center of the room, and Phil swiveled, his eyes hard and bright. He was reaching for her when Kara picked up the heavy wooden cutting board from the counter and brought it down on his head.

The two women stared at the sprawled body. When Rachel spoke, she had to raise her voice to be heard over the indignant barking of the dogs.

"My hero."

"You weren't so bad yourself," Kara said. She tossed the board onto the counter. "Hitting him was no trouble at all, I enjoyed it. Yours was the dirty part of the job."

"Not really. I knew you'd stop him, somehow."

"Thanks," Kara said simply.

"Thank *you*. Shall I call the police?"

"Why go to all that trouble? It's late and I'm tired. Wake him up and get him out of here." She filled a glass with water and was about to dump it onto the face of the fallen man when she paused. "Wait a minute. Did you say he carries a gun?"

"I don't think he carries it."

"Hold this." She handed Rachel the glass and calmly investigated Phil's jacket pockets. "Looks like you were wrong," she said, straightening.

"My God."

"I doubt he'd have used it," Kara mused. "Carrying it made him feel big and brave and macho."

"I'm going to let the dogs in."

"I'll do it. They'll shake themselves all over that dress."

Directed by Kara, the dogs were happy to assist in the resuscitation of Phil. When he started to stir and groan, Kara shoved them out of the way and finished the job with a glass of cold water.

"Get up," she ordered. "And pay close attention."

Propped against the door, spattered with muddy water, his eyes rolling from the gun Kara held to the attentive dogs, Phil listened.

"This is your last chance," Kara finished. "You show your face around here, or within a hundred yards of Rachel, once more and I'll have you locked up for life. Don't think I can't do it. You've got exactly sixty seconds to get to your car before I set the dogs on you. One— two—"

After he had stumbled out, Rachel closed and bolted the door. Kara dropped limply into a chair. She was still holding the gun; realizing this, she placed it carefully on the table. Her hands were shaking.

"Are you all right?" Rachel asked anxiously. "You were so cool, I didn't think—"

"Yeah, I'm all right. Reaction." Kara covered her face with her hands, shook herself, and then smiled. "Wow. I was so mad I didn't realize how scared I was. How about some wine for us heroes?"

"We deserve it. Just wait till I see Adam," Rachel said furiously. "I'll give him some wine too—the whole bottle, on the top of his thick skull. Fine protector he turned out to be, sneaking out without a word. Where could he have gone?"

They found Adam's note on the floor under the table. One corner had been chewed, presumably by Figgin, who was willing to taste anything, but it was still readable and it was, for Adam, positively wordy. "Had to run an errand. I won't be long. You'll be all right. Keep the dogs in. I'm sorry, but this is absolutely necessary. All that rain. I'll be back soon. By midnight at the latest."

But midnight came and went and Adam had not returned.

fourteen

They didn't wait up for him. Not exactly. But when Rachel went to bed she left her door open, and started from light, uneasy slumber whenever she heard a noise. Some of the noises came from Kara, who was doing what Rachel had done—going to the window or the door in the hope of seeing the wanderer return.

Kara had refused to move to one of the upstairs bedrooms, despite the fact that it had been her window Phil had used as a means of entry. "I forgot to close and lock it this morning," she admitted. "Careless of me. I won't make that mistake again."

"And besides," Rachel had said, with only a hint of sarcasm, "you have Alexander."

Alexander was still wandering aimlessly around the room sniffing and bumping into things. Occasionally he gummed a chair leg out of pure frustration; he couldn't believe the owner of the new, interesting smell had gotten away from him.

"I'm glad Phil didn't hurt him," Rachel added, more charitably.

"He probably didn't even notice him." Kara picked the dog up. "If Alexander is asleep it takes him a while to pull himself together and get moving."

"You aren't going to take him out, are you?"

"Not me. I've had enough excitement for one night. If a shadow moved out there I'd drop in my tracks. Anyhow, it's easier to mop up a puddle than dry a soggy, muddy dog. I guess we should roll up the rugs and spread some newspapers on the floor."

Since the scatter rugs were antiques, hooked or braided, Rachel agreed that they should.

"I told Cherry she was crazy to put these things here," Kara grumbled as they piled the rugs on top of the blanket chest. "It's a wonder Tony didn't break his neck."

"She wanted the room to look pretty for him."

"I know." Kara sighed. "Why are nice, decent people so stupid about the ones they love the best? Doing the wrong things, saying the wrong things, hurting one another, and always with the best of intentions . . . He does love her, you know. And even if he didn't, he'd never leave her and the kids."

"You don't have to tell me that."

"Just thought I'd mention it. Oh, for God's sake, go to bed. And don't worry about Adam, that beat-up old wreck of yours has probably broken down somewhere and he can't find a phone or a tow truck."

Rachel went. In addition to Alexander, Kara had the gun, which would be a good deal more useful in a case of real emergency. Rachel wondered whether she would actually fire it even if a brace of burglars appeared in the room. She hadn't needed a gun to handle Phil.

Earlier they had investigated the upstairs apartment together, fearing Phil might have left some unpleasant memento. They found nothing out of the way until Rachel opened her closet door and saw the pink peignoir lying crushed on the floor.

"Your mother must have paid a pretty penny for it," Kara said, after Rachel had explained its origin and restored it to the hanger from which it had . . . fallen? The possibility that Phil might have handled it, thrown it on the floor in a perverse fit of rage or jealousy, made her skin crawl.

The gun had not been fired. Rachel kept telling herself that as she lay awake, listening. She hadn't mentioned that particular nightmare to Kara because she knew it was ridiculous. Adam wasn't lying dead on the street, with the rain beating down on his open eyes. The gun had not been fired. They would have heard a shot. Her car was gone, he hadn't returned.

Where could he have gone? The errand must have been important or he wouldn't have behaved so irresponsibly—though she had to admit that Adam's definition of important might not be the same as hers. A list of possibilities, some logical, some wildly fantastical, circled endlessly through her mind. A secret conference with Pat? Surely not. Adam wouldn't have to leave the house, they could talk on the phone. Another meeting of the witches, or a private consultation with Stargazer? He had taken so much kidding on that subject he might be embarrassed to admit resorting to Wicca . . . but he had said he'd be back by midnight. A shopping trip, for more magical supplies? There were all-night drugstores and markets . . . but he'd have been back by this time, he wouldn't chase all over the county late at night trying to track down something stupid like purple candles or esoteric herbs.

There are other things. Things that don't come from stores.

The inner voice might have been hers or the voice of That Other. They shared the same knowledge. Graveyard dirt, coffin nails, other ingredients even more obscene . . . They were obtainable, if one knew where to look. Adam knew. "Plenty of them around here," he had said. Thanks to the advice in the book from which he had read to her, he also knew what equipment he would need—ropes, flashlights, pliers, shovels—and a sweatband. "Digging is hard work." He had said that too. The author of the book had recommended taking several friends along, but Adam wouldn't—couldn't—involve anyone else. He was strong enough to do the job alone. Or so he would believe.

Rachel got up and tiptoed to the front window. The rain fell harder now, a solid veil of transparency through which she saw no moving object. It was a quarter past two in the morning.

She slept, finally, out of sheer exhaustion—a troubled sleep shot with disturbing dreams. When she woke, nudged into consciousness by a cold nose in her face, sunlight lay bright across the bed and the massive bulk of Figgin lay heavy across her chest.

Then she remembered and shot out of bed, dumping Figgin unceremoniously onto the floor and moving so fast his lunge at her bare ankle missed.

Adam's bed had not been slept in. Rachel scrambled into jeans and shirt and headed down the stairs, without brushing her teeth or washing her face.

Adam wasn't in the family room either. Stretched out on the couch, coffee in hand, Kara was watching the news. Normally she didn't do that. Rachel knew why she was doing it this morning.

"Anything?"

"No." Kara waved the remote at the set, which went black. "I've watched the same local news twice. Not that I expected anything had happened."

"Yeah, right. I'm calling the police, Kara."

"Let's discuss it first. Now, Rachel, another five minutes won't matter. Have some coffee. I agree, I completely agree, we must notify someone. The only question is, who?"

"The police." Rachel reached for a cup.

"What police? The station? You tell the typical sergeant your boyfriend has been out all night and he'll giggle behind his hand. Tom? Maybe. If we can locate him. But I'm not sure Adam would thank us for dragging him into it. I'd rather talk to Pat first."

"Pat," Rachel repeated. "He's not a policeman."

"Drink your coffee," Kara said, trying not to smile. "I'm not taking this lightly, believe me, but I'm sure Adam is all right. If he had had a serious accident it would have been on TV. The local news broadcasts adore car crashes."

"It might not have been a car accident. If he went somewhere isolated and remote—it was dark, not even starlight—the rain pouring down—muddy and slippery underfoot—if he fell . . . "

"Dark and muddy?" Kara's level brow furrowed. "What sort of place did you have in mind? Have you remembered something?"

"No." The idea was insane, the product of worry and fevered imagination.

Kara's forehead smoothed out. "Men do this sort of thing, you know. Mark has done it to me, every husband and every son has done it to some poor damned worrying woman. When they finally turn up they get all wide-eyed and indignant when you scream at them. They couldn't find a phone or they didn't have a quarter or they didn't want to wake you in the middle of the night."

"Yeah, right," Rachel repeated. "When I get my hands on him . . . "

"Good. Normal reaction. Even if we convince the cops there is cause for alarm they won't have the faintest idea where to begin looking for him. Pat will be here pretty soon. If he doesn't know where Adam went—and it wouldn't surprise me to learn they were in cahoots—he may be able to hazard an educated guess. Does that make sense?"

"Yeah," Rachel said. "Right."

"Go wash your face."

Rachel had just stepped out of the shower when she heard the dogs. Pat was early. Or could it be . . . She scrambled into her clothes and went running downstairs, her hair flying out behind her.

It wasn't Adam. She could hear Pat's voice, raised in a shout. When she reached the family room she saw that Ruth was there too. The older woman's smile and outstretched hands were eloquent, but she was unable to express her sentiments because Pat was still bellowing.

"No, dammit, I haven't the ghost of an idea where he might have gone. Some wild goose chase, I suppose. He has no goddamn business chasing off on his own without consulting me! So help me, I'll tear his head off when he shows up. Of all the stupid, useless—"

"Shut up," Rachel said. She didn't raise her voice, but Pat stopped talking and stared at her in astonishment.

"We waited for you because Kara thought you might have a sensible suggestion," she went on cuttingly. "I might have known you'd just yell. I'm going to call the police, as I should have done a long time ago."

Pat gave her a malevolent look. Before he could reply, Ruth said, "We must do that, certainly. But first—have you looked in his room to see what he might have taken with him? Did he say or do anything last evening that would indicate where he might have gone?"

"A sensible suggestion at last," Kara said. "No, we didn't look. We had a busy night."

"You certainly did," Pat muttered. "Why didn't you call the police then? Oh, hell, this is no time for Monday morning quarterbacking. That little encounter can't have any bearing on Adam's disappearance; he had gone before Whatsisname entered the house."

Ruth looked troubled. "If he was angry enough to lie in wait for Adam . . ."

"Not without his gun," Pat said contemptuously. "He wouldn't tackle Adam barehanded. Anyhow, the car's not here. Come on, girls, think. Adam must have said something; reticent he ain't."

"He kept mumbling about the change in the weather," Rachel said. "It seemed to bother him." Rain on untrimmed grass and weeds, water trickling down in the excavation, turning dirt to gluey mud . . . This time the grisly image would not be dispelled: Adam face-down and motionless in the hole he had dug, mud blocking his mouth and nose, water rising around him. She was about to speak when the dogs rose and hurled themselves howling at the door.

No one else moved. When the door opened four pairs of eyes focused on the unspeakable object on the threshhold.

His face and hands were clean, scrubbed pink as those of a baby, and he had made some effort to smooth his hair. Every other part of him, shoes, pants, jacket, was covered with a layer of dried mud that reminded Rachel horribly of the gray film on the quilt. Her pent breath went out in a gasp that seemed to empty not only her lungs but her entire body.

Pat was the first to move, and Rachel realized he had been more concerned than he had admitted. Grabbing Adam by the shoulders, he shook him violently. Flakes of mud rained onto the floor.

After a few incoherent epithets, Pat got to the point. "Where the hell have you been?"

"In jail," Adam said. It seemed to dawn on him, somewhat tardily, that he was in disfavor. Looking at Rachel, he inquired hopefully, "Were you worried about me?"

"It was the rain," Adam explained, when they finally let him talk. Kara had refused to let him trail mud through the house, so he had stripped in the pantry and put on the clean clothes Pat hurled at him, along with a few well-chosen adjectives. Kara had added her comments, and even Ruth had said severely, "It was very thoughtless behavior, Adam."

The only one who had not spoken was Rachel, and Adam kept glancing at the sofa where she sat, hands folded, face expressionless.

"I'm really sorry," he said, for the fourth time. "I didn't think you'd even notice I was gone. I expected to be back by midnight, but I had to get right out there, because of the rain."

"Out where?" Pat inquired. His voice was ominously mild.

"The cemetery. Pat, you've got to—"

Rachel was incapable of speech, but Pat seldom suffered from that

difficulty, and he was as familiar as she with the literature of the supernatural. His voice rose to a pitch that rattled the windows. "Jesus
Christ, Adam! Have you lost your mind? If the newspapers find out
about this you'll never get tenure. Desecrating a grave? Tell me that's
not what you were doing. Tell me I'm wrong."

"You're wrong," Adam said. "Rachel, don't look like that. Did you
think . . . "

"I'm wrong," Pat repeated.

"Yes. Listen to me, will you, this is important. We've got to stop
them. An injunction or a restraining order or something. It's Saturday,
but they may—"

"Stop whom from doing what?" Pat took hold of his head with both
hands. "No, don't answer that; start at the beginning. Dammit, boy,
didn't anybody teach you how to organize a report? God knows I
tried!"

"Okay." Adam pondered, his eyes fixed on the cup he held almost
hidden in his big hands. "It started the day we went to see Miss Ora's
house. The lot next to it was under construction, or about to be. Mrs.
Wilson said it had been sold—the last of the original property to go—
and it was a reasonable assumption that the builders were going to put
up more little crackerboxes like the other houses on the street."

He stopped to sip his coffee and Pat said impatiently, "You're overdoing the organization. Get to the point."

"Well, I like watching construction crews," Adam said. He sounded
meek and looked repentant, but there was a glint of amusement in his
eyes. "All those great big machines. So I wandered over to see what
they were doing. Had to stretch to look over that high fence. They
weren't encouraging rubberneckers.

"Nobody was working that day. The ground was frozen solid, and I
suppose the holidays had disrupted the normal work schedule. Something caught my eye, though. They had covered it with a tarp, but
there was a strong wind blowing. One corner of the tarp had come
loose."

He took a dainty sip of coffee, watching his mentor over the rim of
his cup. Pat growled, and Adam continued, "I went back another time
for a closer look. What I saw confirmed my hunch, but I didn't have a
chance to investigate. The ground was still too hard to dig, and some
guy came along and ran me off."

"Dig," Pat repeated. All at once he looked very thoughtful.

Adam put his cup down. There was no sign of suppressed amusement on his face now; it was set and anxious. "It's a cemetery, Pat. An old cemetery. You've got to keep the construction crew away till we can check it out. The State Code says burials must be shown on site plans, but it doesn't demand a preliminary survey. Builders don't like to report finding cemeteries because they know it will halt construction; they have to remove the remains or leave the site undisturbed, and either one could cost them money. There isn't much visible; they could claim they didn't notice it until afterward, and once it's gone, there's no way—"

"Are you sure?" Pat asked.

The question sounded reasonable to Rachel, but it infuriated Adam. "God damn it, Pat, are you questioning my expertise? I worked at Annapolis and Williamsburg, not to mention Turkey and Guatemala and God knows where else. I know a goddamn cemetery when I see one! I'm an expert on cemeteries!"

"You are," Pat admitted. "I apologize. So you went back last night—I know, I know, it was the rain. Warmer weather, a thaw, the ground softening. If the temperature holds, they could start work next week, after the holidays." He grinned. "So what happened? You got caught?"

"They had a night watchman. Not much of one. He was about this tall." Adam held his flattened palm an improbable three feet above the floor. He went on in an aggrieved voice, "I didn't think he'd come out of his nice comfortable trailer in that filthy weather and in the dark, and I was absorbed in what I was doing, and the rain made so much noise I didn't hear him, and . . . Well, the little son of a gun tackled me."

"A little son of a gun three feet tall overpowered you?" Pat inquired.

"I didn't want to hurt him."

"Oh."

"Anyhow, he had a gun. And as luck would have it, a police cruiser came along while we were arguing. They took me in to the station."

Pat's grin faded. "And you sat there in the slammer all night? Why, for God's sake? Even if they wouldn't release you on your own recognizance you could have called me or Kara, or mentioned Tony, or demanded to see Tom, or—"

"It was late. I didn't want to bother anybody."

I couldn't find a phone, I didn't have a quarter, I didn't want to bother anybody. Rachel wondered if Adam realized how pathetic that excuse sounded: I didn't think anybody would care enough to worry about me. She got up, crossed the room, and slapped Adam resoundingly on the cheek.

"Don't ever do that again!" she shouted.

Adam's face lit up.

"This is stupid," Pat grumbled, resisting Ruth's efforts to help him into his coat. "Everything is closed, it's not only Saturday, it's a holiday weekend. The builders won't be able to start work before Monday, if then."

"It has to be done." Adam's voice was as inflexible as steel. "Five minutes' worth of action from a backhoe or bulldozer and there won't be anything left except rusty nails and rotted scraps of wood."

"And splintered bones," Pat murmured.

"If that. They disintegrate quickly in that kind of soil."

"Oh, all right. I'll give it my best shot. But I'm damned if I'm going to waste the whole day on this. I'll be back in a couple of hours. Don't do anything till I get back! Is that clear?"

"Loud and clear," said Adam.

After he had gone the others sat in silence for a time. Kara was the first to speak.

"Why is this so urgent, Adam? Do you think that old cemetery has some connection with our problem?"

Adam looked at her in surprise. "I'd have done my best to halt construction anyhow, on general principles. But—well, yes, I do think there may be a connection. Remember what Pat said when we were talking about why Rachel should have been affected just now—that there might be another factor we knew nothing about? Work began in that vacant lot a few weeks ago. It disturbed graves that had been untouched, forgotten, for over a century. No—" he held up his hand, stilling Kara's incipient objection—"let me finish. The connection is unproven, I admit. But that property has been in the same family for three generations or more, and that takes it back a long way. Miss Ora was almost ninety. Her grandfather, who built the house, could have been born as early as 1850. The quilts date from approximately the same time, if we can believe Miss Ora's account of their origin."

"Grandpa didn't build the house until about 1890," Kara objected. "Surely the cemetery is older."

"Not only older—abandoned, overgrown, and forgotten by that time. There was a war, remember? I assure you," Adam said soberly, "the southerners I know remember. A lot of men died in that war, a lot of things were destroyed. But the land itself endured. There must have been an older house on that property. After it had been destroyed, by the ever-popular damn yankees or by natural causes, Grandpa built himself a new house in a new location, but on land that had been part of the original grant—as was the cemetery."

"Wait a minute," Kara said. "There's a gap in your reasoning. What makes you think that land was part of the property that had belonged to Mary Elizabeth's husband? We don't know where the King plantation was located. Gerhardt wasn't related to the Kings, he came from out of state. He needn't have bought the land from them."

"There's a gap," Adam admitted. "But it's not as wide as you think. I can bridge it logically, and if we search in the right places we can probably find the proof."

"Gerhardt was related to the Kings," Rachel said. "Is that it?"

"Foiled again." Adam clapped a dramatic hand to his brow. "I keep trying to impress you and you keep anticipating my brilliant deductions."

"Stop being cute," Kara snapped. "The names aren't the same. How could Gerhardt be—"

"By marriage," Rachel said. "It's difficult to free ourselves from traditional patrilineal thinking, isn't it? The quilts came down from mother to daughter. Why not the land, or part of it? In many cases it would pass directly from their fathers to their husbands as part of their dowry, so the deeds wouldn't list their names."

"And," Adam added triumphantly, "don't forget that Mary Elizabeth had only one child—a daughter. Her husband couldn't have married again, he died before she did."

"Died in battle," Ruth murmured.

"Or of dysentery, disease, or unskilled surgery. It wasn't a romantic war for the men who fought it," Adam said soberly. "Point is, if he didn't survive long enough to take a second wife, his only heir would be Mary Elizabeth's daughter. She had to marry somebody; why not a man named Gerhardt?"

"It's logical, but unproven," Kara said stubbornly.

"I don't have to prove it." Adam glowered at her. "I'm not trying to get Mrs. Wilson admitted to the Daughters of the Confederacy, for God's sake. The quilts prove that Miss Ora was descended from Mary Elizabeth. Logic suggests that the house and the cemetery were on part of the King estate. That's enough of a reason why it must be investigated."

"I agree," Ruth said firmly. "Is it possible that Mary Elizabeth herself is buried there?"

"I hardly think so." There was a note in Adam's voice that made Rachel look sharply at him. He shifted uncomfortably. "Do we have to wait for Pat?" he demanded. "We could at least get things set up."

"If there's something you want to do, go ahead," Ruth said placidly. "He'll yell, but you're used to that."

Adam's gloomy face brightened. "I have a few ideas. I'll go get my notes."

"I may as well attend to Alexander before we get started." Kara went out with him.

Despite Ruth's apparent friendliness, Rachel felt a little uncomfortable with her. Murmuring an apology, she was about to follow the others when Ruth said, "I want to talk to you, Rachel. Do you mind?"

"I was just going to finish dressing. I haven't braided my hair—"

"I don't blame you for resenting me."

"I don't," Rachel said. "I understand how you feel."

"Then you are a remarkably forgiving young woman." Ruth smiled wryly. "I've been reluctant to come here because I was ashamed of myself. My reaction was stupid and unthinking. This isn't the same sort of thing we encountered before, I should have known that. We aren't part of this pattern; our involvement is only peripheral and my worries about Pat were absurd."

Rachel wondered what Ruth would say if she knew about the incident Pat had preferred not to describe to his wife. Pat had been right; it had been she, not he, who had reacted abnormally. But an observer, especially a biased observer, might well have interpreted his abrupt movement and her frantic struggles quite differently, and Ruth had good reason to be biased.

Ruth went on. "Distancing myself from the situation for a while may have been a good idea, though. The rest of you are too involved; I think you may have overlooked some of the practical aspects. You're behaving as if the world were coming to an end on Monday afternoon—as if you must resolve the situation by then or give up. That's foolish, you know."

"I must be out of this house before they come back," Rachel said flatly.

"That would probably be best. But you don't have to jump off the edge of the world. Pat will keep digging at this, I know him, and Adam won't quit either. I suggest you come to us on Monday."

Rachel started to expostulate, but Ruth stopped her with a raised hand. "Hear me out. We can easily think of an excuse that will satisfy Cheryl—Pat needs a knowledgeable assistant to help with his book, you've fallen behind on your work and he's offered to help—something like that. Adam can come too. He usually stays with us during the holidays."

"Holidays?" That word opened up another subject, one that hadn't occurred to Rachel. "But he has a job, hasn't he? He'll have to go back to it."

"Didn't he tell you what he does?"

"I . . . never asked." Rachel's eyes fell. "I never even bothered to ask."

"The answer would take some time." Ruth sounded amused. "Adam gets around, as Pat says. He's teaching next semester, but classes don't start till the third week in January. You don't have to decide immediately, Rachel, but think seriously about my suggestion. Whatever you decide, we're not going to let you walk out of our lives."

The last sentence—affectionate, unmistakably sincere—was almost too much for Rachel. Fortunately Kara came back with Alexander in time to keep her from breaking down. It was impossible to be sentimental around Alexander.

She made her escape, leaving Ruth and Kara to bicker amiably about the dog.

Her fingers were too unsteady to cope with a French braid or a braid of any other variety. Burrowing in the bureau drawer in search of a hair clip, she thought of Ruth's offer. It had been sensible and practical—a lot more sensible than the end-of-the-world scenario the rest of them had been following—but it wasn't a final solution. It wouldn't separate her from Cheryl and Tony. The families saw a good deal of one another.

Hearing a thud and a curse from the hall, she opened her door and saw Adam trying to retrieve a book he had dropped without losing his grip on the other books and parcels he carried.

"I'll get it," she said.

"Thanks."

When she straightened she saw he was watching her like a dog that is uncertain as to whether it will be patted or scolded.

"Are you still mad at me?" he asked.

"I wasn't mad. Well, yes, I was, but only because I had been worried. I'm sorry I hit you."

"Any little demonstration of interest is gratefully received. Does that count as the third time?"

"Don't be so humble," Rachel said irritably. "You should have hit me back."

She spoke before she thought; seeing his face change, she tried to think of some way of retrieving her blunder, but there was none, and no way of apologizing. Except . . .

She had to stand on tiptoe and pull his head down in order to reach his mouth. His lips were stiff with surprise at first, but they were quick to respond and not at all humble. Swaying and off balance in every sense, Rachel caught hold of his shoulders to steady herself, and the impulsive kiss turned into something she had not intended or anticipated. Adam dropped the books and wrapped long arms around her, but when she pulled away he made no attempt to hold her.

"I'm sorry," Rachel said.

"Feel free to apologize again the same way." It took him two breaths to complete the short sentence.

"I mean, I'm sorry for—for everything. I had no right—"

"I don't mind your knowing." He knelt and began collecting the books. "The only reason I didn't tell you was because it's a pretty boring story."

"I wouldn't say that." Rachel made no move to help him, though he was clumsier than usual. After adding insult to injury, she could only think of one means of reparation. "It's not as boring as my story. You must have wondered why I was so ungracious about the Christmas gifts."

"None of my business," Adam muttered, without looking up.

"I was sulking. I've been sulking for four years, ever since my mother married again. I don't even remember my father; he walked out when I was two. Twenty years later, after she had raised me, single-handed and without a nickel's worth of help from him, my mother finally found a man she could care for, and went back to England with him. I was jealous."

"That's understandable." Adam rose, clutching his armload. His eyes were warm and sympathetic.

"Maybe. It was also selfish and small-minded." Rachel removed the topmost book from the tottering pile.

"Thank you," Adam said.

He wasn't thanking her for helping him with the books. "You're welcome," Rachel said softly, and led the way downstairs.

"Here we are," Adam announced unnecessarily. "Kara, will you please clear . . . Oh, hell!"

His uncertain grip gave way and papers, books, and arcane paraphernalia spilled across the table. Kara leaped to rescue a tottering glass, and with a look of pained resignation Adam bent over and detached Alexander from his ankle.

"I thought you said he never bit anybody more than once," he remarked, holding the vibrating, grumbling bundle out at arm's length.

"I said hardly ever. Bad boy, Alexander." She put the dog down and started him off in a different direction while Ruth and Rachel cleared the table.

Adam began to arrange his materials into groups. Rachel had seen the purchases but the other women hadn't, and they stared in mounting disbelief.

"Black candles?" Kara said tentatively.

"Where? Oh. We don't need those now. What happened to the white ones?"

"They must have rolled off the table." Kara collected them from the floor. "Adam, what are you doing?"

"I think that's everything," Adam muttered, inspecting his arrangement. "Okay. I found six recipes for unhexing, and a couple of others that are described as cures."

"What's the difference?" Ruth asked.

"Damned if I know. Unless the first variety turns the curse back on the witch and the second just removes it. Do we care?"

He didn't seem to expect an answer; he went on without pausing for breath. "The first one . . . Wait a minute. I forgot the milk."

"It's in the fridge," Kara said. Her eyes were slightly glazed.

Adam got out the jug. "It's only half full. Damn, I should have bought more, we'll need four or five gallons. I better make a quick run to the store."

"I'll go," Kara said. "I think a little fresh air would do me good. Just tell me why you want it."

"Southwest magic," Adam explained. "It's for unhexing clothing, which is more specific than anything else I found. You wash the thing in milk and hang it out overnight in freezing weather."

"Why, for God's sake?"

"The rationale eludes me," Adam admitted. "Any ideas, Rachel?"

"Purity? Milk is white." If she didn't allow herself to think about why they were doing this it became an intriguing if childish game.

"It's as good a guess as any. So we do that tonight, after we've tried the other things. Don't go yet, Kara, I may have forgotten something else. The same book also recommended burying the garment. That's a last resort, obviously. Now here . . . " He indicated a group of objects. "These are voodoo preventives against conjure: silver, red pepper, salt, and nails. They're supposed to be tied up in a 'hand' or bag of red flannel. Do you have any red flannel around, Kara?"

"Red flannel is not often used for elegant vintage garments," Kara said dryly.

"Add it to the list, then. Here's another one we can try, though it's most effective when performed at midnight on a night of full moon. Light the white candle, burn cloves, pine, or sage (I've got 'em all) in an incense burner and repeat the following incantation thirteen times . . . Where's that book?"

"Never mind," Kara said. "That one sounds pretty feeble to me. What else?"

"Okay. Here's one for unhexing a house. You sprinkle powdered nettle and hex-breaking powder—"

"What?" Kara snatched the little packet from his hand and looked at the label. "It does say 'Hex-breaking powder,' " she reported, raising both eyebrows.

"They carry it in all good occult shops," Adam said seriously. "Then there are the standard religious symbols. Crucifix, cross, prayer, holy water. How did Pat do with the holy water, Ruth?"

"No luck yet," Ruth said. "Father Christopher is out of town, and he's the only priest in the area who will talk to Pat, much less listen to a wild story like this. Do you want me to try?"

"You're awfully cool about this," Kara said, almost accusingly.

"I've been here before." Ruth smiled, but her blue eyes were shadowed by memory. "And this isn't like the other time. It's not so . . . Oh, I don't know what I mean. There was one thing we learned, or thought we learned—I don't know whether Pat mentioned it to you, Adam. Religious symbols aren't effective unless the—the entity against whom they are directed believed in them. I'm not expressing that very well . . . "

"I see what you're getting at." Adam appeared struck by the idea. "But practitioners of black magic abjure Christianity, they don't deny it; the rituals that insulted and degraded Christian symbols implicitly acknowledged the power of those symbols. This—woman—must have been raised a Christian. What are the chances of finding a Jew in the American south in the mid-nineteenth century?"

"Slight," Kara said. "What difference does it make? I'm willing to try anything. We'll douse the damned quilt with unhexing powder and draw crosses all over it and throw in a few ankh signs for good measure. What else have you got?"

"Less than I had hoped. I found a lot of spells for cursing people, only a few for removing a curse. Some of them were too ludicrous to consider. Unless Rachel is willing to stand on her head and count backward from one hundred."

He was trying to lighten the atmosphere, and to some extent he succeeded; Kara laughed and Rachel forced a smile. "I couldn't do it, but it isn't as silly as it sounds. The whole thing is a question of belief, isn't it? What you do isn't as important as whether you believe in its efficacy."

"Can you think of anything else?" Adam asked. "You're the expert."

"No, I'm not. I wasn't looking for curses as such, only for superstitions relating to sewing."

None of this matters. None of it is going to work.

They did wait for Pat. He was the expert, and as Adam frankly admitted, he wasn't prepared to risk Pat's fury if he disobeyed a direct order. Pat wasn't gone long, and when he came slamming into the room they could tell his errand had been ineffectual.

"I told you everything was closed. Even the goddamn police—"

"Come now," Ruth said. "The police don't shut down over the holidays."

"No," Pat admitted grudgingly. "But there was hardly anyone there. They're gearing up for the usual drunken drivers and wild partying, I suppose. I asked for Tom and was told he was busy. Busy!"

"That's okay," Adam said. "You tried."

"I'll get back on it Monday morning. We could always go out to the site and chain ourselves to the backhoe."

From the look on Adam's face Rachel knew the idea had already occurred to him. He'd do it, too, she thought.

Pat didn't see the look; he was examining Adam's collection with interest. "Not bad. You did learn something from me after all. What's the white candle for?"

Adam explained. Pat grinned. "That's Wicca, isn't it? Well, it won't hurt to try, I suppose."

"Can you think of anything I've forgotten?"

"Of course."

"Of course," Adam repeated. "For example?"

"Expulsion of demons, subcategories one through three," Pat said promptly. "West Africa, India, and eastern Europe. Beating drums, yelling and screaming, slashing the air with knives and whips. Subcategory four, Southeast Asia. Take a pig on the roof and kill it—"

"Pat," his wife protested.

"Then there's the ever-popular use of a scapegoat," Pat went on. "Drive the demon into an animal and kill it. We could use Alexander."

"That's not funny," Kara said coldly.

"No." Pat sobered. "Don't quiz me, Adam, I've forgotten more things about witchcraft and cursing than you ever knew. Let's get started."

Rachel hung back, allowing Kara to remove the mutilated quilt from its wrapping and stretch it out on the table. Masked and gloved, the others gathered around, and the air of tension, the intent concentration on the faces bent over the table, reminded Rachel of a team of surgeons preparing to operate. How do I know this is a waste of time, she asked herself. I do know.

But when Pat's deep voice began to speak her hands twisted tightly together. He was speaking Latin. She only understood a few words:

Pater Noster, Deus, in nomine tuo . . . From where she stood she could see his hands moving, as if he were sprinkling the surface of the fabric. Adam's unhexing powder?

He finished the prayer and raised his now empty hands. They shaped a symbol Rachel knew, and an involuntary shiver ran through her.

"Nothing," Pat said, in his normal tones.

"What did you expect, smoke and flames?" Adam demanded.

"Damned if I know. Let's try the herbs. St. John's wort is a popular specific against witches."

He went about the process as methodically as if he were carrying out a series of scientific experiments, accompanying each action with speeches in a variety of languages. Once he paused to remark, "Nothing like a good Catholic boyhood," before breaking again into sonorous Latin.

Rachel withdrew a little at a time until she was standing several feet away. Something made her feel, not threatened or apprehensive, just mildly uncomfortable. Was it the words he recited? Words had power, they were an essential part of any spell. Pat had said that. Or was it she who had told the others? She understood some of what he was reciting. They weren't all prayers. Names she had read and half remembered—Hecate, Astarte, Cybele, Isis—female deities, protectors and guardians of women. *A clever idea, but it isn't going to work either.*

None of them had noticed her retreat except Adam, who kept glancing anxiously at her. She gave him a reassuring smile and sat down in the rocking chair.

If they had asked her she would have told them it was a waste of time. She knew why they had not, why they were content to have her stay at a distance. Rocking and watching, she realized that Adam wasn't the only one who was awaiting—fearing, perhaps—a reaction from her. Pat was facing her, on the opposite side of the long table. He didn't have to turn his head to see her.

She was, as he must know, the most likely means of testing his procedures—the canary in the coal mine, the dog whose keener hearing could detect sounds inaudible to the human ear. He was too sophisticated and skeptical to expect a cheap display of demonic pyrotechnics, like the ones in horror films. The only way he could judge the effectiveness of what he was doing was by her reaction. She saw that he was perspiring heavily and once, when she shifted position, he looked up sharply. She smiled at him and shook her head. She could feel the words like rain touching her bare skin, some so light as to be barely perceptible, a few stinging a little, like small pellets of hail; none strong enough to hurt.

Pat had not overestimated the extent of his knowledge or his thoroughness. His voice had grown hoarse and strained when he finally stopped and stepped back from the table.

"Let's take a break. I'm getting claustrophobic."

"Shall I wrap it up again?" Kara asked.

Pat hesitated, and then threw his hands wide in a despairing gesture. "Don't bother. There are several more things I want to try, but at the moment I can't think straight. I feel as if I'm suffocating in this damned mask."

The others were as anxious to leave as he. Ruth was gray with fatigue and tension; forgetting Rachel, Pat put his arm around his wife and led her out, cursing himself for his thoughtlessness and demanding why she hadn't told him she was getting tired.

Adam went to Rachel. "Everything all right?"

"Fine, thank you," she said, smiling.

The smile and the courteous response seemed to bother him. "Let's get out of here," he said curtly. "Kara?"

Pat had settled his wife in a chair and was making tea, or trying to; he was still looking for teabags and swearing at the kettle for refusing to boil faster when the others joined them. Kara dropped onto the sofa and blotted her face with a tissue.

"I could use a little something myself," she said. "I don't know why I'm so tired. Rachel?"

"I'm fine."

"Are you hungry?" Adam asked.

"I am, now that you mention it." Rachel rubbed her forehead. The headache wasn't severe, just a dull discomfort. "Did we have lunch?"

"No, we didn't," Kara said. "No wonder we're all feeling weird."

"I'll make sandwiches," Adam offered.

"Forget the sandwiches." Pat presented his wife with a cup and saucer. "Let's go out to dinner. My treat."

"None of the restaurants will be serving for another hour, and we'll never get a reservation on New Year's Eve," Ruth said, surreptitiously blotting the spilled tea.

"I know a place," Pat said, smiling ominously.

"Not one of your awful diners," Ruth protested.

"I don't care where we go, so long as we go out," Kara said suddenly. "We all need to get away from here for a while. Someplace loud and noisy and vulgar."

"That's the sort of place Pat has in mind," his wife said resignedly. "Darling, maybe you had better call first."

"No need. Joe knows me, he'll fit us in. Hurry up, I'm hungry too. Don't fuss over your faces, ladies, you're a lot better groomed than Joe's usual clientele."

The sun was setting as they headed out of town; by the time they reached the restaurant, some ten miles south of Leesburg, darkness had fallen. Curls of magenta and green neon proclaimed the presence of the Casa Cassidy, and Kara, who had been silent during the drive, burst out laughing.

"My God, Pat, you sure can pick 'em. The sign is awful enough—"

"What's wrong with a few shamrocks?"

"They wouldn't be so bad without the Santa and the reindeer and those thousands of Christmas lights."

"You said you wanted something vulgar. I aim to please."

The bar was already crowded with people getting a head start on their celebration, but Joe welcomed Pat with a raucous shout and found a table for them.

"It's got everything," Kara said happily. "Red checked plastic table-cloths, plastic flowers in a plastic vase, even a candle in a Chianti bottle. I haven't seen one of those since Mark and I were courting."

"He'd love this place," Pat said.

"Yes," Kara said. "He would."

Pat insisted on buying a bottle of wine and then a second—"At ten bucks a crack I guess I can afford it"—and by the time they finished the first bottle and a gargantuan plate of antipasto the atmosphere was a good deal more cheerful. In his wool plaid shirt, his hair rumpled and his glasses riding low on his nose, Pat looked like one of the boys, instead of a learned professor. Rachel was sitting next to him; while the others were engaged in a spirited debate on Italian versus Irish cuisine, she caught his eye, which was fixed on her.

"This was a good idea," she said. "You weren't thinking only of food when you suggested it, were you?"

"Elementary psychology. Prolonged tension leads to arguments, tears, and inefficiency. But there's nothing wrong with food," he added, as Adam offered them a basket of bread.

He waited until they had finished eating before rapping on the table and calling the meeting to order.

"Okay, Rachel. I thought it the better part of wisdom to leave you out of the proceedings this afternoon, but it's high time we consulted you. I'm not going to ask you any questions and I don't want you to force it. Is there anything you want to say?"

"It was a waste of time."

"Ah. Are you speaking in your professional capacity, or as . . . or otherwise? Shut up, Adam, she has sense enough to know when to stop."

"I don't know," Rachel said slowly. "It was something I felt. That it was a waste of time."

"You were right."

"Then why the hell did we spend the whole afternoon on it?" Adam demanded angrily.

"Because we had to try, you opinionated young idiot. Do you want coffee?"

"What?" Adam glared at the hovering waiter. "I don't care. Yes."

"I'll have an espresso," Kara said. "And add my curses, you should excuse the word, to Adam's. What are you going to do now?"

Pat leaned back and loosened his belt. "Honey, I've just begun to fight. We haven't got to the really serious stuff yet."

"Such as what?"

"Such as dissecting the damned thing. Rip out every stitch, reduce it to a pile of scraps." Rachel moved involuntarily, but didn't speak. Pat glanced at her and went on, "The methods that offer the greatest hope of success will result in the destruction of the quilt. Fire is the most favored counteractive, and we may have to resort to that, but not until after we've tried everything else. There are certain . . . dangers involved in burning it."

"I thought we had tried everything else," Adam said.

"Good God, no. I haven't tried Pennsylvania Dutch un-hexing spells, or voodoo, or the peculiar methodology of the Trobriand Islanders. Drink your coffee. It's time you young folks went home to beddy by."

Pat insisted on singing as they drove home. "Auld Lang Syne" had never been rendered with greater feeling. Rachel joined in; she knew the song well enough to be able to sing and think at the same time. She had to get to the quilt before Pat started his "serious stuff." What she wanted to do wouldn't take more than ten or fifteen minutes, but she would have to wait until after Adam was asleep. She couldn't risk telling him, he was already antagonistic and suspicious.

They had almost reached the house before Pat returned to the subject with an abruptness that made Rachel wonder if he had somehow read her mind. "Try your milk routine tonight, Adam. It's probably not worth a damn, but a good researcher doesn't overlook anything. We'll be there bright and early tomorrow morning. With holy water."

Rachel bit back an exclamation of angry protest. It would be almost impossible to do what she had to do after the quilt had been hung, dripping, on a clothesline in the backyard. She'd have to think of some way of getting Adam out of the house for half an hour. An errand of some kind . . .

"Aren't you coming in?" Adam asked, opening the car door.

"No. It's New Year's Eve, and I'm going to celebrate by checking a few more references and then taking my wife to bed."

"Really, Pat." Ruth sounded more amused than offended.

"You're a disgusting old man, Pat," Kara said, laughing.

"What's disgusting about being madly in love with your wife?"

"Nothing." Kara leaned forward and kissed Ruth's cheek. "Good night, my dears. See you tomorrow."

She started toward the house. Rachel was about to follow when Pat called to her. "Rachel."

"Yes?"

"Happy New Year, kid."

"Happy New Year."

He meant it as a promise, and such was the force of his personality that she almost believed it—until Adam opened the door and she saw the man who was waiting for them.

Tony.

fifteen

She had anticipated everything but this. The unexpectedness of the disaster was as stunning as a blow against defenses that were too new and fragile. The crack was hairline-thin, but it was wide enough for what waited. First a trickle, then a sudden flood, it filled her as liquid fills a container, compressing her consciousness into a small area impossibly remote from the centers of speech and movement. Her parted lips never shaped the words they would have uttered.

"Tony!" Kara ran to her brother-in-law and threw her arms around him. "What are you doing here?"

"I live here, remember?" Tony said. "I might ask what you're doing here. I thought you and Mark would be out tonight getting drunk with the hotshots of Washington."

Kara's face went blank as she tried to come up with a plausible explanation. Fortunately for her, Tony didn't wait for an answer. "In fact, brilliant detective that I am, I deduced you were here when I went into what I thought was my room and stepped on unmistakable evidence of the presence of Alexander. I managed to limp away before he attacked."

"Oh, God, I'm so sorry." Kara sank down onto the floor next to his chair. "I was going to destroy the evidence and clean the room, but we didn't expect you till Monday."

"Didn't you get my messages?" His eyes moved from her to the form that stood rigid and silent next to Adam. "I called twice."

Rachel had unplugged the telephone in the workroom. They had spent the entire afternoon there, and no one had thought to check the answering machine. Another link in the chain.

Standing behind her, one hand near but not quite touching her shoulder, Adam said, "Something has happened."

"Yes. It's good news," he added quickly, as Kara looked at him in alarm. "Cheryl and the kids are fine, this is something else. Why don't you two sit down and relax—you look like a couple of statues—and I'll tell you about it."

She let Adam lead her to the couch. He sat down beside her. "They found the burglar."

"You got it." Tony's lips twisted wryly. "Calling it good news is rather callous, but it can only come as a relief to Rachel."

"To all of us," Kara said. "What do you mean, callous? We should break out the champagne. Where did they find him?"

"Less than twenty miles from here, in the woods. Champagne might be in bad taste," Tony said. "He'd been there for a long time. We're not sure how long yet; the coroner's office is backed up because of the holidays."

"Dead." Adam made it a statement. "How—"

Kara didn't allow him to finish. "They dragged you all the way back here for that? I thought Tom was handling the case."

"Somebody had to identify him as the alleged thief. I didn't want Rachel to do it, he was . . . not a pleasant sight."

Lines of fatigue and strain marked his face. The hasty, unexpected journey must have been difficult for him. He had gone to all that trouble to spare a virtual stranger, a woman who meant nothing to him. A woman named Rachel, reduced to a faint flicker of awareness, helpless as a fly in a spider's sticky web.

The lips she no longer controlled smiled at Tony. "Thank you," they said.

"All in a day's work." The lines of strain smoothed out as he returned her smile, relieved she had taken the news so quietly. "To be truthful, I was glad of an excuse to get away. My mother was driving me nuts, shoving eggnog at me every half hour and smothering me with pillows."

"You look terrible," Kara said bluntly.

"Thanks. I could use a drink, at that. Why don't you break out the scotch, Kara? It's New Year's Eve and I think we're entitled to a modest, tasteful celebration. Unless you kids were planning to go out?"

He raised an inquiring eyebrow at Adam, who glanced at the woman beside him on the couch.

"No, we kids weren't," she said pleasantly. "Sit still, Kara, I'll play bartender, and then Tony can have the floor. I have a feeling he hasn't told us the whole story."

"Most of it. If you want details . . . The body was found early this morning by a couple of kids out hunting. They practically stumbled over the corpse, it was uncovered except by the brush into which it had fallen. Like good citizens they immediately reported the discovery, and one of them brought in the wallet they had found—lying next to the body, he said. When Tom saw the name on the driver's license, he called me."

"Wait a minute," Adam exclaimed. "You knew his name?"

"We were pretty sure he was the guy we wanted, yes. It was mostly a process of elimination; there were several possibles, but when we called on one Eddy Whitbread, we found he hadn't been heard from for over a week. His family hadn't reported him as missing, since he had a habit of disappearing for days at a time. There are several other children, and Tom got the distinct impression the parents were relieved when Eddy took himself off. He'd been in trouble before. Anyhow . . . " He paused, drank, and grinned. "You have a generous hand with the booze, Rachel. Anyhow, his disappearance confirmed our hunch that he was the man we wanted. We assumed he'd skipped town, but he may have been dead all this time. A couple of weeks, from the condition of the body."

"How did he die?" Adam asked. The glass of wine he held was untouched.

"Impossible to tell without an autopsy. I gave myself the pleasure of inspecting the body fairly closely, though, and I didn't see any bullet holes or deep wounds. Most of the damage seemed to be postmortem. Could have been an accident."

He let his head rest against the back of the chair. The position bared his throat—he was coatless and tieless, his shirt open—and Rachel's eyes were drawn to the stretched tendons and smooth skin.

"That's too much of a coincidence," Adam said, frowning.

"They happen." Tony sat up. "There is another guy involved. We think we know who he is, but we've got no proof, and with his presumed accomplice dead, we may never get it. However, our suspect is not the violent type—no previous record except the usual juvenile pranks—and right now he's probably scared out of his socks. If he sits tight he may get away with this, much as I hate to admit it."

"Unless he killed Eddy," Adam muttered.

"I don't think he did. There's been very little violence in this business when you stop and think about it; they didn't intend to kill the old lady, and Eddy turned and ran when Rachel caught him in her room that night. I don't believe she was ever in serious danger." Tony finished his drink. "So," he said amiably, "what have you guys been doing for entertainment?"

The interlude had given Kara time to come up with an explanation for her presence that sounded reasonable—the sale, the end-of-year inventory, the fact that she hadn't expected Mark back so soon. Tony's raised eyebrows indicated that he wasn't entirely convinced, but she didn't give him time to ask questions.

"I think you ought to go to bed, Tony, you look exhausted. Do you want another drink?"

"One more and I'll fall flat on my face," Tony admitted. "I guess I will hit the sack. But I refuse to sleep with Alexander."

"I'll move him, and my things," Kara said.

"There's no need for that, I can sleep upstairs. I'm not that helpless."

Kara gave the others an agonized look. "No, no, this is the simplest way. I didn't bring much with me, it will be easier for me to change rooms. Give me a hand, Adam?"

"Sure. Relax, Tony, it may take a while to swab the deck. Alexander has been shut in there for hours. Coming, Rachel?"

"Don't bully the girl," Tony said. "They don't need you, Rachel. Maybe I will have another drink, if you'll do the honors."

The mouth of the woman he addressed curved gently. *It was easier now, the muscles answered to her will, the memories were accessible, almost part of her—and so useful.*

She prepared his drink as she had the others, strong and undiluted except by ice. When she offered him the glass, Tony shook his head. "I don't want a drink, I just wanted an excuse to talk to you alone." She stepped back, and he said angrily, "Don't look at me like that! Sit down—please. I don't blame you for despising me, but all I want to do is set things straight."

"I don't despise you," she said softly.

"You have every right to. I've been thinking about what I said to you the day we left—about you moving out—and feeling like a louse. I couldn't discuss it on the phone, there was always somebody around. I still can't imagine what came over me that night, but pinning the blame, even part of it, on you was unconscionable. You don't have to leave. I don't want you to leave. Cheryl is crazy about you, the kids like you, and I . . . I think we could be friends if you'll give me a chance. Will you?"

"Yes."

"Thanks. You won't regret it, I promise. I—oh, for God's sake, Kara, I thought you were going to take that damned dog upstairs."

"He has to go out and then have his din-din," Kara said indignantly. "I don't know why you are all so mean to poor Alexander."

The dogs retreated, cringing, into the pantry and a flurry of cats soared up from the floor to the tops of various pieces of furniture. Adam came in carrying a wad of reeking newspapers, and Tony burst out laughing. "I rest my case."

He did finish his drink, and Rachel persuaded Kara to join him while Alexander ate his din-din and Adam trudged back and forth with mops and buckets and clean sheets and towels. Tony's mood had relaxed; he exchanged friendly insults with Kara and kidded Adam about his talent for housework. He kept smiling at Rachel. She kept smiling at him.

Finally Adam announced that the room was fit for human habitation, and Tony reached for his crutches. Adam hurried to support him as he swayed, and he shook his head ruefully. "I shouldn't have had that last drink. Thanks, Adam. I won't need any pills tonight, I'll sleep like the dead."

A shiver ran through Rachel's body. She looked down at her clasped hands.

"I'll go with our drunken friend and make sure he doesn't fall over," Kara said. "Back in a minute."

After they had gone out, Adam collapsed onto the sofa. "God. Now what are we going to do?"

"About what?"

"What do you mean, about what? The bed canopy is still lying on the floor, we've ruined an expensive piece of merchandise belonging to his wife, and we were planning to spend the whole day tomorrow carrying out mystic rites, complete with chanting. You can hear Pat chanting half a block away."

"Maybe you should call Pat."

"I already did, from the bedroom extension. He said not to worry, he'd think of something."

"I'm sure he will."

"Are you okay?" Adam reached for her hand. "You've been sitting around like a stuffed doll all evening."

She let her hand rest in his, neither responding nor rejecting. The others hadn't observed anything unusual in her behavior. She should have realized that Adam might. She had to reassure him, he was the only one who presented a threat. He hadn't drunk as much as Tony and Kara.

She shifted position, leaning back, kicking her shoes off and tucking her feet under her. The movement brought her head closer to his shoulder. "I'm so confused I can't think straight," she murmured. "Seeing him here was such a shock, and then he kept asking questions. I was afraid to open my mouth for fear of saying the wrong thing." She laughed. "I almost lost it when he asked what we'd been doing to amuse ourselves."

Adam's worried frown smoothed out. "I know what you mean. My worst moment was when he said he'd sleep upstairs. I was remembering that bed canopy, which is still on the floor, and wondering how in God's name we could explain what happened. Thank God, Kara is a quick thinker."

"You weren't so slow either," she said softly. She drew her thumb slowly across his palm and felt his fingers tighten.

She had thought she would have more time, but Kara wasn't gone much longer than a minute. She threw herself into a chair and let out a long sigh. "So far so good. He's all tucked in and dead to the world, poor guy. He thinks my marriage is breaking up, which has him all upset, but he was too tired to lecture me tonight."

"I'm sorry," the other woman said.

"Stop apologizing and think. We need a plan. Pat was no help, he kept saying leave it to him. Smug son of a gun."

"My mind is an absolute blank," she said. "Maybe we should sleep on it."

"You do look tired," Kara said. "Go to bed. Adam, you'll have to take the rap for ruining the canopy; you could say you tripped and fell against it . . . No? I guess it isn't very convincing. Oh, hell. Maybe we can come up with something brilliant tomorrow. I'm going to bed too. Alexander, where are you?"

Adam dragged him out from under the table and handed him over. "Where's the key to the workroom?" he asked.

Kara looked at him in surprise, and then laughed. "I forgot. Are you really going to give that quilt a milk bath?"

Adam stared back at her, his mouth set in a stubborn line. Kara shrugged. "I left the key in the lock. Maybe I'd better come with you."

"No need. I'll be careful."

"See that you are. And for God's sake try to get it off the line before Tony gets up, in case he looks out the window."

"I will." Adam's stiff pose relaxed. When he went on, Rachel knew he meant the words for her. "It won't do any harm, as we keep saying. Don't worry. We'll figure out what to do tomorrow."

She wasn't worried. There was no need to think about tomorrow. By tomorrow it would be over.

She lay still in the darkness, waiting. Waiting quietly, without impatience or urgency.

She had heard Adam come upstairs a short time ago. He had paused outside her door; seeing the light was out, hearing no sound from within, he had moved on. Give him an hour, she thought calmly. Or perhaps two hours. Long enough to fall deeply asleep. She was in no hurry.

The old woman had been right, there was no such thing as coincidence or accident. Every event, however random in appearance, formed part of a design too vast and too alien to be comprehended by limited human understanding. Events that were, on the surface, unimportant and meaningless—Rachel's choice of a thesis topic, Tony's decision to respond to a call he should never have answered—these and a dozen other strands in the web led inexorably toward a nexus in time, when the invisible hands of the weaver would draw the threads tight and complete the pattern. It had been predestinated and foreordained; their efforts to prevent the inevitable end had been as futile as the struggles of flies caught in a spider web.

In deadly patience she watched the illuminated numbers of the clock flash on and off. Two hours now since Adam had gone to his room. There had been no sound for over an hour. Time to get on with it.

She had taken off her shoes but had not undressed. Slowly she went to the door and eased it open. The hall light was on. The door of the room Kara occupied was closed. She had assumed it would be, because of the dog, and she didn't doubt that Kara was sound asleep. She had had quite a bit to drink. Adam was the problem. His door was ajar, as she had expected.

She stood in the open doorway listening and watching, until Adam's door edged a little farther open. Figgin squeezed his portly form through the opening and padded toward her. She had expected that too. Picking him up, she put him in her room and closed the door. The turkey sandwich she had brought upstairs would keep him quiet long enough. It wouldn't take long.

She waited for another sixty seconds, counting them off, to make sure the cat's movement hadn't wakened Adam. Hearing nothing, she went to the stairs and descended them, placing each foot carefully on the outside of the tread to avoid a squeaking board.

There was no sound from the family room. The dogs wouldn't bark, they were accustomed to hearing people move around inside the house. One of the wall sconces was just outside Tony's room. That was all the light she would need.

The door squeaked slightly, but he didn't stir. She saw him more clearly than the dim glow should have allowed, as if another kind of light surrounded him. He was lying on his back, one arm across his chest, the other hanging limp off the bed. She stood looking at him for a moment, memorizing the features she would never see again—the mouth relaxed in sleep, framed by the cavalry-style bravado of his mustache, the tousled golden hair, streaked with paler gold where the sun had bleached it . . .

Something buried deep in her mind whimpered and made a last

frantic effort to fight free. "It's all right," she whispered, soothing it. "It will soon be over."

Her feet moved lightly and surely toward the wardrobe. The gun was there, where Kara had put it, on a high shelf. Sooner or later she would remember it and remove it, if Tony didn't find it first. Sooner rather than later—probably the following day. Kara wasn't usually careless about such things, but she had had a lot on her mind that evening. Tomorrow the gun would be gone. Another thread in the weaving . . .

Her fingers fumbled for a moment before they found the proper grip. Phil had insisted that Rachel handle the gun, had showed her how the safety worked and how to aim.

She heard him coming, though he could move quietly as a cat when he chose. She turned, without haste. It was too late, she was ready—arms extended, one hand bracing the other, the muzzle pointed at the sleeper's chest.

"Rachel!"

"Don't wake him," she said softly. "That would be cruel."

"I had a feeling . . . " He lowered his voice; it was a deep, shaken sound, half-groan, half-whisper. "Mary Elizabeth wasn't the only one you—she—wanted to harm. It was his blood on that scrap in the quilt, wasn't it? One of the nail clippings too . . . Rachel—darling—can you hear me?"

"It's too late." The taste of salt on her parted lips . . . Someone was crying. The tears streaked down her cheeks but her hands were steady as stone. "You can't stop it now. Don't come any closer. I don't want to hurt you."

He was closer than she had realized, almost within arm's reach—perhaps within his reach, his arms were longer than those of most people. The light from the hall fell across his face, scoring the harsh lines of it with deep shadows. The lines writhed, shifting, as he weighed the risks and tried to decide what to do.

Then the lines smoothed out and his clenched hands loosened and his breath went out in a long slow expiration. He took one step back, and then another. "You won't do it," he said quietly. "You can't do it. Put the gun down, Rachel, and come here to me."

The threads of the unfinished pattern stretched and grew taut, poised and quivering, before they slipped smoothly into place. The

gun fell to the floor and Rachel turned blindly into Adam's outstretched arms.

She woke to find herself lying on her own bed with Adam holding
her, and with no conscious recollection of what had happened after
she stumbled into his embrace. He was fully dressed and sound asleep,
but the moment she stirred he came awake. His arms tightened and he
studied her face anxiously.

"It's all right, honey. Nothing happened."

"How did I get here?"

"You don't remember?"

"I remember everything up to . . . It is all right," she said, thinking
how inadequate the trite phrase sounded. There should have been
trumpets. "Did I faint?"

"I guess that's what it was. You were completely out of it and limp as
one of Megan's floppy stuffed animals—except for your hands. I
couldn't pry them loose, even after I had carried you upstairs and tried
to put you on your bed."

Her hands were relaxed now, resting against his chest. Rachel
opened his shirt and saw the marks her nails had left, even through the
wool fabric. Her lips touched each of them in turn and came to rest on
the largest bruise.

Adam groaned. "Don't do that. A polite 'thank you' will suffice."

"Who is Rosamund?"

"I haven't the faintest idea," Adam said wildly. "What do you think
you're—"

"You wrote her a letter."

"Oh. Oh, that. A former teacher. Old. Retired. She likes to get—"

"That's all right, then." Rachel kissed his throat and chin and jaw,
and then his mouth, and finally his arms closed around her and his
lips shaped themselves to fit hers.

She didn't hear the knocking until Adam breathed into her ear,
"There's somebody at the door."

"Mmmm," said Rachel.

"It's probably Kara."

"Who cares? Don't stop," she added dreamily.

"It's now or never," Adam said, on a breath of stifled laughter.
"Release me, you shameless hussy. I didn't lock the door."

"Oh, hell."

She watched him move toward the door, wondering how she could ever have thought him clumsy and homely. Even his back looked wonderful.

Kara didn't so much as blink when she saw Adam, large and looming and *there;* she had other things on her mind.

"Did you get that quilt off the line?" she demanded.

"No, I forgot. Guess I'd better."

Adam stretched and yawned, and Kara said suspiciously, "You look like the cat that ate the canary. What's going on?"

"Nothing," Adam said. "Nothing at all. Isn't that wonderful?"

"You're drunk. Dammit, Adam—" She stopped, cocking her head to listen. "That's Tony, what's he doing up so early? I've got to get down there. Hurry."

The activities of the next few hours reminded Rachel of one of the more improbable plots of light opera, with characters running on and off the stage, constantly interrupted and being interrupted, never completing the conversation that would resolve the ambiguities and bring the play to an end. The conspirators were unable to exchange more than a few whispered sentences. Tony was rested and bright and in a convivial mood; he wanted to talk to all of them. Distracting his attention while Adam sneaked out to retrieve the quilt and restore it to its place involved maneuvers that would have been funny under other circumstances. The phone kept ringing—Cheryl, demanding to chat with everyone in turn—Mark, who had heard of Tony's arrival and announced he was coming out to take them all to dinner—Tom, wanting to discuss the case with Tony and angling for an invitation, which he didn't get.

"There are too damned many people here already," Pat said disagreeably. He and Ruth had arrived shortly after eight, and Adam's disjointed references to the events of the previous night had left him totally bewildered and wild with curiosity.

"The more the merrier," Tony said. "It sure is good to be home."

His affectionate smile included Rachel, who returned it with interest. She knew she was behaving like an idiot; she couldn't seem to stop smiling. Her behavior worried Pat. He kept staring nervously at her.

Mark's arrival finally gave them the chance they wanted. He and Tony settled down to watch a football game, and since Mark favored the Patriots and Tony was a fanatical Redskins supporter, they graciously allowed the unconverted to withdraw. Kara refused to be in the same room with them. "They yell all the time," she explained.

The others retreated to the workroom. Pat settled his wife in the rocking chair and himself in the only other chair the room provided.

"Talk and talk fast," he growled. "I'm on the verge of a stroke."

Cross-legged on the floor, with Rachel next to him, Adam talked. As he later said, he had never had or was likely to have such an attentive audience.

Kara was the first to comment on the story. Her voice shook. "I could kill myself for forgetting about that gun. You took an awful chance, Adam."

"I didn't think of it that way. It was just the only thing to do."

"The pattern had to be worked out," Ruth said. "Completed."

"So it's really completed?" Kara asked. "She's gone?"

"She was never here," Rachel said. "Not until the very end. What came through to me were isolated memories or emotions—strong enough at times to obliterate my own consciousness—but they weren't all of her, only the feelings that had lingered. At first I couldn't even remember them. Later . . . "

"You began to identify with her," Pat said. "I was afraid of that. I didn't mention it because the warning itself might have put the idea into your head. But it was already there. As time went on she became increasingly part of you—"

"No, it wasn't like that at all. I always saw her as something apart from me, and when I visualized her, she was so . . . so small. Crouched, hiding—on the defensive. The first time you questioned me she reacted as any threatened creature might do; terror produced unthinking violence. After that night she could only work with me and through me. It took me a long time to realize that the emotion I had felt most often and most strongly wasn't hate. It was fear."

The expletive that burst out of Pat brought a murmur of reproach from Ruth. "I was applying it to myself," he explained. "That was what I felt, the day I . . . " He cleared his throat self-consciously and glanced at Ruth. "I didn't tell you about that, honey. I was afraid it would upset you. I—uh—well, I grabbed Rachel by the shoulders, I was just going to give her a friendly little shake, the way I do with all the girls—"

Perched on the table, feet swinging, Kara said, "I hate it when you do that."

"You do? Why didn't you say so?"

"We put up with your grosser habits because you're so adorable in other ways," Kara said with a grin. "I didn't want to hurt your poor little feelings."

"Go to hell," Pat said amiably. "Anyhow, she reacted as if I had made a really gross advance. It scared the—uh—the devil out of me. That wasn't you reacting, was it, Rachel? You were reliving an experience of hers."

Rachel nodded. Even now, with Adam's hand warm on hers and her friends around her, the memory was painful. "I remember thinking the night the burglar was in my room, 'You can fight back.' She couldn't. Except—" She indicated the bundle that contained the mutilated quilt. "The hate and the fear were there. She sewed them into the quilt. But the hair and the fingernail clippings and the other trappings of black magic were rather childish, really; feeble substitutes for action. The things I did under her influence weren't directly homicidal either. The canopy was the most dangerous, but it was a very haphazard way of killing someone. It might have fallen of its own accord, or caused minor injuries. No one would have taken more than a single bite of the cranberry sauce, the pieces of glass were large enough to be visible. The black liquid in the bleach bottle—"

"Dye," Pat said. "I got the report yesterday. Black dye and Drano. It would have ruined the laundry and raised blisters on Cheryl's hands if she had spilled it."

"Spiteful and childish," Rachel said. "Like the grit in Cheryl's makeup. Oh, she hated them all right—the woman who had taken her lover, and her lover too, after he cast her off. But she would never have attacked either of them directly. Adam saw that last night. I didn't stop her, I couldn't have stopped her. She made the decision—a decision she never had a chance to make in life. Something happened to prevent it, something that broke the pattern."

"She died?" Ruth suggested.

"Something worse, I think. Murder or suicide. A natural death wouldn't have left such an imprint on time. She died believing herself guilty. Guilty and damned."

"It does make sense," Pat said grudgingly. "In the literature of the supernatural, violent death is a standard explanation for psychic survival. It's the fear I don't understand. Why couldn't she fight back against something like attempted rape? Women had few enough rights at that time, God knows, but defending their virtue—"

"You're missing it, Pat," Adam said. "It seems obvious to me, but maybe it's because I know something you don't. That cemetery next to the old lady's house? It was a slave cemetery."

"What does that have to do with . . . " Pat's jaw dropped. "My God," he said feebly.

Kara stiffened, her eyes widening. "My God is right. After all the nasty cracks I made about your chauvinist prejudices . . . I know about African-American quilts, they're quite different from the Anglo-American variety, a different tradition, one that has been overlooked and undervalued until recently. Our quilts weren't in that tradition, so it never occurred to me that . . . But I should have remembered about the sewing women. Slaves; skilled seamstresses who did much of the endless sewing required to clothe and equip a large household. The mistress couldn't have done all of it herself. That would explain the bride's quilt! Mary Elizabeth didn't make it for herself; her sewing woman made it. Her slave—a woman of extraordinary talent, whose skills would have been noticed and encouraged—"

"Wait a minute!" Pat waved his arms wildly. "Never mind the quilts, I want to hear about the cemetery. I am not going to ask you how you know, you sneaky little bastard, I am going to ask why the hell you didn't tell me this before."

"Since you aren't asking me how I know, I'll tell you," Adam said calmly. "The burials weren't those of field workers; they wouldn't have rated even such paltry memorials as I found. These people were probably house slaves. The coffins, what was left of them, were plain, cheap pine. The builder had covered the ones he found, but he hadn't buried them deep. I also found two stones. That was the giveaway. They were small and crude, with no ornamentation, just the name and the dates. A first name, like that of a—a beloved pet. One of the names was Elijah."

He paused, looking at each of their faces in turn, watching their expressions alter as they anticipated what he was going to say.

"The other name was Rachel. She was seventeen years old."

· · ·

They buried the mutilated remains of the quilt, and the things it had contained, in a corner of the MacDougals' dead garden later that night. Kara and Mark were spending the night with Tony. When Adam announced that he and Rachel were going out for a while, Tony had given them a paternal grin and told them to have a good time.

Kara had declined the invitation. "I've had enough black magic to last me for a while. And I think I need to spend some time with my husband."

Clouds moved in slow procession across the moon; the light dimmed and brightened. The wind whispered in the branches of the enclosing trees. It would rain before morning.

"Hurry up," Pat ordered. "Ruth is shivering."

"I'm not cold," Ruth said. "The wind is rising."

Adam was, of course, doing the digging. "How deep?" he asked.

"Good and deep," Pat said. "I hope you realize, Rachel, that you could blackmail me for years. If my so-called colleagues ever heard about this—"

"We decided this was the right thing." Rachel held the quilt cradled in her arms.

"I agreed, didn't I? That should do it, Adam."

Adam drove the shovel into the ground. It stood upright, quivering. "Do you want me to—"

"I'll do it." Rachel knelt and lowered the tightly wrapped bundle into the hole he had dug. Rising to her feet, she gathered a handful of dirt from the piled-up earth and let it fall. She nodded at Adam, who began to fill in the excavation.

"There is something of her there too, isn't there?" Pat said quietly.

"Her hair," Rachel said. "She used it to veil her rival's face and feather the arrow that pierced the two hearts. Long, dark hair. I was going to remove it before you destroyed the quilt, but perhaps this is better. I think we should say something. All I know is 'Now I lay me down to sleep,' and the Lord's Prayer. Pat?"

It was an odd, brief little ceremony, and after Pat's deep voice had faded into silence they started back to the house.

"How about a nightcap?" Pat asked.

"My dear, how inappropriate," Ruth exclaimed.

"Why? We're celebrating the triumph of good over evil, life over death, heaven—if there is such a thing—over hell. Let's hope she made it. Poor little devil," Pat added. His voice was gentle, as if he were speaking of a hurt child, and Rachel thought that her namesake might have had worse epitaphs.

Adam politely declined the invitation. "It's late."

"Not that late," Pat began. Then an evil grin spread across his face. "Oh, I see. Run along, then, my children and enjoy yourselves. I have nothing to offer that could possibly compare with—"

"In that you are correct," Adam said. "The thing is, we've got to be up early."

"Why?" Pat demanded. "Kara will be there, and Ruth and I will come and help you clean the house and hide the evidence."

"You mean you'll stand around and watch while the others do the cleaning," Rachel said. "Adam and I won't be there. We'll be chained to a bulldozer."

sixteen

Easter was early that year and Adam had come to spend his spring break with the MacDougals. The meeting had to be sub rosa, but since Rachel was now living in Manassas, Kara was the only one who had trouble getting away. She was the last to arrive and she came in grumbling.

"I had to tell Mark I was going to see Mrs. Grossmuller. He follows me every place I go these days, even from room to room, but he detests Mrs. G."

"Is everything all right?" Ruth asked.

"Oh, sure. The doctor says I'm healthy as a horse. Mark is just being cute. He says he's going to insist on a couvade. What's a couvade? I didn't want to admit I didn't know."

Adam laughed. "It's a custom in some tribes, where the expectant father takes to his bed when his wife is about to deliver, and pretends he's the one having the baby."

"The dirty dog," Kara exclaimed. "I suppose he gets all the sympathy, while she—"

"No, no, it's classic sympathetic magic," Adam said. "Taking on her pain, making it easier for her."

"Huh," Kara said skeptically. "No couvade for Mark. I'm beginning to wonder about him. None of you guys mentioned the quilt business to him, did you?"

"Of course not," Ruth said. The others shook their heads.

Kara went on, "He's getting awfully superstitious. He didn't want me to see Mrs. Grossmuller—muttered something about the evil eye."

"That's normal behavior for an expectant father," Ruth said with a smile.

"She is a little uncanny," Kara admitted. "Do you know what was in the last lot she brought us? Baby clothes. A whole layette, filthy and crumpled as usual, but exquisite. All hand-made. It laundered beautifully."

"Are you going to keep it?" Rachel asked.

"I think I will. I wondered if maybe she made it herself."

"That's sweet," Ruth murmured.

"If you'll all excuse me I'm going over to Joe's and have a few beers with the boys," Pat said caustically. "I thought this was supposed to be a business meeting. You two babbling about babies, and Rachel and Adam . . . Get your hands off him, girl, can't you show a little decent restraint in the presence of your elders?"

"I haven't seen him for three weeks," Rachel said, unabashed.

"And you haven't done anything for the past three months except knit socks for him."

"They're beautiful socks," Adam said loyally.

"They're hideous," Pat said. "Why purple?"

"It's my favorite color." Adam stuck out his large feet and gazed admiringly at his socks. They were very purple.

"If she doesn't stop knitting hideous socks and get down to work she'll never finish that dissertation," Pat grumbled.

"If I don't, the world probably won't come to an end." Rachel grinned at Pat, who snarled wordlessly back at her. This wasn't the first time they had discussed the subject. Sobering, she removed herself from Adam's lap—the position was distracting—and settled down next to him. "I'm having trouble deciding exactly what I want to do. The original subject is out. I can't deal with it dispassionately now, and anyhow, I haven't been able to find any concrete examples—except the one I can't use."

Adam wrapped a long arm around her and squeezed her shoulders.

"Maybe you'll think of something this summer while we're in England."

"Is that definite?" Pat asked.

"Yep. The grant came through. We'll spend a couple of weeks with Rachel's folks before we go to Somerset. They're dying to meet me," he added complacently.

"Have you prepared them for the shock?" Pat inquired of Rachel.

"They're dying to meet him," Rachel said with a grin. "I told mother how much he admired the peignoir. She's decided he has excellent taste."

Pat made the expected remark about purple socks, and then silence fell—a comfortable, friendly silence that anticipated without fearing what was to come. Dust motes danced in the sunlight that spilled across the floor; through the window Rachel could see the willows on the lawn, branches spread with the green haze of new buds.

Adam was the first to introduce the subject. "So they got Rocky?"

"He's been arraigned," Pat answered. "Tony admits he isn't sure they can convince a jury. Most of the evidence is circumstantial."

"It seems so obvious," Rachel said. "I can't think why it didn't occur to us. No ordinary sneak thief would have known about the quilts or their value. It had to have been a friend of Rocky's."

"It did occur to me," Pat said. The others made disparaging noises, and he amended the statement. "It would have occurred to me if I'd given any thought to the problem. I mean, for God's sake, we had more pressing matters on our mind. As you say, it was obvious—certainly to the police. Eddy was on the basketball team with Rocky, one of his buddies. Of course Rocky denies ever having discussed the quilts with his friends. The only concrete evidence they have is the hair, and the defense will probably question the validity of the DNA process. There wasn't much, only a few hairs."

Rachel shivered. Tom hadn't told her about the hairs caught under the old woman's broken nails. Miss Ora had fought back. The ugliest part of that image was the possibility that she had seen the face of her assailant and recognized him.

"Hair again," Kara murmured. "Ironic, these coincidences . . . Including the fact that Mrs. Wilson's inheritance from Auntie will be spent on Rocky's defense."

"Can she inherit?" Ruth asked. "I thought one wasn't allowed to profit from a crime."

"She didn't commit it," Pat answered. "And she probably believes, fiercely and wholeheartedly, that he is innocent."

"The coincidence I can't buy is the cause of Eddy's death," Kara said. "Snake bite? Snakes are dormant during the winter."

Adam shrugged. "There were a couple of unseasonably warm days."

"Yeah, sure," Kara muttered.

"Nature is unpredictable," Adam insisted. He looked uneasy, though, and his next question was not as much of a non sequitur as an outsider might have supposed. "Anything new on the cemetery?"

Pat shook his head. "Still a lot of squabbling going on. It's unlikely it will ever be excavated. The question of how to deal with human remains is too sensitive, and these are fairly recent remains, in archaeological terms."

"If they were my ancestors I wouldn't want them picked over by a bunch of nosy anthropologists," Adam agreed. "At least we were able to stop the construction; that would have been real desecration. I suppose the builder offered to relocate the graves?"

"That was one suggestion, yes," Pat said. "Several other groups are opposed to it. Whatever the final decision, nobody will ever get a look at what's inside those coffins. I can't fault that, but it's a pity we'll never know what happened to her."

"What more could we learn from those poor broken bones?" Rachel demanded. "I don't want them disturbed, I want her left in peace. I know what happened. I can't give you the kind of proof Pat would consider convincing—"

"How do you know what I'd consider convincing?" Pat interrupted. "Give me a break, kid. I've swallowed a lot of unconventional theories in my time. I never asked you how many of her memories you received—"

"You hinted a lot, though," Rachel said.

"And you ignored the hints."

"I had to get things straight in my own mind before I could talk about it," Rachel said soberly. "The memories were fragmentary and out of sequence, and there were times when I wasn't sure whether the thoughts that passed through my head were mine or hers.

"The impressions that were the most difficult to interpret involved a big, burly man with a heavy beard. The man wasn't her lover—we may as well give her lover a name, he was unquestionably Mary Elizabeth's husband, Charles. The other man had hurt her, and she was terrified of him. I think he raped her when she was hardly more than a child, and continued to abuse her sexually until he tired of her or died. According to Pat's genealogical research, Mary Elizabeth's father—Rachel's owner— died in 1858. That would fit.

"Mary Elizabeth inherited everything he owned, including Rachel and the other slaves. As a wealthy heiress, she must have had a lot of ardent swains. She took her time about deciding; she was probably smart enough to realize that it was more fun being a sought-after belle than a wife.

"Charles was one of her suitors—a younger son, from a North Carolina family, as Pat discovered. While he was courting Mary Elizabeth, he saw Rachel. She couldn't reject him any more than she could have refused the old man, but he was young and handsome and at first he was kind to her. It's no wonder she came to care for him—and he, I think, cared for her. In his way . . .

"Mary Elizabeth had known about Charles and Rachel, and had turned a blind eye. Gentlemen had their needs. But once she decided to marry him, she wouldn't tolerate the continuation of an affair with one of her own slaves, in her own home. She didn't trust Charles— probably with good reason—so Rachel had to go.

"I'm prejudiced, of course, but Mary Elizabeth really was a monster. She told Rachel what was going to happen to her—and then sent her back to work. There was a lot of sewing to do before the wedding, and Rachel was the best seamstress in the county, perhaps in the state. They believed in long engagements then. For months, perhaps for a year, Rachel worked on that quilt and on the delicate garments of Mary Elizabeth's trousseau, and thought about her own dreadful future.

"Is it any wonder that the quilt radiated fear and helpless rage and hurt and despair? It must have relieved her feelings a little to invent ingenious ways of hiding threatening images in those pretty appliquéd pictures. Acquiring the hair and other bits of human detritus would have required ingenuity too. They are, and were used as, ingredients of black magic, but I don't think they were as important as her hatred. It permeated every thread of that quilt.

"And it worked. Coincidence, we would say, that Mary Elizabeth died in childbirth and Charles during the war. But the magical significance of knots and tightly tied stitches in preventing childbirth is documented—and Charles also died young.

"According to the tombstone Adam found, Rachel died in 1859. She didn't live long enough to see the curse fulfilled. But she knew it would be, she believed in the power of her magic, and that made her, by her own definition, a murderess. Having taken her revenge, she killed herself. I would have, given the alternative—to be sold to a stranger, a man who would have the right to use her as he pleased."

"They were going to sell her?" Ruth said, horrified. "If she had been born and raised there—forced to leave her family, perhaps her parents—"

"I came across a case that has some interesting parallels," Rachel said, opening the book she had brought with her. "This girl had been 'brought up like a lady.' She could embroider, read and write, dance and play the piano—and all this she had learned from the family that owned her and treated her as if she were their own. But she had become proud and above herself; so, to humble her, they took her to be sold."

"God." Kara looked sick. "It's beyond comprehension. Bad enough to treat any human being like a piece of merchandise, but after raising her like their own child—"

"That girl's very success and talent destroyed the slave-owners' assumption of innate superiority," Rachel said. "That was why they had to get rid of her, she would have been a constant reminder of a truth their narrow minds could not admit. Mary Elizabeth had an even stronger motive for 'humbling' Rachel. I think she was jealous. Charles was marrying her for her money, but he had cared for Rachel—as much as he was capable of caring for anyone. Not enough to risk losing a wealthy bride by defending Rachel, though. She appealed to him, and he denied her.

"Suicide was Rachel's only defense, her final gesture of defiance. She could cheat Mary Elizabeth of the pleasure of witnessing her humiliation, and claim the right to dispose of her own body."

"It's psychologically valid," Pat admitted. "And violent death does break patterns. Why couldn't it have been murder?"

"Mary Elizabeth would have preferred to see her live and suffer. I doubt any of them would have wantonly destroyed a valuable piece of property." Rachel's lip curled. "A trained sewing woman could bring over a thousand dollars. And Rachel had . . . other qualifications."

"Youth and beauty," Adam said, tightening his grasp on Rachel.

"You're a hopeless sentimentalist," Pat jeered. "We'll never know what she looked like. She was young, certainly. Poor little kid . . . " He stopped to clear his throat and glared at the others. "Frog in my throat."

"Sure," Kara said, with an affectionate smile.

"Enough of this sloppy stuff. Who wants coffee?" Pat rose stiffly to his feet. "Damned arthritis . . . There's no proof of any of this, you know. No proof, even, that the girl in that forgotten grave was the quilt maker."

"Sure," Kara said again.

"You haven't sold the other quilts yet, have you?" Ruth asked. "I'd like to buy one of them."

"Ten percent off to you," Kara said with a grin.

"What do you mean, ten?" On his way to the kitchen, Pat turned to scowl at her. "Dammit, we're kin. Twenty percent or no deal."

"Oh, all right." Kara scowled back at him. "But Rachel gets first choice. We're giving her one as a wedding present."

"I want the patchwork," Rachel said promptly. "The Carolina Rose."

There was no proof. But she knew who had made those quilts, and when people admired hers and asked about the maker, she would tell them what she knew.

The sunlight strengthened, stretching long warm fingers through the room. Out in the garden purple and golden crocuses and the small blue flowers called "glory-of-the-snow" covered a certain spot like living patchwork.